REBORN FREE

The Eternal Emperor's eyes opened. He found himself in a cold, sterile place. Naked. A flash of panic. Had mistakes been made? Was he now that mewling waffler he had grown to hate?

No. He remembered . . . Yes. He must be on Earth, and Poyndex had performed his duty. The Emperor yet lived.

He allowed his mind to wander, still half-anesthetized. But even stuporous, he realized that he no longer felt watched. He no longer felt he had to guard his every thought. The link was broken.

Now he was alive. Now he could rule as his fate intended. Now he was free.

The Eternal Emperor smiled.

By Allan Cole and Chris Bunch
Published by Ballantine Books:

The STEN Adventures:
STEN
THE WOLF WORLDS
THE COURT OF A THOUSAND SUNS
FLEET OF THE DAMNED
REVENGE OF THE DAMNED
THE RETURN OF THE EMPEROR
VORTEX

A RECKONING FOR KINGS
The Shannon Family Saga
Book One: A DAUGHTER OF LIBERTY

VORTEX

Allan Cole and Chris Bunch

A Del Rey Book

BALLANTINE BOOKS • NEW YORK

A Del Rey Book
Published by Ballantine Books

Copyright © 1992 by Allan Cole and Christopher Bunch

All rights reserved under International and Pan-American Copyright Conventions. Published in the United States of America by Ballantine Books, a division of Random House, Inc., New York, and simultaneously in Canada by Random House of Canada Limited, Toronto.

Library of Congress Catalog Card Number: 91-92387

ISBN 0-345-37151-8

Printed in Canada

First Edition: June 1992

Cover Art by Bruce Jensen

To
Andy AFFA Anderson
and
Harry Harrison

A pair of Stainless Steel Rats

"When your fear cometh as desolation,
and your destruction cometh as a whirlwind;
when destruction and anguish cometh upon you."

—Proverbs 1:27

CONVECTION

CHAPTER ONE

THE SQUARE OF the Khaqans brooded under storm clouds knuckled black in the sky. A weak sun crept through those clouds, picking out flashes of gold, green, and red from the towering buildings and domes.

The square was immense: twenty-five square kilometers solid with gaudy buildings, the official heartbeat of the Altaic Cluster. On the western edge was the lace-pattern fan of the Palace of the Khaqans—home to the old and angry Jochian who had ruled over the cluster for a hundred and fifty years. For seventy-five of those years the man had labored on this square, lavishing billions of credits and being-hours. It was a monument to himself and his deeds—both real and imagined. Almost as an afterthought there was a small shrine park in a forgotten corner of the square in memory of his father, the first Khaqan.

The square sat in the center of Jochi's capital, Rurik. Everything in this city was huge; the inhabitants were forever scurrying about, reduced in scale and spirit by the size of the Khaqan's vision.

Rurik was quiet this day. Humid streets emptied. Beings huddled in their tenements for mandatory viewing of the events about to unfold on their livie screens. All across the planet Jochi it was the same.

In fact, on all the habitable worlds of the Altaic Cluster humans and ETs alike had been cleared from the streets by loudspeaker vehicles and ordered into their dwellings to punch up the livie cast. Small red eyes at the bottom of the screens monitored their required rapt attention. Security squads were posted in every neighborhood, ready to kick in the door and haul away any being whose attention flagged.

3

At the Square of the Khaqans itself, three hundred thousand beings had been ordered in for public witness. Their bodies formed a black smear around the edges of the square. The heat from the living mass rose in waves of steam and drifted up into the menacing clouds. The only movement was a constant nervous shifting. There was not one sound from the crowd. Not the cry of a child or a cough from an Old One.

Heat lightning branched over the four gilded pillars that marked each end of the square and the enormous statues honoring Altaic heroes and deeds hunched over it. Thunder boomed and echoed under the clouds. Still the crowd held its silence.

Troops were formed up in the center of the square, weapons at ready, eyes scanning the crowd for any sign of danger.

At their backs loomed the Killing Wall.

A sergeant barked orders, and the execution squad clanked forward, walking heavily under the burden of twin tanks strapped to each being's back. Flex hose ran from the tanks to a two-meter-long tube held by each squad member.

Another order, and hands sheathed in thick fireproof gloves flexed the triggers of the flamethrowers. Molten fire dripped from the ends of the tubes. Gloved fingers tightened, and a howl rent the air as flame exploded out and against the Killing Wall.

The squad held the triggers back for a terrible moment of heat and acrid smoke. The flames hammered at the wall in heavy waves. At the sergeant's signal, the fire stopped.

The Killing Wall was unmarked, except for the deep red glow of superheated metal. The sergeant spat. The spittle exploded as it touched the wall. He turned and smiled.

The execution squad was ready.

A sudden squall erupted, drenching the crowd and sending up hissing clouds of steam from the wall. It stopped as quickly as it had begun, leaving the crowd miserable in the humid atmosphere.

There was a nervous buzz here and there. Among so many beings, fear can keep the silence only so long.

"This is the fourth time in as many cycles," a young Suzdal yipped to his pack mate. "Every time the Jochi police come hammering on the door to call us out to the square, I think, this time they're coming for us." His little snout was wrinkled back with fear, exposing sharp, chattering teeth.

"It's nothing to do with us, dear," his pack mate said. She rubbed the thick furred hump that protruded above her muzzle against the adolescent male, spreading soothing hormone. "They only want the black marketeers."

"But all of us do it," the frightened Suzdal yipped. "There's no other way to live. We'd all starve without the black market."

"Hush, someone will hear," his pack mate warned. "This is human doings. As long as they're killing Jochians or Torks, we mind our own business."

"I can't help it. It feels like what some humans call Judgment Day. Like we're all doomed. Look at the weather. Everybody's talking about it. No one's seen anything like it. Even the Old Ones say it's never been like this on Jochi. Freezing cold one day. Blistering hot the next. Snow storms. Then floods and cyclones. When I woke this morning, I thought it smelled like spring outside. Now look." He pointed at the heavy black storm clouds overhead.

"Now, don't get yourself overwrought," his pack mate said. "Not even the Khaqan can control the weather."

"He's going to get to us eventually. And then . . ." The young Suzdal shuddered. "Do you know one being who has been executed yet who was *really* guilty? Of anything . . . big?"

"Of course not, dear. Now, be quiet. It'll be over with . . . soon." And she rubbed more hormone into his fur. Soon the chattering teeth were still.

There was a crash and a boom and howl of music over the great loudspeakers, so loud that the foliage in the scattered parks of the square shivered with the beat. The gold-robed Khaqan Guard trotted, spear formation, out of the palace. At the apex of the spear was a floating platform bearing the Khaqan on his high-back, gilded throne.

The whole group quick-marched to a position just near the Killing Wall. The platform settled to the ground.

The old Khaqan peered about him with suspicious, rheumy eyes. He wrinkled his nose at the close smell of the crowd. An ever-attentive privy aide caught the gesture and sprayed the Khaqan with his favorite sweet-scented incense. The old man pulled a decorated flask of methquill from his belt, uncorked it, and took a long drink. It quick-fired through his veins. His heart raced and his eyes cleared along with his enthusiasm.

"Bring them out," he barked. It was an old, shrill sound, but it put the fear of the cowardly gods who tended this place into his servants.

Orders were whispered down the line. In front of the Killing Wall, metal hissed on oiled bearings, and a dark hole yawned. There was a hum of machinery, and a wide platform rose up to fill the hole.

There was a long, audible shudder from the crowd when they saw the prisoners standing there in their chains, blinking in the dim light. Soldiers hustled forward and prodded the forty-five men and women to the wall. Metal bands emerged from the wall and clamped them into place.

The prisoners looked at the Khaqan with stunned eyes. He took another pull on his flask and giggled with the heat of the methquill.

"Get on with it," he said.

The black-robed inquisitor stepped forward and began reading the names and confessions of each of the assembled felons. Their list of crimes boomed over the loudspeakers: Conspiracy to profit . . . Hoarding of rationed goods . . . Theft from the markets of the Jochi elite . . . Abuse of office to profit . . . On and on it went.

The old Khaqan frowned at each charge, then nodded and smiled at each disposition of guilt.

Finally it was done. The Inquisitor slid the charge fiche into its sleeve and turned to await the Khaqan's decision.

The old man sipped at his flask, then keyed his throat mike. His shrill, raspy voice filled the square and buzzed on the livies in the billions of homes in the Altaic Cluster.

"As I look at your faces, my heart is moved with pity," he said. "But I am also ashamed. All of you are Jochians . . . like myself. As the majority race in the Altaics, it is for the Jochians to point the way. By good example. What are our fellow humans, the Tork, to think when they hear of your evil deeds? Much less our ET subjects, with their looser grip of morality. Yes . . . What do the Suzdal and the Bogazi think when you Jochians—my most prized subjects—flaunt the law and endanger our society by your greed?

"These are terrible times, I know. All those long years of war with the filthy Tahn. We suffered and sacrificed—and, yes, died—in that war. But no matter how heavy our burden, we stood by the Eternal Emperor.

"And later—when we believed him slain by his enemies—we struggled on, despite the unfair burdens placed on us by the beings who conspired to assassinate him and rule in his place.

"During each of these emergencies, I asked your help and your sacrifice to keep our lovely cluster safe and secure until the Emperor's return. As I believed he would, all the time.

"Finally, he came. He disposed of the evil privy council. Then he looked around to see who had remained steadfast in his absence. He found me—your Khaqan. As strong and loyal a servant as I have been for nearly two centuries. And he saw you—my children. And he smiled. From that moment on, the Anti-Matter Two flowed again. Our factories were alight once more. Our starships soared to the great market places of the Empire.

"But all is still not well. The Tahn wars and the actions of the traitorous privy council have sorely tested the Eternal Emperor's resources. And ours as well. We have years of hard work ahead of us before life can be normal and prosperous.

"Until that time comes, we must all continue to sacrifice the comforts of the present for the glorious life of the future. All of us are hungry now. But at least there is food enough to sustain. Our AM2 allotment is more than most, thanks to my close friendship with the Emperor. But it is only enough to keep commerce alive."

The Khaqan paused to wet his throat with methquill. "Greed is the greatest crime in our small kingdom now. For in these times, isn't greed nothing more than murder on a mass scale?

"Every grain you steal, every drop of drink you sell on the black market, comes from the mouths of children, who will certainly starve if greed is left unchecked. The same for our precious

AM2 supplies. Or the minerals for tools to rebuild our industry, and the synthcloth that keeps us from the elements.

"So it is with a heavy heart that I sentence you. I have read the letters from your friends and loved ones, begging my mercy. I wept over each one. I really did. They told a sad tale of beings gone wrong. Beings who have listened to the lies of our enemies, or fell into callous company."

The Khaqan wiped a nonexistent tear from rimless eyelids. "I have mercy enough for all of you. But it is a mercy I must withhold. To do otherwise would be criminally selfish of me.

"Therefore I am forced to sentence you to the most disgraceful death known, as an example to any others who are foolish enough to be tempted by greed.

"I can allow only one small concession to self-weakness. And I hope my subjects forgive me this, for I am very old and easily moved to pity."

He leaned forward in his chair as the livie camera dollied in until his face filled one side of the screen for the viewers at home. It was a mask of compassion. On the other side of the screen were the forty-five doomed beings.

The Khaqan's voice whispered harshly. "To each and every one of you . . . I'm sorry."

He cut the throat mike and turned to his privy aide. "Now, get this over with quick. I don't want to be out here when the storm breaks." And he eased his old bones back into the throne to watch.

Orders were shouted, and the execution squad took up position. Flamethrower barrels were raised. The crowd drew a long breath. The prisoners hung dully against their bonds. Thunder crashed overhead from the clouds.

"Do it," the Khaqan snarled.

The flamethrowers roared into life. Solid sheets of fire burst out at the Killing Wall.

In the crowd some beings turned away.

A Suzdal pack leader named Youtang barked in disgust. "It's the smell that gets me most," she yipped. "Puts me off my rations. Everything tastes like cooked Jochians."

"Humans smell bad enough without being parboiled," her assistant leader agreed.

"When the Khaqan started these purges," Youtang said, "I thought, so what? There's so many Jochians, maybe it'll thin their ranks some. Leave more for us Suzdal. But he kept at it. And I got worried. Pretty soon, he's going to have to start looking elsewhere for his examples."

"He thinks the Bogazi are stupidest, so they'll probably be last," her assistant said. "We'll be purged just before them. The Torks are human, so if he sticks to whatever it is he calls logic, they're probably next."

"Speaking of Torks," Youtang said, "I see one worried-looking friend of ours over there." She said "friend of ours" with disgust. "Look. It's Baron Menynder. Jabbering at some other human. Jochian, by the cut of his clothes."

"It's General Douw," her assistant yipped, excited.

The Suzdal pack leader pondered for a moment. The human she was looking at was a short, squat being with a pure bald head. The beefy face was ugly enough to belong to a thug, but Baron Menynder affected spectacles that made his brown eyes large, wide, and innocent.

"Now, what would the Khaqan's defense secretary be doing talking with Menynder? Couldn't be professional advice, even though Menynder had the same job once. But he's past it now. His time was four or five defense secretaries back. The Khaqan fired or killed all the rest. Clot, that Menynder is a canny old being," Youtang mused almost to herself. "Got out just in time. And he sticks to his own business and keeps his head low."

She studied the situation a little longer, getting a closer look at General Douw. The Jochian appeared an ideal general, well over two and a half meters high. He was sleek and athletic, at least next to the tubby Menynder. His sliver-gray locks fitted his head like a tight helmet, in stark contrast to Menynder's bald pate.

"Douw must be liking what he's hearing," the Suzdal pack leader finally said. "Menynder's been going nonstop since we started watching."

"Maybe the old Tork is feeling extra mortal these days," her assistant said. "Maybe he has a plan. Maybe that's what the discussion is all about."

The work at the Killing Wall was done. There were only ashes where the condemned had once stood. At the western edge of the square, the Suzdals could see the Khaqan and his guards disappearing into the lacy palace. In the center, the soldiers were being formed up and marched off a platoon at a time.

Youtang watched the two humans in deep discussion. An idea stirred. "I think we should join them," she said. "One thing about Menynder is that he's a clotting great survivor. Come on. If there's a way out of this alive, I don't want the Suzdal to be left behind."

The two beings edged through the crowd.

The storm broke. Shouts of pain and terror echoed across the square as hailstones hammered out of the clouds, bursting like shrapnel.

The loudspeakers blared dismissal, and the crowd erupted out of the square.

Menynder and General Douw hurried away together. But by the time they reached the main gate, the two Suzdals had caught up with them. The four paused in the shelter of an enormous statue of the Khaqan at the edge of the gate. A few words were exchanged. Then nods of agreement. A moment later the four hurried off together.

The conspiracy had been launched.

CHAPTER TWO

"AN APERITIF, M'LORD?" a voice purred in Sten's ear.

Sten brought himself back to reality, realized he'd been preening like an Earth peacock in front of the oak-framed mirror on the wall, and covered a blush.

The owner of the voice was female, black haired, invitingly constructed and costumed, and was holding a tray of fluted glasses. The flutes contained a black, slightly bubbling liquid. "Black Velvet," she said. Indeed you are, Sten thought. But he said nothing, merely lifted an inquiring eyebrow.

"A combination of two Old Earth spirits," she continued. "Earth champagne—Taittinger Blanc de Blancs—and a rare brewed stout from the island of Eire. Guinness, it is named."

She paused and smiled—a most personal smile. "You should enjoy your stay here on Prime, Sr. Ambassador Sten. As a member of the household staff, it would be my disappointment were you to leave . . . dissatisfied."

Sten took one glass, sipped, and said his thanks. The woman waited, found nothing further, smiled once more—a more formal smile—and passed on.

You are growing old, Sten thought. Once upon a time you would have admired, asked, and gotten either a turndown or an acceptance for later. Then you would have downed six glasses to stagger you through this idiotic ceremony. But you are now an adult. You do not get drunk because you think parades are foolishness. Nor do you leap for the first beautiful woman who presents herself.

Besides . . . that smiling servitor was certainly an Intelligence—Mercury Corps—operative who quite possibly outranked Admiral (Inactive-Reserve) Sten (NI).

Finally, at the moment he was not in the mood for a fling. Why not? While part of his brain puzzled, he tasted. Odd combination. He had tasted fermented and augmented effervescent grape juice before, although it had seldom been this dry. The other liquid—Guinness?—added a sharp, solid bash to the taste, not unlike a pugil stick to the head. Before he left Prime he would drink more of these, he resolved.

Sten moved back until his shoulders touched the wall—old habits as an Imperial assassin died hard—and looked about the monstrous chamber.

Arundel Castle rose triumphant over its own ruins. Built as the Eternal Emperor's grandiose living quarters on the Imperial world of Prime, it had been destroyed by a tacnuke as part of the Tahn's unique way of beginning a war sans preliminaries. During the ensuing Empire-wide battle, Arundel had remained in symbolic ruins, the Eternal Emperor headquartered in the vast warren under the desolation.

When the Emperor had been assassinated, Arundel had been left as a memorial by his killers. It had been rebuilt upon the Emperor's return—even more lofty and looming than before.

Sten was in one of the castle's antechambers. A waiting room. A waiting room that could have served handily as a hangar for a fleet destroyer.

The room was packed with fat cats, military and civilian, humanoid and otherwise. Sten glanced once more in the mirror and winced. "Fat cats" was slightly too apt a phrase. Now that you have finished the Emperor's latest bidding, he thought, you need to get back in shape. That sash you were admiring but a minute before with all its decorations *does* accentuate a bit of a paunch, does it not? And the wingtip collar serves to give you another chin. Don't you hope it's the collar?

The hell with you, Sten told his backbrain. I am happy at the moment. Happy with me, happy with the world, happy with where I am.

He looked yet a third time in the mirror, returning to the train of thought interrupted by the servitor. Damn. I am still not used to seeing myself in diplomatic drag. Instead of some kind of uniform, or at least a disguise. This outfit, this archaic shirt, coat with a forked tail that stretches nearly to my ankles, these pants that reach down to shiny low-top boots . . . this is still strange.

He wondered what would happen if the Sten who *was*—that poor clottin' orphan from that slave company world who was lucky and quick with a knife—looked into that mirror and it became that fictional favorite, a timescreen? What would that young Sten think as he peered into it, knowing he was looking at himself in years to come?

Years? Many more than he'd like to total.

What an odd wonderment. Especially here. Waiting on the pleasure of the Eternal Emperor, to be congratulated and awarded for service at the highest level.

Yes. What would that younger Sten think? Or say?

Sten grinned. Probably—other than 'Why the clot didn't you follow up with Black Velvet?'—a grunt of relief. So. We're clottin' alive. Never thought we'd make it. Without thinking, his right hand moved over and touched the rich silk of his coat.

Under that—and under his diamond-studded shirtsleeve—was still the knife. Surgically hidden *in* his arm. Sten had built it—had grown it and then "machined" it on a biomill—as a slave laborer on Vulcan. It had been his first possession. The knife was a tiny, double-edged dart, contoured to fit no other hand but his. Needle-pointed, it could cut an Earthdiamond in half with only blade pressure. It may have been the most deadly knife that man, with his infinite fascination with destruction, had ever built. It was kept in place by a surgically rerouted muscle.

But it had been more than a year, no, almost two years since it had been drawn in anger. Four wonderful years of peace, after a lifetime at war. Peace . . . and a growing sense in Sten that he was finally doing the task he was suited for. Something that did not involve—

"How correct," a voice said in a flat, lethal monotone. "You always *did* remind me a bit of a pimp. I see you have become one. Or at least dress like one."

Sten growled back to reality, arm dropping, fingers curling, the knife reflexing down into its killing slot; stepping away from the wall, left foot coming back, poised on toe, weight centered, slight crouch . . .

Clotting Mason.

Correction. Clotting Fleet Admiral Rohber Mason. In full dress whites, his chest a blaze of decorations, all of them well earned and probably no more than one-third of the hero buttons Mason deserved. He had never bothered to get that livid scar that ripped across his face removed. Sten figured he probably felt it added to his charm.

"Admiral," Sten said. "How is the baby-slaughtering trade?"

"It goes well," Mason retorted. "Once you learn to shorten your lead and range, it's simple."

Mason and Sten hated each other for no known reason. Mason had been one of Sten's instructors back during flight school and had done his best to make sure Sten never graduated. Mason was considered by his students as an unmitigated bastard. The students were correct. And, unlike the livies, after graduation Mason's heart of stone was not revealed as a pose. Under the granite was ten-point steel.

During the Tahn war Mason had risen to admiral. He had many qualities: He was brilliant. A tyrant. A master strategist. A killer. A brutal disciplinarian. A leader who backed his subordinates to the grave and beyond. For instance, when he was unable to find just cause to wash Sten out of flight school, he graduated him with the highest marks. Mason was possibly the best tac pilot in the Imperial Forces. Second best, Sten's pilot-ego growled.

Fiercely loyal to the Emperor, he had survived the privy council's purges through luck and meanness. Now he was no doubt carrying out Imperial orders as he had in the past—efficiently and savagely. Yes, Sten thought, there had been peace. But only compared to the nightmare of the Tahn war. Beings still died.

"I heard you'd become the Emperor's messenger boy," Mason said. "Never could understand how a *real* being could stand living in a world where everything's gray and there's no truth."

"I've gotten to like the color," Sten said. "It doesn't stain the hands as much as red. And it washes off."

A booming voice broke the mutual glower. "Gentlebeings, your attention, please." The buzz of polite diplomatic chatter died away.

"I am Grand Chamberlain Bleick." The speaker was a ridiculously costumed, undersized being, speaking in the loudest smarmy twitter Sten had ever heard. Of course. He had a throat mike and porta boomer.

"We want to ensure that all of you noble ones receive the correct recognition, and that this ceremony proceeds as planned. Therefore, we must adhere to the following rules. The awards will be presented in descending order of merit. A subordinate will announce each category.

"When your award is called, you will form a single line here, at the entrance. When the annunciator"—Bleick indicated a being in red flummoxry—"announces your name, you will enter the main chamber. You will walk directly forward approximately seventeen steps, where you will see a line graven on the floor.

"The Emperor will be standing on the far side of that line.

"If you are the only recipient of an award, stop directly in front of the Eternal Emperor. If you are one of a group, proceed directly to the line and stop next to the nearest being on your left.

"Please stand at attention.

"An Imperial aide will read the citation for your award. A second aide will physically give you the award, either on a sash or she will pin it directly to your uniform. If there is an error, please try to cover any pained reaction. The ceremonies are, of course, being taped for subsequent broadcast to your home worlds.

"Additional copies, I might add, may be secured through my office at a reasonable fee.

"There are no scheduled recipients for any of the Imperial Privy Household Orders. The next ranking are hereditary awards: dukedoms, baronetcies, and the like. Those who are receiving one of those . . ."

"Hereditary," Sten breathed in surprise. His lips did not move, nor did his voice reach beyond Mason's ears. It was a talent learned in military formations and prisons.

Mason, too, had the talent: "The Eternal Emperor has seen fit to find many new and unique patterns to reward those who serve him well." His voice was quite devoid of irony.

"But—"

"Not only does it please the red-tape bastards," Mason said, "but their bureaucratic bosses, as well."

The disapproval both men felt never showed on either's face. But strong sentiments *did* materialize a few meters away.

The man was huge and very white—from his flowing mane to his sweeping muttonchop whiskers and formal court dress. He also looked to be slightly drunk.

"Right lot of mad idiots," he said in a voice that rolled like thunder. "Clottin' titles make a yearlin' think he's automatic blood stock. Give unproven whelps ideas, that does! First time I heard of such drakh!

"By haveen, th' Emp's slippin', allowin' all this formal dancin' by this crew of scrotumless ijiots! B'dam' if I'll take part in any such monkey dancin'. Tell th' Emp, if he wants—''

Whatever Whiskers was about to suggest for the Emperor was swiftly broken off as four very, very large humans slid out of nowhere and formed a mini-cordon around the man.

Sten heard more protests, but most smoothly the man was brought under control and guided—he was too large to be frog-marched—out a nearby exit.

The four men were wearing a new, police-type gray uniform that Sten could not recollect having seen around Prime or the palace before. He saw one of their shoulder tabs, a round black and gold patch with a gold *I*, and the letter *S* scrolled around it.

"Who were the eighty-sixers?" he wondered in that monotone to Mason.

"New security element. Internal Security. The limit of my knowledge or curiosity."

"Who are they organized under? Mercury? Mantis?" Sten's natural curiosity sprang from his former—at least officially—membership in both organizations.

"I say again my last . . ." Mason's voice was louder, frostier. "Goons, gestapos, and guessers have never been my province."

Sten found it polite to follow the ebb as awardees formed up, walked through the door, and vanished.

Hereditary orders . . . Meritorious orders . . . Decorations (military) . . . Decorations (civil) . . .

Sten stopped in front of the chamberlain, who consulted his list. "Sr. Plenipotentiary Sten, you will be the only being honored with this award today. You may enter."

Sten walked toward the high gaping doors, and two beings in those red suits—and, Sten thought, some kind of whitish artificial hair—opened the doors.

A voice blared: "The Most Honorable Sten . . . of Smallbridge."

The yawning Award Chamber was now filled with those who had already gone. Sten smoothed forward, at that slightly slower-than-normal pacing every diplomat learns that shows best on the livies. He formed a dignified expression on his face.

Most Honorable, he thought. Very interesting. As I recall, I was only Very Honorable the last time I was at court. Does Most Honorable give me a bigger paycheck?

"Ambassador Plenipotentiary Sten fulfilled the highest standards of the Imperial Service, at considerable risk to his own personal safety, in a recent mission to mediate between the Thorvaldians and the inhabitants of Markel Bat. Not only was peace preserved, but a new era of tranquillity was brought to the cluster. He is to be honored by being named to a new ranking, A Companion of the Emperor."

Which meant, Sten thought, whatever the Eternal Emperor wanted it to. Which was anything except an Imperial Privy Household Order—whatever *they* were. At least those obnoxious clots hadn't actually gotten around to killing each other. Nor had he found it necessary to kill any of them, tempting as it had been at times.

None of these thoughts appeared on Sten's face. Nor did his expression change as he walked toward that line, his eyes sweeping the huge chamber.

Up there . . . the iris in the chandelier . . . a tracking gun turret. That huge portrait—a one-way screen with a riot squad behind it, most likely. There, and there. At belt level. To either side of that line . . . hidden laser projectors.

On each side of the Awards Chamber's doors were paired Gurkhas. Quiet, small, brown men, faces blank, in dress uniform, their slouch hats' chin straps held just below their lower lips. And, holstered on one hip, each had a miniwillygun. On the other hip the lethal, slashing kukris that helped make the Gurkha the most feared and respected soldier in the Empire. Plus there were about ten more of those gray-clad Internal Security types scattered through the room.

So? Wouldn't you put on a little bit more security if some clot had gone and killed you a few years earlier?

A man stood alone just beyond that line.

The Eternal Emperor.

Dark hair. Blue eyes. Well muscled. He looked to be, at the oldest, in his mid-thirties. No, Sten corrected, his eyes made him out to be a bit older.

But certainly not old enough to be what he was—the man who

for over a millennium had single-handedly built this Empire, the Empire that stretched beyond any beings' visualizations, the Empire that had almost been destroyed and now was being reassembled.

Sten came to rigid attention. The Emperor looked his personal envoy up and down, then nodded in formal approval.

The two Imperial aides—the one who had recited the citation, and the other, who was holding some kind of medal in an open, velvet case—stepped forward.

Then the Emperor broke tradition. He turned to the aide and took the award from its case.

He stepped close, looping the decoration over Sten's neck. "Forty-five minutes," the Eternal Emperor monotoned, in a prison whisper just as skilled as Sten's. "Backstairs . . . my chambers . . . we need a drink."

CHAPTER THREE

STEN STEPPED ONTO the security grid. At the Internal Security officer's signal he offered his palm to the identification beam. The grid hummed into life, and Sten was bathed in a glow of colors. Somewhere in the bowels of Arundel a whole host of facts was collected: Sten was being analyzed by the most sophisticated snooping equipment in the Empire.

The first level was ID. As soon as Sten's palm print was checked and rechecked, his bio was being scanned for any potential animosity to the Emperor. That information was checked a third time against the latest Mercury Corps records, up to date within the past twenty-four hours.

The second was organic. His system was analyzed for any possible bacterial or viral threat to Sten's boss. It had been possible for a long time to build a living germ warfare bomb.

The final level was for weapons, from the obvious hide-out gun or blade, to the not so obvious surgically implanted explosive. Or, in Sten's case, the knife in his arm. He knew that when the scanners caught it, his authorization for bearing such a weapon in the Emperor's presence would override any alarm.

Sten got the okay, stepped off the grid, and headed along the corridor for the Emperor's quarters. He was feeling edgy about the upcoming conference with his boss. It had been a long time since the two of them had had a face-to-face. Something extra-important must be up.

But that wasn't what was bothering him. It was the supertight security that made him nervous—an odd thought from the man who had once headed up the Emperor's personal bodyguard. Then he had fretted at any lapse, worried at the Emperor's tendency to plunge off into crowds, or sneak away for a private adventure.

Sten didn't blame the Eternal Emperor for clamping down hard after what had happened. But now that he had gained a great deal of experience as a public man himself, Sten also knew it was dangerous for any being in authority to adopt a bunker mentality. The tighter the screen, the harder the job of the villain, admittedly. But it also could make it tough for the guys in the white hats.

And as for the Internal Security beings he had seen so far, Sten had picked up a bit of a skin crawl. Why, he couldn't say. The closer he got to the Emperor's presence, the more the IS personnel bothered him. They were all so . . . vaguely familiar.

When he saw the tall, fair young man at the door, Sten got it. The man was a twin of the Emperor—as were all the men he had seen since he had entered the Emperor's private apartments. The main physical difference was that they were taller.

He grudgingly admitted that this arrangement made good sense. Individually, the IS guards resembled the Emperor enough to draw any assassin's fire. And in a group around him, they were a living shield.

The IS officer clicked his boot heels together as Sten approached. "You are expected, Ambassador Sten," he said in soothing tones that were in odd contrast to his stone face. Suspicious eyes measured Sten. Compared. Sten was a little hurt to see the suspicion replaced with self-satisfaction. The clot thought he could take Sten with ease.

"You can go right in," the IS officer said.

Sten's muscles and reflexes tingled with memory, as he played his own measuring game. The man's eyes narrowed. He *knew* what was going on.

Sten laughed. "Thanks," was all he said. The door whisked open and he entered. He saw the startled look on the man's face as he realized his worth had been found sadly lacking. Sten could take him with ease. Sure, he was a little slower. Out of practice. But it would be no problem at all.

The stregg hit the Black Velvet, thought about making trouble, then was seduced by all that smoothness. Sten felt his belly warm to a cheery glow.

The Eternal Emperor beamed at him, then refilled the shot glasses with the fiery drink the Bhor had named after an ancient enemy. "As our old Irish friend Ian Mahoney says, 'This one's just to let the Good Lord know we're serious.' " The Emperor downed another shot.

Sten followed his lead. If the boss wanted the meeting to be boozy, then Sten had little choice but to participate—with feeling. Besides, the Eternal Emperor had been right. As usual. Sten really had needed a drink.

"Now, let's see about that dinner I promised you," the Emperor said. "Until further notice, Ambassador, you are in charge of keeping the glasses full."

He began bustling about that marvel of low-tech goodness married to high-tech speed he called his kitchen.

"A difficult duty, sir," Sten said, "but I will do my very best." He laughed, refilled their glasses, and carried them to the counter. He took his usual position perched on one of the tall stools.

Sten sniffed the air appreciatively. It was a mixture of vaguely familiar smells but with a tantalizing mystery to them. The Eternal Emperor could give a master chef lessons. Even Marr and Senn, the greatest banqueters in the Empire, grudged this.

The Emperor favored re-creating the recipes of ancient Earth.

Though from the Emperor's perspective, the recipes weren't so ancient, Sten thought. He had ruled for three thousand years.

Sten sniffed the air again. "Asian?" he guessed. He was no mean cook himself. He had picked up the hobby—inspired by his boss, perhaps—whiling away long hours at dreary military posts where the food was even duller than the company.

"You're only thinking that because it's complex," the Emperor said. "Although there are some influences, I guess. But the other way around. The Chinese *were* the best cooks. These folks, however, gave them a run for the money. Some people say they were even better. I go back and forth."

He palmed a spot at the counter's edge and a refrigerated shelf slid out, revealing an array of jars and pots of good stuff. He stacked them on the counter.

"The theme tonight is India," the Eternal Emperor said. "Sort of goes along with the job I've got in mind for you."

He smiled. Sten had seen his boss in friendly moods before, but never quite so downright jolly. Uh-oh. Another impossible task. Sten was only mildly bothered. The potential difficulty intrigued him. But he couldn't fold up too easily.

"Not to be contrary, sir," Sten said, sipping at his stregg, "but I was hoping for a little leave time." He saw a flicker of irritation on his boss's face. Good.

"Don't push it," the Eternal Emperor snapped. Sten was alarmed to see the irritation building to quick fury. "I'm sick and tired of negatives. Don't you people get it? I'm holding this thing together with spit and baling wire and . . ." The Emperor's voice trailed off.

Sten watched him bring the anger under control. It was a definite fight. The Emperor shook his head and gave Sten a sheepish grin.

"Sorry," he said. "Pressures of the job and all. Sometimes it makes me forget who my old friends are. My *real* friends." He toasted Sten and sipped his stregg.

"It was my fault, sir," Sten said. His instincts told him it was important to take the blame. "The smell of all that good food got to the lazy side of me."

The Emperor liked that. He gave a sharp, too-right nod, and went back to work—and the subject.

"My current pain in the ass," the Emperor said, "resembles the place this food comes from. Within the borders of India there were more people of more different opinions than just about any place on Earth. It was one mass of hate groups who had been at each other's throats so long they had forgotten about what pissed them off in the first place. I take that back. Actually, they remembered all too well.

"A Hindu or a Sikh could tell you to the day and the color of the sky what atrocity the other guy's great great-grandfather had committed."

He slid over a bowl filled with a greenish-looking mass. "It's dhal," the Emperor said. "A kind of a bean—or in this case, pea—dish. It's deliberately bland. To give balance to the rest. Clear the palate every bite or so. I made it up yesterday. All we have to do is reheat."

"About this problem child," Sten prodded.

"Right." The Emperor took a hit off his stregg. "I could have used another example besides India. But their food was mostly potatoes—and pig when they could get it. They made a helluva sausage, though. Wrapped in flour and fried. But I didn't feel like sausage."

Sten sniffed the ingredients the Emperor was assembling into some kind of order. "India will do just fine, sir," he said.

"The place I'm sending you is the Altaic Cluster," the Emperor said.

Sten frowned. He was only slightly familiar with the cluster. "The Jochians, among others, right? But, I thought they were among the best allies we have on board."

"They are," the Emperor said firmly. "And I want them to stay that way. Trouble is, the Khaqan—which is what the fellow who runs the joint calls himself—is up to his ass in alligators."

The Emperor held up a mound of cubed meat. About two pounds worth, Sten noted. "This is goat," the Emperor said. "I had a field constructed for him and his brothers and sisters. Had the field planted with the same stuff his ancestors ate in India—

mint, wild onion, you name it.'' He plunked the mass into an ovenproof casserole.

"The Khaqan is getting old and a little past it," the Emperor went on in his typical veer back and forth between subjects. Except that over the years Sten had noted there really was no veer at all: Each topic always had something to do with the other.

"Anyway," the Emperor continued, "the trouble is mostly his fault . . . Still, I can't afford to lose him."

Sten nodded agreement. Whoever this Khaqan was, the Altaic Cluster was an important ally. Worse: It was damned close to Prime. "What's threatening him, sir?"

"Just about everything and everybody," the Emperor said. He started shaking out spices over the lamb. "A little ginger," he said, shifting to the recipe again. "Ground cloves, cardamom, chili, cumin . . . heavier than the others . . . couple of squeezes of garlic, and ye olde salt and pepper."

He dumped in some yogurt and lemon juice, and stirred up the whole mess, then set it to the side. He started frying onions in peanut oil.

"There are three separate species in the Altaics," the Emperor said. "Split four ways. And all of them are sons of bitches. First, there's the Jochians. Human. The majority race. The Khaqan is a Jochian, natch."

"Right," Sten said. That was the way things usually worked under one-being rule. Present company excepted. There were far fewer humans than other species in the Empire.

"Their top world is Jochi, which is where the Khaqan hangs his head. It's the center of the cluster. Anyway . . . to the other villains in this piece . . ."

He dumped half the fried onions on the lamb and mixed it up. He pulled the rice off the range. The water had been boiling for about five minutes. He drained the rice, stirred it up with the onions, and spread it out over the lamb.

"A little butter drizzled on the top," the Emperor said, "and . . . voila! I call this Bombay Birani, but basically it's an old goat stew." He slammed on a tight-fitting lid, popped the casserole into the oven, and set it for bake.

"Now, I'm going to cheat," the Emperor said. "The way this

is supposed to go is, you set it at 380 degrees. Bake one hour. Then cut it to 325 and go for an hour more.''

Sten tucked those figures away, along with the rest of the recipe.

''But Marr and Senn, bless their souls, have come up with a new oven. Cuts real time half or more. And I can't tell the difference.''

''About those other villains, sir?''

''Oh, right. Okay, we've got the Jochians. Human, as I said. Besides being the majority race, they've got one of my old trading charters. I gave it to them maybe five hundred years ago. It was a wild and wooly frontier area then.

''Which brings me to the Tork. Human, as well. Old boom-town types.''

Sten didn't know exactly what the Emperor meant, but he got the drift.

''The Torks hit the cluster earlier when Imperium X was discovered in the region,'' the Emperor went on. ''Miners. Ship jumpers. Storekeeps. Joyboys and joygirls. That sort. Except, when the Imperium X played out, they stayed on instead of drifting to the next glory hole.''

Imperium X was the only element that could shield the Anti-Matter Two particle. AM2 was the fuel that had built the Empire. And it was under the rigid control of the Eternal Emperor. So much so, that when the privy council had assassinated him, all AM2 supplies had automatically stopped. For six years the privy council had searched fruitlessly for its source. In the meantime, the Empire had plunged toward ruin—a state Sten was currently engaged in helping to turn around. Although sometimes he wasn't sure he would see it happen in his lifetime.

''Of course, the Torks objected when the Jochians showed up. These merchant adventurers smacked some heads together, showed them my charter—and that was that.

''Time passed, and the Jochians fell apart a little. Turned into not much more than separate worlds—city-states. The current Khaqan's father pulled things back together a couple three hundred years ago.''

Sten made no comment. It was frontier justice. He had used a little of those old ways to bring the privy council to bay. "What about the other two species? Natives of the cluster, I assume?"

"Correct. They break down into the Suzdal and the Bogazi. Don't know much about them. They probably have the same touchy points as any other beings. Apparently when the Torks arrived, they were just climbing off their own home worlds and had discovered one another.

"They had pitiful spaceships. But they were doing a good job of knocking each other off when the Torks came along. Didn't have to do too much ass kicking. Star drive has a way of putting any backward being in awe."

Sten could imagine the shock. Here you had just managed to struggle up the tech ladder from stone to space. You look around at the waiting stars, feeling pretty good about yourself. You're standing at the top of your history, right? No one who has ever gone before has accomplished as much.

Then, wham! Aliens—in this case, human—show up with all their fancy gadgets, plus weapons, all of which can blow you back to flaking stone chips. Plus, marvel of all marvels, they can jump from one star to the next, from system to system. Even cruise the galaxies with ease. AM2 drive. The greatest achievement in history.

For the first time, Sten imagined what it must have been like when the Emperor arrived on scene many centuries before with AM2 under his arm. It would have rocked any civilization that existed, put them on their knees begging to see the light.

The Eternal Emperor was musing over some half-remembered ingredient. "Cilantro," he said. "That's the ticket." He crumbled some leaves into a dish of chopped up cucumber and yogurt.

Yes, Sten thought. AM2 plus the secret to eternal life . . . It must have really been something.

It was an incredible dinner. Unforgettable. As usual.

There were mounds of food all over the table. Dhal and cucumber cooler. Three kinds of chutney: green mango, Bengal, and hot lime. Real hot lime. Little dishes of extra hot sauces and tiny red peppers. And fresh griddled flat bread—chapaties, the Emperor called it. Plus the Bombay Birani. Fragrant steam rose from the casserole.

"Dig in," the Emperor said.

Sten dug.

For long minutes they just ate, savoring each bite and washing it down with what the Emperor swore was Thai beer.

When starvation was no longer threatening, the Emperor speared a hunk of goat with his fork and held it up to examine it.

"About my old buddy, the Khaqan," he said. He popped the goat into his mouth and chewed. "He's a tyrant of the first order. And I won't deny it. Trouble with being a tyrant is you can never lose your moves. You can't let the lid up a little to allow the steam to escape. If you do, your enemies take it as a sign of weakness. And you've got trouble.

"You also can't get sloppy. Or senile. The Khaqan, I'm afraid, is getting sloppy. He may even be getting senile, for all I know. I *do* know he has every life-support system available close by. Constant blood and organ purging, hormone implants, that sort of thing. With luck, he can live long enough for me to take the time to figure out what happens next. Right now, I'm too busy."

Sten nodded. He could only begin to imagine just how busy the Emperor was. Sten wasn't privy to the big picture. But from his assignments—diplomatic brushfires all—and his circle of knowledgeable friends, he had a hazy idea.

The Empire had been crumbling when the Emperor returned. Whole regions had been without any AM2 for a long time. With the cheap power gone, industries collapsed. Rebellions erupted. Beings were forced to fend for themselves in all sorts of ways.

The Eternal Emperor had been scrambling ever since, plugging up leaks where he could. Abandoning some areas entirely. Pulling in his sphere and clamping on rigid economic and military controls. And there were many new faces among his allies. Beings with whom he had no past history. Questioning beings. Frightened beings who looked at their miserable populations and shored themselves up against constant conspiracies and coups.

"I've given the Khaqan a lot more AM2 than he deserves," the Emperor said. "But he's been squandering it. Putting it to building big monuments to himself, instead of using it to feed his people. They're getting sick of it.

"I even warned him about his behavior. A year or so ago our ambassador to the Altaics rotated out. It was routine. What wasn't routine is that I haven't named a replacement yet."

That was a fairly heavy duty gig against the Khaqan, Sten thought. "I'm surprised he didn't wake up," he said.

"So am I. Like I said, he's old. Set in his ways. But if he goes under, all the doubting Thomases among my allies will get the jitters. Demand more AM2. Which would blow the clot out of the economy."

Sten understood. All money was pegged to the value of the basic power unit of the Empire. Produce more, inflate the money. Produce less, and it deflates. Here there was a double whammy: since there was less power, fewer goods would show up at market. So all prices would shoot up, leading to more scarcity. Black markets. And finally, restive populations.

The Emperor was walking a helluva tightwire.

"Who's the Khaqan's likely successor?" Sten asked.

The Emperor sighed. "No one. He has no living heirs. And he's also a micromanager. Decides on every detail, from how much water there should be in the main palace pool to the rates the gravcabs can charge. He discourages any initiative. As a capitalist, the Khaqan is so-so. As a CEO, he stinks."

The Emperor swilled more beer. "However, he's getting pretty desperate, now. He's been begging me for some sign of support. Show his people I'm in his camp. Along with the AM2, of course."

"And you want me to be that support?" Sten said.

"Right. Put on a big show for him. You're one of my top heroes. Medals. Honors. Victories. In the field of battle and the halls of diplomacy and all that hogwash. I'll have my media people make a big deal of it. Not that you'll need much of a buildup." He looked at Sten. But instead of smiling, he looked thoughtful. Sten decided he didn't want to know what his boss was thinking.

The Emperor broke off and grinned. "Take anybody you want—your pals the Bhor, some crack troops, your usual crew of experts, whatever. Just make sure everybody sparkles. And to make this a rcal show-the-flag exercise, I want you to take my personal ship. The *Victory*."

Now *that* brought a grin to Sten's face.

The Emperor laughed. "I thought you'd like that."

The *Victory* was purportedly a dream ship. A new class battle-wagon/tacship carrier built to the Emperor's specifications. Regal as all clot. To impress the natives, he said. Everything about it was ultraluxury, from private crew quarters to the Emperor's personal suite.

"Now, this is what I call a great job description," Sten said, toasting his boss. "Now. If you want kisses and hugs for the Khaqan in public, what's my attitude when we're alone?"

"Chilly politeness," the Emperor said. "Real reserved. Scary as you can make it. I want him to see my eyes in yours. Tell him I've promised to put in a new ambassador right away. However . . . I also want some progress on who his successor is going to be when he kicks. That way, I can start some private discussions with *that* fellow. See if we can't make life a little more pleasant—and stable—in the Altaics when the old boy is gone."

Sten nodded that he understood the drill. He also realized that the Emperor would be wanting his opinion on who that successor ought to be.

"One more thing," the Emperor said. "Tell him I'm putting him on my personal invitation list. The short list. I'll expect his visit in a year or so."

"He'll like that," Sten said. "More propaganda for the home folks."

"Yeah, he will," the Eternal Emperor said. "But he's not going to like what I have to say. In private."

And he speared the last hunk of goat. He snipped it from the fork with sharp white teeth.

Sten didn't feel sorry for the Khaqan a bit. He sounded—in Kilgour's words—like a "right bastard."

CHAPTER FOUR

"AH'LL GIE TH' poss'bil'ty y' may hae saved me," Alex grudged. "Nae, lad. Tis m'shout this round."

He got up, walked to the bar, paid the barman, and brought back the tray. Four mugs of beer and four single shot glasses of clear liquid. Sten indicated the shot glasses with a questioning finger.

"Quill. Nae stregg. Thae's none ae that off the Bhor Worlds or away frae th' Emp's palace, so this'll hae t' cure the dog."

Sten was still a little skull-fried from his marathon dinner–drunk–orders group–plotting session with the Emperor some days earlier. Obediently, he dumped one shot down his throat, gagged politely, and chased it with a beer.

"Y'll note, Ah'm but bein't civil an' keepin't y' company," Alex said as he did the same. "Dinnae be haein' th' thought Ah'm still a wee alky. Gie it all up, Ah did."

The two of them sat, anonymous in gray shipsuits, near the back of a spaceport bar near Soward City's vast spacefields. The bar was a businesslike hum of sailors getting drunk enough to transship, or drunk enough to realize they had finally ported, and the whores and hustlers were helping both sets toward their missions.

"I really did save you?"

"Oh, aye," Alex said. "She was wee, she was wily, she was gorgeous, and she e'en had her own money."

"Maybe you *should* have married her."

"Ah clottin' near did. Th' banns were read. Th' hall wae hired. Ah found a sky pilot thae'd go through the ceremony wi'oot gig-glin'. Ah'd e'en introduced her t' m' wee mum."

29

"What did *she* think?"

"She consider't, an' said thae i' Ah hadda marry, still so young an' barely beyont th' cradle as Ah am, she c'd live wi' th' lass."

"I say again my last: maybe you should settle down. Start thinking about the next Laird Kilgour of Kilgour."

Alex shuddered gently. "Ah dunno, lad. Thae wae a moment . . . but then Ah thought a' myself, years gone, brain gone i' Ah e'er had one t' begin wi', teeth gone, chewin' on pap, puttin' milk i' th' brandy, wi' bairns bouncin' around an' all. Cacklin' on aboot how th' old days are gone, an' modern clots dinnae lift a candle t' th' mighty ones thae're gone, men frae the old days, when men were men an' th' sheep ran like hell.

"Disgustin'. Clottin' disgustin'. So Ah considers . . . looks at your signal . . . writes oot a well-reasoned arg'ment an' slips out th' back afore dawn."

"Mr. Kilgour," Sten said. "An act of cowardice! You at least should have stayed and explained."

"Rotate around it, lad. Th' way th' lass impress't m' mum was by beatin't her ae arm wrestlin.' Ah'm mad, but Ah'm noo daft."

Sten checked the time. "We're due at the *Victory* in ten minutes. Let's drink and get."

Kilgour blurred into motion, old battle reflexes reappearing. The beer and alk on the table vanished. He burped politely, rose, and started toward the exit, threading his way between tables, Sten in his wake.

Alex's way was blocked by a very large quadruped, whose gray hide looked as if it would make an acceptable suit armor. The being emptied the large plas balloon he had been sniffing and bounced it away into a corner. All three of his—her? its?—eyes glared around separately, then settled on Kilgour. The being's twin manipulating arms flexed.

"Men! Don't like men!"

"Ah dinnae either," Alex said equably.

"You man."

"No."

"What you?"

"Ah'm a penguin. Frae Earth. A wee slickit cowerin't birdie thae lives on herring."

Sten ran through various ET handbooks, trying to ID the being. Nothing in his memory had four legs, three eyes, two arms, a dim brain—last undetermined for certain, given probability said being was blitzed—stood two and a half meters tall, weighed several squillion kilos, and had a terrible attitude.

Oh, yeah. Not very vestigal claws on the arms.

Sten felt mildly sorry for the being.

"You not penguin."

"An' how d'ye know, lad? Y' dinnae hae th' look ae a passionate penguin pervert aboot y'."

"You man."

"Look, son. Y're tired. Y'hae a bit t' . . . snuff, snort, swill, or suck. Hae y'self ae sitdown, an' Ah'll buy y' a wee new balloon."

"Don't like men! I hurt men! First I hurt you, then hurt him."

"Ah well," Kilgour said. "Sten, y' bear witness t' m' wee mum Ah'm noo goin't out an' gettin' in th' bloody frae like Ah wae a cub again."

"I'll tell her."

"Ah knew Ah c'd rely on you."

The being was reaching for Kilgour's neck—what little neck the tubby man had.

Kilgour's hands circled the being's arms, just where a wrist would be on a humanoid. And he levered down. The being scrawked in pain and collapsed down on what were maybe knees, just as gracelessly as an Earth camel. Kilgour, still holding the being's "wrists," stepped forward—and the quadruped collapsed back into a sprawled, seated position.

"Noo," Alex said. "Y' see how easy pacifism is, when y' put y'r mind t' it?"

"If you're through playing, Mr. Kilgour?"

"Ah'm through, Admiral. But Ah hae t' buy m' friend his round. As Ah promis't."

Kilgour, an upright and honorable man from the high-gee world of Edinburgh, Sten's long-time aide and accomplice and one of the Empire's most highly trained elite commandos, *did* keep his word—and bought the now quiescent monster a balloon before they left for their inspection tour of the Imperial battle cruiser *Victory*.

" 'Tis all i' th' the leverage," was his only explanation to Sten. "Like tearin' a phone book apart."

"What's a phone book?"

" 'Tis quite a ship," Alex said, three hours later.

"Aye," Sten agreed. He took off the sensor hood he had been wearing and stopped his run through of the *Victory's* tertiary and redundant TA systems.

Alex's eyes swept the room before he spoke. There weren't any crewmen within earshot, and the com box wasn't picking up. "Perhaps Ah'm gettin' old," he went on, still tentatively, "but the way this scow's set up's noo like it would have been back in the—the old days."

"You mean before the Emperor's assassination."

"Aye," Kilgour said. "Thae's a bit too much flash ae filigree f'r this to suit th' *old* Emp. Or am I rememberin't th' past ae better'n it wae?"

"I've been thinking the same thing," Sten said. He touched keys, and the computer obediently threw a three-meter hologram of the *Victory* into the air over the mess table they were sitting at. Another key combination, and the computer began peeling the hologram, displaying the new battle cruiser from all angles and deck by deck.

"Ah'd heard this wae t' be a 'maphrodite," Alex said. "But it looks more like a three-way or four-way arrangement t'me."

Sten nodded agreement. He wasn't happy, on a number of levels. First was the entirely pragmatic consideration of the *Victory* as a warship. Sten had experience with tools, vehicles, and ships that were ostensibly dual- or multiple-purpose. Almost without exception that meant that the tool did quite a number of things badly, and nothing well.

Battle cruisers, for instance, were based on aeons-old designs of ships that had enough muscle to beat up almost anything—except battleships or monitors—and enough power to run away from the biggies. Quite frequently, though, it worked out that the class was too slow to be able to catch and destroy smaller ships, and played hell getting away from the monsters. Plus, once the ship was caught, its armament, quite capable of bashing a stray destroyer or such, was too light to damage a battleship, and its defensive systems, active or passive, were too weak.

Sten had gone through the builder-promised specs on the *Victory*, cross-correlating them with the actual performance the battle cruiser produced during its trials. Unless the Imperial procurement people were on the take—not an impossibility, but not very likely—it looked as if the *Victory* might be an effective weapon.

The problem was this tacship capability the Emperor had evidently decided was vital. The *Victory*'s rear third was dedicated to hangar/weapons/quarters for a complete tacship flotilla—three squadrons of four ships each. The tacships were Bulkeley-II class ships, developed and refined during the Tahn war. They were just-over-hundred-meter-long needles of destruction. They were built to get in at speed, hit hard, and get out. Anything else—crew comfort, defensive capabilities, armor—was secondary or nonexistent. Sane pilots hated the tacships—they required constant hands-on pilot response and were unforgiving, as in kill you, of the slightest error. Sten loved them.

So on one hand the *Victory*'s added capability was something Sten appreciated. But it also meant that the rear spaces were flying time bombs, packed with sensitive explosives, fuels, and weaponry. The large hangar and maintenance areas meant any hit in those spaces might destroy the battle cruiser. Plus the *Victory* was more than a bit blind and defenseless around the stern. "Thae'll be a problem," Kilgour had observed. "Means thae i' we cannae break an' run, we'll haè t' retreat backwards, clutchin' our bustle an' flailin' wi' our wee ladylike brolly."

That image of Earth Victorian times brought up the *Victory*'s final oddity: complete luxury. Sten already knew the ship had been outfitted for luxury—even the lowest-rank wiper had his own tiny compartment. Paneling appeared to be wood and stone on many of the passageways. The kitchens could efficiently prepare and serve Imperial conference banquets with no strain.

Sten appreciated this to a degree. A lean, clean fighting machine might sound good in the livies, but Sten knew from his tacship experience that after three or four weeks into a mission, one thing *not* appreciated was a fresher one had to squeeze oneself into to degrease the body. Especially if that fresher just happened to have a sharp corner cleverly located where elbows and knees went.

But then there was the Imperial Suite, which included living quarters large enough, it seemed, for an entire Imperial court, plus guest area and troop support sectors, including armories and gymnasiums. Sten was glad to see the latter—he was still aware of the smallish handles he had previously noted in the Imperial mirror.

The Imperial Suite—if that was the correct label for such a large area—covered the upper quarter of the *Victory* between the tacship decks to the forward command spaces for the *Victory*'s own crew. A frontal cross-section would show the Imperial area as a T, the figure's leg extending deep into the ship's center. Like all flagships, the *Victory* was designed and built so the Imperial—or flag—quarters were independent of the warship's own areas. For thousands of years every admiral had known he was a better captain than the flagship's own captain, and would frequently drop the larger concerns he was paid to worry about and play skipper-for-a-day.

Yes. Sten agreed with Alex that this Imperial Suite was a bit much. The heads had gold fixtures. The basins were real marble. The bedchambers were richly upholstered. As for the beds themselves, particularly the ones—plural correct—in the Imperial private quarters, Sten wondered how they would be described in the inventory:

BED, Mark 24, perhaps. *Multiple-user-capable. Structurally reinforced to allow occupants limitless creativity. Bed fitted for hydraulic modification while in use, which includes adjustment overall area from polyhedron to circular to conventional; vertical adjustment of any portion of bed for height. Internal and external multiple capabilities, including, but not limited to, internal illumination, external illumination, holographic projection, holographic recording. Includes refrigeration and snack area. Includes full communication capability. Overhead rack (can be hidden) capable of supporting as many as three beings. Fitted for light*

*array to include, but not limited to, stroboscopic or holographic
imaging.*

The owner of such a bed, Sten summarized, would be listed as
orgy-qualified and -experienced.

The Emperor?

Sten did not give a damn—but it was odd that during his time
as captain of the Emperor's Gurkha bodyguard, he hadn't noticed
that the Eternal Emperor seemed particularly sex-driven. He
hadn't thought much about it, but sort of guessed that after a few
thousand years maybe the possibilities had been completely explored.

But now?

Hell, he was not even sure he was right—it wasn't as if Sten
had personally explored every inch of Arundel Castle to ensure
that what was listed as a storeroom might not, in fact, have been
an Imperial bordello.

The problem was going to be, Sten thought, sleeping in that
bed himself. Why you puritanical little clot, his mind jeered.
There have been times, he prodded himself, that he'd been known
to roll about in a big pile with friends. And speaking of which,
his thought went on, who's going to see you sleeping in that
humongous great bed, anyway? You might as well have been a
clottin' castrato of late.

Sten brought himself back to the issues at hand. "Mr. Kilgour," he said, "I'm not at all sure what this goatrope they call
the Altaic Cluster is going to be. But I'm getting the idea our boss
isn't giving us all these goodies just because he likes my legs."

"Prog: ninety percent," Alex agreed.

"Which means I'll be needing all my assets. So, uh, do you
think it'd be a proper utilization of your talents, Laird Kilgour,
for you to skipper this solid-gold whorehouse?"

Kilgour appeared taken aback. "Me? But thae's an admiral
rank. Twa-star, Ah'd hazard. An' th' highest rank Ah e'er held,
last time Ah meter-metered the matter, wae but wee warrant."

"I don't think that would present a problem," Sten said. "And
it wasn't what I asked."

Alex considered. Then slowly shook his head. "Ah dinnae

think so, lad. But Ah'm touched ae the thought. T'now, thae's nae been a Kilgour been an admiral. 'Ceptin' the pirates, a' course.

"M'mum'd be pleased, an a'.

"But . . . nae. Marchin' swabs here an' bye, pushin' all this steel aroun' th' sky . . . thae dinnae tweak m' testes. Ah'm more int'rested in all thae clots we're goin' out to straighten oot—Ah think thae's m' main talent, skipper."

Sten was very damned elated. Beyond the value he placed on Kilgour's friendship and quite literal back-guarding ability, he knew that the man whom the Emperor called Sten's personal thug had real talents at diplomacy, situation analysis, and solution breakdown.

Then a notion crossed his mind. Sten grinned—it was just a shade farcical. But it would bear consideration.

He shut down the computer and stood up. "Come on, Laird Kilgour. Let's go back to the bar and see if that rhino's ready to buy us a round."

Alex came to his feet, then frowned and checked the wall-chrom. "Nice thought, boss. But we cannae. We'll be haein' vis'tors back ae our quarters."

"Visitors? Kilgour, are you running another number on me?"

"Noo, lad. Hae y' e'r, e'er known me to stick ae match under y'r breeks jus' t' see how high y'll jump?"

Sten didn't even trouble with an answer, nor with kicking his "diplomatic adviser" in the slats.

"I shall be entirely gotohell," Sten said.

"Is that all you're going to say? No 'Clottin' Kilgour did it to me again?' No 'But duty calleth, M'lady, and I must away?' "

"Nope."

Sten crossed from the entrance to his suite in Arundel Castle to the sideboard. "Best I can do," he said, "is I just came from a room I'd like to show you, someday."

"Do I get an explanation?"

"Nope."

"Do I get to see that room?"

Sten did not reply. He picked up a decanter and eyed its contents.

"Stregg?"

"Yes . . . stregg."

"It's early—but I'll have one if *you're* drinking."

Sten found two corrosion-proof shot glasses, poured them full, and took one across to Cind. She half sat, half lay on one of the room's couches.

Sten had met Cind many years earlier under circumstances both would have preferred to be different. Cind was a human woman, a descendant of the warrior elite who had once defended the religious fanatics of the Lupus Cluster, known as the Wolf Worlds. Sten had overturned that corrupt and militant church government during his days as an undercover Mantis Section operative.

When the bodies stopped bouncing, Sten had decided—with the Eternal Emperor's ex post facto grudging approval—that the victors and new champions of the Wolf Worlds were the Bhor, the excessively nonhuman, obsessively barbaric, insistently alcoholic gorillas who were native to the cluster.

Cind grew up in a failed warrior culture—and studied war. Studied war until it became her love and her obsession. She joined the Bhor and became a warrior—sniping and ship-to-ship boardings among her specialties.

Part of her youthful obsession was the superstalwart that had destroyed her own Jannissar culture. A man of myth named Sten. Then she met him. And found he was not the bearded ancient she had envisioned, but a still-young, still-vibrant soldier.

In hero worship, she found her way to his bed. Sten, however, was in shock after a combat mission had led to the death of his entire team and had no interest in romance, especially from a seventeen-year-old naïf. Yet somehow he had managed, entirely accidently, not to make Cind feel like a fool or himself like a complete idiot.

During the fight to destroy the privy council, they met again and again—but always professionally. Somehow, they became friends.

Then, when the Emperor returned and the privy council was destroyed, Cind traveled with Sten to her home worlds, the Lupus Cluster. Their perceptions of each other had changed during this time. Still . . . nothing happened between them.

And when Sten left to assume his new tasks as Imperial ambassador plenipotentiary, Cind soldiered on, but with less of an interest in hands-on slaughter than in studying the causes and results of war.

Now both soldiers sipped stregg, shuddered, and sipped again.

"I assume," Sten said, "that you've arrived as part of my Imperial circus and diplomatic mission to the Altaic Cluster."

"Is that where we're going? Alex said the AOR was classified."

"It is. You can draw the area briefing fiche from Mr. Kilgour."

Silence in the room. The old sexual tension between them warmed that silence.

"You look well," Sten said.

"Thank you. Since the last time I saw you, I decided I should become more familiar with civilian dress."

Sten admired—she had done her homework. Cind, just past twenty, trim in the conservative four-piece suit, hair close-cropped, makeup just enough to enhance without being seen, would have been taken by most as a CEO of a top multiworld corporation.

No one could have seen—and few besides Sten would have theorized—that the heel on her dress flat was the haft to a hideout knife, that her pouch contained a miniwillygun, and that her necklace could do double duty as a garrote.

Cind eyed him. "Do you remember the first time we met?"

Sten gurgled stregg through his nostrils, a distinctly unpleasant sensation.

Cind laughed at his reaction. "No, not that time. Before . . . at the banquet. I was in the receiving line."

"Uh . . ." Sten thought back. The woman—then girl—had worn . . . seemed to him she had just been wearing a uniform of some sort. But he felt he would be an utter ass if he so said.

"I wore walking out semidress," she said. "But that wasn't what I first chose."

It was now Cind's turn to look away, as she blushingly described the sleek sex-outfit she had paid nearly a campaign's bonus for, put on, and then ripped off and thrown away.

"I looked like a clottin' joygirl," she said. "And . . . and later,

I figured out all I really knew how to look like—how to be—was a soldier. Which also meant a soldier's whore, I guess.''

And there it was again, Sten thought. For some reason Cind was able to say astonishing things to him, things that other women had only said deep in intimacy and after long knowledge. And it was the same for himself as well, Sten realized.

He also realized that he wanted to change the subject. ''May I be formal?'' he asked.

''You may, Admiral.''

''Not Admiral. This time around, I'm a civilian.''

''Very good.''

''Why so?''

Cind smiled once more. Oh, Sten thought. No chain-of-command drakh. No ''It's not military kosher to want to hold hands with a lower (higher) ranking soldier.''

''I am in a most uncomfortable position,'' Cind said, stretching into a more comfortable position and thus placing Sten in a slightly *un*comfortable position. ''I am a major now.''

''Congratulations.''

''Perhaps. Would you like to meet my ranking private?''

Sten waited. Cind rose, went to an adjoining door, and opened it. ''Private? Post!''

There was a sudden clashing of leather, and a creature lumbered into the chamber. Just 150 centimeters tall, it must have weighed around 150 kilograms—twenty more than the last time Sten had seen the horror. The creature's knobbed hairy paws brushed against the ground, as did its enormous brush-tail beard, as the monster pushed its great trunk semierect and bellowed.

''By my mother's beard,'' came the shout. ''Here are you two, ambassador and major, drinking all of the stregg, and leaving a poor, thirsty private, who loves you like a brother, to die of thirst, forlorn, abandoned in the outer darkness.''

''What,'' Sten said, ''in the name of my father's—your father's, hell, Cind's father's—frozen buttocks are *you* doing here, Otho?''

''I am but a simple soldier, following in the way of a warrior, as the great gods Sarla, Laraz, and—who the clot's that other worthless godling? oh yes—Kholeric have told me.''

''He's been into the stregg,'' Sten said.

"He's been into the stregg," Cind agreed.

"Bring in the rest of the motley crew," Sten said. "Buzz down for Kilgour. Tell him to have the kitchen stand by for a buffet in-chamber. Tell him to order up more stregg, some of that horrible stuff the Emperor calls Scotch, and, oh yes, indeed, a case of—hell, whatever goes into a Black Velvet. And get his butt in here with a good thirst. Now, Otho. How many goddamned Bhor do I have?"

"Only a hundred and fifty."

"Oh, Lord," Sten said. "And we're still weeks from departure. Major Cind, have you arranged billets for your beings?"

"I have. There's an entire wing set aside on a new officers' quarters, just inside the Imperial grounds here. Set up for clean and black work."

"So the Bhor won't be able to get out and maim, pillage, and loot Prime?"

"With luck."

"Good. Now, Private Otho. Pour us all a drink, and explain. Quickly."

Sten needed an explanation, because when he had last been in Otho's brawling company the being had been a chieftain, the ruler—if a Bhor could be said to rule anything save by acclamation—of the entire Lupus Cluster.

Now here he was as a rear-rank warrior, as if he were a young Bhor whose beard was yet to sprout.

"I didn't know," Sten said, after the third stregg, but before Kilgour and the rest of the Bhor had descended on him and sobriety vanished into the night, "you beings had second childhoods."

"Don't be a scrote," Otho growled, refilling his horn. "First —the Lupus Worlds are at peace. Clotting well better be, if they don't want to get killed.

"Which is good—I guess. But it is a meatless plate, my friend. Back then, back when we were being exterminated by the Jann, I never dreamed how *boring* peace can be. So I ran away to join the circus."

He sighed—or Sten arbitrarily assigned the value of "sigh" to the alk- and stregg-laden gas blast that erupted from Otho's bowels to typhoon across the table. "And I am becoming civilized."

"Say clottin' what?" Alex said as he entered, and Otho's tale was interrupted by the obligatory roars, shouts, embraces, liquid kisses, and toasts that made a Bhor greeting synonymous with second-degree assault.

Then the Taittinger and Guinness arrived. Sten was forced to demonstrate Black Velvets to his guests. Otho said the stuff was weak mix for suckling babes. Alex preferred his Guinness straight from the pump and drunk in Eire. Cind touched her flute to Sten's. They drank, and their eyes held the moment.

Then Sten brought the conversation back to some kind of a track. "Otho, you said being here had something to do with your becoming civilized."

"By my father's icy arse, so it does. Using human standards, even. If I am civilized . . . and a great leader—which, considering my beard is yet uncut, I may be—then I am now spending my wilderness years. Which I understand must be spent among primitive beings.

"I found a fiche recently, the biography of what, evidently, you humans consider a great being. His name was Illchurch, or some such. Now, when he had done his first stint as a leader, where did he spend his wilderness years?"

Otho gestured with his glass, sloshing drink over the edge. "I'll tell you where. Among a primitive Earth tribe he called Americans. Since I could find no remnants of such a tribe, I decided to settle for what must be the second best primitives . . ." Otho raised his glass in toast. "To the human race."

CHAPTER FIVE

"I WOULD LIKE," Sten said formally, "to request the pleasure of your company this evening."

"The pleasure is mine, sir. How many troopies do I bring for backup?"

"One more time. May I buy you dinner, m'lady?"

"Oh. Just a moment, I've got to check the 'dex . . . yes. I'd be delighted, Sten. How formal is this place?"

"Sidearms should be unobtrusive, but color-coordinated. At . . . 1930?"

"*Seven*-thirty it is," Cind said, and broke the connection.

"And dinnae we look pretty, lad. Are we wooin' or spookin' t'night?"

"A little of both."

"Ah." Alex brushed nonexistent lint from Sten's raw silk shirtjac. "Well, y're set up on th' far end. Sh'd Ah hae extraction set up, or will y' RON?"

"My God," Sten said. "I never realized the joys of being an orphan before. Mother Kilgour, I don't have any idea of whether I'm remaining overnight anywhere, whether I'm even going to get kissed, and what concern is it of yours, anyway?"

"Ah'm mere remindin' you y' hae a 1115 wi' th' Emp tomorrow, f'r final briefing."

"And I'll be there. Anything else?"

"Noo . . . yes. Y'r scarf's all crookedy." Kilgour straightened it. "An' as m' mum useta advise, dinna be doin' aught you cannae stand up in church an' tell th' deac aboot."

"She really said that?"

42

"Aye. An' now y' ken why th' Kilgours are nae a church-goin't clan."

Kilgour slid out. Sten made a fast final check—damn, but I seem to be spending a lot of time in front of mirrors lately—and he was ready. He tucked a hideout willygun into a chamois ankle holster, curled his fingers twice—the knife came out of its arm-sheath easily—and he was ready for a night on the town.

There was a tap on the door.

"It's open." He wondered what new, last-minute harassment Kilgour had come up with. But no one entered. Instead, again came the tap.

Sten frowned, crossed to the door, and opened it.

Three small, well-muscled young men stood there. They wore civilian clothes—but their suits all looked as if they had been issued by some central authority.

They were Gurkhas. They snapped to attention and saluted. Sten started to return the salute, then caught himself.

"Forgive me, honored soldiers. But I am no longer a soldier."

"You are still a soldier. You are Sten. You are still Subadar."

"I thank you once more," Sten said. "Would you come in? I have but a few moments."

Sten ushered them inside. The three stood in uncomfortable silence.

"Shall I send for tea?" Sten asked. "Or whiskey, if you are off duty? I must apologize for my bad Gurkhali. But my tongue is rusty."

"We will have nothing," one said. The other two looked at him and nodded. He was now their appointed spokesperson.

"I am Lalbahadur Thapa," he said. "This man is Chittahang Limbu. And this one here is Mahkhajiri Gurung. He thinks he is of a superior caste, but do not let his arrogance trouble you. He is still a good soldier. All of us carry the rank of Naik."

"Lalbahadur . . . Chittahang . . . you bear honorable names."

"They are—were our fathers. This Mahkhajiri's father runs the recruiting depot on Earth. At Pokhara."

Havildar-Major Lalbahadur Thapa had fallen saving the Emperor's life from assassins years before. Long ago, Subadar-Major Chittahang Limbu had replaced Sten as commander of the Gurkhas—at Sten's request. Chittahang had been the first Gurkha to command the unit, establishing a tradition.

Gurkhas, in addition to their other virtues, had very long memories, at least as regards their friends and enemies.

"How may I serve you?" Sten asked.

"A notice was posted in the Administration Office, saying that you desired volunteers for a special mission, and any member of the Imperial household was invited to apply."

"You?"

"There are twenty-four more of us."

"But . . ." Sten sat down. He felt as if somebody had sucker-punched him in the psychic diaphragm. He regained equilibrium. "Gurkhas serve only the Emperor."

"That was true."

"Was?"

"Only cows and mountains never change. We discussed this matter with our captain. He agreed that serving the Emperor by helping you with your mission, whatever it is, would be *sabash*— well done."

"This volunteering was done," Sten said carefully, "with Imperial permission?"

"How could it be otherwise? The notice ended with 'In the Name of the Emperor.' "

Gurkhas could be very naive on occasion. Sometimes it was theorized they were deliberately so, using blankness as a device so they could do exactly as they had previously decided.

Sten thought that if the Emperor did not know—and approve— of their request, all hell might break loose. After all, one of the most impressive Imperial boasts was that after the assassination the Gurkhas had refused service under the privy council, returned to Earth, and waited for the Imperial return.

Sten didn't let this potential ego problem show on his face or in his words. Instead, he beamed. "I am most honored, gentlemen. I shall speak to your commanding officer and to your *bahun*, and begin the proper ceremonies."

Fortunately the Gurkhas were not obsessed with long ceremonials, so Sten was able to usher the three men out in a few mo-

ments without offending anyone's dignity. Then he allowed
himself a few minutes of ponderment and one stregg.

Damn, he thought. Why me? Why this? I think I'd better walk
very small when I bring this up to the Emperor. Then the thought
leapt:

But if it works out—and I go in with some Gurkhas—the Emperor is sure going to get the flash he said he wanted. Plus, his
backbrain chortled, I won't have any trouble keeping my back
covered . . .

Cind had no idea what was going on.

First Sten had asked her out—socially. Then he had made that
strange remark about sidearms being unobtrusive but color-
coordinated.

She had chanced a fast call to Kilgour, a man she felt was on
"her" side. Maybe. And whatever "her" side was anyway, which
she was none too sure of.

Of course, the Scotsman had been less than no help.

"You remember, Mr. Kilgour, a conversation we had some
time ago," Cind began. "When you said I was, uh, too young
and striking to play spy?"

Alex thought back. Vaguely. "Ah do."

"Sten invited me to dinner this evening. I have the idea that
. . . this is about half professional."

"Thae's a good startin't point, lass. Th' puir waif canna do
naught thae's not work-related. 'Twill lead him t' an early grave,
Ah'm fearit."

"Where are we going?"

"Y'mean morally, collectively, or historically?"

"I mean where is Sten taking me for dinner? And how should
I dress?"

"Ah. I misunderstood. Th' place is secure, an' y'should dress
cazz. Cazz dressy. Carry heat i' y' wish. Ah would. But y're
safe."

"You'll not tell me any more."

"A course not, Cind. Dinnae Ah think—an' Ah'm tellin't th'
truth—y' hae moves aboot y', giein' thae y'did some growin't
since th' last we've seen y'? Dinnae Ah think, were y' noo so

young, an' you an' Sten in love, Ah'd take y' home m'self to meet
m' mum? So why sh'd Ah denigrate y' an' start tellin' y' wha's
goin't on, when deep down, y' ken already?''

Without waiting for a response, Kilgour blanked the screen.

Clotting men, Cind thought.

Clotting . . . and then she deciphered Kilgour's brogue. Love?
You an' Sten, emphasis Sten? Of course she probably was in love
with him, assuming love was something that made you not sleep
well at night, build entire castle complexes in the clouds and then
move into them, and behave generally, if you didn't watch yourself, as if you had just injected an opiate.

But . . .

But Sten? Love?

Clot men, she decided, was a safer and more productive way
to think.

At least now she knew how to dress.

Cind's outfit was a whisper of sensuality, a simple collarless
garment with a deep V dip on the neckline, a close-fitting waist,
and a slight flare just above the knees. There were no buttons,
zips, or velk to suggest how it stayed together. The waist had a
plain belt-tie. Of course, like all "plain, simple, well tailored"
garments, it had cost Cind a quarter of her last proficiency bonus.

What made it special, besides the cutting, was the fabric itself.
Mantis Section—the ultraelite operational section of Imperial Intelligence—wore the ultimate in camouflage uniforms. They were
phototropic, changing colors to match the background the soldier
was next to.

A civilian had bought marketing rights to this fabric and then
modified it. The material remained phototropic—but it reflected
the background of five minutes earlier. The color recorder and
time delay were part of the garment—the belt, on Cind's dress. It
also held a strip computer with a simpleminded color wheel that
could override the phototropic commands so the wearer would
not suddenly find herself wearing a pink dress against an orange
background. The belt further contained sensors that muted or
increased the color response to match the current light level. On
a random factor, it sent strobe images to certain panels and, just

to make sure the garment's audience stayed interested, occasional real-time flashes of what lay beneath, when panels would go transparent for eye-blink flashes. Those transparencies could be programmed to match the wearer's modesty. Or, in Cind's case, to never show the knife sheathed down her backbone or the mini-willygun in the small of her back.

Cind met Sten dressed to kill, in several ways.

And for once the male animal didn't screw up. Sten not only noticed and complimented her outfit, but asked intelligent questions—as if he were really interested—about how the cloth worked.

Still better, he brought a complementary flower.

Flower was not quite the right word. Aeons earlier, an Earth-orchid grower, exiled from his native tropics, had developed the ultimate *oncidium* orchid—many, many tiny little blossoms on a single stem, crossbred with a native chameleonlike and highly adaptable plant form. The result produced a living bouquet—a necklace—that exactly matched its wearer's garb.

She gave Sten a moderate kiss and a hug in thanks. And, as she pulled away, she allowed her little fingernail to trail across his neck and down his chestline.

She did not want him to think, after all, that she was a *total* virgin . . .

The bar-restaurant was secreted in an industrial cul-de-sac not far from Prime World's Embassy Row. Sten missed the turnoff and had to bring his rented gravsled—he had politely rejected the garish official transport he'd been offered—back for another approach. The building sat by itself, isolated in gloom, almost impossible to see. But as the gravsled grounded, bright lights flared.

Cind blinked in the glare. The lights seemed less intended to illuminate the path than to allow those inside to see approaching visitors. There was a very small sign halfway up the curving walk:

The Western Eating Parlor. Number Two.

"Not a very exotic name," she observed.

Sten grinned. "There are wheels within wheels here. Supposedly this joint started back on old Earth, way, way back. Like pre-Empire back. Outside a city called Langley. It catered to an exclusive clientele, the story goes. Which hasn't changed in all these centuries.''

"Okay, I'll bite. Who're the customers?" She raised a hand before Sten could answer. "Don't tell me. But give me a hint.''

"Okay. Take the first letter of each word in the name: *T-W-E-P.* "

"Twep," Cind sounded.

"Long *E*," Sten said.

Oh. Like in the old archaic term "Terminate With Extreme Prejudice." Cind had heard the term used by elderly intelligence types. Officially sanctioned murder.

Inside, the restaurant was a hush of real leather, murmured conversation, and skillful service.

The maître d' was a horror.

Half of his face was gone, replaced by a plas mask. Cind wondered how long he must have been without medhelp—it was very rare to see, at least in what passed for civilization, someone whom reconstructive surgery did not take on. He didn't notice Sten and Cind for a moment. He was supervising two busboys, who were covering a large blast hole in the paneling. Then he greeted the newcomers as if they were strangers. "May I help you, sir?"

"She's clean, Delaney."

Delaney grinned with the half that remained of his face. "Indeed she is. I have an upstairs snug, Cap'n. An' your friend's at the far bar. I'll bring her up.''

"You've been here before?" Cind whispered as Delaney led them through quiet luxury.

"No. Delaney and I go back a ways."

Delaney's hearing was very sharp. He paused. "FYI, the captain lugged me off a mountain once. A real big mountain. During a bad time. When I wasn't computin' real well." His fingers touched where his face was.

"I had to," Sten said. "You owed me money." A bit embarrassed, he changed the subject. "What happened to the wall?"

"You ever operate with an octopots with a service name Quebec Niner Three Mike? Called herself Crazy Daisy? Kinda cute if you go for cephalopods.''

Sten thought, then shook his head.

"She retired as OC, outa Mantis 365," Delaney added helpfully. "Mostly out of NGC 1300 Central?"

"Must've been before my time—wait a minute. Was three-six-five the guys who stole the sports arena?"

"That's them."

"Okay. Know the team. Never met her. But isn't she on some renegade list?"

"You must be thinking of somebody else," Delaney shrugged. "She's clean-up with anybody here."

"Sorry. Didn't mean to interrupt."

"Anyway, she was in this afternoon. Celebrating something. Kept climbing out of her tank and floppin' up and down the bar. Gettin' nasty. Pourin' down shots of jenever cut with dry ice. Anyway, she'd bought herself a toy. Old projectile weapon she'd had made up. Called it a goose gun. Anyway, she decided she wanted to show it around. I maybe shoulda said something, but—

"At any rate, she showed off how it loads—she'd had some special rounds built up for it—and then she says it'd put a hole in the wall you could throw a human through.

"Guy down at the end—ex-Mercury REMF Analysis, shoulda stayed quiet—says drakh. So Daisy blew a hole in the wall 'n started throwing the guy at the hole. He was right, and the hole wasn't big enough. But Daisy kept trying. I had to tell her to knock it off and go home after three, four tries."

Cind hid her giggle. Delaney led them into a small room and seated them.

"You'll have what, skipper? Scotch, or are you streggin' tonight?"

Sten decided to be reasonable. "Scotch. It's early."

"Do you pour Black Velvet?" Cind asked.

"We pour *anything*. Or if it doesn't pour, we'll get you the needle, the inhaler, or a suppository blank. And I'll tell Aretha—that's the name she prefers to use—to come on up." He left.

"This," Cind said, "is a spook bar? Correct?"

"It is. Mostly Mantis."

Every profession had its own watering holes, from politicians to pederasts. And each had its own requirements. The Western

Eating Parlor was an almost perfect intelligence operative's bar. Situated in a capital—*the* capital, in fact—it was unobtrusive. It would serve its retired or active clients any of the exotics they had become fond of on a hundred hundred worlds. All of the help had some degree of intelligence background, from Delaney the maître d' to the barman who was the son of a recently deceased planning type who was waiting his appointment to the appropriate university, to the busbeings who might just have done some contract wet work in the past. The Parlor was unbugged; it was kept that way with frequent, sophisticated sweeps. The press were discouraged, except for those journalists who needed deep background and would never blow a source.

The Parlor, like the dozens of other spook bars, gave its clients not only a chance to get radically unwound, but a chance to pick up on new information or what a new assignment *really* might bring down on the hapless operative whose control had been less than generous with the facts.

That was why Sten had asked Alex to book dinner at the Parlor. The Eternal Emperor was being entirely too generous with things for this to be anything other than a nightmare assignment.

Aretha sleeked into the room and curled onto an oversize ottoman, hooves tucked underneath her. She—question mark—might have been taken for a sextuple-legged herbivore, considering the swept-back, needle-sharp horns, the brown-white-striped fur coat, and the hooves on the first and rearmost set of legs. But when she put her head back and bayed amusement, the prominent canines and cutting premolars and molars said otherwise. She ordered mineral water to drink—Sten and Cind immediately put their drink intake at "nurse"—and a slab of animal tissue, pounded and raw. Sten had charbroiled Earth salmon, a relatively new addiction, with butter and dill sauce. Cind also sampled Earth salmon. Raw.

Aretha briefed them—as only a Mantis field operative could. Sten was grateful that she spoke through a synthbox after the initial, polite greetings. Translating someone else's speech, even when it was in one's own tongue, could get wearisome, especially if the speaker had a dual diaphragm and evidently was at home in a language with glottal stops and sibilants.

She knew of Sten and his reputation and said she would help as much as she could. She assumed this woman had a need to know. Helping, she went on, would best be done by her kicking Sten in the genitalia, ensuring that he could not take this posting.

Three years earlier, Aretha had been deputy military attache at the Imperial Embassy on Jochi, she said. She was recovering from a minor case of zagging when zigging was indicated. Sten estimated her rank at lieutenant colonel.

"Nightmare," she went on. "A nightmare indeed.

"First let me tell you about the humans, my dear ambassador-to-be. Horrible. Horrible. Horrible. Former miners, with all of the forethought and logic that means. Go to any length to prevent regulation, then howl like a spavined pup when the material being mined runs out.

"As a culture, the Torks have enough imagination to want everything, but not nearly enough brains to achieve it. So that means they will willingly deny anyone else possession of these same mostly imagined treasures. Because the Altaic Cluster can only be considered a treasure if you have a way to package and export hatred and ethnocentrism.

"Consider the Jochians. Perhaps you did not know they were once a self-named Society of Adventurers. Given a charter to plunder by our own Eternal Emperor, long may he wave."

"I know that." Sten did not feel it necessary to tell Aretha that the information had come from the Emperor himself.

"Adventurers—pirates at one time. Then their culture swashbuckled itself down into anarchy and city-world solar systems until the oncoming of the Khaqan. The first. There have only been two.

"The Khaqan was also a liar and a thief and a back-stabber. The thing was, he could do it faster and better than any other Jochians. So he rose to the top. Like scum on a pond.

"He either died or was murdered by his son, the present Khaqan. Who has all of his father's talents at chicanery, and a fondness for building monuments to himself to the exclusion of all logic, needed public works, or continuing the social umbrella. And the Empire did nothing about his excesses while I was there. Possibly the Emperor had larger problems. Certainly, he would have heard almost nothing about how severe the problems really were.

"Unfortunately, our beloved Emperor had appointed an ambassador whose talents—I should not think anything less than complimentary, but allow me to say that in two E-years of intense observation I thought Ambassador Nallas's primary talent was lunch."

"What about the cluster's other beings?" Sten asked.

"Merciful clouds, they manage to fit in very well with the humans. First we have the Bogazi. Have you ever seen a livie on the planet Earth?"

"I've been there."

"That is right. I forgot. Think chickens."

"What?" Sten said.

"Mean chickens."

Sten chortled, almost spraying Cind with Scotch.

"I am not even beginning to jest. Fowllike. Large. Two and a half meters tall. Bipedal. Hammer beaks. Beaks lined with teeth. Two arms—hands most capable of weapons use or strangulation. Retractable spurs. Not chicken temperament, however. Except under times of extreme duress, when panic seems to be the correct measure, and they rush back and forth and to and fro, flailing about with all these wonderful evolution-provided weapons.

"They seem to have evolved from an aquatic bird. I understand, however, that in common with chickens their drumsticks are most tasty. We were not, unfortunately, in a position where a little sedate galluspophagism could be accomplished.

"They group like feline carnivores—one male, five or six females. The grouping is called—I am not making this up, either—a coop.

"The male is smaller, weaker, and marsupial—their young are born alive, by the by. Extremely colorful. The females hunt, so they have natural camouflage—not phototropic, such as your quiet assistant, but nearly as effective. They're highly democratic—but you should hear the discussions before a decision is reached. A rookery. You will enjoy them."

Sten *was* enjoying Aretha's descriptions and company. The food came. They ate.

"Sten has given me all the fiche," Cind said, halfway through her sushi inhalation. "What about the fourth set of beings—the Suzdal?"

"You could—I could, at any rate—almost get used to them. Think of a protomammal that evolved. Originally a pack carnivore. Small. A meter and a half to two meters. Six beings to a group. Attractive beings—quite gold in color."

"Why'd you have a problem with them?"

"If I believed in racial memory, which I do not, or if my home planet has fossils of small, pack-hunting carrion eaters, which it does not, I would offer that as an explanation.

"I cannot. Perhaps their language—an incessant yapping—is what is bothersome. For certain what *is* loathsome is their violence. The Suzdal like to kill. A prime social pleasure is turning an animal loose on open terrain and hunting it down. In packs. It would almost seem that *they* have an Ur-memory.

"Whatever it is, the Suzdal fit in perfectly with everyone else in the Altaic Cluster—beings who hate each other, and have hated each other for so long they forget why. But that does not stop them from a little considered genocide whenever possible."

"Wonderful," Sten said. He worded his next question very carefully. "I have heard reports that suggest that the Imperial energy shipments are . . . being diverted."

"You mean someone is stealing the AM2," Aretha said. "They are. Or rather, the Khaqan is."

"Where's it going?"

"Not sure. I attempted to learn—and found my esteemed ambassadorial leader a stumbling block. Some of it, I think, is going to the Khaqan's cronies within the cluster. Some of it is being outshipped, and the profits used to build his monuments. More is just disappearing."

Aretha finished her dinner and had a final sip of mineral water. "You have no doubt been told of the Khaqan's infatuation with large, ornate structures. But until you see for yourself just how massive an edifice complex he has, you will not believe it."

"I thank you, Aretha. It would seem to me—and this must stay QT—that the most logical way to keep the lid on the Altaic Cluster is to quarantine all four races to their own sectors. At least, kept at arm's length, they can't manage a pogrom a week."

Aretha whinnied laughter. "You were not told."

"I evidently have not been told several things," Sten said.

"Many, many years ago, the Khaqan decided to settle this terrible problem. So he intermingled these beings."

"What?"

"He arbitrarily chose resettlement. A nation of Suzdal, for instance, that rose against him would be moved, once the rising was suppressed. Frequently their new home would be in the middle of Bogazi worlds."

"Oh, drakh," Sten said. He poured himself a drink—straight. He started to drain it, then offered the decanter to Cind. She shook her head.

"Even more amusing," Aretha went on, "the Khaqan formed various militias. Each of a single group of beings."

"That makes no sense," Cind said.

"Oh, but it does. If you use each group of militia only against their traditional enemies, it keeps the anger focused everywhere except on you—the Khaqan. Another advantage is that these militia forces, stationed worlds and light-years away from their native sectors, are not only potential hostages, but keep the home worlds from being able to easily mount a revolution or civil war."

There was a loud crash, what sounded like gunshots from downstairs, and then whooping laughter. Aretha looked longingly at the door to the snug.

Sten smiled. "Thank you, Colonel. I owe you one. Now, if you'd ask Delaney to bring up the bill?"

"Would you permit me to buy you a drink downstairs?"

"I don't think so," Sten said. "I've got an early morning, and the . . . gentleman I'm seeing might not appreciate his favorite ambassador sporting a mouse."

With a whicker of pleasure, Aretha was out the door and headed down the stairs. In a second, Sten and Cind heard an even louder crash.

"I hope this place has a back door," Cind said.

"It does," Sten said. "Have you ever heard of a spookery that didn't?"

* * *

Sten's tongue caressed down Cind's neck, following the cleavage of the dress. Cind sighed . . . deep in her throat . . . near a growl. His hand moved along the inside of her thigh.

Their rented gravsled was on autopilot, holding a westering speed of barely fifty kph, and an altitude of nearly six thousand meters, out of any traffic lanes. Sten had managed to turn on all coll-sensors before the two of them tumbled, locked together, into the wide back.

Sten's hand found her belt buckle and fumbled. Nothing happened. "I feel like a teener," he said.

"You should," Cind murmured. "You tell me all about that enormous Imperial bed—and then hurl me into a rentawreck's backseat like we were flashing pubescents. Serve you right if a cop overflew. I can see it now," she murmured into his ear. "Hero Ambassador Found With Nude Bodyguard."

"But you're not . . ."

His fingers suddenly became capable.

"Yes, I am," Cind said throatily, as the dress came away and the nipples of her small breasts shone dark in the moonlight.

Their lips came together, tongues moving smoothly as if this were long-rehearsed and never the first time, and then her warmth caught him and drew him down and in for the eternity.

CHAPTER SIX

THE ATMOSPHERE IN the Imperial study was autumnal. There was no alk or stregg in sight. Sten felt himself very definitely in the V-ring as he came to the end of his Altaic mission briefing and sped through the last few items.

"Coding . . . SOI . . . emergency procedures . . . all that's here in the fiche. We're ready. The *Victory* can lift within three E-days when victuals and ordnance are boarded.''

Sten put two copies of his fiche on the Emperor's desk. They were coded and marked for the highest security access. The Emperor ignored them.

"You seem," he said, "to have also done an excellent job of picking your personnel for this mission. Your longtime aide—the heavyworlder. The Bhor. Their commander. Most photogenic. And an excellent way to avoid . . . foreign entanglements."

Whoever had had the meeting before Sten's must *really* have crapped in the Emp's mess kit. But Sten was used to vile temper from his superiors and paid no mind. "One more thing, sir. Also regarding personnel."

"What else do you want?"

"A skipper for the *Victory*. I think you've arranged it so that I'm going to be very busy on Jochi."

"Is there somebody you want?"

"Fleet Admiral Rohber Mason. He's currently awaiting reassignment here on Prime."

At first the idea had come to Sten as almost a joke. Then, on further consideration, it seemed a better and better idea. Mason might run a tyrannical ship, but the morale of the *Victory*'s crew was not especially of concern to Sten. Keeping himself alive was—and Sten knew that Mason the martinet was as capable of that as anyone. Besides, he knew that the admiral would follow orders. He was mildly curious to see whether it would bother Mason to serve under a man he disliked. Probably not—Mason almost certainly had the same feeling for all sentient beings. Sten himself had learned as a Delinq and then a soldier that one did not have to be friends with someone to task with them.

"Mmm. Very well. But you have a habit of wanting my best."

So the Emperor had heard of Sten's prospective Gurkha recruits. "Yessir. And that brings up something else. I've had twenty-seven of your Gurkhas volunteer for this mission."

"And you told them?"

"I told them that if this was in accordance with Imperial policy, they would be welcome. They seemed to feel your approval had been tacitly granted."

The Emperor swung his chair around and stared out the window at the sprawling castle grounds. He said something that Sten could not make out.

"Pardon, sir?"

"Nothing."

Silence. Then the Emperor swung around again. He was smiling. He chuckled once.

"Having a few Nepalese along," he said, "would certainly suggest to the Altaic beings that your mission is taken very seriously—and that you have access to the very highest levels, wouldn't it?"

Sten did not answer.

"Take them," the Eternal Emperor said. "It will do them good. We probably should start a program of rotating the Gurkhas into temporary outside field duties. Give them experience—and keep them from getting stale."

"Yessir."

"I think," the Emperor said, "you have done an excellent job of preparing yourself and your team for this mission. I wish you success . . . and luck."

He stood and held out a hand. Sten shook it, then came to attention and saluted—even though he was in mufti. Very smartly he about-faced and headed for the exit. No parting glass, he thought absently. But he was more intent on what his mind suggested the Emperor had said, when his back was turned: "So everything changes . . ."

The Emperor held his ceremonial smile until the doors closed behind him. Then he dropped it. He stood for a long moment looking at the door Sten had gone through before reseating himself and keying the chamberlain to allow the next catastrophe to enter.

Sten stopped at Arundel's Admin Office long enough to have them issue orders transferring Mason to the *Victory*, and to tell the Gurkhas' CO that the volunteers' request had been approved and that they should pack their kit and report aboard the next day. Then he headed for his gravsled in a truly sour mood. Hell. He should have told Lalbahadur Thapa to go sit on one of Nepal's eight-thousand-meter peaks until his pubes froze, and take his twenty-six friends with him.

And having somebody slither around and find out that he and Cind were not sleeping solo—not that they'd kept their building relationship particularly secret—he didn't like that, either.

Sten *knew* that the Emperor had survived as long as he had by keeping his Intelligence the best available. He knew that every retainer in the Imperial household had had at least some intelligence training, and most of them were ex-specialists. And he guessed it made sense to know whether your ambassador plenipotentiary was available, booked, or in area-wide lust.

But he did not like it.

As he went down the broad steps to the parade ground, he automatically touched his forehead, returning the salutes of the posted sentries. Too many goddamned nosy people in this world, he thought resentfully. He suddenly snickered. He guessed spooks never did like it when somebody looked under *their* sheets.

There was another gravsled waiting beside his, a nearly exact duplicate. That was strange . . . Sten's transport was a sleek, stretched, blazingly white luxury item that reeked official muckety, from its assigned driver and guard—one of Cind's Bhor—to the small ambassadorial flags mounted on each corner of the vehicle, to the phototropic bubble roof. Not uncommon on Prime. But Sten's diplo-yacht was emblazoned with the Imperial crest on a solid red slash on either side of the vehicle's doors.

The other gravsled lacked only ambassadorial markings to be a clone of Sten's. The door came open . . . and Ian Mahoney stepped out.

Mahoney was ex-head of Mercury Corps, ex-head of Mantis Section, the man who had plucked Sten off the factory world of Vulcan and recruited him into Imperial Service. Mahoney had gone on to command the elite First Imperial Guards Division, then to become overall commander for the final assault on the Tahn. Then, when the Emperor had been killed, Mahoney had begun the drive to destroy his assassins, the privy council.

The Empire regained, Mahoney had been given an assignment much like Sten's: to be one of the Emperor's roving troubleshooters, with ultimate authority.

The task of trying to piece the ravaged Empire back together was enormous. So Sten and Mahoney had only seen each other twice during the intervening years, and even those two occasions had been briefly seized moments.

Mahoney mock-scrutinized Sten's shoulders. "I can't make out the epaulettes," he said. "This time, do I outrank you, or do you kiss *my* ring?"

Sten laughed, and wondered why he suddenly felt so good. He realized there were very few people he could talk to openly, let alone consider a bit of a mentor, even though he had pulled Mahoney's butt out of a crack as many times as Ian had saved him.

"Damfino," Sten said. "I'm not sure what pay grade I'm getting this time around. Let's stick with me calling you 'sir'—that way I won't have to be apologizing for old habits. Time for a drink?"

Mahoney shook his head. "Unfortunately, the path of duty calls, and it is a stony path indeed. I am due to make a rather more meaningless than usual speech before Parliament shortly. And much as I'd love to stomp to the podium, belch stregg, and start by damning all politicians' nonexistent souls to the Pit, I think the boss"—Mahoney jerked a thumb up at the Emperor's apartment—"would have words with me."

"Clot," Sten said. "You and I fought the war to end wars, and they *still* won't let us do any malingering."

Mahoney frowned, seemingly deep in thought. "Why don't we kill a few minutes before my speech? It'll give us a chance to talk, plus get a little exercise, which we both could use. Have these poor excuses for politicians' hearses meet us over there—if you have the time."

"I have the time."

"Wasn't it around here," Mahoney said, "where the Emperor had his workshop? Building . . . what were they?"

"Guitars," Sten said.

"Wonder why he never rebuilt the shop, after . . . his return?" Mahoney asked.

Sten shrugged. He had really wanted to blow some steam off, but so far Mahoney had kept the conversation relentlessly trivial.

"Those were some days, weren't they . . ." Then Mahoney's casual tone changed. "Damn, but you take hell's own time tracking down, boy. Keep the smile on the face. We're just beyond parabolic mikes now, but there's a long-range eye that's up on one of the battlements. It can read lips."

Sten's bobble lasted for only a microsecond. Then he became the total professional. "How do you know we're clean?"

"I have a copy of all security plans—and changes—to Arundel. Woman in the tech department owes me a small favor."

"What's going on?"

"Damn, Sten, but I wish I could answer that straight on. Or that we had more than two minutes before we're in range of the next pickup. Because I'm not all that sure. But things . . . just aren't right. Haven't been, as far as I can see, since he came back." Mahoney grunted. "Or maybe I'm just becoming a senile, paranoiac old man. But the fault, from my seeing, is the Emperor."

Sten almost slumped in relief. There it was—somebody else saw something.

"And if I try to give you specifics, you'll think I'm past it," Mahoney went on. "Because . . . It's all little things. Little things that lead to big things."

"Like the new Guys in Gray," Sten wondered. "This Internal Security?"

"That's a bigger thing. Still bigger is that they don't answer to Mercury or Mantis. And it's strange that the closer they get to the Emperor himself, the more they look like they're his damned sons or something. Time!"

"Right. Just getting tired. But lately, retiring back to Smallbridge has sounded better and better," Sten picked up smoothly. "Let the world go by and all that."

"I always said you lack ambition," Mahoney said.

"And lacking it more the older I get."

"Clear," Mahoney said. "Have you spent any time around court?"

"Not really."

"It's being taken pretty seriously these days," Ian said. "It used to be a place the Emperor had to stash obnoxious or stupid people with money or clout. Give them a title, tuck them here on Prime, and they can't stir up any trouble back home. Most of them now are still prancing peacocks. But it seems that the Eternal Emperor spends more time in their company. Plus there's starting to be some people here who aren't popinjays.''

''What does that mean?''

''I don't know,'' Mahoney said.

''Have you noticed the Emperor's temper's on a short fuse these days?'' Sten asked.

''You see,'' Mahoney answered, starting to spread his hands helplessly and then changing his mind, ''drakh like this—like whether he's being cranky—I don't even know if it's important. Maybe he was always like this. Maybe he's just pushing too hard, trying to put this crumble of an Empire back together. I . . . I truly do not know,'' Mahoney said once more.

''That's the other question,'' Sten said. ''Maybe the real question, and what's been eating at me. *Can* this clottin' Empire be saved? Or did the combination of the Tahn war and the privy council batter it too much?''

''Clean it up . . . three, two, now . . . Again, Sten, the only answer I have is DNC—insufficient data.''

They walked on, as the path wound toward the artificial mountain the Emperor had built with the ostensible reason of keeping him from having to look at the clots in Parliament, talking of this, and that. At last Mahoney announced that they were outside any bugs, and asked about Sten's current assignment.

''We've got ten minutes now, so give me the full details.''

Sten did. Mahoney mostly kept silent, except for an occasional shake of his head or grunt.

''Now, there's a fine example of what I've been groping at,'' Mahoney said. ''The Altaic Cluster. .Good analysis by the boss, yet you wonder why he let it go on for so long. Blame it on being busy with bigger catastrophes.

''What's bad is that he told you to go out there and lay sacred hands on the Khaqan and bless his hustle. He could just as well, and possibly more wisely, have sent you out to get a feel for the problem and *then* reach a solution as to whether to reinforce the old thief or just send in Mantis to cut his throat.

"Now there's a point that just occurred to me, thinking out loud as I am. It's as if he doesn't quite have the same patience or depth.

"Oh well," he said. "Oh well."

"The problem is," Sten said, smiling a bit ruefully, "is that the Emp is, as far as I can see, the only game in town."

Mahoney did not answer him. "I'm sure it'll all straighten out," he said obliquely. "Now. We're coming up on range of more bigears. Let me take care of *my* business. I didn't go to all this clottin' trouble because I particularly care about your pissant personal problems. There's chaplains for trash like that."

Sten laughed, feeling a great deal more cheery. Mahoney was using the old Mantis "sorry you're bleeding to death but could you do it in another color, since I always hated red" hard-edged sympathy.

"First, here." Mahoney's hand brushed Sten's, and a square of plas passed between them. "That's body-temp sensitive. Keep it close. If you drop it it'll char."

"What's on it?"

"A very elaborate, very complicated computer program, and its two brothers. Get to any Imperial computer terminal that's cleared for ALL/UN input, and key the codes in. The first one will wipe *all* references, anywhere in the Imperial records, including Mantis and Imperial Eyes Only, to one Ian Mahoney. The second does the same for Sten, No Initial; the third for that thug Kilgour. After wiping, it then mutates in all directions, destroying as it goes."

"Why the hell would I need *that*?" Sten said in complete shock.

Mahoney didn't answer. "One other thing. And listen close, because I am only going to say it once, and I want you to bury it in your backbrain.

"If the drakh comes down—*really* comes down, and you will absolutely know what I mean if it does—start by going home. There's something waiting."

"Small—"

"Think, goddamn it," Mahoney snarled. "You've got your

head up like you were a straight-leg trainee. That's it. Four tools, maybe. Or four parts of an old man's degenerating into senility?''

Mahoney chortled suddenly. ''. . . said, 'you clot, the line was there's *hope* in her *soul*.' ''

Mahoney laughed. Sten, more than familiar with situations when sudden merriment sans joke was required, also laughed. ''Fine, Ian. If we're telling old stinkers, here's one of Kilgour's, which I won't even begin to try in dialect.''

As his mouth began the words to the half-remembered joke, Sten forbade himself a guilty look back over his shoulder at Arundel Castle . . . and concentrated on jokes, obscene, scots, stupid.

Days later, Ian Mahoney stood in the shadows near a spaceport hangar. Far across the field a violet flame plumed into the night.

The *Victory* lifted smoothly on its Yukawa drive until it was a thousand meters above Prime. Then its captain shifted to stardrive, and suddenly there was nothing but silence and night sky.

Mahoney stood for a long time looking up at that nothing.

Luck, lad. Better than mine. Because I'm starting to think mine's running thin.

And I hope you learn it may be time for this town to hunt up another game—and find out just what exactly it could be.

CHAPTER SEVEN

THERE WERE ABOUT twenty beings cloistered in the room. The atmosphere was conspiratorial. Thick with talk—and smells. The sweet musk of the Suzdal. The mint /fish odor of the Bogazi. And the methane and ammonia aroma of humans.

''Like privies smell,'' the Bogazi male clicked. ''Own privies.''

"Shush. Might hear," one of his wives warned. She fussed over him, tucking a stray feather back into his fabulous tail display. His name was Hoatzin.

He tapped the big hammer of his beak against hers, showing pleasure. "Humans I study in books only," Hoatzin said. "Some in school I see. But not close."

He waved a delicate grasping limb at the humans in the room. "This *very* close. Like it. Not smell. Like study close." Hoatzin was a teacher, as were most males in his society. They reared the young. Their domain was the nest and the book. For the wives, it was the hunt.

Hoatzin looked over at the main table with pride. This is where the leaders of each group held forth, seeking a way, or, at least, agreement to agree. His chief wife, Diatry, was one of the four. She was speaking now.

"In circles we talk," she said. "Big egg circles. But big nothing in egg. Could all night stay. Talk and talk. Still egg not hatch." She peered down the hammer beak at the much smaller forms around her. Even by Bogazi standards she was tall: nearly three meters.

The Suzdal pack leader made a tooth display. The dim light glittered all along the sharp edges. "Summed up like a true Bogazi," Youtang said. "Forget the flesh. Get to the bone of the thing." The flattery to a former enemy was not intended. Youtang was getting weary of all the fencing. She would probably be surprised to learn that she had one other thing in common with the Bogazi: In their hatred of the smell of humans, they were sisters.

The general sighed. He wasn't sure how he had let himself be talked into this meeting. Except that the Tork, Menynder, was notoriously persuasive. Douw was frightened. What had started as an information-only probe had developed into a full-scale engagement. The current griping irritated him. As the Jochian secretary of defense, he certainly had the most to lose.

"What *more* am I supposed to say?" Douw gave his shoulders a helpless shrug. "That conditions are intolerable? Of course they are." He looked nervously around. "I mean . . . *some* conditions are bad. On the other hand . . ."

"There's a foot," Menynder broke in.

PARK AND TURNE
ZANFEE VALLEY
AIRDRIE AB
T4A 2E4
403-945-2503

DEBIT SALE

APPROVED 00

Appr Code: 203993
DEBIT CHQ
5592**************5815
AMOUNT $3.15

THANK YOU / MERCI

MERCHANT COPY

"What?" Douw's face was a blank.

Like a cow, Menynder thought. A silver-haired cow. "This isn't a staff meeting, General," he said. "Every being here has a life on the line. We gotta start talking plain. Otherwise the risk isn't worth it."

He motioned around the room. "I told you the place was clean. I had it scoured for bugs stone by stone. Now, so far I have provided a safe place to meet. Right in the middle of the squeakiest clean Tork neighborhood on Jochi." He ticked the rest off on his fingers. "Youtang stuck her neck out contacting the Bogazi. And Diatry, here, is probably on the Khaqan's *Most Suspicious* list, so she risked it even coming out of her roost."

The Tork shifted his heavy weight in the chair. "Face it, General, if he knows we're here we are already dead. Now, let's go."

Douw soaked this up, slowly churning it through his conservative military mind. Menynder was right.

"After close observation of the Khaqan," he said quite formally, "I have come to the conclusion that he is insane."

No one laughed. Every being in the room realized the step Douw had just taken. It was almost as if the words had been delivered in a courtroom.

"Furthermore, I believe he has become a danger not only to himself, but to all the beings living in the Altaic Cluster." The general sucked in breath and let it out in a great whoosh. There. It was done.

The room erupted.

"I'll say he's insane," Youtang said. "Killed every one of his own cubs, didn't he?"

"One hatchling was trouble," Diatry said. "With rebels he plotted."

"Sure. But what about the others? Three daughters and a son. He killed them all. Afraid they wouldn't wait until he died for them to try to take over." Youtang was especially outraged by this sin. The Suzdal were highly protective of their young.

"In gluttony he lives," Diatry said. "Food. Drink. Sex. Money. Power. Too much of all he has. All over Altaics, roosts are cold. Markets they are empty. Stores outside we line. For hours and hours. What a life is this?"

"Drakh. That's what," Youtang snarled.

"What do we do about it?" Menynder pressed.

"Do? What's to be done?" Douw asked.

Menynder boomed laughter. "Well, from the looks of things in this room, we're all pretty much in agreement that the old buzzard has to go."

"Three questions we must decide," Diatry said. "One: Do we kill? Two: If kill, how? Three: Once gone, who rules? In these I am correct, yes?"

There were no arguments.

"Let's start with the last part," Menynder said. "Speaking as a Tork, I'm tired of us getting short-ended because we're a minority. Whoever takes the Khaqan's place is going to have to deal with that."

"I agree," Youtang said.

"Same for Bogazi," Diatry said.

"What if we felt out Dr. Iskra?" Menynder wondered. "He's respected all over the cluster. And he has a rep for seeing all sides of a problem."

Iskra was a member of the Jochian majority. But he was a famous professor who had made his mark in Imperial circles. Another plus was that he was currently the Emperor's territorial governor of one of the conquered Tahn regions.

There was a long silence, as the beings in the room pondered the suggestion.

"I don't know," Youtang said finally. "Lots of smoke. Not a lot of substance. I mean, who knows how he really thinks?"

They all turned to see what General Douw had to say about the proposal. The general's brow was furrowed with thought. "Do you really think we need to kill the Khaqan?" he asked.

There was a frustrated murmur around the room, but before anyone could speak, the door crashed open.

Every being in the room lost a lifespan as they looked up to see their worst nightmare: the Khaqan. Standing in the doorway. Flanked by gold-robed soldiers. Riotguns leveled.

"Traitors!" the Khaqan roared. "Plotting my murder!"

He strode forward, face a bloodless mask of death, bony finger jabbing like a specter to pierce each heart, emptying lungs and defecating organs.

"I'll roast you alive," the Khaqan shrieked. He was at the table now, his fury pouring over them. "But first, I'll take you apart—small piece by small piece. And I'll feed the pieces to your children. And I'll feed them to your friends. And they'll be the ones who stand at the Killing Wall."

He gathered up the fury into a chest-bursting balloon and shouted: "Take them to my—"

Sudden silence. Everyone stared at the Khaqan. His mouth was a wide *O*. His eyes bulged. The death face had turned swollen red. Even the soldiers were gaping at him.

The Khaqan plunged face forward on the table. Small bones cracked. Blood gouted from his mouth. Then the body slowly slid to the floor.

Menynder squatted beside him and put a practiced hand to the Khaqan's throat.

He stood. Removed his spectacles. Cleaned them. Put them back on.

"Well?" Oddly, the question came from the captain of the guard.

"He's dead," Menynder announced.

"Thank God," the soldier said, lowering his weapon. "The old son of a bitch had gone looners."

CHAPTER EIGHT

THE AMBASSADOR AND the warrior lay entwined in bed asleep. Naked limbs had curled around each other until the two bodies resembled an ancient Chinese puzzle knot, of the erotic variety.

The ambassador's groin was covered with the warrior's barracks cap.

Through the thick insulated walls of the ambassador's suite the distant sounds of a shift change could be heard. Somewhere in the bowels of the *Victory* a pump shuddered into life and began filtering the fluids in the hydroponic tanks.

The blond curls of the warrior stirred first. Long lashes fluttered open. The warrior peered into the face of the sleeping ambassador. The warrior's eyes roamed downward to the barracks cap, then lit with mischief. Little teeth flashed in a crooked grin.

Cind carefully untied her portion of the knot. Sliding her lovely limbs out of Sten's embrace, she knelt on the Eternal Emperor's yawning bed. There was room for a whole division of lovers on its silky smoothness. But for what Cind had in mind, the vast playing field was a waste.

She gently lifted the cap away. Her slender fingers reached for their target. Blond head and soft lips dipped downward.

Sten was dreaming about Smallbridge. He had been roaming the snowfields that spread from the forest to his cabin by the lake. For some reason he had been dressed in battle harness—tight battle harness. Odder still, the harness was cinched over his naked flesh. It wasn't uncomfortable or anything. Just odd.

Suddenly, he was inside his cabin, lying by a crackling fire. The harness was gone. But he was still naked—and something wonderful was going on. Then he realized he was asleep. And dreaming. Well, it wasn't all a dream. Not the naked part. Or the wonderful goings on. Then the fire crackled louder.

"Ambassador, your presence is requested on the bridge!" The fire was talking.

"What?" This a murmur.

"Ambassador! Do you hear me?"

"Go away, fire. I'm busy."

"Ambassador Sten. This is Admiral Mason. If you please, I need you on the bridge."

The wonderfulness abruptly stopped. Sten opened his eyes, suddenly in a sour mood. His mood curdled more when he saw Cind's rounded curves and disappointed face. Her lips formed the word "Sorry." She shrugged.

Sten palmed the switch of the com unit on the built-in bedside stand. "Okay, Mason," he said, doing his best not to snarl, with little success. "Be right there."

Cind started laughing. Sten's frown deepened. Clottin' Mason.

"Give me the order," Cind said, "and I'll trot out a firing squad and have him shot."

Sten finally saw the humor and joined her laughter. "Do I get to torture him first?" he snarled. "I know just where I want to start." He clambered off the bed and started to get dressed.

"I'm off shift for another two hours," Cind said. "So if you're back before I have to shower . . ." She let the rest trail off suggestively.

"I'll hurry," Sten said.

Two hours later, he checked the clock, thought wistfully of Cind, and turned back to Mason.

"Maybe we're drowning our own sensors," Sten suggested tentatively. "The *Victory* is pretty new. Not much time on the engines. Leaky baffles, perhaps?"

The scar on Mason's face purpled. He had personally checked the scans on every flex nut and seam. No way would he allow some slipup to embarrass him in front of this son of a Xypaca. He would rather eat drakh for rations.

"I had it happen on my first tacship," Sten lied smoothly, knowing what Mason was thinking. He wasn't needling the man. After all, Mason was in charge. Sten just wanted the problem solved. "It was brand new and barely broken in when Mr. Kilgour and I got it."

Sten indicated his heavyworld friend, whose technical knowledge had been commandeered by Mason's com officer. The two were conferring, hands flying over the com center panel. Buzzwords thickened the air.

"The designer hadn't factored the effect broken-in engines would have on the baffling," Sten said. "Blew clot out of our reception. Transmissions, too."

Mason's scar returned to normal color. "Good thought," he said. "I'll check it." He gave orders to his chief engineer, mentally kicking himself for not thinking of it first.

A few minutes later word came back. "That was no good," Mason said. He was too professional to gloat. The admiral wanted the problem solved, too. "You were right about the leakage. But it's minor. Not enough to foul things up."

Sten nodded. He had only been hoping. He looked over at Kilgour and the com officer, wanting to ask how they were doing. But he kept his lips buttoned. Not his place.

"Anything to report?" Sten heard Mason ask his com officer.

The com officer and Kilgour exchanged looks. "He'd better tell you, sir," the officer said.

"Ah wae puzzlin't i' it twere th' bafflin' myself, sir," Kilgour said. "But thae'd on'y mess wi' transmission. The talkin'. Nae the hearin'."

"Except for some stray old radio echoes, sir," the com officer told Mason, "there's not one thing being broadcast on the whole planet. Jochi is silent, sir. Not even any livie feed. And you know how broad *those* bands are? I've tried every kind of transmission I could think of to rouse someone, sir. Sr. Kilgour threw in a few ideas of his own. I double-identified the *Victory*. I even pointed out that his majesty's personal emissary was on board." He gave Sten a worried nod. "Still no answer."

"Anything from the other worlds in the system?" Mason asked.

"Negative, sir. As silent as Jochi. But the funny thing is . . ." His voice faded.

"Yes? Speak up, man."

The com officer looked at Kilgour and licked his lips. Kilgour gave him a reassuring nod.

"It's real spooky, if you don't mind, sir. There are no broadcasts, as I said. But every scanner we've got going is just showing a flicker of life. As if everybody on Jochi was tuned in at the same time. Listening. But not talking."

"Th' silence hae a wee echo t' it, sir," Alex said. "Like a specter m' ol' gran conjured t' frighten us bairns wi'."

Mason gave Alex a withering look, then turned to his com officer. "Keep transmitting," he said.

"Yes, sir."

The com officer keyed the mike. "This is His Imperial Majes-

ty's battleship *Victory* calling. All receiving stations are requested
to respond."

Keyed off. Waited. Got silence. Tried again. "This is His Imperial . . ."

Mason motioned to Sten and strolled to a quiet corner of the
bridge.

"I don't understand what's going on," Mason said. "I've carpet bombed half a planet, and even out of the smoking ruins some
poor bassid managed to get on the air. Spotty transmission, yes.
Silence, never."

"There's only one way that I can think of to answer the question," Sten said.

"You mean, land anyway?"

"That's what I was thinking."

"But the Emperor wanted a big show. Honor guard. Me in
dress whites, you in tux and tails, and the whole band playing to
idolizing crowds as you and the Khaqan greeted one another."

"I'll arrange something later," Sten said. "The Emperor is
worried about this place. I'd rather forget the show and find out
what's happening." He shook his head for effect. "Can't imagine
what he'd say if I came back and said, Sorry, sir. Mission abandoned. Seems the inhabitants of Jochi got the throat plague, or
something."

"I'll land," Mason said. "But I'm going to full alert. And clear
for action."

"I am in your capable hands, Admiral," Sten said.

Mason snorted and went back to the com center. Sten slipped
quietly off the bridge.

"Some ghost, Kilgour," Sten said. He wiped the sweat from
his brow and pulled his collar up to protect his neck from the
fierce Jochi sun.

"Mayhap' th' wee specter hae a bomb aboot him," Alex said.

Sten took another look around the Rurik spaceport. Except for
his party, there wasn't a being in sight. No one living, anyway.
He thought he saw a charred stump lying in the rubble about a
large bomb crater. Or maybe it was just an optical trick of the
heat and the lung-drowning humidity.

There were similar craters all over the spaceport, as well as the fire-blackened outlines of what must once have been a few parked tacships and a lot of combat cars.

There was a sudden howl of air, and a small whirlwind touched down, sucking up bits of rubble as it cut across the ground. In the odd behavior of cyclones, large and small, it ran around the edge of the immense crater in the center of the field. Another bomb hole. A big clottin' bomb. The hole was where the control tower had once stood.

The twister lifted off and was gone.

"Now we know the answer to why no one was talking," Sten said. "Everybody's too scared. Didn't want to be noticed."

"But they're all a listenin', though," Alex said.

Sten nodded. "They're waiting to hear who wins."

Heat lightning flashed. Then there was a heavy roll of thunder. His Gurkhas suddenly lifted their willyguns. Something—or someone—was coming. Sten could make out a small figure edging around the ruins of the control tower. Cind and her scouts? No. They had reconned off in the other direction.

"Still on'y one ae them," Kilgour said.

"Maybe it's the band," Sten said dryly.

Gradually the small figure got larger. Sten could make out a squat, barrel-chested human, sweating copiously in the heat. Picking distastefully at his sodden clothing, the man tromped steadily onward. In his left hand he was tiredly waving a kerchief-size white flag.

"Let him past," Sten told the Gurkhas.

They parted ranks, and the man lumbered gratefully to a halt in front of Sten. He took off a pair of antique spectacles. Blew on the lenses. Wiped with the flag. Put them back on. Looked at Sten with his oddly magnified brown eyes.

"I hope you're Ambassador Sten," he said. "And if you are, I'm real sorry about the lousy reception." He looked around at the bomb craters. "Ouch. I guess they really went at it."

He turned back. "You *are* Ambassador Sten, aren't you?"

"I am." Sten waited.

"Oh. Forgive me. The heat's getting to my old Tork head. I'm

Menynder. About the only one you'll find around here to speak for my people."

He wiped a sweaty hand on damp clothing and with an embarrassed grimace held out his hand.

Sten shook. Then he pointed around at the signs of destruction. "What happened?"

Menynder sighed. "I hate to be the one to break the news, but . . . the Khaqan is dead."

Sten had to yank fast into his diplomatic bag of tricks to turn the gape that was growing onto his face into professional surprise.

"Clottin' what?" Kilgour said. "An' who kill't th' ol'—"

"Natural causes," Menynder assured them. He eased his collar away from his neck. "I was there myself. Saw the whole thing.

"It was a terrible experience. We were all just about to sit down to . . . dinner, and the Khaqan keeled over on the table. Dead. Just like that." He snapped his fingers.

"There was an autopsy?" Sten asked coolly.

"Lord, did we have an autopsy," Menynder said. "Nobody wanted to . . . I mean, under the circumstances, we thought it wise. Two teams worked on him. And we really pored over those reports. Just to make double clottin' sure." He fingered the collar again. "It was natural causes all right."

"When is the funeral?" Sten asked. This had torn the whole thing. The Emperor would not be pleased.

"Uh . . . kind of hard to say. You see, we all agreed to agree until the final coroner's report. Things sort of fell apart before we got to talking about a funeral." Menynder indicated the bomb craters. "If you see what I mean."

Sten did.

"I don't want to point fingers," Menynder said, "but the Jochians started it. Squabbling among themselves over who was to be the new Khaqan. The rest of us weren't consulted. Although we told them plainly, *before* the shooting, that we had some ideas of our own."

"Naturally," Sten said.

"Anyway, when the Jochians ran out of hot words, they started fighting. We all hunkered down. Then a stray shell landed right in the middle of a Tork neighborhood. It was . . . pretty bad. My home world thought it best to send a militia."

"Oh?" Sten said.

"Just to protect my people. Not to get into anything with the Jochians."

"How did that work out?"

"Not well." Menynder sighed. "I didn't think it would. There have been some . . . ahem . . . sharp exchanges, if you know what I mean."

Sten could see just fine.

"Of course, once our militia showed up, well the Bogazi and the Suzdal militias decided their folks needed protecting, too."

"I figured that," Sten said. It was getting worse and worse.

"Okay, you've got the picture. Now, I've got some real bad news for you," Menynder said, checking his timepiece and looking nervously around the spaceport.

"Och, so thae's th' braw news, i' it?" Kilgour growled, liking it even less than Sten, if that was possible.

"See, everyone's been glued to the emergency bands, praying for the cavalry to show up. We *all* heard your broadcasts. Folks probably overloaded the Jane's fiche, checking out the *Victory*." He pointed at the sleek craft behind Sten that was the Emperor's ship. "Personally, I already knew. Pride myself in keeping up at my old trade. But I had only vaguely heard of you." He nodded at Sten.

Sten cursed under his breath, remembering the com officer saying he had tried everything.

"So . . . I'm the cavalry," Sten said.

"You got it, Ambassador," Menynder said. "I checked the Imperial *Who's Who*. Pretty impressive. Hero soldier. Hero diplomat. The Eternal Emperor's main man. At least, that's how it's playing on Jochi."

Sten could imagine. This was not good. Definitely not how he had planned this miserable day.

"Everybody's on the way now," Menynder said. "I hustled like clot to beat them. And they're going to want your ear. They'll kick reptile snot out of each other trying to rip it off your corpse, if they have to."

Menynder let this sink in a second before going on. "See, whoever has you, is top dog." He winced. "Gotta watch myself. Some of my best friends are Suzdals."

"I assume you had some sort of a plan," Sten said. "Otherwise you wouldn't be here."

"I sure did," Menynder said. "Although I might have trouble convincing you of my good intentions."

"Ah. I see," Sten said. "You were thinking we could go have a nice quiet word in some safe Tork neighborhood. Am I right?"

Menynder grinned. "What the clot? It was worth a try. If not, maybe you better get out of here. Fast."

Sten ignored this. Thinking. He got a glimmer.

"How far to the embassy?" Neutral turf. No one would dare fire on or even near the Emperor's embassy.

"Clear across town," Menynder said. "You'd never make it."

There was a grind and heavy clank of tracks. Sten jolted up to see an armored ground vehicle push its way through rubble. A small flag flew from a standard next to the tank's chain guns. Sten didn't have to ask. It was Jochian.

There was a cry from the other side of the field. Sten turned to see Cind running like the wind, her Bhor scouts right behind her. She was yelling some kind of warning and gesturing at a low building behind her.

Mortar dust suddenly sprayed out from the building. The entire front collapsed. Another track emerged under a rain of metal and brickwork. The track was also armored. It had chain guns and flew a flag—Jochian, as well.

Cind panted up to Sten. "And that's not all," she said, pointing at the track. "There's more of them. Plus soldiers. And from the sound of things, a great big mob on its way."

The tracks' main gun turrets suddenly swung around. They had spotted each other. Simultaneously, their guns opened up, hurling spent uranium AP shells.

Admiral Mason's voice crackled over the *Victory*'s outside speakers. "I suggest we leave, Ambassador," he said.

Sten agreed. He turned to Menynder. "You better make yourself scarce," he said. "Good luck."

"We're going to need a lot more than luck," Menynder said.

And he puffed away for cover. Sten and his group sprinted to the ship and thundered up the ramp.

Behind them, first one track exploded, then the other. A mortar round slammed in. More tracks appeared. Guns blazing.

Braced against the gees exerted by the *Victory*'s fast takeoff, Sten watched the battle scene shrink away from him on the bridge's main screen.

Some welcome, he thought. Now, how the clot was he going to unravel this muck-up?

Sten huddled with Mason in the admiral's cabin, trying to figure out what to do next. As they worried over several possibilities—ranging from poor to plain stupid—the reports kept flooding in. Jochi was no longer silent.

Sten's eyes swept over a sheaf of transcriptions the com officer had handed to him. "They've gone mad," he summarized. "Everybody's calling everybody else all kinds of obscenities. Prodding the other guy to come out and fight like beings." He read on, then gave a low whistle and lifted his eyes. "Which they are doing." He tapped one report. "A Jochi militia caught some Torks in a building. They wouldn't come out to be slaughtered. So the Jochians burned it around their ears."

"Wonderful," Mason said. "Plus we have so many riots going on that the algo computer has scorched its wires running progs on how fast this thing can spread." He snorted. "So much for diplomacy. Proves my own private theories on the behavior of the average citizen. The only thing any of them understand is a good shot up alongside the head."

"I don't think that would work here," Sten said dryly. "The Emperor wants their hearts and minds. Their scalps won't do him a clottin' bit of good."

"Still . . ." Mason said.

"I know," Sten said. "With these folks it's damned tempting. Unfortunately, what's happening right now was triggered by our arrival."

"I'm not taking the blame for this," Mason said, a little hotly.

Sten sighed. "No one's asking you to, Admiral. It's my ass the

Emperor will want on toast. Although, if it gets much worse, he may not be satisfied with *just* mine."

Mason opened his mouth to retort. Sten raised his hand, silencing him. He'd had a sudden thought. "My father used to tell me about this beast," Sten said. "A mule, I think he called it. It was a sport. A mean and stubborn sport. Said the only way to get its attention was to hit it with a board, first."

"I already suggested something along those lines," Mason said.

"Yeah. I know. But for these beings, a hit on the head may be too subtle . . . Okay. Try this idea on for size . . ."

Mason leaned closer as Sten sketched in the broad outlines of his plan.

The Jochi mob was pressing close on the Bogazi barricade, showering rocks, debris, and taunts on the small group of neighborhood defenders. The shops on either side of the broad main street of Rurik were blank eyes of shattered glass. Many of them were gouting flames.

Overhead, the midday sky was black with threatening storms. Heavy clouds jostled one another, triggering thick blue arcs of electrical fire.

A tall Jochian rushed the heap of furniture and scrap timber that made up the barricade. He hurled a grenade, turned, and ran for safety.

A burst of fire cut him down. At the same instant, the grenade went off. The explosion shrapneled through the Bogazi. There were screams of pain and anger.

A big female Bogazi hurtled through the gap cut by the grenade. Spurs jutting out from her forearms, she snagged two Jochians. She brought the big hammer beak down once. Twice. Skulls cracked like pollution-thinned eggshells.

She dropped the corpses on the ground and turned for another victim. A heavy bar swung against her throat. The Bogazi flopped beside the two corpses.

More Bogazi came pouring out. In a moment, the main street's storm drains would be awash in blood.

There was a sudden banshee howl from overhead. A heavy

wind blasted along the street, battering the crowd with dust and small debris. The mob stopped in midriot—and gaped upward.

The gleaming white body of the *Victory* swept down the boulevard toward them. Not high in the sky, but just below the roofs of the high-rise buildings that lined the street, a looming bulk never meant for the heart of a city.

Close to the barricades the howl grew louder, and the warship went into a hover on McLean Drive, close enough for the mob to get a good long look at the Imperial emblem on its sides.

This was the Imperial presence—mailed fist and looming overlord in one.

"My God, would you look at that," a Jochi chemical worker breathed.

"Maybe now, justice we get," a Bogazi said.

"Wait up! What's he doing?" another awe-stricken Jochian said, absently tugging at a Bogazi's sleeve.

The *Victory* settled still closer, until it was no more than twenty meters overhead. The crowd huddled under the dark cloud of its body. Engines stirred, then the ship slowly began to move forward, straight down the broad avenue.

The two sides of the conflict gaped after it for a moment or two. Then they turned to stare at one another. Makeshift weapons tumbled to the ground from hands and grasping limbs.

Above them, the black sky was suddenly bright blue. Sun painted lacy clouds a multitude of colors. The air was fresh and tasted of spring.

"We've been saved," a Jochian said.

"I knew the Emperor wouldn't abandon us," said another.

Someone shouted from a rooftop: "The ship's heading for the Imperial embassy."

The spell broke and the mob, laughing and shouting in relief, rushed after the ship.

The *Victory* sailed slowly along just above the pavement. Below it, the street was suddenly jammed from side to side with a sea of beings. Bogazi and Jochians and Suzdal and Torks, all mingled together, joking and slapping one another on the back.

Thousands of other beings leaned from the windows of the tall buildings, cheering the *Victory* and its majestic flight.

All over Jochi—in fact, all over the entire cluster—beings stopped what they were doing and rushed to witness the arrival of the Emperor's man.

By the time the ship reached the Imperial embassy, there were literally millions of beings surrounding its broad, gated grounds. And there were billions more watching on their livies.

All hostilities had ceased.

Inside the *Victory*, Sten quick-brushed his clothes. Cind ran her fingers through his hair, pushing strands into place.

Alex looked at a livie screen and the enormous crowd waiting outside. "You're a bleedin' Pied Piper, young Sten," he said.

"Don't say that," Sten said. "He got paid off in rats. Or house apes, and I don't know which is worse."

A crew member tickled the port controls. The port swung open. Sten felt the fresh breeze on his face. He heard the thump of the ramp settling to the ground.

"Okay," he said. "Now let the bastards come to me."

He stepped out into a torrent of cheers.

BOOK TWO

CAT'S CLAW

CHAPTER NINE

"I'VE NEVER BEEN one to kill the messenger bearing bad news," the Eternal Emperor said.

"Yessir," Sten said.

"In this case, however," the Emperor continued, "it's a good thing I've known you such a long time."

"Yessir," Sten said.

"You get the point that I am not pleased?"

"I do, Your Majesty," Sten said. "Absolutely . . . sir."

The holo image of the Emperor wavered as Sten's boss crossed to the antique drinks tray in his study and poured himself two fingers of Scotch.

"You have something to drink there?" the Emperor asked a bit absently.

"Yessir," Sten said. "I thought it best to haul along my own supplies." He took the hint, hooked a bottle of Scotch off the desk of the previous ambassador, and poured himself a drink.

The Emperor mock-toasted: "I'd say confusion to my enemies—but if they get any more confused we'll all go into the drakh head first."

He drank anyway. Sten followed suit.

"You know there's no way I can keep this from getting out?" the Emperor said. Sten didn't answer. It had not really been a question.

"There's already reports in the media hinting at a building crisis in the Altaics. Wait'll they find out how bad things really are." The Emperor refilled his glass, thinking. "What really hurts is I've got some crucial agreements in the works. Agreements hinging on strong confidence in the Empire. The slightest sign of a hole in the structure I've rebuilt is going to put those agreements into decaying orbits. And . . . when one fails . . . then a lot of other things come into doubt.''

Sten sighed. ''I wish there were some way I could paint a more hopeful picture, Your Majesty,'' he said. ''But this is probably the stickiest assignment I've ever handled for you. And it's not really begun.''

''I'm sensible of that, Sten,'' the Emperor said. ''The Khaqan just picked a lousy time to die.'' He sipped his drink. ''You *are* sure someone didn't help him along?''

''I've gone over all the reports,'' Sten said. ''And it's pretty clear how and why he died. It was an aneurysm. An artery blew a cork. The only thing I'm not sure of is the circumstances.'' Sten was thinking of Menynder's claim about a dinner party honoring the Khaqan. ''Personally, I don't think it matters that much. If there was some kind of conspiracy in the works . . . well, from what I've seen it wouldn't be all that unusual.''

''I agree,'' the Emperor said. ''In fact, if there was no sign of a conspiracy, I'd be damned suspicious. Fine. Let's leave the circumstances alone—for the time being.''

''Yessir,'' Sten said.

''What we have to do,'' the Emperor said, ''is get this thing under control fast. If the whole Empire is going to be watching, I don't want anyone to think I'm going to be less than firm about this. There are going to be some who'll say I screwed up. There are going to be others who'll say I've lost my moves . . . since I got back. And then there'll be those who are just hoping I've gotten soft so they can stir up trouble. So, with that in mind, I want to set the tone of how to handle things right from the start . . .

''Which is this: If anybody moves we don't like, smack them down. We install a new government. Immediately. With my *full* support. Once this is done, there will be *no* objections. Not in my earshot, anyway. And, if there are loud or violent quarrels with my decision in the Altaics, then I want them silenced. Fast. With whatever it takes. I will suffer no humiliation in this!'' Slam went the Emperor's hand on his desk. Even through the holo speakers it sounded like a shot.

Abruptly the Emperor stopped steaming and gave Sten a thin, unfelt smile. "I want to be damned sure both my enemies *and* my friends know I will not be fooled with."

"Yessir. I . . . agree, sir . . ."

"Do I hear a silent 'but' in your agreement?"

"Not with your overall point, Your Majesty. Not at all. This is no time to show hesitancy. However, when you briefed me on this place, you weren't exaggerating about how contrary these people are. Even if we use a big hammer to nail this together, I think we'll still need to be real careful how it *goes* together."

Sten hesitated, trying to read the Emperor's face. It was blank. But not necessarily angry blank.

"Go ahead," the Emperor said.

"As you know, sir, I've talked to all the leaders—at least the beings who *say* they are the leaders. Until I get some better analyses, based on immediate HUMINT, I'll just trust in my instincts: This thing can split a lot more than four ways. Clot, it already has. When I arrived two Jochi factions were firing on each other at the spaceport."

"Listen to those instincts," the Emperor said.

"Soon as I showed up," Sten continued, "all of these faction leaders, human and ET, clawed their way to the embassy, each one begging to be made the new honcho. I made them wait for official invitations. Called them in one by one."

"And took your good time about it, too," the Emperor said. "Made them cool their heels and ponder their sins against me. I like how that was handled."

"Thank you, sir," Sten said. "Frankly, now that this place has come apart once, I'm real doubtful it can be put back together again. Not the way it was before.

"They're all sitting in their neighborhoods now, sir. And on their home worlds, as well—with nothing to distract them but their personal problems. Picking over wounds. Thinking things can somehow be different. And in this case, sir, just the thinking might make it so. Of course, each of these beings sees some kind of personal vision of paradise for his own group. Personally, I think it's going to be sheer hell around here for a long, long time."

"Unless we fix it," the Emperor said.

"Unless we fix it, sir," Sten agreed.

"To begin with," the Emperor said, "I'm giving you a battalion of Imperial Guards. That ought to help make the glue stick."

Sten jolted. "So much . . . sir? I was hoping for maybe one Mantis Section. If we stay a little lower profile, and if things don't work out . . . we take less blame. Besides, sir, I really believe I can do better with scalpels than a hammer."

"I can't take that chance," the Emperor said. "You're getting a battalion. I'm already a target of ridicule. Fine. I'll be a big damned one. Also, I have another reason."

"Yessir," Sten said.

"Any other thoughts?" the Emperor asked.

"Yessir. Out of this whole sorry lot, I *do* have one pretty good candidate to take over. If only temporarily."

"Who?" The single word had a guarded edge to it. Sten didn't realize this, however, until later.

"Menynder, sir. The Tork. He's a tricky old buzzard. But he's the one being everybody seems to respect. His enemies list is real short. And I think he could get people to listen long enough for things to take hold. Pick up their own momentum."

"Good choice," the Emperor said. "Except . . . like you said, he's probably just a temporary solution. I have a permanent fix in mind." He took a casual sip of scotch. "The man's name is Iskra. Dr. Iskra. He's a Jochian."

Sten furrowed his brow. He'd heard it. Vaguely. Enough to know Iskra commanded a great deal of respect. But Sten was so new on the ground that he would just have to take the Emperor's word on Dr. Iskra's sterling qualities.

"I've already spoken to him," the Emperor said. "One of my ships is picking him up now. He should be with you in a few cycles. He's the other reason I'm sending a battalion of guards. Dr. Iskra asked for them. He'll use them as personal security. At first."

"Very good, sir," Sten said. His antennae for trouble gave a bit of a quiver over Iskra's request for the troops before he'd even seen the Altaics and evaluated the current situation. He pushed the worry to the back. But he didn't lock it away.

Also, the only thing that mattered was that this whole thing worked. Sten had picked up exactly none of the Imperial Foreign Office's traditional bad habits, such as placing ego in front of solution.

"Anything else?" the Emperor asked. He seemed restless, anxious to be on to other things.

"No sir."

"Then . . . until your next report . . ." The Emperor leaned forward to touch a button on his desk.

But as the holo image of Sten in the Jochi embassy chamber thinned, the Emperor quickly checked the expression on Sten's face. It was properly respectful. And then Sten was gone.

The Eternal Emperor absently picked up his drink and sipped, deep in thought. Total concentration was one of the many abilities he had fine-tuned over his many centuries. He gave the subject of Sten a full five seconds of that concentration.

Was he loyal? Without question. In the Emperor's absence, Sten had been the architect of the plan to depose the privy council. The keystone of the alliance he had created was absolute commitment to the Emperor's memory.

Yes, Sten was loyal. And the Emperor had given him many honors. But few beings realized just how great a hero Sten was.

For perhaps the first time, the Emperor was aware that he was fortunate Sten was on his side. For some reason, the thought was not entirely comforting.

The Emperor tucked that nugget of discomfort away. Later, he would fit it into the larger puzzle. He pulled his mind back from its task.

There was another man whose assistance he required. Of the very silent—and deadly—variety. Yes. He must take no chances in this Altaic matter. No chances at all.

CHAPTER TEN

THE LIVIE CASTS were filled with reports of Sten's razzle-dazzle with the *Victory*. The Emperor's spin experts flooded the media with dramatic pictures of the ship's progress over awed Jochi crowds and the hero's welcome Sten received when he landed at the embassy.

Much was made of the calming influence the Emperor's flag had on the poor hysterical beings of the Altaic Cluster. The death of the Khaqan came almost as an afterthought, with appropriate sad words from the Emperor, mourning the demise of "a dear friend and trusted ally."

There were the usual assurances from key aides that order had been restored, and that the Emperor's people were "Working closely with local leaders to assure an orderly transition of government."

Sten sighed as he palmed the switch cutting off the livie anchor in mid-toothy charm. He had expected the Emperor's damage-control campaign. Which—no surprise—was highly effective. Unfortunately, the spin the Emperor's teams were putting on events was so optimistic that Sten feared that a minor hiccup might be viewed as total disaster.

A situation he was doing his damnedest to prevent. Sten bent his head to his task, ignoring the buzz of techs in the embassy com room working under Alex's directions. For the tenth time he struggled with the diplomatic note. The problem was, how was he going to tell General Douw, Menynder, Youtang, Diatry, and the other Jochi leaders that they had been cut out of the loop? That the new Khaqan had been chosen—without consulting them?

Dr. Iskra was on his way. And Sten would have to tell the group soon, or he would be in an especially embarrassing situation.

He could see it right now: "Good afternoon, gentlebeings," Sten would say. "I'd like you to meet your new despot. Comes highly recommended. In fact, I think you may all even know the gentleman. Sorry I didn't mention it sooner. But the Emperor doesn't trust a single one of you. And could give a clot if you live or die. Just so long as you do it quietly. Now . . . If you'll excuse me . . . I'll repair to the barricades whilst you good beings fight it out amongst yourselves." And he would take off as fast as a Jochi twister.

Oh, boy. This was going to be near impossible to put a good face on. However, there was no getting around it. The note would have to be written, yes. But the real deed must be done in person.

Sten's mind started to cramp. He looked up to see how Alex was coming along with his little spy mission. Not for the first time, Sten marveled at how many of their old nasty skills the work of peace involved.

His eyes swept the bank of screens filling one wall of the embassy com room. "Coom on, y' wee Frick & Frack," Alex coaxed, tickling some controls. "Be't ae good bat."

Kilgour had made a preliminary scavenging survey of the embassy to see what goodies the previous ambassador had left behind. The first pass was immediately useful. Stashed in the basement storerooms, he found hundreds of tiny robotic monitors. They were winged—and looked a lot like bats. Alex dubbed them Frick & Frack One through One Thousand or so, in honor of the live batlike beings who snooped for Mantis operations. He had recharged the monitors' powerpaks, consulted with his team of techs and experts on the Jochi culture, programmed in patrol sectors, and sent the bats aloft to spy.

They were broadcasting pictures right now of scores of scenes all over Rurik. And those pictures told a different story than the Emperor's livie casts.

Yes, calm had been restored. But only compared to the mess Sten encountered when he first arrived. The screen in the upper left-hand corner showed the scene outside a Jochi military compound. Peaceful . . . on the surface.

But as Alex coaxed his little snooper closer, Sten could see several armored tracks. Idle, but ready to go in an instant. Maintenance crews were hard at work on others. He could see gravlifts hauling in ammunition and supplies.

The screen below it displayed a rebel Jochi force undergoing intense drilling and training. Another, a Tork encampment, bristling with arms and hot talk.

There were similar scenes on other monitors: Suzdal and Bogazi barricades being rebuilt and strengthened; militias patrolling neighborhood streets, in one case pointedly ignoring a group of adolescents filling glass jars with pilfered flammable fuel.

The main market district of Rurik was empty. Shops were buttoned up tight, some with hired thugs as guards. Sten saw gangs of young beings swaggering through the streets looking for trouble and loot. One of Alex's bats swooped past a blasted-out storefront. Figures hauled out valuables by the armload. In this case the looters were soldiers, with a few police sprinkled in.

"Aha, wee Sten," Kilgour said. "Here's th' lass Ah wae blatherin' aboot." He threw the projection to one of the larger, center wallscreens. Sten saw a joygirl exiting an alley. The screen's map inset showed she was near a Jochi military compound. A wolf whistle shrilling through a speaker told him just how close.

The view shifted, and Sten could see several soldiers reacting to the scantily clad woman. The joygirl stopped and posed with hand on hip, bosom and other goodies jutting. A soldier called to her. The joygirl gave a pouty flip of her head, swiveled on shapely heels, and ankled back into the alley.

The soldiers looked at each other and laughed. Two split away to follow.

"Now watch this lass at work," Alex said, tugging at a tiny joystick as he sent the bat soaring over the alley. The soldiers had caught up to the girl. Bargaining was in progress. Finally, price agreed on, the joygirl leaned against the alley wall. Fumbling with his clothing, and joking with his buddy over his shoulder, the first soldier advanced.

As he was lifting the joygirl off her feet, there was sudden motion, so quick that Sten almost missed it.

The joygirl had some hefty friends. They clubbed the soldiers down. By the time the joygirl had finished straightening her scant tunic, the soldiers' unconscious bodies were being stripped of weapons, uniforms, and IDs.

Sten watched the joygirl and her group head off to set up another trap. "How many does this make?"

"A score or so. But on'y since Ah've been countin'. She's verra quick. Got a few more lads jus' t' haul th' stuff t' the rebels."

"Jackrollers for a Free Jochi, huh?" Sten said. "It'd almost be funny, if I didn't think any minute now the lid was going to blow off the pot.

"The big pain is that there isn't much we can do. Except sit tight, hope for the best, and jawbone the locals to be patient. And wait for Dr. Iskra to show up."

"When first we met, young Sten," Kilgour said, "you were nae such a honey-tongued liar. Ah'm pleased a' y'r progress."

"Thanks . . . I think," Sten said. "Trouble is, now I've got to be really creative." He tapped the diplomatic note he was composing. "When Iskra arrives there's going to be some pretty pissed off beings."

"Y'll do fine, lad. Liars like us'r made, nae born. Otherwise, our dear mums'd ice us when we were bairns."

Sten groaned in agreement. But what choice did he have? He knew that just as long as relative calm lasted on Jochi, so the rest of the cluster would stay at "peace."

The joyous enthusiasm that had greeted his arrival had lasted about as long as the sudden spring weather—which had almost immediately turned foul. Tempers rose with humidity. Black clouds bunched under that humidity. Moods bounced from euphoria to headache gloom. Which, Sten was already learning, pretty much described the nature of all the beings on Jochi.

A few hours before dusk on the second day, a whole snake's nest of cyclones appeared above the Rurik skyline. The twisters roared around in the strange nonlogic of the inanimate. Dashing for the city. Scaring clot out of everyone. Then retreating. All the while, sucking up trees and topsoil and outbuildings—which did nothing to lessen the fear. Suddenly, they sped off and were gone.

Ever since then the citizens of Rurik had been casting nervous looks at the horizon. And at one another.

Then, just the previous day, winter had returned with a cold snap as if the spring and then the humidity and heat had never been. Another part of the wonders of Jochi.

Sten went back to his lying scribbles. "'. . . Whereas the Eternal Emperor . . . in his deep affection for all the beings of the Altaic Cluster . . .'"

"Holy clot! Look't thae!"

Sten's head bounced back up. He looked where Alex was pointing. The center monitor screen was complete confusion. Sten strode over to get a closer look.

A whole mass of beings was parading in front of some institutionlike structures; evidently built by the late Khaqan, the structures were heroic in size and drabness. To Sten, they looked like giant beehives tied together with sky-high walkways and beltways.

"It's the Pooshkan University," an earnest young tech said. Sten recalled that her name was Naomi.

He groaned. "Students? Oh, no."

"Aye. W' hae hormone trouble, lad," Alex said. He twiddled with controls and suddenly a dozen views of the university leapt up on the main screen.

Here, uniformed campus cops were being hauled out by young beings and dumped through the main archway. In another section of the campus, Sten could see students smashing through what appeared to be a glass-fronted cafeteria. In half a second a wild food fight erupted.

Teachers were fleeing for cover, not too successfully ducking hurled food and other debris. Bonfires were being set all over the campus. Fed, Sten was sure, with the records of any students who happened to be failing.

He also caught glimpses of naked flesh through bushes and trees and heard squeals of joy as some of the students protested in a more passionate manner.

A huge barricade was being erected at the main gate of Pooshkan University. There was enough logic to the tumble of junk that Sten was sure engineering students had to have been involved. Which took planning.

Further proof of this was the sudden unfurling of carefully

printed banners. The banners demanded many things. But mostly they demanded: "Democracy Now!"

"Wonderful," Sten said. "The one thing nobody in this place is going to get."

He peered closer at one of the views of the students—and he realized just how odd these students were. To begin with, it was a mixed group. As many Suzdal and Bogazi youths as there were Jochians and Torks. Second, they were all working—rioting, actually—together. This almost never happened on Jochi, much less in the rest of the cluster, where segregation was a prized fact of society's status quo.

"What kind of a place is this?" Sten asked, noting as he did, just how well fed—and clothed—these young beings appeared.

"Gie us a reading, lass," Alex said to the young tech.

Naomi shook her head. "I don't have to look it up. Pooshkan is *the* premier university of the cluster. That's where all the top beings in the Altaics send their sons, daughters, chicks, and pups."

"Rich kids," Sten groaned. "Double wonderful." Then he shrugged. "Oh, well. Sounds like a local problem to me. The cops will handle it."

"Oh-oh," Kilgour said.

"What's with the oh-oh?" Sten hated to ask.

"Wish't an' y'll receive't," Alex said. "Th' wee pigs are comin' out. An' spritely."

Sten saw a phalanx of cops moving toward the main gate, complete with helmets, riot shields, electric prods, and—he saw a small track moving in—tear gas.

"Clot!" was all Sten said.

"An' here come the Lookie Lous," Kilgour said, pointing at crowds of adults gathering at the edge of the campus. Some were shouting at the cops. Some at the students. Some at one another. The onlookers were definitely segregated into tight knots of angry ethnics.

"Hell with it," Sten said. "Still a local problem. No way are we getting involved."

As he spoke, the com board lit up with incoming calls. Alex's people started fielding them. ". . . Imperial embassy. Yes, we've heard of the disturbance at the university. No, the ambassador has no comment . . . Imperial embassy . . . the Pooshkan riot? Yessir. No sir . . . Imperial embassy . . .''

Totally disgusted, Sten grabbed his scribblings and started for the door. "Don't call me unless it gets worse," he yelled over his shoulder. "In fact . . . don't even call me—"

"You best take this one, lad," Alex said, proffering a com set.

"Who is it?" Sten asked, almost snarling.

"A wee bairn frae Pooshkan," Alex said. "In fact, it's thae one." He pointed at a monitor screen, which showed a close-up of an imperious young Jochian. A handsome boy despite a tendency to lard about the jowls. Sten could see him talking into a com set that apparently was connected to the embassy board.

"Th' ringleader, methinks," Alex continued. "Milhouz i' th' name he gives."

Naomi whistled. "Student president," she said. "His parents are on the board of the Bank of Jochi."

It dawned on Sten just how dicey this Pooshkan place was. A bloodied nose would be viewed as pure murder in some quarters.

"Yes, Sr. Milhouz," Sten said into the com unit, smooth as glass. "This is Ambassador Sten speaking. How may I help you?"

As he listened to the young voice jabbering away in his ear and saw the flushed, excited features on the monitor screen, Sten knew he would have to break the first rule he had set himself in Phase One of this operation. Which was: Do not leave the embassy. Make them come to you.

"You may expect us in a few minutes, young man," he said, and broke connection. As he turned back to the board, he saw that Cind had entered the room. From the look on her face, he could see she had a pretty good idea of what was going on.

One of the monitor screens showed students hurling a shower of debris at the cops.

"This damned thing could be the spark that sets off the big ka-bang," he told Cind. "So, here's the drill. I'll need about ten Gurkhas. Maybe fifty Bhor. But we want to go at this real low profile. Concealed weapons. No uniforms. We don't want to act like storm troopers."

"Pretty tall order for the Bhor," Cind said. "Especially Otho."

"If this works right," Sten said, "everybody will be so curious about Otho and the others, they'll be too busy gaping to cause trouble. Alex?"

"Ready ae you are, lad," Kilgour said.

"Okay, boys and girls," Sten said. "We're going back to school."

CHAPTER ELEVEN

THE DAY WAS bright and bitterly cold as Sten and his crew moved through the Square of the Khaqans. He gawked along with the others at the monuments towering over them. He felt like an insect marching through a land of giants.

"I keep waiting for one of them to step on me," Cind said, in an odd echo of his own thoughts.

"By my mother's long and knotty beard," Otho rumbled, "the man had ego enough for a fleet of us."

Otho lifted a hairy paw to shield his eyes from the glittering domes and brooded at a particularly awesome display of bad taste. It amounted to a platform resting on the shoulders of a dozen statues. The statues—easily twenty meters high—were of perfectly formed male and female humans, probably Jochians. They were stark naked. Posed on top of the platform was an idealized statue of the Khaqan swathed in golden robes. He held a torch aloft, complete with eternally licking flames.

"I could understand the man if he built drinking halls," Otho finally said. "It's much more useful to a boasting being. Besides, if you set a good table and are not stingy with the stregg, no one minds a braggart." He peered at Sten with his bloodshot eyes. "Not that I am one to follow this practice. I prefer my guests to extol my deeds."

Sten pointed at the legend inscribed in one corner of the display. It read: TO HE WHO LIT THE ALTAICS WITH HIS GLORY. Under it, in smaller letters: From A Grateful People.

"Maybe he had a similar idea," Sten said. "Except he dispensed with the good times for one and all."

Otho's massive brow beetled at him. "This is why I said a drinking hall would make better sense. For a being who ruled so long, this Khaqan knew nothing of leadership."

Sten laughed agreement and motioned his group onward. He had decided it would be better to walk to Pooshkan University. It wasn't far from the embassy, and walking would certainly be lower profile than a phalanx of armored gravcars.

Besides, the first rule Sten had adopted as he learned the ropes of diplomacy was that it was important not to become isolated. He knew many ambassadors whose feet had never touched real ground. They were whisked from the steps of the embassy to state chambers to banquet and back again, for their entire tour of duty. He had also noted that their advice was invariably wrong.

In this case, he had found the scene on the street to be no different from what he had seen on the com room vid screens. Except, emptier. But the *feel* was different, there in the bright sunlight and sharp cold. His breath steamed. Shadowy figures ducked out of sight as his team tromped along, wary hands and paws near weapons belts.

Everywhere Sten looked there was a gigantic portrait or statue of the Khaqan, peering down on the mere mortals who must tread the avenues to their inconsequential appointments.

Especially unnerving was the low sound of thunder that rumbled continually behind the distant mountains. It definitely added an edge to one's mood.

Sten kept that in mind as he mentally prepared himself for young Milhouz and the other student agitators.

All those thoughts had vanished, however, when they entered the Square of the Khaqans. The sheer size of it would stagger any normal being's imagination. Just as the blinding colors fuddled the senses. It was a difficult place to get any kind of perspective. Turning away from a garish pillar, the eyes would clear, only to be confronted by a monument so large it made one dizzy.

Despite the sheer size of the square, Sten felt frighteningly closed in. With good reason. His professional eye noted that the square was built for maximum crowd control. Then he saw the Killing Wall. He didn't have to ask what it was as he looked over its black smoothness. A monument of hatred. Of power gone mad.

A sudden helplessness gripped him. He felt far too small for the task. His mind told him that was silly. The square had been designed to elicit exactly that response. Still, the feeling was difficult to shake.

At last they reached the far exit. Pooshkan University was just beyond. As Sten heard the low chanting of angry students, his mood instantly lifted and spring returned to his step. At least this was something he could confront. And maybe even solve.

"Th' cops're stokin' up their wee courage," Alex said. He had gone on ahead with a Gurkha squad to scout the situation. "Th' gravlighters're pourin' by th' minute. Wi' reinforcements. An' the brass're well back oot a harm's way i' th' mob should break through."

"Worthy warriors all," Otho snorted. "They lead from the rear. Even to attack children. I tell you, my friend, there is no honor in this place. I swear to you I will feel no joy when I break their heads."

"Now, Otho," Sten soothed. "Breaking heads is not your job description. This is a diplomatic mission, remember?"

Down the street they could all see and hear the squalling confrontation that was their mission. Sten professionally estimated that there were about a squillion beings about to go at it, tooth, nail, tear gas, and guns. There came a thunderous shower of rocks falling on the cops' riot shields. Oh, yes—and rocks as well.

"I promise I will use no more than this, my friend," Otho said, shaking a clenched ham of a paw. The other Bhor rumbled in agreement.

"Your orders," Cind snapped at Otho, "are to use nothing but open hands. Or elbows and knees. Light kicking is also permissible."

There was a long silence as Otho peered at this small thing

issuing orders. Cind stared back. "Is that understood . . . Private?" she said.

Laughter boomed from Otho. "By my father's frozen arse cheeks," he said, "open hands it is." He glanced at Sten and wiped moisture from the edge of one bloodshot eye. "She makes me proud," he said. "She proves the worth of Bhor training and ideals."

As Otho struggled with his emotions, there were more loud shouts down the street. A police bullhorn rumbled a warning. And there was another rock shower.

"Dinna be bawlin't, m' great hairy beast ae a friend," Alex said. "W' hae a riot to tend to. Remember?"

"We're going to have to get to it first," Cind said, indicating the confused mass of beings jamming the street and the arched entrance to the university.

Then Sten heard a familiar voice. "Beings of Jochi," it thundered over a porta boomer, "listen to the pleas of your children . . ."

It was young Milhouz. Sten spotted him standing high off the ground, on the base of yet another heroic statue of the late, not so great Khaqan.

"We bring you a message of hope and lo—" And the voice cut off as a group of shielded cops charged the students. There were screams of pain and anger, which were overridden instantly by a roar from the crowd of adult onlookers.

Then there were cheers and some laughter as the charging cops abruptly changed course and beat a hasty retreat. Milhouz flashed a victory sign.

But Sten could see that the victory would be short-lived. The cops were humiliated now—and even more scared than before. He could see that they were about to renew the assault, this time in massed and deadly force.

He nodded to Cind. "You know the drill."

They moved forward. Alex took a flanker's role, moving with the Gurkhas around the cops. Cind took some Bhor to cut between Alex and the angry crowd of adult civilians. Sten, Otho, and about twenty Bhor went straight up the middle, through the cops.

"Ooops! Pardon me," Cind said, as she jabbed an elbow into

a burly Tork dockworker. "How rude of me," she apologized, neatly clipping a Suzdal in the jaw.

"So very sorry," Lalbahadur Thapa said, as a sharp toe made contact with the shins of a towering Bogazi. He squeezed his slim figure past two more and trod heavily on the toe of a mammoth Jochian, blocking his path.

"My fault," Alex said as he leaned a shoulder into a cop and sent him tumbling against his mates. His arm swept back in awed reaction to his own clumsiness. Another cop went sailing. "Och! Thae must've smarted. F'rgive me, lad."

"Coming through," Sten shouted. A knee lifted and caught a crouching cop in the behind. The cop went mask first into the ground. "Sorry about that. Imperial business, you know."

A thick cop arm circled Otho's neck. Two more came at him, riot sticks raised to strike. "By my mother's beard," he said, "my boot wants tying again." He leaned forward to do the deed, and the cop went sailing over his head—right into his charging colleagues.

Someone had Cind by the shirt. A big someone. She jabbed him in the eye with a finger. The big someone howled in pain and let loose. "I don't know what's wrong with me today," Cind said. "I'm so clumsy."

A Suzdal snapped at Chittahang Limbu. The little Gurkha grabbed it by the ear just as the jaws reached his throat. He twisted. The Suzdal went with the twist, tumbling over into his pack sisters. "I am such a silly man today," Chittahang mourned. Then, under his breath, he muttered, "Yak pube."

"Make way! Imperial business! Make way!" Sten shouted. Remarkably, it was working. Most of the cops parted to let them through. Those that didn't got an elbow or a heavy Bhor slap.

Alex came upon two cops beating the bejabbers out of a small student. Without pause, he lifted them from the ground and slammed them together. He let go. They fell to the ground. Unconscious.

"Och, no. Ah hope Ah dinnae go an' break y'r wee heads. Sten'll hae m' hide f'r it." He moved on.

Otho and four Bhor broke through to the statue. They turned—like living armored tracks—sweeping a wide, clear space around them. A few seconds later, Sten was in the center of the clear space. A few seconds more, and the whole group had taken up formation around him.

Sten looked up at Milhouz. The young Jochian's jowls were flushed with astonishment.

"Sorry I'm a little late," Sten said. "Now. If you'll give me that thing, I'll have a little chat with these good people."

He indicated the porta boom in Milhouz's hand. The young Jochian stared at him, mouth open. Then he nodded and handed Sten the boomer.

"I can't believe you did that," he said.

"Neither can I," Sten said. And he turned to face his public.

"First . . . we demand respect for the dignity of all species of the Altaic Cluster," Milhouz said, stabbing a finger at the document that he and his fellow students had drawn up.

"I don't think anyone would argue with that," Sten said. He glanced around the cafeteria table at the other student leaders. They were all very young, all very solemn.

Strange, Sten thought, how much youthful beings looked alike. Whether Suzdal, Bogazi, or human, they had those great wide innocent eyes and round helpless faces. Terminally cute, Sten thought. Which, come to think of it, was an odd bit of universal genetic programming. The probable reason parents didn't kill their young at birth.

"Second," Milhouz continued, jowls flapping like a small, burrowing rodent, "the equality of all species must be the cornerstone of the future government."

"The Emperor's record is pretty clear on that," Sten said dryly. "He's a noted champion of equality."

"Still must be said," the Bogazi student broke in. Her name, Sten remembered, was Nirsky. From the way the other Bogazi males fawned on her, he assumed she was pretty.

"Then, say away," Sten said.

Milhouz cleared his throat for attention. "Third. All militias must return to their home worlds. Forthwith."

"I suspect that will be high on the agenda of any new authority," Sten said.

"You're patronizing us," Milhouz complained.

"Not at all," Sten said. "I'm merely underscoring a fact." He kept his features bland.

"No one ever listens," the Suzdal yipped. He had been introduced to Sten as Tehrand.

"Yes. That's right. We stayed up all night hammering out these demands." The speaker was a Tork. A very lovely Tork, who obviously doted on young Milhouz. Her name was Riehl.

"I'm listening," Sten said. "I went to some trouble to get here, remember? Now, why don't you go on?"

"Fourth," Milhouz continued, "we demand amnesty for all students at Pooshkan who participated in this blow for freedom. And this must include us—the members of the Action Committee."

"I'll do my best," Sten said, meaning it.

"Not good enough," Nirsky said. "Promise, you must."

"Promises are easy to make," Sten said, "but hard to secure. Once again—I'll do my best."

Milhouz's face took on a look of saintly purity. "I'm willing to take my chances," he said. "I'd gladly lay down my life for my ideals."

"Let's not get carried away," Sten said. "No one's life is at issue here. All I'm saying is when the new government is in place, some people might not take too kindly to the damage you've caused.

"There may be charges. Fines. A little jail time at the most. Which, by the way, I'll do my damndest to prevent. But they may not listen to me. So, be prepared."

Squabbling erupted. Sten leaned back in his chair as the students tossed his comments back and forth. Tehrand shot him a threatening look, Suzdal teeth gleaming. Sten paid him no mind, just as he ignored the thirty or more other students in the room, many of whom were also giving him the evil eye.

Although he had elected to meet with the group alone, he doubted there was much they could do that he couldn't handle, should the situation turn nasty.

"I'm sorry," Milhouz finally said, "but that demand is not negotiable."

"What if it's refused?" Sten asked.

"We'll burn the university to the ground," Riehl said, her pretty features flushed with resolve.

"I wouldn't advise that," Sten said. "In fact, I really wish you'd consider making no threats at all. It'll give me more leeway to negotiate with the police."

"One week only," Nirsky said. "Then burn we must."

"We all agreed," Tehrand said. "We voted on it."

"So have another vote," Sten said. "You can say it's in light of new factors Sr. Sten has brought to your attention."

"Democracy doesn't work that way. All votes are final," Milhouz said pompously. "Which brings us to the next and most important demand . . .

"The rule of the Khaqans must end. In fact, the rule of any form of tyranny must end. We demand a new order. Only through democracy can the problems of the Altaics be finally resolved!"

"To further this end," Riehl said, "we have drawn up a list of candidates acceptable to the Pooshkan Action Committee."

"Hold on," Sten said. "Tell me more about this 'approved' list. Doesn't sound too democratic to me."

"Oh, but it is," Milhouz said. "In its purest sense."

"And he doesn't mean that primitive theory where *every* being gets to vote, no matter how . . . undeserving." Riehl gave Milhouz a melting look. Sten figured Milhouz for the list of the "deserving."

"I see," Sten said. He made diplomatic *hmmm* noises. "How interesting you should think that way."

"Good. You understand my point," Milhouz said, taking this for acceptance. "Let's be frank. Most beings—meaning the, well, uneducated classes—want to be told what to do." He leaned forward, impassioned. "They feel . . . uncomfortable with weighty decisions. They want structure in their lives. It makes them . . ."

"Comfortable," Sten helped.

"How astute of you, Sr. Ambassador. Yes. That's the word exactly. Comfortable. And happy, as well."

"Educated ones know best," Nirsky said.

"A long-known fact," Tehrand yipped.

"There can be no tyranny if you have an educated elite, is what

Milhouz says. Isn't that right, de—ahhh. Isn't that right?'' Riehl blushed at almost revealing her feelings.

Milhouz gave her a warm pat on the thigh, letting his hand linger. "Yes. I did say . . . something like that. But, I'm no genius. Others mine the same field.'' He gave Sten a very solemn look. "So the thought isn't entirely original.''

"How very modest of you,'' Sten said.

"Thank you, Ambassador. Anyway . . . back to the point of our . . . manifesto. We believe the new leaders of the Altaics should be chosen from all the great families of the cluster. The most educated Suzdals, Torks, Bogazi, and Jochians—like myself.''

"Would success at this university help in their . . . qualifications?'' Sten ventured.

"There is no greater laboratory of learning than Pooshkan University. So . . . that goes without saying.''

"I should have guessed. How foolish of me,'' Sten said.

"Although we do see a great need for improvements here,'' Riehl said. "Many of the courses are . . . incorrect in their thinking.''

"I assume the overhaul of the university is also among your demands?'' Sten asked.

"Absolutely.''

"And you'll burn the university if they don't?''

"Yes. Who to stop us?'' the Bogazi said. "My brood most important. If someone hurt me—much trouble.''

"The same with all of us,'' Riehl said. "It's a good thing for those cops that you came along. If they had done something stupid . . . why, our families would have destroyed them all. Believe me.''

Milhouz handed Sten the sheaf of paper that was the Action Committee's manifesto. "Those are our demands. Take them . . . or leave them.''

Sten drew the moment out very long. "Then . . . I'm leaving,'' he finally said. And he rose to go.

The room erupted in total panic.

"Wait,'' Milhouz said. "Where are you going?''

"Back to the embassy,'' Sten told him. "I'm no good here.

Besides, this is really none of my business. It's definitely a local problem. So . . . if you'll forgive me . . . I'll go watch what happens to you next on my livie screen. With a nice stiff drink to warm my belly.''

"But you can't leave!" Riehl shouted, nearly in tears.

"Watch me," Sten said.

"But police will—"

"Kill all of you," Sten said. "They're pretty mad. I don't think it'll take much to set them off. Your pedigree will probably just make them madder. You know how cops get? Touchy. Very touchy.

"Funny, isn't it? You people think you're rioting. But the cops riot instead. Happens every time.''

"What do you want from us?" Milhouz wailed. His jowls were white with fear.

Sten turned at the door. "Better question. What do you really want? And don't give me that manifesto business.''

There was total silence.

"I'll tell you what," Sten said. "I'll see if somebody will talk to you. Give your views a fair hearing.''

"Someone . . . important?" Milhouz asked.

"Yeah. Someone important."

"A public hearing?"

"I don't know. Maybe."

"We want witnesses," Tehrand yipped.

"I'll ask," Sten said. "Now . . . will that do? A fair hearing of all your views. To be taken into account by decision-making people. Okay?''

Milhouz glanced around and saw slight nods of heads. "It's agreed," he said.

"Good." Sten headed for the door.

"But . . . if they don't at least listen . . ." Milhouz was trying to pull some pride in for the group.

"You'll burn the university to the ground," Sten finished for him.

"In one week!" Milhouz snapped.

"I'll keep that in mind." And Sten was gone.

CHAPTER TWELVE

STEN RETURNED TO the embassy in a mood that could only be livened by a few ax murders.

He took one look at that lying diplomatic note still only half-written and sent the burn pad spinning across the room.

Juvenile as all hell. Also, not nearly satisfying enough.

He thought about kicking the desk over but caught himself in time, considering the mass of that enormous wooden block big enough for the Khaqan's tastes and noting, also, that its legs already were scarred, trophies of previous ambassadorial self-mutilations undoubtedly resulting from dealing with the charming, altruistic, visionary residents of the Altaic Cluster.

Sten next thought of ordering Admiral Mason to his quarters in hopes of provoking an off-the-record punchup but settled instead for a loud feral growl, aimed out the sealed window at the slamming rain from the storm that had settled in over Rurik.

There was a chortle.

And a giggle.

Sten did not turn.

"An' dinnae y' hae pity ae th' lad," Alex's voice crooned. "Discoverin' he's th' wee one whae hae Imperial custody ae an entire *cluster* ae Campbells?"

"And this," Cind said, her voice equally sincere, "is the brave Sten. The great warrior I grew up worshiping. The man, legend had it, that led all of the beings in the Lupus Cluster to peace and plentitude, never losing the smile on his lips or the song in his heart."

Sten still did not turn.

"Is there one clottin' being in this whole clottin' cluster who isn't out to clottin' murder every other clottin' being?'' he demanded. ''Is there clottin' *anybody*, from these pampered appararatchik fools who think they're innalekchuls and students to those clots running around with their clotting private armies to these clotting imbeciles who're trying to play button, button, who's going to wear the clotting throne to this clotting imbecile Iskra that our Eternal Clotting—'' He broke off, found out that his lungs were pumped airless, inhaled, then went on, a bit more carefully, considering Cind's presence: ''—that we're supposed to hand the clotting keys to the clotting kingdom to, is there *anybody* who has one lousy cc of the milk of human kindness hidden somewhere about his/her/whoever's person?''

''Tsk,'' Alex mourned. ''Th' clottin' language. In frae of a clottin' laird an' all.''

''Somebody pour me a drink.''

''Not yet, skipper. P'raps y' dinnae want alk runnin' aroun' y'r system.''

Sten finally turned around. Both Cind and Kilgour were wearing Jochi civilian clothes. Poor-people-type civilian clothes. Dark colored.

They had Jochi cloaks over their arms.

Even more interesting, both of them were wearing combat vests. Each vest held a small com link, a cut-barreled, collapsing-stock willygun in an underarm sling, two spare magazines of the ultralethal AM2 rounds, and a sheathed combat knife. The vests would be invisible under the cloaks.

Even better, Kilgour had a bulky parcel under one arm, a parcel that was wrapped in a third cloak.

> ''Atween th' dark an' th' twilight
> Whae th' night's beginnin't t' glower,
> Com't a pause in thae day's occupations.
> Thae's know't ae th' Thuggee's Hour.''

As he recited, Alex unrolled the parcel, revealing it was, as Sten had hoped, a set of indigene civilian clothes, a weapons-equipped combat vest, and a pair of phototropic coveralls.

Kilgour continued:

"Ah ken i' th' close below me
Th' clatter ae tippie-toed feet
Th' thunk ae a dagger thae's buried
An' deathrattles soft an' sweet."

"You two clowns are going out and play Sally-Down-the-Alley spook games, and leave me here with the paperwork."

"A noble ambassador," Cind said, "can't be out in the cold and wet dealing with common turncoats."

"You are right. I've got to keep track of my new station. Kilgour, did you remember my kukri?" Feeling slightly more gleeful than he had in some time, Sten doffed his ambassadorial tunic.

"Y'll be wantin' th' Mantis cammies underneath, boss. I' th' event we're blown."

"What do you have?"

"Y' ken one ae the Emp's complaints, or so y' relayed to me, wae that the Khaqan wae black-marketin' the AM2. Sellin' it out-system t' pay f'r his edifice complex, aye?"

"So?"

"Assumin't thae villainy ne'er changes, the villains mere look f'r new bosses, Ah had th' notion it might be braw an' productive t' find a wee bit aboot how thae black-market conduit work't."

"Very good. Very clottin' good," Sten approved. "At least somebody around here's thinking. Lord knows it isn't me. So who's this lovable citizen who suddenly wants to sell his cluster's leadership down the pike?"

Alex explained. The Mercury Corps station chief for the Altaic Cluster, a relatively junior and inexperienced operative named Hynds, holding the usual cover slot of cultural attache, had put one of his better Jochi agents in motion.

How good, Sten wanted to know. Kilgour shrugged.

"Our wee spook thinkit A Level. But frae his reports, an' th' one debriefing I sat in on, th' agent's nae better'n B. Howe'er, we're dealin't, boss, wi' whae tools're on hand. Ah dinnae hae time yet t' be doin't m' walshingham.

" 'T any rate, Hynds' agent claim't he's got one ae th' schemin't smugglers who's doin' his nut frae gettin' cut out ae th' pie."

"Do you have any verification or any second source that this canary who wants to come in and sing is anything better than somebody who wants to pick up a few Imperial credits for a creative lie?''

Kilgour looked injured that Sten could suspect him of credulity, but continued his explanation.

The man they were supposed to meet claimed to have been the owner/captain of a small shipping line that had been used by the Khaqan to move AM2. Hynds' agent had obtained fiche of one of the line's ship logs and two lading fiche from the man.

''A course, th' cargo wae listed ae pears, plums, poppies, or some such, but th' destination wae in'trestin'. It went t' th' Honjo, who're ne'er backward t' buy AM2, wi'oot askin't too close whae th' home ae origin was.''

''Thin,'' Sten evaluated.

''No drakh,'' Kilgour agreed. ''Plus meetin' ae night. In ae t'r'ble part ae town. Wi' nae heavy backup allowed. Thae's why Ah hae guns. An Ah hae th' notion Cind might be a braw part ae th' discussion. An' y'self, assumin't y' still hae wind enow t' keep up.''

''Let's go.'' Sten grinned. The prospect of a little action, even though it would almost certainly be meeting some lying sort in a back alley who'd try to sell them wolf tickets, was energizing.

''You realize, Captain Cind,'' he said, ''that a certain Private Otho's going to make us cut our beards off just for general principle for excluding him from a situation that might include a bit of mayhem?''

Then he thought of something else. ''Just how *do* we go? Suddenly remembering that I'm an ambassador and can't just go slithering stage right without someone noticing.''

Cind looked smug. ''While you've been out playing Diplomacy with the Bumf Brigade, I thought it might be appropriate to see how secure our bedroom is. And I would suspect the former ambassador of a slight taste for the strange.''

Cind crossed to the light controls and forced one up-down toggle sideways. A panel hissed open.

''Ah,'' Sten said. ''What's life without a secret passage?''

''Running from here past our bedroom,'' Cind explained. ''Then down back along the wing the clericals and junior staffers are quartered in. It goes underground just next to where the kitchen is, I think, and then surfaces as part of the rear wall.''

''Wi' peepyholes an' doors into th' maidservant's bed. Th' lad wae a romantic,'' Kilgour said.

''A pervert,'' Cind corrected.

''An' whae's th' difference?'' Kilgour wondered. ''A'ter you, skip. Cap'n, if y'll go next, Ah'll walk drag. Y' dinnae hae t' worry, by th' bye, aboot bugs. Thae's no one knows aboot th' passage 'cept Cind an' myself.''

Kilgour was very wrong . . .

The meet was almost four klicks from the embassy. The streets were nearly deserted except for an occasional gravsled moving very slowly through the blinding storm, and once or twice a being scurrying along on some no-doubt cursed errand.

Their route led them to and through Rurik's enormous public transport terminal. As they approached the terminal, Sten wondered why all transport terminals were situated in slums. Which came first? Or did transiency encourage transients?

The paired cops just inside the entrance glanced at them, identified the trio as an urban peasant, his wife, and a friend or distant relative and of no interest. Kilgour led Sten and Cind on a circuitous route through the huge building. Benches were filled with beings who, it appeared, had been waiting endlessly. Some slept. Some ate. Some read. Some stared at the blurry entertainment or transport-status screens. More just stared. On Rurik, being able to wait in line without going mad from screaming boredom was more than an art form. It was a necessity.

They stopped beside a refreshment stand. There were no hot drinks available, but three varieties of summer ices could be purchased. The only food for sale that Sten could see was a thin broth made from tubers, and the tureens were filthy. Rancid fat floated on top of the soup.

Cind, still considering herself a student in espionage, studied the other two as they, in turn, studied the people around them without seeming to pay attention.

So far, the run appeared clean, although Sten knew there was little possibility of detecting a full-scale effort to track them, with each tracker following only momentarily before passing them along to the next agent.

Finally Kilgour shrugged hopelessly, pointing up at one line on a transport status screen that was blinking: SERVICE SUSPENDED INDEFINITELY DUE TO WEATHER. Muttering inaudibly like a proper peasant who had just been told he could not go home again, he led them toward an exit.

They were passing a door marked OFFICIAL ONLY when Alex's head jerked a signal and he darted sideways through the door. Cind was caught by surprise, but Sten had her by the shoulder, and they were following Kilgour. The door closed behind them, Alex booted a jamming wedge into the jamb, and they were in an echoing dank stairwell with an open gate and rain below.

Hand signals from Kilgour. You, Cind. On point. Down the stairs, outside, secure the exit.

Cind flowed silently down the stairs like mercury, cloak opening slightly, gun hand on her weapon's grip, finger carefully near but not on trigger, ready to pull the gun into firing position. She slipped out into the night and went instantly flat against the wall.

She found a moment to admire Sten and Kilgour. Again, she was learning from these two. She had never been around combat teams where the order-giver was the one most familiar with the conditions and immediate problem, not the one with the highest rank.

Sten came out the door and was flat against the wall on the other side. Alex followed.

He, too, found spare brain for a personnel evaluation: Th' lass fits, dinnae she? She dinnae ken, but she'd fit wi' th' best ae Mantis noo. Ah reck Ah'll hae t' tell Sten Ah gie m'blessing.

Then he, too, was out in the pelt of rain, and they were moving at the double down a maintenance access road and into the slum streets behind the terminal. A block away they took cover in a doorway and held, waiting to see if they were pursued.

The street stayed rain-dark and empty. Kilgour nodded with satisfaction. He took a bug sensor from his vest and quickly swept all three of them. Nobody had planted them as they went through the terminal.

"How did you know that terminal door would be unlocked?"
Cind asked.

"Ah, lass," Kilgour said. "Ah thought brighter ae y'. Who
d'y' think unlocked it? Who do y' think hung that 'official' sign?
Dinnae y' gie me credit f'r m' craft?"

He didn't wait for an answer. "Noo. Straight t' meet our new
friend."

They moved on, staying close to the buildings. They went unnoticed—in this area, everyone moved as if he either had a secret
or a stash, or was a footpad.

The slum they were moving through was a vertical desolation
row, monstrously huge, as was everything else on Jochi. The
buildings had been constructed over a hundred E-years earlier as
high-rise flats for administration workers, fitted with enough con-
veniences and luxuries to prevent those who greased the Khaqan's
wheels from being too unhappy. Time had passed. The buildings
deteriorated. The government workers found cleaner, safer, newer
quarters. The poor moved in. The McLean lifts stopped, and
there were many, many flights of stairs to climb. The building
supervisors were afraid or venal. And one of the curses of Jochi
struck—Jochians were good at building things, but never seemed
to consider that buildings, roads, or monuments needed maintenance.

Now, windows were shattered or boarded. The upper stories of
the buildings were mostly dark. There was only the occasional
flicker of light from a squatter's fatlamp or a thieves' lair.

The buildings' facings had been intended to look like stone.
Now they hung, peeling, or lay in great slippery sheets across the
cracked paving. Garbage littered the streets and was piled high
in the buildings' service lanes.

Their route led them near one of the rivers that ran through
Rurik. It was less a river than a moving slough, shallow and filled
with junk and abandoned vehicles that had been pushed off the
high bridge that spidered overhead.

Probably years earlier the embankment had been a nice place
to stroll on holidays or on summer evenings. Not now. Sten decided he was not fond of this situation whatsoever—assuming this
was where the meet with the agent had been set. If it was on that

bridge, that was an excellent place for a trap. And *under* the bridge, next to the river? Sten shuddered. Not even Alex, with his supreme and usually justified confidence in his cunning, his heavyworld muscles and his experience, would go into that midnight nightmare.

Or so Sten hoped.

"Here's the drill," Kilgour explained. "Ah tol' this wee agent Ah was noo a dumber, an' was bringin't backup. Thae's you, Cind. Ah dinnae say where y'd be, so Ah'd be apprec'tive i' y'd vanish into yon shadows, an track wi' me as Ah hike.

"Ah'm to stroll doon th' bank, an' th' finkette's t' make the meet. Ah dinnae like th' plan, but th' lad wae skitterish. Boss, i' y' agree, y'll be th' invisible fly i' th' haggis. Hie y' doon noo o'er th' retain't wall, an' gie me cover. Frae in front, i' y' please."

"Thanks, Kilgour. I flog it through river mud, and I've got to move faster than you?"

"Aye. An' quieter. Thae's whae y're a wee admiral, an' Ah'm noo but a puir agent-runner."

Sten checked his gun. It was ready.

"I' y' feel aroon i' th' vest, y'll find a wee corn'copia ae grenades. Bester, flare, frag, blast."

"What's the prog for trouble?" Cind whispered.

"Nae bad. Or Ah'd hae wee Sten carry a howitzer. Nae more'n seventy percent. Enow talk. Go."

Watching the embankment closely, one might have seen a shadow. A shadow that moved. But it was a trick of the light from the bridge, light dimly seen through the slashing rain. The shadow that was Sten oozed over the retaining wall onto the river's "beach."

Pure mire. Sten's foot sank into something that probably had been sentient a bit more recently than the muck. His nose wrinkled. Getting soft, son. Remember, back in Mantis training when they had you low-crawl for half a kilometer through an open sewer line—and then announced the freshers were off limits when your training patrol returned to base? A sickener, it was correctly termed in Mantis slang.

Sten realized he was a bit stiff, a bit out of practice at snoopery, as he lurked on, a wharf rat looking for carrion. Behind him, through the hiss of the rain, he dimly heard Alex's deliberately slammed boot heels on the embankment's paving.

Cind held close in to the shuttered buildings across from the embankment, flitting from shadow to shadow, about fifty meters behind Alex the Target.

Kilgour shivered, but not from the cold rain sheeting down. How many times had he skulked toward a meeting with some local agent? Scores, Laird Kilgour, he thought. An' hae y' e'er not felt th' chill crawl 'tween y'r shoulder blades, waitin' for the sights to cross an' th' round t' slam home?

Ahead of him was a tiny building, next to a shattered lamppost. The building might have been a transport stop or a policeman's watch box.

Movement. Alex's fingers considered the cutdown gun slung in his vest, but found the miniwillygun holstered in the small of his back more subtle. He edged the pistol's safety off, even though no one could have heard the click through the storm noise. Ball of finger touching the trigger, he held it ready, the weapon's muzzle just inside his cloak. Without realizing it Alex centered himself, legs slightly crouched as he moved on, foot coming clear of the ground sweeping in, almost touching his other ankle, then out, weight coming down on the ball of his foot, then the other leg moving forward.

The shadow was man-sized. It moved once more. Lightning shattered behind him, and Kilgour's finger tightened on the trigger. Then he relaxed. The shadow became a man, wearing a hooded ankle-length raincoat. In the flash, Kilgour had seen the man's empty hands outside the coat's sleeves.

Contact.

"An' thae sun break't through th' darkest clouds," he said, cursing himself for his imbecile choice of passwords that had seemed quite clever back in his warm, dry office.

The waiting source—the shipper—*should* have responded with "So honor peereth in the meanest habit."

Nothing but storm howl.

Over the wall, some meters beyond the watch box, Sten went to Condition Red. The cloak's frogs ripped away, and the cloak dropped away into the muck, as his hand pulled the stubby gun off its harness and his thumb spun the selector down off SAFE past FIRE, past BURST, to AUTO, other hand yanking the stock full open, tucked under arm, down on one knee in the slime, eyes moving, moving, for targets.

Perhaps he had seen something. Perhaps there had been a momentary flicker of reflection from above the man, a shiny wire, or perhaps there was nothing.

Kilgour hissed shock, mind snapping orders to his reflexes. Nae, nae, dinnae go doon an' flat, body. Y're i' th' death zone.

Y' hae a couple seconds, lad. More'n enow time.

Contact had not answered, because Contact was very dead. It was somewhat close to normal, in Kilgour and Sten's shadow world, to learn that the oppos were on to your agent by finding him with an extra smile. And hanging by a wire noose from a lamppost wasn't all that uncommon a form of execution. But when the body was propped up, waiting for you at a meet . . .

Ambush.

Alex snapped the grenade out of his vest pocket, thumbed the impact fuse on, and sidearmed the tiny bomb overhead, to the right, just as he spun into motion, three leaping steps coming for a high jump. He dove forward, airborne, then slammed down on the rain-slick pavement, skating forward a meter, an' Ah need more time i' th' gym, because Ah'll hae bruises ae th' squeeze box t'morrow.

I' there *is* a t'morrow, he thought, as projectile fire shattered toward the watch box.

Triangulation, Sten analyzed. They've got us from three sides. This is a serious hit . . . as his finger came back on the trigger and he blew one potential assassin in half.

Cind had gaped for a microsecond at the space where Kilgour had been.

Then Kilgour's grenade, mortared high into the air with heavy-world muscles, hit the brownstone sixty meters above and some meters ahead of her—and detonated.

The front of the building peeled off, bricks cascading over the second murderer, just as Cind's AM2 round made the cascade a decent burial instead of self-defense.

The third member of the team was just bringing the trigger back for his second shot when Kilgour had him in his sights and snapped a round. The round whip-cracked past the third man; Kilgour's mind muttered about clottin' pistols beyond arm's reach, and his left hand had the pistol butt cupped for stability and two rounds double-tapped out—and the third man was dead, as well.

The team was moving—Sten up toward the retaining wall, Kilgour rolling like a beachball across the street toward some rubble, and Cind crouching first in one doorway and then in another. Kilgour jammed the pistol back in its holster and snapped his willygun into firing position.

The thunder from that lightning blast crashed across them, and Sten realized he had been counting in his mind: The lightning burst was only two kilometers away, and a bit more than six seconds have passed since we saw the shadow was a man.

Ambush. Why? Just to tell Kilgour that another intelligence group was watching him? Melodramatic way to announce the info—this contact, even if he had been a genuine smuggler, had given them nothing. Not a very professional organization, either. Pros never hit each other. It wasn't necessary once one had closed off the leak or potential leak.

Whatever. They could analyze who, what, and why later. Now it was time to extract. Run like hell. Sten wasn't worried about Jochi cops showing up—he doubted their dedication to real police work at best and knew damned well they wouldn't patrol this district except in watch-size formation. But it would be embarrassing for the Imperial ambassador to be seen in a vulgar brawl like this.

Sten started up, instinctively taking command even though the run had been Kilgour's thus far.

His mind had time to absorb the *klang*, his eyes time to see a flicker from behind and above them, on that bridge, and the mortar round *blapped* into the river mud, muck spraying, but killing shrapnel damped.

Then the automatic weapons opened up. High-rate projectile as bullets sheeted in a *wheep* into the mire just beyond him, and Sten wriggled back over the wall, rolling, landing on a shoulder; then he saw the muzzle flashes from the third-story window across from him. Willygun up, swearing at the short barrel, lousy accuracy, no time for the sights, he skeet-gunned a long burst through the muzzle flashes, and the weapon kept firing, dead hand on the triggers, as the gunner fell, pulling the gun over with him, the rest of the gun's magazine emptying itself in the sky. Gunfire shattered on from two other guns.

Sten found himself next to Kilgour, both of them trying to marry that wonderful sheltering pile of rubble, a pile that was getting smaller as the mortar's gunner corrected his aim, and a second bomb blew against the pavement.

"Th' bastards're serious, boss."

They were—this went far beyond an acceptable if extreme attempt to remove a problematical intelligence specialist. When the first hit failed, the cover should have disengaged and withdrawn. Whoever these beings were, this was a full-blown military ambush, eager for some Imperial corpses, regardless of the expense.

The army, Sten wondered. No. They weren't players—at least he didn't think so. Not yet, anyway.

Where the clot was Cind? His question was answered as a grenade blew a long-boarded window open, and she shouted, "Covering! Move!"

Sten slammed Alex's butt, and Kilgour was on his feet, hurtling forward and diving into the abandoned shop. Sten sprayed a burst in the general direction of death; infantry muscles took over, and he was dashing forward, coming in as Alex blasted covering fire, and he was through the window, recovering, to one side. Cind came through the window like a bounding Earth marten in the snow, a spatter of rounds accompanying her.

Their momentary shelter would soon become a death trap, Sten knew. At least, he thought, they didn't have to worry about running out of ammunition. Not for a day, anyway—each willygun's tube magazine held 1400 one-millimeter balls of shielded AM2.

Again, the mortar's gunner corrected his aim, and another bomb *klanged* out of the tube and arced toward them, and Sten gnawed drakh-smelling carpet just like so many rats had before him.

The gunner's range was long—the bomb exploded above them, against the building's face. Bricks avalanched down, just as they had from Kilgour's grenade.

"By the beard of my mother," Cind said absently, "but that's the first good thing that's happened since the party started."

She was right—the opposition had just given them an adequate breastwork to fight behind. But Sten was chortling. "Your mother's what?"

"Clot off," Cind said. "You see what happens when you run away and get raised by Bhor?"

"Speakin't ae which," Kilgour said, "Ah could but wish f'r a few ae thae gorillers ae th' moment, aye?"

"Yeah. Right. You wish for Bhor, and I'll wish for a back door. Guess which one we'll get," Sten said.

They were up and sliding toward the back of the building, barely able to see in the gloom, stumbling through overturned refuse.

"Any idea who doesn't like the way we comb our hair?" Cind asked. Neither man had an answer. The way this Cluster thought, it might be almost anyone.

At the rear of the shop, Sten found the back door. It had been closed off with heavy timber X-ed over the door and spiked down. Not a problem, Sten thought, with Kilgour's proven grunt-and-groan talent.

About one second later, their enemies also found the back door, and a grenade shattered against it, punching holes in the panel. Sten saw movement outside through the blast holes and sent a burst and then a bester grenade after it. There were screams, which were chopped off as the grenade exploded. The bester grenade blanked time for anyone caught in its radius—two hours worth of unconsciousness, and the victim had no knowledge that even a second had passed.

"Y're bein't merciful, skip."

"Like hell," Sten snarled. "I got the wrong clottin' bomb. You just rip and tear, since you got us in this sorry mess in the first place."

"Ah," Kilgour said. "Thae's days—an' nights—th' magic dinnae seem to work."

He grabbed, one-handed, one of the X-braces and pulled. The heavy plank—and the rest of the door—came away.

"You can leave the rest of the building," Sten said.

The three edged out through the hole. Sten looked at the four men scattered around the door. Human—which meant Tork or Jochian. Duow's faction? Or maybe that other group of Jochians whose goals and leaders Sten was still to hear from? Insufficient data. All four of them wore coveralls without insignia.

"Noo. Le's roll this up. Thae's no more pleasure or sport t'be gain't, an' thae's still baddies left."

Sten took point, and they doubled away, down the alley, moving as fast as they could and still keep complete silence.

Their luck ran out in two separate catastrophes. The storm quite suddenly stopped, just as suddenly as it had broken. Worse, the sky cleared, and two of Jochi's moons three-quartered at them.

"Cind, do the Bhor have a weather god?" Sten wondered.

"Schind. He rules ice storms."

"Drakh."

Then their second ruin struck. A searchlight beam pinned the team like insects. Sten imagined the three of them silhouetted like an old photo negative, then all three of their weapons chattered and the light blew, hissed, died, and was dark, and they were flat behind the stripped, torched, and abandoned wreck of a gravsled.

"I saw 'um," came a surprised shout. "Thet bit one. Hez that Imperial we'b seed in livie!"

Sten swore. This would take some explaining.

First to these provisional power-grabbers on Jochi. Sten also thought his Eternal Emperor might hear of the incident and have some questions as to why his ambassador plenipotentiary had been out farting around on a completely unnecessary bit of cowboyed intelligence.

Oh well. At least they wouldn't get killed now. And maybe Sten could figure a way out of the Imperial flaying.

Then: "Th' gamclotting ambassador?"

"Yah."

"Kill the scrote! Now!"

"Ah dinnae ken who's daft enow t' wan' to ice th' Emp's lad," Alex said, "but w' kin sort th' villain out later. Back. Th' way we came."

A small infantry rocket round crashed against the wall above them—and that way too was sealed.

"We're sandwiched," Cind announced. "Anybody know how to levitate?"

"Be serious. Ah dinnae hae e'en a wee chuckle noo, let alone lev'ty."

They were well and truly trapped.

Solid rounds chewed up the gravsled above them.

"How come," Sten wondered, "when you see the livies, and the hero ducks behind a stupid gravsled, all the slugs ricochet instead of punching right on through like in real life?"

Nobody answered.

The return fire stopped. They heard the shuffle of feet coming in.

Cind lifted her gun. Sten shook his head, and she saw the kukri blade gleaming in the moonlight.

Cind's combat knife slid out of its sheath.

There were four attackers.

Number One saw nothing—Cind's knife was anodized flatblack, and there was no reflection as the blade went home under his rib cage, into his heart, and the man's momentum sagged him forward.

Number Two heard nothing as the two minikegs Kilgour called fists slammed against the side of his head, and his skull eggshelled.

Number Three had a moment to blink, then that curved shortsword of the Gurkhas clove him, slashing his shoulder blade apart, snapping ribs, and burying itself in his stomach.

Number Four had too much time. He had time to shove his rifle sideways, into Sten, sending him stumbling back, hand coming off the gore-slick kukri handle, and then the gun's barrel was aiming.

Sten let himself fall back into a crouch, right hand dropping, fingers curled, death sliver coming out of his armsheath.

Left hand braced, he slashed near-blindly—in a knife fight do anything but think about things.

Too much time . . . and Four saw his gun barrel cut in half.

Too much time . . . and Sten recovered, blade coming down and then flashing up into Four's solar plexus, flashing up, intestines spilling as he gutted the man like a fish.

Sten's knife was reflexively bravo-wiped on the corpse's coveralls, then went back into his arm.

He ripped the kukri free from Three's body, avoiding looking at the man he had so neatly eviscerated. Another one, Sten. Another one on the long list.

Cind and Alex were awaiting orders.

Sten picked up his gun and tapped its stock. The other two nodded. It took ten minutes for the enemy to realize that even though there had been no shrieks or gunfire, the four they had sent in would not be coming back.

They sent seven men in next.

Sten let them get within four meters of the gravsled before he signaled. Fire spat—and seven bodies were shattered on the paving.

The third wave came less than two minutes later.

Grenades paved their way, blasts crashing against the alley walls.

"Thae're no playin' fair," Alex said.

"I'm not planning to let them take me," Cind said.

"Nor I," Sten said. "But there's no gain in suicide."

"We're waitin', lad. F'r a wee idea."

Sten considered . . . and as he did, thunder drumrolled and the storm smashed in again. He swore. Five minutes earlier and . . .

Very well, he thought. Use what you have. Add some confusion. "Kilgour. Can you get a grenade among 'em?"

Alex considered. "Close."

"When it blasts . . . we go. Fifteen meters, go flat, grenade again, and we'll go in on them."

Cind and Alex looked at him. There was no expression on either of their faces.

"With no one to drink our souls to hell," Cind sighed, unclipping a grenade from her harness and coming to a crouch.

"Ah well, Ah well," Alex sighed. "A' least we're noo dyin' in bed."

He set his gun down, readied a grenade, and came half-up, into classic throw position. A braw cast, he thought, thumbed the button, and threw.

The grenade hit, bounced, and exploded, barely a meter short of the enemy position, and the three were up, as lightning opened hell's gates for them and thunder tympanied and Cind ululated a

Bhor war cry and they were charging, three against—against who knew how many.

Sten, pure bluff, pure rage, bellowed: "Ayo . . . Gurkhali!" As good a battle shout as any to die with.

The ululation echoed against the brownstones.

And the Gurkhas heard him.

And attacked.

A brown wave of men came out of the night, guns spattering fire, and then they were closed with the enemy. The men spun in sudden confusion at the attack from their rear, and the Gurkhas gave up their guns and slashed in with the kukri.

Two Gurkha fire teams ran past Sten and the others, each with a light crew-served automatic weapon. Moving in pure drill, they went down and opened up, fire roaring down the alley and unsealing that end.

By the time Sten realized he was alive and would stay alive— or, at least, make it out of this stinking alley—none of his attackers could say the same.

The rain felt wonderful on his face. Cind's shoulders as he squeezed them were the most comforting thing he had known. Alex's beam was the friendliest expression he had seen.

Portable torches gleamed from where the enemy's position had been. The three stumbled toward them.

Mahkhajiri Gurung was waiting for him. "Sir, you were very hard to find. This district we found very confusing. I wish you would have summoned us sooner. And when you go out next, would you wear a locator?"

"How," Sten realized, "did you even know I'd left the embassy?"

Mahkhajiri shrugged. "After Mr. Kilgour find secret passage, we did, too. Even though he did not bug passage, we did.

"You see, we are not as good as Mr. Kilgour, and cannot sense in our deepest sleep if some assassin came to attack you in that passage. We Gurkhas need all the help we can get."

Sten, Cind, and Alex looked at each other.

"All right," Sten said finally. "So you know everything. I guess the only question I could have is where are the Bhor?"

"Up on the bridge. Out on the embankment. There were many people with guns we thought should be dealt with.

"The Bhor wanted that honor. We agreed, since they are far more capable of diplomacy than we are."

That would mean no prisoners out there, either.

"I want," Sten said, "a gravsled and back to the embassy and a drink."

"Waiting," Mahkhajiri Gurung said. "In the street."

With a nod, Kilgour pulled Sten aside as they walked down the alley. "Lad, thae was a bit closer'n Ah'm comfortable wi'. Dinnae it be time to be noo studyin't war no more?"

"It is."

"Y ken, Ah know, th' mos' interestin' thing aboot this evening?"

Sten did. Someone had knowingly tried to kill the Eternal Emperor's ambassador plenipotentiary. Not in the heat of battle, but by direct order.

Any rational being would know that such a murder would produce the most immediate and most lethal response from the Emperor.

Sten realized that there were people—factions—here on Jochi that made the lunatics he had been dealing with appear to be sane, peaceful beings.

And so the question would be, who did this semiarmy belong to? Mortars . . . automatic weapons . . . men attacking like trained, or at least semitrained, soldiers.

They belonged to somebody.

Sten would wait for the howls of outrage, wondering what conceivable cover story someone would find for the bloody death of one or two companies of gunmen.

But over the days that came, there was never any mention of the incident.

Not from anyone.

Including Rurik's police force.

CHAPTER THIRTEEN

THE PROPOSAL WAS very brief. It was handwritten on three pages of what appeared to be antique paper. The bloodless man sitting across from the Eternal Emperor finished reading it and replaced the pages on the desk.

"Your comments," the Emperor asked.

"Interesting, sir." A neutral tone.

Unsurprising, since everything about Poyndex was neutral. He had formerly been head of Mercury Corps—Imperial Intelligence—in the final days of the Tahn war. An efficient, passionless soldier, he had continued serving under the privy council. Later, in a piece of internal politicking, he had been made the junior member of that council.

But when the Emperor returned, Poyndex betrayed the council to the Empire. All he asked—he knew all he *could* ask—was for his life. He had had nothing whatsoever to do with the assassination of the Emperor. Nor had he publicly had any part in the various purges and atrocities ordered by the council.

The Emperor took his offer—and the privy council's back was appropriately poniarded, and Poyndex disappeared into the hinterlands of the Empire.

"You show no surprise," the Emperor said.

"Sir . . . May I speak frankly?"

It was the Emperor's turn for silence. Poyndex chose to interpret that as permission.

"I am only surprised that I am still alive, Your Majesty. When you ordered my return here to Prime World, I was sure—"

"No," the Emperor said. "If I had wanted your corpse, it would have been done silently and at the time of maximum ire. I decided the interregnum would not be memorialized by show trials. Besides, I remember you as being a most efficient chief of Intelligence.

"Now I have need of your services. I want you to take over this newly created entity, Internal Security. It is to be run somewhat differently than Mercury. Its operatives have been and will continue to be recruited from nonmilitary channels. They are required to swear an oath of fealty to me, personally, rather than to the Empire. Their tasks and duties will be known to me alone. The only duty they have been tasked for, in public or classified records, is my protection. Which I plan to give the widest possible interpretation to.

"All IS missions will be assigned by me, and their accomplishment will be reported to me. There will be no other elements in the chain of command. The unit will have the highest priorities in its missions. All reports will be single-copy Eyes Only or orally delivered. There will be no records kept in Imperial Archives. Now . . . your response?"

"There is not much of a choice, Your Majesty." Poyndex said. "Just knowledge of the existence of this unit could be . . . embarrassing. And . . ." He tapped the proposal on the desk. "This plan, and the problem it is intended to solve, is certainly something that must never be common knowledge."

"Your reasoning is correct. You are, in fact, the only being besides myself privy to both the problem and my projected solution," the Emperor said. "But before you accept, I have a single question.

"What is to keep you from betraying me, as you betrayed the council?"

There was a very long silence. Poyndex stood and paced.

"I will answer that, sir," he said, "even though I prefer not to ever discuss my own personality quirks. I find the subject . . . embarrassing. Perhaps, if you will allow me, a story—a parable— will help."

Poyndex took a breath. "In Spyschool One, they tell the story about a famous spymaster. Serving an ancient Earth imperator. He is credited with creating modern espionage, in fact—where each man spies on his brother and is spied upon. His ruler, impressed, wanted to reward him. The man wanted but one thing—the baton of a field marshal.

"His emperor was shocked at the request, and refused. Spies are not given the rewards of honest soldiers. Nor—he did not add—should they be given public fame."

"The man's name was Fouché, and the dictator's name was First Napoleon," the Emperor said.

"You know the incident, sir. Well, it is told to discourage the budding young intelligence specialist from wanting fame or public glory. And I thought I had taken it to heart and learned to suppress whatever need I had to appear in the public prints, together with other feelings that lessen a reasoning being's efficiency. But when the late Sr. Kyes made his offer to elevate me to the privy council, an offer made very much to serve his own interests I learned, I discovered I was still ambitious. After the privy council's—and my own—downfall I corrected this weakness."

"Did you?" the Emperor wondered. "Ambition is a hydra."

"Does it matter, sir?" Poyndex asked. "Because unlike those dunders on the privy council, I doubt if you would ever expose your back to me."

The Emperor nodded. Enlightened—or fearful—self-interest was an acceptable motivation. Especially for the tasks he planned to set Poyndex.

"I accept your assignment, Your Majesty. Of course I do. In fact, I am honored."

"Good. There will be other people assigned to you. Some of them will come from . . . equally gray backgrounds. And some of them will be given missions you will have no need to know about."

"I understand, sir."

"Just like that one." The Emperor indicated the proposal. "I have three questions on my proposal," he went on. "Do you need to know any more about this device?"

"No, sir. And I would refuse to listen if I did. Just knowledge of this is risky enough to endanger my continued survival."

"Do you think the task can be accomplished?"

"Yes," Poyndex said flatly. "We've had far more elaborate work done on doubles, triples, and defectors, Your Majesty."

"Good. Very good," the Emperor said.

"We will need about a month to assemble the personnel, sir. Probably two cycles for the work itself, and of course, complete seclusion," Poyndex said.

"I have already thought of that." The Emperor reached across the desk and picked up the proposal. He took a firestick from his desk, ignited it, and held it to the paper. The papers instantly flamed into sheets, and then were gray ashes.

"The site will be ancient Earth."

Poyndex rose, saluted, and was gone.

The Emperor stared after him. It was a pity he would never offer Poyndex a celebratory drink, or make him dinner when a plan was complete, as he had done with Ian Mahoney or Sten.

But that had been long ago, and this was another time.

CHAPTER FOURTEEN

"Y'R MUG'S SCREW'T up like a basset, young Sten. And Ah dinna ken y'r worry," Alex said. "Th' hae no choice in th' matter. 'Tis th' Emperor's command."

"That doesn't make it any easier," Sten said.

"I agree with Alex," Cind said, a Bhor fascist at heart. "I know you don't like just flat out announcing to these people their fate has been determined. A new leader is on the way and they'll just have to like it or choke on it. But I don't see any way to sugarcoat it. Those *are* the facts, and they'll just have to live with them."

"It wasn't sugarcoating I was looking for," Sten said.

"Make up your mind fast, lad," Alex said. "Our friendly four will be here any minute."

"Here's how I see it," Sten said. "When Dr. Iskra arrives—and I still don't know exactly *when* he is going to arrive, damn it—anyway, when he arrives and takes command, things can go into the drakh in a hurry. What if everyone tells the Emperor to put his new fearless leader where the sun is mortified to go?"

"The Emperor would crush them," Cind said flatly.

"Probably," Sten said. "Still. Beings have done stranger things. Up to and including mass suicide. I guess they don't quite believe it will really happen to them."

Sten reflected on the millions of dead and the awful destruction the Tahn had caused themselves.

"I want to do this right," he said. "Otherwise, we'll end up with a six-way civil war on our hands. I want the Emperor's choice to stick. Make them worry about refusing to go along with Dr. Iskra."

Cind didn't get it. "If they're all *that* crazy—and from what I've seen, all the species in this Sarla-forsaken cluster are certifiably insane—wouldn't worry just aggravate the problem?"

Alex was thoughtful. "Nae s' fast, lass. Our Sten i' sharpenin' his Mantis wits." He turned to Sten. "C'd we no make't personal, lad? Fear alone c'n make a man braw. But, add guilt t' fear and y' oft find a lurkin' coward."

Sten looked up at Alex. And the light bulb dawned. "Why kiss me, Dr. Rykor," he laughed.

"Ah'm no so blubbery," Alex sniffed.

But Sten wasn't paying any attention. He was hastily drawing up a game plan. Just as the outline took shape, the com line buzzed.

It was time.

"Before we begin, Sr. Ambassador," General Douw said, "the four of us would like to express our—" The silver-haired Jochian glanced nervously around the sterile room Sten had chosen for the meeting. "—our appreciation for your . . . ahem . . . hospitality."

Sten ostentatiously glanced at the time display ticking away on the far wall. It was the only decoration. "My pleasure," he said, sounding bored. He drummed his fingers on the table.

"We know you're a busy man, Sr. Sten," Menynder said, peering at him amiably through his antique spectacles. "So, as soon as we got word you wanted to see us, we got together to hammer out a little presentation."

"Oh?" was all Sten said.

"We're extremely proud of this effort," the general broke in. "In fact, I personally view this as an historic moment." He pushed over a sheaf of documents. "Herewith is our plan for a new government. All four of us have signed on. I think you'll be impressed with our efforts."

"Must only clear with home worlds," Diatry, the Bogazi leader, said.

"I can guarantee the Suzdal," Youtang barked.

Sten frowned at the documents and prodded at them with a suspicious finger.

"Something wrong?" Menynder asked. The old Tork's alarm bells were going off. They had ting-a-linged a bit when he had walked into this white-on-white room. It was decidedly unfriendly. Reminded him of an interrogation room. He also noted the walls were thick enough to be scream-proof. The only furniture was the long, bare table they were seated at. And five hard chairs.

"Are you *sure* you want to give this to me?" Sten asked, poking at the offending documents.

"Of course we're sure," General Douw said. "This is the blueprint, I tell you, the blueprint of our future."

Sten just stared at him.

The general got a little panicky under the stare. He turned to Menynder. "That's what *you* said, isn't it?"

"Quiet, General," Menynder warned.

"Why should I be quiet? We're here to air our views, correct? To be firm, but fair. We agreed, right?"

"You talk, talk, talk," Diatry said, picking up which way the wind was blowing. And it was definitely smelling.

But Douw was still on his self-destructive course. "I'm not

going to take all the blame," he whined. "It's not my fault! Sr. Ambassador, please . . ."

"You want to remove these?" Sten asked, shifting to a gentle tone and pushing the documents back toward the general. "I'll pretend I never saw them."

"Sure! No trouble. Lot of drakh, anyway," Douw babbled, hauling the sheaf of papers back.

"What is your pleasure, Sr. Ambassador?" Menynder said. "How can we make your mission easier?"

"Two things. The first is a mere matter of curiosity. The Eternal Emperor's curiosity, I might add."

"Which is?" Menynder asked.

"The dinner party you had for the Khaqan. On that tragic night."

Stone silence in the room. Gotcha, Sten thought. He let the silence lay there for a long time.

"You four were among those in attendance, correct?" he asked at last.

"Uh . . . well . . . I arrived awfully late," General Douw said.

"Then you were there," Sten said. A statement.

"Certainly, I was. Nothing suspicious about that, is there?"

"Who said anything about suspicion?" Sten asked. He gave Douw a quizzical "Why are you acting so guilty?" look.

"Quite right," Douw said. "I mean, you didn't. I mean—"

"Yes, Sr. Sten. We were all in attendance," Menynder broke in.

"Odd," Sten said.

"Friendly gathering only," Diatry said. "Is strange to have friendly gathering only where you come from?"

Sten ignored this. "And the Khaqan gave no sign he was ill?" he asked. "A little pale and weak, perhaps? Or . . . maybe a show of temper?"

"Why'd he be angry?" Youtang yapped. "It was merely a social evening."

"I think he very happy before he die," Diatry said. "Not angry. Tell big joke. We laugh. Ha. Ha. Then he die. We all very sad this happen. Cry boo hoo."

Sten shifted course again. "I've gone through his appointments calendar," he said. "And the dinner wasn't listed."

"It was, uh, a last-minute thing," Menynder said quickly.

"I guess that explains that little mystery, then," Sten said.

"That's what was bothering you?" Menynder asked. "The appointments calendar?"

"Not me," Sten said. "The Eternal Emperor. Remember?"

"Yes. Of course," Menynder said. He took his glasses off and wiped them with the kerchief from his pocket. "Any other little mysteries we can clear up?"

"No. I don't think so. Oh. Yes. One more thing. The place where this famous dinner occurred? Who'd it belong to?"

"A friend of mine," Menynder said. "The Khaqan wanted privacy. I arranged it."

"In a Tork neighborhood?" Sten asked.

"Why not?"

Sten stared at Menynder. He let that stare linger until Menynder began to sweat. Then he moved his gaze from face to face, studying each being closely. He wound up the tension until it was a supertight ball of kinetic energy just waiting to be released.

Then he let it go. "Why not, indeed," Sten said.

He pretended not to notice as four very worried beings whooshed out air.

"Now, for the main reason I've called you all together," Sten said.

Douw, Menynder, and the two others bent close to hear Sten's words. He had their complete attention.

"After careful study and long consideration, the Emperor has found a solution to your dilemma. And I think you will all agree it's pure genius on his part."

"I'm quite sure it is," Douw said, not giving a damn at that second.

Menynder was wiping sweat from his brow while Diatry and Youtang were busy mentally ticking off the sins Sten had failed to sniff out.

"Gentlebeings," Sten said, "I'm pleased to announce the Emperor has handpicked the being who will lead you into a new era of good fortune . . .

"His name, gentlebeings, is Iskra. Dr. Iskra." Sten looked mildly around the room. His game plan had worked. There was not the slightest sign of objection.

"Good choice," Menynder said. "In fact, I remember his name being mentioned the night of that dinner we were discussing earlier. Isn't that so, General Douw?"

Douw shuddered. That clottin' dinner again! "Yes, quite so. And, we're honored the Emperor took a personal interest in our small affairs."

"When is he expected?" Menynder wanted to know.

At that moment, a big ship smashed overhead and plunged for the spaceport. The crack of a shattered sound barrier rocked the embassy. Oh, clot, Sten thought. Just in time. He continued, however, without missing a beat.

"As we speak, gentlebeings. As we speak."

CHAPTER FIFTEEN

DR. ISKRA ARRIVED with an impressive amount of pomp, even if the circumstance was a bit premature. Sten would have preferred that this construct of the Eternal Emperor, this dictator-in-waiting, would have arrived a few cycles after the various in-place schemers had figured out that none of them were about to be the nominated replacement—and had time to decide how they would play the new hand.

But Sten had learned eons before, early in his Imperial Service, that it was a valuable lesson in real life to wish in one hand, crap in the other, and then watch to see which one filled up first.

That rumble portending Dr. Iskra's arrival was fortunately an overflight. Sten had time to scrag Alex and the Gurkhas and have Cind find enough nonstregged Bhor to present an Impressive

Package at the spaceport. He also made sure to bring two livie operators from the embassy, in case no one else remembered to document this historic event.

Two heavy cruisers hung over the landing field, McLean generators hissing, their destroyer screens and picket tacships darting around them. Four fleet transports settled down on the field. Ramps dropped and gravlighters flitted out, scattering a rim of security troops as they went. Other troops formed an inner shield within the square formed by the transports.

Sten, Alex, and Cind watched with a critical eye.

"Th' Guard," Alex said, "*still* dinnae hae recov'rd frae th' war an' th' priv'tations ae th' privy council."

"Alex," Sten observed mildly, "did it ever occur to you that *no* unit we've ever been assigned to is now qualified to hold the bullocks of the lowliest private we knew? At least the way we remember it?"

"An' whae's th' matter wi' thae?" Kilgour asked in injury. "Tis nae but th' truth, aye?"

"Aaargh." Sten stalked forward—flanked by an Impressive of Gurkhas and Bhor—as the largest of the cruisers landed in the middle of the square formed by the transports.

A rigid color guard had doubled out of the cruiser and was drawn up, on line, by the time Sten arrived at the cruiser's ramp. The cruiser's commander and the commander of the Imperial Guard battalion saluted Sten. The battalion came from the Third Guards, a unit Sten had never operated with, nor knew much about. Once, a long time before, his cover on a Mantis operation had been as a dishonorably discharged officer of the Third Guard, and he wondered, amused, if that cashiering was somewhere in the unit's records. Imperial Intelligence tended to set up cover stories very carefully. Sten hoped not—he never wanted to explain to this Guard's colonel, an efficient-sounding if somewhat thick individual named T'm Jerety, why the Imperial ambassador plenipotentiary had in the dim past been cashiered for atrocities, ambiguity, and angst, or whatever crimes his cover identity had required.

A dry, hot wind swept across the field as Dr. Iskra walked down the cruiser's forward ramp.

No one's expression changed. On the part of the newly arrived Imperial forces it came from familiarity. Sten was impressed, however, with the professionalism of his own crew. All he heard was a low sigh from Kilgour, a suppressed sinusoidal squeal from Otho, and a sotto voce comment from Cind, who was going to *have* to relearn her Bhor-taught freebooting ways and dreadnought tongue:

"Clot," came the whisper. "He looks a hanging judge who wears rubber panties under his robes. Rubber and pink lace."

Her description was apt.

Dr. Iskra at twenty meters was very unimpressive. He was not tall. He was thin. He wore nondescript, baggy civilian attire that any zee-grade livie would have costumed its absentminded professor in. A professor, Sten decided, of Undercurrents of Subconscious Thought and Priapic Imagery in Agrarian Nonrhyming Poets You Never Heard Of. Balding, in an age when natural body hair was an easily added or subtracted cosmetic item. What hair he had was combed or slicked over his pate as if to hide it.

At twenty meters, a figure of fun or pity.

At three, the image changed, Sten thought.

Dr. Iskra menaced. Sten could not tell why. It might have been the hard gray glare from eyes that never seemed to blink or look anywhere but into your guts. Or it might have been the tiny pinch marks around Iskra's lipless mouth. Or that none of the lines on his face would fit a smile.

Iskra was flanked by the usual civilian aides/disciples that any politician-in-exile collects.

Sten bowed a salute. Iskra did not return it.

"You are Sten, yes? Very well. Enough of this ceremony. There is much work to be done. I want immediate transportation to the palace, yes?"

"I have embassy gravsleds standing by," Sten said.

"No. No." Iskra turned to Colonel Jerety. "I want six heavy gravlighters. I will ride in the second. The first should have flags mounted as decoy. One company of your battalion should secure the route. I want a second company on zone security awaiting my arrival at the Square of the Khaqans. I want a third company to secure the palace itself. My chambers, of course, will be those used by the late usurper. See that they are cleared. And I want one guardsman per servitor, until I have had a chance to have my servants screened.''

Colonel Jerety saluted and shouted orders, apparently unaware that most statesmen either knew nothing about security, or wanted the least amount between them and their adoring populace. Or, perhaps Jerety was used to such demands from Iskra by now. Sten wondered if Iskra also had a food taster on his staff.

Iskra turned back to Sten. ''As I said, there is much work ahead of us. Please accompany me to the palace, so that we may discuss the proper manner of implementing my assumption of authority, so the minimum of order is lost.''

Sten bowed once more. His face was as blank as Alex's, Otho's, or Cind's.

Awaiting them in the Square of the Khaqans was a claque. Since all of them were human, it must have been assembled by either Douw or Menynder. Most likely, considering how long it usually took the secretary of defense to come to full drive on anything, it was one of Menynder's cheering sections.

Iskra went slowly, knowing he was being recorded by the livie crews, up the sweeping steps to the palace's main terrace. He turned and looked down at the cheering minicrowd. Sten wondered if he would make a speech. But Iskra just nodded jerkily, as if accepting no more than his due, and turned to the waiting officialdom, which included the full gaggle of Jochi leaders, plus the Bogazi and Suzdal representatives.

His eyes swept them as thoroughly as any camera. And as emotionlessly. Again, he nodded.

''Thank you for welcoming me home,'' he said. ''Tomorrow we shall meet to discuss how those of you who are qualified will help me implement our New Order for the cluster.

''Now, I am tired. I will eat, rest, and go over my notes. Someone from my staff will contact you as to the exact time and place of our conference.''

Without waiting for a response, he swept through the open two-story-high doors that led into the palace. Sten followed.

Several Guard officers and one scared Jochi palace flunky were inside.

"I am—" the flunky began.

"You are Nullimer," Iskra interrupted. "You were majordomo to the Khaqan. As was your father. And your father's father served the pig that bred the Khaqan."

Nullimer looked ready to faint.

"You also," Iskra went on, "once warned *my* father at a court function that the Khaqan was speaking ill of him."

Nullimer blanked, obviously not remembering the incident, then covered.

"Yes," Iskra went on. "And you will be rewarded for that, even though your warning was not taken with sufficient gravity. I can only hope that you will serve me as faithfully as you did that evil one."

Nullimer started to his knees. Instantly Iskra was beside him, lifting him up. "No, man. There shall be no kneeling in this New Order."

Iskra turned, as if now addressing the claque outside, or the dignitaries still milling about out on the terrace. "You see? Everything is known. And everything shall be rewarded." His voice lowered. "Or punished."

Then, more strongly: "Everything!"

He spun back to the majordomo. "You have heard. Now, go. Tell the kitchen I will eat. I will give this officer here my weekly menu."

Nullimer, alternately flushing and beaming, managed to stumble from the chamber.

Iskra spoke to one of his aides. "After that, he will serve me well. But have his quarters fine-combed—in the event my assessment was in error."

The aide nodded and passed Iskra a printed list. Iskra handed it to one of the Guard officers.

"This is what I eat," he said. "Please have the kitchen made aware. And inform them that this diet, of course, shall not apply for banquets or special occasions."

Iskra pinned an expression that could be considered a smile on his face for an instant, then swept on.

Sten couldn't resist. He stopped beside the Imperial soldier and glanced at the list. It was one cycle's worth of menus, with the note that at the end of a cycle the menu was to be repeated. He had time to see one day's offerings:

Morning
Black bread
Herbal tea

Midday
Vegetable soup
Mineral water

Dusk
Lung soup
Nut cutlet
Garden salad, undressed
Cream torte
One glass, nonvintage Rurikdoktor white wine

Before Bed
Digestive crackers
Herbal tea

Sten hoped that any conferences with the Imperial ambassador around mealtime would be considered a special occasion. Especially the evening feeding. Sten hoped that the lung soup was to remind Iskra of his poverty-stricken days in exile. Gods forbid he actually *liked* it.

But that cream torte? Perhaps that was Iskra's one allowed indulgence? Sten, if someone had made him dictator-elect, would have thought in terms of concubines, strong drink, hallucinatory substances, or bad company. But each tyrant to his tastes.

Iskra was waiting, looking impatient. Sten hurried to catch up.

"This, I assume, was the Khaqan's bedchamber?"

"It was," one of Iskra's hovering aides said.

"Then it shall be mine. However, I shall wish some changes."

"Of course, Doctor."

Iskra looked thoughtfully around the huge chamber. "First, get rid of that obscenity of a bed. I will not be succumbing to the sexual practices of that worm. You know what I sleep on. Those pictures. Have them removed. Give them to a museum, or have them burnt. It doesn't matter. We will have little time for gross representations of the miserable past.

"Have them replaced with a wallscreen on that wall; a map projector on that one. Fiche storage and book cases on the other walls. We shall have that fireplace punched out, into the next room, which shall be my battlechamber.

"Now. Leave. You, J'Dean. Return to the Imperial ship. Inform the rest of my staff they may relocate to this palace. Have the Imperials provide security for their passage."

The aide nodded—just as jerkily as Iskra. Perhaps it was their own version of a salute. He withdrew. Doors closed, and Iskra and Sten were alone.

There was no preamble. "You have been in communication with the Eternal Emperor?"

"I have," Sten said.

"He has given you instructions? That I am to be given your fullest and most complete support, without questions?"

"I must correct you, doctor. To prevent a future misunderstanding. I was ordered to provide full support by the Emperor. However, I am not, nor is any member of my embassy, under your command. We are here in the Altaic Cluster representing the Emperor, the Empire, and its interests and its citizenry. We are also here, under Imperial instructions, to ensure that the peace is kept and a stable government is in power."

"Different words," Iskra said. "The same meaning."

Sten chose not to participate in the debating society. "May I ask your immediate intentions?"

"I intend that this cluster shall live in peace, as you said moments ago. I further intend that the brutalities, injustices, and evils of the Khaqan and his lickspittle underlings shall end immediately."

"Admirable intent," Sten said, forcing some warmth into his voice.

"Thank you."

"You have used the phrase New Order twice in my hearing," Sten went on. "What, precisely, does that mean?"

"You are not familiar with my writings? With my analyses?"

"Apologies. But I have been busy of late, trying to keep small points of light from becoming firestorms. And I learned of your imminent arrival only recently."

"You *must* read them," Iskra said earnestly. "Otherwise, it is impossible to understand the Altaic Cluster, let alone to help me rule it."

"Then I shall. Immediately. But—what you just said. You intend to rule this cluster. Forgive my ignorance. But what form will that take? To be exact, how representative will your government be?"

"Very," Iskra said firmly. "It shall bear no resemblance whatsoever to the Khaqan's tyranny. But one thing, Ambassador Sten.

"Since you are from a civilized world, do not make the mistake of becoming anthropomorphic about the beings of my cluster."

Civilized world, Sten thought. Vulcan? A man-made planet of slave labor and sudden death? He kept his face blank as Iskra continued.

"Understand that none of us, Torks, Jochians, Suzdal, or Bogazi, have ever known democracy. Beings here may rave about it, but it is an inconceivable idea in reality to them. Much like expecting someone who is blind from birth to envision a sunset, yes?

"So my New Order means a certain amount of direction. Guidance. That is the only way for us to find eventual freedom. Not in my time, of course, nor probably that of my sons yet unborn.

"But it will come.

"That is the oath I swore on my father's grave, and reconsecrated myself to, when the Khaqan murdered my brother.

"The Altaic Cluster will be at peace. And my sacred trust will be fulfilled—no matter the cost to this generation! There can be *no* true heroism or godhood without sacrifice along the path!"

Dr. Iskra's eyes glittered red, reflecting the sun setting outside.

CHAPTER SIXTEEN

"WHY," ALEX KILGOUR wondered, "do Ah hae th' feelin' ae a' thae an' ae a thae's a roarin't crock?"

He gestured at the wallscreen, which showed the terrace of the Khaqan's palace. I must learn to change the labels, Sten told himself. Iskra now wears the crown.

On the terrace stood Dr. Iskra, hands raised, a slight smile on his face as below him the packed square boomed with cheers.

Behind him stood the Altaic power structure. The humans, at least, all showed the same expression of pleased relief on hearing of the assumption. Sten was not familiar enough with either the Bogazi or Suzdal to understand their emotional projections. So that big meeting, he thought, must have been just the obligatory change of command speech, as when one took over a new unit and was required to meet the unit's lower-ranking officers and make nice. Then, later one announced the terror and that heads were to roll.

The cheering stopped, and Iskra resumed his speech.

". . . a time of healing. A time for all of us to abandon the past, the dark shadows of vengeance, and strike out boldly together to secure the future for ourselves and for generations to come.

"We are all Altaics. We share the same systems. The same planets. But instead of realizing our common destiny we waste our substance in feuds begun for forgotten reasons. We hate our neighbor because his genetic code differs from ours. But we all came from the same universal plasm, no matter our species, race, or home planet.

"You know me.

139

"You know the justice and honor I represent.

"You know I have spent years in exile, fighting in every way I knew to bring down the abhorrence that was the Khaqan. And I succeeded."

"Aye. Jus' you an' a wee attack ae apoopoplexy. Next he'll be claimin't t' hae created AM2 an' Scotch, as well."

"Now it is time for our next task. Now it is time, and past time for all of us—"

Sten palmed the mute switch, leaving Iskra to gesticulate in silence. He and Alex were alone in the embassy apartments assigned to Sten, apartments that were security-sealed and constantly checked for bugs.

"You think it's a crock," he told Alex, "because it is." He indicated a large pile of fiche and abstracts.

"Y'hae dredged throo all ae th' doc's natterin's, a'ready?"

"Read a couple. Had the rest abstracted. Iskra isn't exactly clear like crystal when he writes. And he's supposed to be such a brilliant speaker."

"Th' clot dinnae do aught t' make my adrenaline adren," Alex agreed.

"Nor mine. As far as I can tell, and I'm surely not a political philosopher, his main theory seems to be first we obliterate anything that the Khaqan did, then figure out what's to come next. This New Order, he says somewhere, 'must remain supple and sensitive to change and challenge.' He's in love with assonance."

"Aye, he is an ass. Ah dinnae ken aboot whether it belongs to wee Nancy or no. An' of course, th' one thae's most supple t' this change is th' good Dr. Iskra?"

"Of course. He's traveled. He's studied. He's done comparative analysis on every political theory going, including the Emperor. I didn't know the Emp picked him as one of the territorial governors of a Tahn solar system after the war. He did well—at least according to him."

"Ah dinnae wonder," Alex said. "Th' Tahn dinnae understand aught but a boot ae' their neck a'ter the rules they grew up wi'. Doc Iskra—clot, e'en a Campbell—would'a likely been deemed liberal.

"Whae about th' real problem? All these races who're nae

happy wi'out they're slittin' another one's weasan? Hae Iskra got a plan to end that?"

Sten shook his head. "He talks a lot about equality. But it sort of works out that some people in the Altaic Cluster are a bit more superior than others."

"An' lemme guess. Iskra, bein' a Jochian, somehow hae th' notion thae Jochians are th' most superior ae all."

"Correct."

"Clottin' wonderful. 'Ware ye ae th' new boss. Same ae th' old boss.' An wee Iskra's th' Emp's han-picked golden boy. Ah dinnae mind he's bein' a dictator, lord knowin' you an' I o'er th' years hae installed a few dozen ae them. But Ah'm nae taken wi' th' wee lad haein' nae th' slightest bit ae subtlety or patience. Ah'll wager he's a lad thae wan's th' world, an' he wants it yesterday."

"I'll live with that call," Sten said. He stared back at the screen and the appropriately enthusiastic beings behind Iskra. "I wonder just what—besides general make-nice—Iskra said to his rump parliament . . . Anybody there you think we can corrupt?"

Kilgour thought. "All ae 'em, in time," he said. "But i' y' want a fly on th' wall yest'day, Ah'd start wi' Menynder. He appears t' hae his eye on th' main chance moren' most. An' a wee bit ae follow-through."

"Agreed," Sten said. "See if we can't make him into a nice reliable source."

"No puh-roblem." Kilgour was silent for a minute. Then, seemingly irrelevantly, he asked, "Did y' e'er gie y'self th' fearful luxury ae wonderin' i' our Fearless Leader's gettin' a wee touch senile?"

Sten flinched, as if an icy blast had touched him. He didn't answer, but went to the bar and poured two large drinks. Not of Scotch; not of stregg. But pure quill alk, as he had grown used to drinking as a field soldier. He handed one to Kilgour.

"If he is," Sten said, after sipping his drink, "and Dr. Iskra is an example, the future's going to start looking like that." He gestured outside the double-paned security window at the huge, building thunderheads that were bringing yet another slashing summer storm down on the capital.

"Dinnae fash, lad," Kilgour said, knocking back his drink, waiting for Sten to do the same, and going for more. "We're th' Emp's spearheaders, aye? So i' this harbringer's a busto, we'll nae survive t' see th' rest."

Sten did not feel reassured. "Now," he said, taking Alex's example and slugging his drink down, "we'll have the fun of seeing just how Dr. Iskra shows his firm hand—and what happens to anybody who disagrees with him."

"Ah hae th' answer t' that one, too," Kilgour said. "Th' clot's an idealist. Which means we'll be wadin't in blood t' our scrotes. Six months an' thae'll be lookin't back an' talkin' aboot how kind, gentle, an' silky th' late Khaqan was. Hide an' watch. Or do ye hae th' desire t' take my bet Isky's nae but a timit, slickit lambiepie?"

Sten shook his head. "Like you say. I'm mad, but I don't think I'm clottin' daft. Other than being here in the first place. No. I don't think Dr. Iskra is going to end up being remembered for his sweetness and light."

"To you gentlebeings," Dr. Iskra said, "I know that I can present the future without need of equivocation. You are professionals, students of the inevitable historical process, and concerned as I about ensuring the glory of the Altaic Cluster."

There was a murmur. It could be taken as the listener chose, up to and including agreement.

There were only fifteen beings in the huge auditorium. It was part of the barracks complex belonging to the unit that had formerly been known as the Khaqan's Own, the purportedly elite unit whose prime function was guarding the late Khaqan's life, possessions, relatives, and friends. The walls were freshly repainted with new murals showing soldiers of the Own serving an offstage master, waiting, chins thrust forward nobly, on barricades against an offstage foe. Helping innocent citizens against offstage disasters. All of the soldiers, and all of the civilians on the mural, were Jochians.

The fifteen beings were among the highest-ranking officers of the Khaqan's military. Not *the* highest-ranking flag officers. Iskra had selected carefully.

Each of them had received verbal orders to stand by for a special assignment. One by one, sans staff or aides, they had been picked up by a representative of Iskra and taken to the secure complex.

All of them were career military. All of them came from long-serving families of what the Khaqan had called "the State." And all of them were Jochians. Iskra had not wanted the presence of the few Torks, Suzdal, and Bogazi who had gotten their stars.

Among them was a tall, silver-haired man. General Douw. He was doing his best to remain unnoticed—until he could see which way the wind was blowing.

"We Altaics," Iskra went on, "are beings that genetically wish for rocks we can cling to as the tides of change wash about us.

"One of those traditions should be—but never was under the Khaqan or his father—the military. The beings who are prepared to defend the state with their lives, unquestioningly. And not just the soldiers in the field, but those who dedicate and sacrifice their entire lives to that service in the services that support them.

"These are the beings whom I, as a babe, grew up somehow, instinctively, loving and respecting. I must confess, and I do not wish it spread beyond this room, that I cried when I discovered that my health would not permit me to serve as a soldier."

Iskra paused, eyes moving over the faces before him. They held on Douw for a moment. Just long enough to frighten the general. Douw nodded and tried to make his expression sympathetic.

Iskra continued. "Of course, when I grew a few more years, and realized the monstrous crimes a soldier was required to commit under the Khaqan, and my father and my revered brother found me mature enough to tell me the truth, knowing I would not chatter it forth in childish gossip, I was very grateful for my illnesses.

"But I have skewed.

"We do not have much time. You fifteen are the men and women I must have for my New Order. You represent the military. Not the rabble the Khaqan called his army and navy.

"And you are all Jochians."

Iskra stopped and let the silence build and become uncomfortable.

No one who had reached flag rank in any military would miss a cue like that.

"I noticed that," a hard-faced woman whose uniform dripped medals said. "Should we draw the conclusions we would like?"

"Which are, General F'lahn?" Iskra led her on, as he would encourage a prize pupil.

"I have read your writings, doctor. And they spoke to me of a cluster where all of us, Torks, Suzdal, and Bogazi are united toward a common goal. A goal that the best, the Jochians, lead, carrying the banner. Or do I misunderstand?"

"You misunderstand nothing," Iskra said. "Which is why I said I can speak honestly.

"This is a new day. A New Order.

"But that is yet to be. What must happen now is a return to peace. We must start from a position where all beings know safety. Security for themselves, their homes, their jobs, and their children."

There was another murmur—this one of definite agreement. General F'lahn would be rewarded for her bravery in walking point.

"Never happen," an admiral growled. "Not so long as we have these pocket armies, these militias, running about, calling themselves soldiers."

"That shall be dealt with, I promise you, Admiral Nel. Either they shall be dissolved, or brought under the command of properly trained officers, or . . ."

He did not finish. Nor did he need to. And the fifteen officers were now beaming openly.

"Yes," Iskra went on. "Just as the eventual New Order will give other beings a sense of place . . . This nonsense at Pooshkan University, for instance."

"Dr. Iskra. The Khaqan committed some terrible crimes. And some members of our military, even to my infinite shame some Jochians, were the assassins. Have you considered this?"

The questioner was the lowest-ranking flag officer present, Brigadier S!Kt. She was also a disciple of Iskra's, who had been driven into retirement. All that had saved her from being murdered by the Khaqan was that she came from an incredibly rich family who had traditionally supported the Khaqan. One of Dr. Iskra's first actions on arriving on Rurik was to "request" that she return to public service.

"I have. And these rapes and murders were monstrous. Against my fellow Jochians, against the Torks, against the Suzdal, and against the Bogazi. Orders are even now being issued for any military people involved to be picked up and questioned closely."

The meeting froze. Douw shrank down in his seat.

But Iskra pasted on his smile. "Of course, if any of you here today happened to be in charge of units involved in these crimes, I fully understand how much deadly pressure you were put under by the Khaqan. None of you, to speak bluntly, are considered anything other than the honorable soldiers you are. Anyone who thinks otherwise shall encounter my severest judgment.

"And I would appreciate your assistance in this matter. Fiche will be provided to you when you leave of the units and officers I propose to investigate.

"If you know any of them to be innocent, and my informants are in error, please advise a member of my staff immediately. And, if there are any criminal individuals or units *not* on the fiche, I would appreciate your including them."

Silence. A few officers—especially General Douw—chanced smiles. The lettres de cachet would be open.

"I think we have an understanding, yes?"

Nods. Larger smiles.

"A final question."

"Yes, General F'lahn."

"Your own family . . . was treated most shamefully."

Iskra's face was stone. "That is another matter. Of no concern to you. Of no concern to the state. Blood is blood. Blood must be answered.

"Those who helped the nightmare worm that called itself the Khaqan persecute and destroy my father, my family, and my brother will be destroyed.

"I know them.

"I have known them for years.

"Lying awake, on my pallet, dreaming of the homeland I

thought I would never see, I saw their faces, and I swore that if I was offered the chance, there would be a reckoning.

"This reckoning is now at hand."

Complete silence in the hall. Then the silence was broken by the applause of the Altaic Cluster—a forearm slammed hard against the body. Applauding the loudest was General Douw.

After all, each of them, and each of their families, had enemies. Blood, indeed, *had* to be answered.

". . . there would be a reckoning. This reckoning is now at—" and the man palmed the recorder off.

"And what will your Imperial master think of that?" Dr. Iskra asked, a note of challenge in his voice.

"The matter should not concern him," the man answered. "The Emperor chose you to rule the Altaic Cluster, after having decided you were the most qualified being. In what manner you choose to consolidate your power is not important, especially when it comes to minor trivia like a purge of the military hierarchy."

Dr. Iskra visibly relaxed. The man allowed him to relax while he went to a table and poured two cups of Iskra's nighttime herbal tea.

"That is assuming," he suddenly said, "that this action is handled as it should be. Which means you should be cautious as to how many private enemies you let these generals add to your list . . . And the matter must be handled immediately."

"It will be," Iskra said. "In the way you outlined as being the most effective. Of course, I have had to provide slight modifications, given the social characteristics of my people."

The man looked at Iskra and decided not to ask further.

The man was the Eternal Emperor's liason to Dr. Iskra, ordered to operate under deep cover. No one beyond the Emperor himself was to know of his existence—especially not any of the Imperial mission on Rurik. That exclusion specifically indicated Sten, the Imperial ambassador.

Sten knew the man.

He was the consummate spymaster, a man who served no one

but himself and his employers of the moment, who had best be the highest bidders.

His name was Venloe.

The man responsible for the assassination of the Eternal Emperor.

CHAPTER SEVENTEEN

THE FOREST WAS far north of Rurik. It began where an equally huge swamp ended, and it stretched for many kilometers, almost to the shore of a nearly tideless inland sea.

In the local peasant dialect, the forest was called "The Place of Smokes." In summer, windstorms swept through the forest, lifting huge clouds of debris high into the atmosphere. In spring and fall, dank fog crawled over the dry, silent land. In winter, polar storms made the "smoke" white.

Near that inland sea, many years earlier, the Khaqan had determined to build himself a retreat. Since everything on Rurik was big, and since the Khaqan thought even more grandiosely than his world encouraged, this retreat was to have included buildings sufficient for his entire court.

The property was surveyed.

Here and there one could still see colored markers that had been injected into tree trunks or stumps.

Roadways had been cleared, but never paved.

The Khaqan lost interest before any construction had been done, and the Place of Smokes returned to its desolation. Now, the forest's only visitors were illegal charcoal burners in summer and fall, and fur hunters in the winter.

They did not stay long. The forest was too huge. Too silent. Too uncaring.

The long line of gravlighters crept along the remains of a road, deep in the forest heart.

Each gravlighter's cargo area was packed with beings, human and ET. Some of them wore uniforms, hastily pulled on in summons to angry door-knocks and now ripped and torn. Others wore only what garments they had been able to grab as they were rushed from their homes or places of duty.

They were closely guarded by beings who wore the same uniform. But all of these guards were human.

The prisoners were silent. Some of them nursed wounds.

The gravlighters turned onto a narrower lane, then again, onto a track. The track opened onto what had been a meadow.

The lighters grounded.

Orders were shouted. The prisoners dismounted.

There were other prisoners still in the gravlighters. They lay, unmoving and trampled, on the lighters' decks. For the moment, these dead or near-dead were ignored by the guards.

Further orders brought the surviving prisoners into line.

Among the prisoners were Acinhow and N'ern. One was a minor prison officer, the other a tax official. Both of them had had time, when being arrested, to grab a few rationpaks, which had kept them alive on the long trip north.

"And now," N'ern whispered. "I see no sign of a prison. Are we to build our own from this forest?"

Acinhow shook her head slightly and indicated with a nod.

Halfway across the meadow were long, open trenches. Earth-moving equipment waited nearby.

Other trenches had been dug beyond them. But these had been filled in. Earth mounded above them in rows.

N'ern's face became gray.

There were whispers as other prisoners saw the trenches. Shouts from the guards for silence.

It took N'ern two attempts before she could speak.

"The children will never—" She broke off.

Acinhow shivered.

N'ern tried once more.

"At least . . . at least," she murmured, "it will be honorable."

CHAPTER EIGHTEEN

STEN WAS UP to his ass in R-O-U-T-I-N-E. Which on Jochi meant a permanent state of borderline panic. Two thirds of the lights on the com board were winking yellow alert. The remainder were red.

His com techs—all schooled as diplomatic ombudsmen—hustled the board. Whittling away at the drakh. Soothing when mere calm words would do. Referring callers to appropriate agencies—knowing it would be some time before *any* Jochi governmental department would be operational. Dispensing small Imperial embassy favors where they could.

Anything worthwhile was boiled into an intelligence monograph and sent on to Sten. So many such reports had been pouring in that Sten had wound up spending his whole morning in the com room, poring over the reports, as well as fielding a stream of calls only an ambassador could deal with.

The first call of the day had been from young Milhouz, urgently wanting to talk to the ambassador. Sten put this at the bottom of the mental stack of things he had to do. Yes, he had promised the Pooshkan students a hearing with someone in authority. After meeting Dr. Iskra, Sten wasn't real sure how to make his promise good.

Later with that. He would figure out something—just as soon as he made sense of all these reports of scattered disturbances all over Jochi. Especially in the neighborhoods and ghettos of Rurik.

There were a few more blood feuds being settled than usual. But no rioting. Some small-scale street maneuvering by the militias. But no shots fired—in anger, at least. A slight increase in looting. Also family violence.

Sten scrolled on. He came to another urgent call from Milhouz. The com officer had boiled the message down to the following: "Have successfully won delay in ultimatum," it read. "Committee has agreed to extend deadline by one more week." Sten noted the com officer was Freston, his most senior and trusted dial-twiddler. Unfortunately, the man was far too efficient, and it had taken Sten to rescue him from a seemingly inevitable and murderously dull career running high-ranking REMF com staffs.

Under *Observations*, Freston had written: "Subject's manner outwardly calm. Voice box tension, however, indicates instability of individual. Sees Ambassador Sten as father figure. *Suggested handling*: Continue firm line. Softer approach will further feed instability."

Clottin' great, Sten thought. A father figure to a spoiled rich kid. He didn't even *like* Milhouz, thought of him as a shrill-voiced toady taking advantage of a group of equally useless individuals. Clot him! He would call back when he was good and ready. Father figure, my clottin' . . .

Sten skipped ahead, musing over other reports. Then he hit another warning. Panic buying had erupted. As well as hoarding. All over the planet, shops that stocked nonperishable food and drink were selling out. Fuel and cooking-oil stocks also were being depleted.

He did not like this. It meant that it was going to take a great deal more than fine-minded speeches for Iskra to convince people that some kind of normal life lay ahead.

Sten gazed at the drakh heaping higher and higher in his bowl. This defied Kilgour's law of drakh hitting the fan. Alex insisted that trouble came in threes. Sten disagreed, even if the axiom came from Kilgour's sainted "mum." It was Sten's opinion that trouble kept coming until you could take no more. Then you got hit twice more.

The com room door hissed open and Cind boiled in. He was glad to see her. But he was not glad to see the look on her face.

"I get the idea you're not here to tell me Iskra's idea of paradise has dawned on the streets of Rurik," Sten said.

"Not unless paradise includes storm troopers and mass arrests," Cind said.

Sten reacted in his best diplomatic manner. "Say clottin' what?"

"I've been checking up on those rumors of people going missing," she said. "They aren't rumors. I've got eyewitnesses. Heads of families—whole families, sometimes—are being grabbed right and left. By Iskra's soldiers."

"What kind of game is that man playing?" Sten asked. "He'll have the whole thing down around his ears before he barely gets started."

One of the com officers signaled him. "I've got another call from young Milhouz," he said. "He's holding right now. He says it's real important he talk to you. An emergency, he claims."

"Sure it is," Sten said. "Lie to him. Tell him I've been stricken with beriberi, or some such. Then get Dr. Iskra on the line. I want to talk to him. Now!"

A few minutes later, the thin-lipped face of Iskra appeared on the center vid screen.

"I understand you have a matter of some urgency," Iskra said.

"I'd like an explanation, is what I'd like, doctor."

"I don't appreciate your tone, Sr. Ambassador."

"I tend to sing in that key," Sten said, "when I hear a leader I am supporting is perilously close to embarrassing the man I answer to. The Eternal Emperor."

"In what manner am I doing this?"

"I have *confirmed* reports, Dr. Iskra, that your soldiers are engaged in mass arrests."

"If you would have asked me first," Iskra said smoothly, "I would have confirmed that fact for you. Save you a great deal of trouble—and misunderstanding."

"Fine. I'm asking."

"Yes, there have been some arrests," Iskra said. "Although, I *do* think referring to them as mass arrests exaggerates the circumstances. For convenience's sake, the accused ones were arrested at much the same time, just as they were transported to and are being held in a single prison—Gatchin Fortress, which is the traditional site on Jochi for those beings in the public eye who have been indicted. I assure you, however, these are merely routine matters involving restoring stability to the cluster. My people want assurances that justice has returned to the Altaics.

"The individuals in question have been accused of various crimes. Some serious. However, to be absolutely frank, I fully expect many of these accusations to prove false. That they are victims of petty beings seeking revenge.

"But, as I indicated, people are demanding trials. Therefore, I shall give them those trials. Fair trials. So that anyone falsely accused can publicly clear his or her name."

This is a great load of drakh, Sten thought. "What about the guilty ones?" he asked.

"Aren't you treading heavily in places you shouldn't go?" Iskra asked. "What business is the justice system of the Altaics to the Imperial ambassador?"

"None at all," Sten admitted. "But I am determined to see the Emperor's orders carried out. Which means he expects a return to stability in the Altaics. Creating new blood feuds, doctor, is not a good way to accomplish this."

"I promise you, Sr. Ambassador," Iskra said, "the trials will be completely fair. And I will be as merciful as possible to the guilty. Does that satisfy you?"

Sten had to say it did. Of course, Iskra was lying. But Sten couldn't afford an open break with the man. He would lose all control, and the mission would be doomed.

"It was a pleasure talking to you, Sr. Sten," Iskra said when they were done. And the screen went blank.

"We'd better increase surveillance," Sten told Cind. "Get more of Kilgour's bats in the sky."

"You'll be needin' more'n Frick 'n Frack," Alex said. Sten jumped. He hadn't heard Kilgour enter. " 'Less m' ears're waxed tight, they're shootin' oop th' univers'ty."

Sten was astounded. "The students? Where'd they get the guns?"

"Ah dinnae think it wae kids doin' th' shootin'," Alex said.

"Clot!" was all Sten said. He raced for the door, Alex and Cind tearing after him.

As he sprinted through the embassy, shouting for the duty company of Bhor and the Gurkhas, and stormed out the door and across the broad grounds, the specter of complete disaster choked his mind. The little twerp Milhouz had been right about at least one thing. If something happened to the coddled young beings of Pooshkan, pure hell would break loose over the Altaics.

Sten could hear the sound of gunfire coming from the university as he reached the embassy gates.

Then he was brought up short. The boulevard outside was barred by many Jochi soldiers. Iskra's men. The soldiers were backed by two armored tracks.

A burly major loomed up at him.

"Get out of my way," Sten rasped.

"I'm sorry, Sr. Ambassador," the major said, "but I can't permit you to leave."

"By whose orders?"

"Dr. Iskra's orders, sir. But please don't misunderstand. It's for your own safety. I have also been instructed to apologize for any inconvenience. You'll be permitted to leave once the emergency has passed."

Sten heard more shots coming from Pooshkan. "Is that the emergency?" he said.

The major shrugged. "Young hooligans are rioting. Committing terrible deeds. Destroying public property. Murder. Looting. Sexual atrocities. It's a terrible, terrible thing."

"Lying clot!" he heard Cind mutter.

"I must see for myself," Sten said.

The major stayed professionally calm. But Sten could see the soldiers tense around him. Someone whispered, and there came the hum of turrets turning toward the embassy.

"I honestly can't permit it, sir," the major said. "Really. It's for your own safety. Please don't press the point and force me to do my duty."

Sten was hollow inside as he turned away. He heard another burst of gunfire and what sounded like distant screams.

What the hell could he do? He thought about Milhouz and those other poor damned rich kids. Sure, he had no use for them. Would have wished them away and out of his life if he could.

If only he had returned Milhouz's calls sooner. If only he had . . .

Aw, clot!

Alex and Cind tried to soothe him as he headed back inside.

There was nothing left to do now—except brace for the backlash.

CHAPTER NINETEEN

THE CHILDREN OF the Altaics didn't die without a fight.

More than twenty-five thousand students had packed the campus when Iskra's forces struck. It started as a feint at the barricade. Sixty club-wielding cops charged the ten-meter-high jumble of rubble.

Caught unaware, the students were rocked back. A squad of cops burst over the side and hammered around them, cracking skulls and breaking limbs.

A pair of young Suzdal broke in among them. Bodies slithering under the blows, sharp teeth ripping at tendons. The cops were driven back. They pretended to regroup for another charge.

The young barricade defenders screamed for help. Hundreds came rushing to the rescue.

At the Pooshkan Action Committee headquarters, Milhouz and the other young leaders heard the screams.

"We've been betrayed," he shouted.

"Come on. We have to help!" Riehl said, voice breaking with alarm. She headed for the door along with Tehrand and Nirsky.

Milhouz didn't respond. He had just caught a glimpse of something out the window. Through a long alleyway between the Language and the Cultural Arts buildings, he spotted the silhouette of a tank, moving down the road that paralleled Pooshkan.

"Milhouz!" Riehl shouted again. "Come on. We've got to stop them!"

Milhouz saw the blur of another armored track go by at speed. He calmed himself and turned to Riehl. She was hovering at the door along with Tehrand and Nirsky.

"I'm going to try Ambassador Sten one more time," he said. "Threaten pure hell if he doesn't stop this."

He moved toward the com line the engineering students had installed and shot a look over his shoulder at his companions. "Go ahead," he said. "I'll be right with you."

The three rushed out.

Milhouz stopped. He turned his head to study the open door, head tilted like a feral animal. He waited a moment, listening to more screams of help from the barricades.

Then he ran to the window and opened it, flung a leg over the sill—and jumped.

At the barricades, the cops were retreating again—this time under a heavy cascade of rocks and timber and pieces of rebar.

Riehl and the two other student leaders raced onto the scene. There were cries of recognition.

At the top of the barricade, young beings were waving for them, calling their names, urging them to help rally the students for the next assault.

Riehl looked wildly back for Milhouz. Leadership was demanded, now, dammit!

"Must go to top," Nirsky chirped.

"Up. Up. Up," Tehrand snarled.

Still hoping her lover would show up at any minute, Riehl ran forward. Young hands grabbed her, hoisted her high, and passed her from hand to hand. Up. And up. Tehrand and Nirsky followed behind her.

She was set on her feet. Riehl peered down at the massed cop force. She turned to face the students and lifted an arm high, fist clenched.

"Freedom for the Altaics!" she screamed.

The students took up the cry. "Freedom! Freedom!"

Above the melee Riehl heard the sound of heavy engines. She turned to see the cops parting ranks, revealing first one armored track. Then another.

The big vehicles lumbered forward. Double-timing behind them came soldiers. Weapons at ready.

The first track stopped. Turret clanked up.

An explosion . . . then another.

Canisters of tear gas arced high and plunged into the mass of students. There were shouts of pain and terror.

Eyes streaming with tears, Riehl held her ground. She shook her fists at the tracks.

Almost on cue, both tracks charged—hitting the barricade full force and cracking through it as if it were paper.

Debris burst upward.

Riehl saw the sharp piece of rebar coming at her, tumbling through the air in slow motion.

"Milhouz!" she screamed.

The rebar took her through the throat. She did a slow doll's fall off the crumbling barricade.

The soldiers opened fire.

Tehrand and Nirsky died where they stood.

Some students fled the onslaught. Others held their ground, only to be chewed apart by the soldiers' fire, or to be crushed under the tracks. Still . . . many apparachniks did their parents proud.

But in the end the soldiers flung them aside and poured onto the campus, firing magazine after magazine into the crowd. The last of the student holdouts finally broke and ran wildly for cover.

The soldiers followed.

As night fell there were still sounds of gunfire coming from Pooshkan. But not concentrated fire. Only single reports—as the soldiers hunted down the children of Jochi and shot them.

One by one.

CHAPTER TWENTY

POYNDEX FELT ONE moment of incredible power.

He had given the Eternal Emperor orders—and the man had obeyed.

Then he caught himself. You are a clotting fool—and worse. I thought you had changed yourself, cut that blind ambition out of your soul like it was a tumor.

With all his strength, Poyndex closed his hand on the rusting barbed wire in front of him. The jagged metal knifed into his finger and palm. After a minute, he released his grip and examined his bloody hand. Let it infect if it is going to, he thought fiercely. Let it swell and fester. Because this crude hunger for real power you feel has almost destroyed you once. And there will not be a second chance.

Poyndex told his body he felt no pain from his hand, and shut off that nerve center's screaming. He looked across the wire, down at the Umpqua River, swirling in spring flood.

This is, he thought, the second time I have been on Manhome, the planet Earth. The first was serving the privy council, which I did well. Especially here, short-stopping that assassination team Sten led. What would have happened, what would have been different, if I had been more alert to the changewinds, and not stopped him? If I had let the privy council die?

You would not have been doing your duty.

True. But might that not have prevented . . . other events?

Who could tell, he thought. Then I would have remained just a colonel, just head of Mercury Corps. Perhaps I would never have come to the attention of the Eternal Emperor when he returned, even though that spotlight hardly showed me in the best light. Perhaps I would have been purged into retirement after the Emperor took power, as so many others have been.

Do not allow yourself to second-guess the past. Learn from it . . . but do not think it could be or should be changed. The present and the future are more important—especially this return to Earth. This comes close to the moment of triumph.

That proposal the Emperor had given him had been very thorough, for all its brevity:

It was necessary for a certain surgical operation to be performed on the Eternal Emperor. Something artificial was to be removed from deep inside his body. But the operation must be planned and conducted without the Emperor ever realizing what was going on.

To Poyndex, that was simple. He had, as he had told the Emperor, dealt fairly frequently with enemy agents who had suicide orders conditioned into them—from physical devices to programmed deathtrauma to the hardest to defuse, psychological bombs that ordered the agent's personality to self-destruct.

He had warned the Emperor that the plan would be initiated without the Emperor knowing the exact moment it began, given the suspected nature of the device in his body. Certain events would occur. The Emperor must not question them, or allow his mind to feel alarmed. He must accept whatever happened as if it were common and natural.

The Eternal Emperor had taken a long moment before agreeing.

Stage One was assembling the surgical team. Years earlier, when Poyndex had graduated from field agent through agent runner to planner, he learned he had held three major myths about the medical profession:

A) A doctor had ethics or a code requiring him to believe in and maintain the sanctity of life. The truth was that a doctor was no more or less idealistic than any other member of society. Which to Poyndex meant without any morality beyond self-interest, profit, or the drooling current beliefs of that doctor's society. It was quite easy to involve doctors in projects on the phsyiology of torture, mass euthanasia, or involuntary sterilization of society's misfits, to name only a few areas that Poyndex had been involved with over the years.

B) The only doctors who would perform "illegal" actions were less than competent. The fact was that he had never found it difficult to recruit the highest level professionals—provided they were given the appropriate sop of "patriotism," or "duty to the Empire," or even, in extreme cases, "duty to life."

C) That after performing the required deed, a doctor might be stricken with guilt or even just a desire to discuss what happened. The fact was that the only guilt Poyndex had ever seen a medico evince was when the mores of the society changed without the doctor being aware of the change, the fee had not been paid, or his malpractice insurance did not cover the deed. And every doctor seemed to hate every other doctor, which kept shoptalk from ever being worrisome.

For this operation, it had taken no more than two hours for Poyndex to find his surgical team. Among them were the best and the brightest of the Empire's doctors. And all of them had been on Poyndex's payroll for years.

The cover story—which Poyndex had planted no more heavily than a casual mention to an OR nurse who was a Mercury operative—was that the operation would be performed on one of the Emperor's doubles. Everyone "knew" the Emperor had doubles, who were sent into high-risk or high-boredom assignments. In fact, there were none and never had been, a blatant stupidity that Poyndex meant to bring up with the Emperor at an early date.

Once assembled, the team was sent to Earth. The Emperor had been right: the site was perfect.

Aeons earlier, the Emperor had decided he liked salmon fishing. He had bought from Earth's government, and from the local government of the province of Oregon, the entire Umpqua River, from its headwaters to its mouth at the Pacific Ocean. Over the decades he had also bought out everyone who lived or worked on or near the river. A few locals were permitted to live and work near the Umpqua—after all, provisions, guides, game wardens, and so forth were necessary. The Emperor then went fishing, using sites that were no more than level ground that a few tents could be pitched upon.

But on that river an industrialist, Tanz Sullamora, had also built a camp. Sullamora, however, had found he couldn't stand either the wilderness or fishing, so his camp had been turned into a luxurious retreat. Sullamora, once the Emperor's most loyal supporter/groupie, became a bitter enemy and the leader of the assassination plot. But he died when that bomb destroyed the Emperor, as well.

His secluded resort became a place where the rest of the conspirators, the self-named privy council, went for consultations.

Now . . .

Now it was where the Emperor went to take a long-needed—as the livies praised—rest from his onerous duties.

This time the Emperor never knew that he had traveled to Earth.

Days before the departure date, his food had been gently drugged with sopors. The Emperor didn't realize he was receding into a fog. He continued to perform his duties and consult with his aides on important issues.

He did not realize that these aides—none of whom he recognized—were carefully trained Mercury Corps operatives, presenting him with problems that grew simpler and simpler. Eventually they were so easy a one-celled protozoa, *Amoeba quaylus*, could have solved them. The entire scenario was a traditional operation, called a reagan/baker, devised to maintain a senile ruler in power as long as possible.

Poyndex and his technicians took the Emperor down and down, until he was unconscious. But they continued the slow dosage, now in an intravenous solution that everyone nursing the comatose being thought was just nourishment.

Poyndex was taking no chances.

Eventually his technicians reported that the Emperor was one stage above the suspended animation the early longliners had used, the animation that had killed most of the passengers and crew on those monster ships that had stumbled out from Earth for the nearest stars before stardrive had been devised, and before AM2 had been discovered to make that drive a practicality.

Poyndex then ordered the Emperor stabilized and transferred to the *Normandie*, the Emperor's yacht-battleship that officially did not even exist.

The Emperor held, very comfortably and safely, in that state. Poyndex felt a bit of pride.

Next, the nature of the device—or devices—hidden inside the Emperor's body should have been examined electronically. Poyndex could not. He was fairly sure there were no antiexamination booby traps on them. The Emperor, after all, could stride through security screens without anything happening.

But he was only fairly sure.

Therefore, feeling as if he were living in the Dark Ages, he ordered his chief surgeon to begin exploratory surgery. The surgeon was further told that the operation must be done at speed, as if he were in a trauma center, with only seconds to keep the patient from dying.

It was well that Poyndex gave those instructions. He had scrubbed and gowned and gone into the operating theater, an arena he was quite familiar with. The first incision opened the body cavity, and Poyndex saw the device. He brushed the surgeon's hand aside and held the back of his fingers against the plas ovoid. It was growing warm.

"Excise it," he snapped.

"But—"

The surgeon's scalpel lased twice, and the device was free. Bastard, Poyndex thought. Got you before you could detonate.

"There. Another one."

"But there's hemorrhaging!"

"Screw that! Cut!"

A second device.

"What are the vital signs?" Poyndex asked hoarsely.

"Stable."

"Good. Doctor, open the rib cage."

The heavy bone-cutting laser made the cut.

"There. Another one. Take it out."

The cuts were made. Poyndex was sweating. There could be one more. But he couldn't just send in the machete team.

"Survey. Scan the medulla oblongata area."

"Yes, sir."

Time stopped.

"There appears to be . . . some kind of short-range transmitting device. Very short-range—one third of a meter. If you wanted an opinion, I'd say it was a very sophisticated encephalograph. But that's all it is.''

Poyndex almost sagged.

''Then that's all. You can slow down. Stabilize him. Stop the bleeding. And button him up.''

''What about these?'' The second surgeon indicated the three man-made devices that had been cut out of the Emperor's body.

''Mine. You did not see them.''

The three plas objects went to immediate tech analysis.

The first devise was a sophisticated bomb, using conventional matter for the detonator and Anti-Matter Two for the explosive. It would have been enough to create a one-eighth-kilometer parking lot with the OR as ground zero. Poyndex grinned tightly. Now he knew where that mysterious blast had come from that went off microseconds after the privy council's assassin had shot the Emperor. The bomb was intended to prevent autopsies, at the very least.

The second device was a combination receiver and booby trap set to detonate if the Emperor was ever cut open. It further contained certain programmed circumstances. It took Poyndex some hours to puzzle out the purpose of the device. The electroencephalograph still in the Imperial skull would continually transmit the Emperor's thoughts. If those thoughts deviated beyond the programmed circumstances, the bomb would detonate.

Interesting, he thought. One way to keep yourself from going insane. Or . . . And he decided not to ponder further possibilities.

The third device was the most interesting. It was a very high-powered transmitter. Its activating mechanism was linked to the Emperor's vital organs. So, Poyndex thought. If the Emperor is killed, the transmitter transmits. Or, he theorized, if the Emperor is tortured into doing something he should not, or drug-conditioned into a certain pattern, or if he becomes neurotic/psychotic beyond the allowable profile—the bomb goes off and the transmitter transmits.

To whom?

To where?

And sometime later, the Eternal Emperor returns.

Poyndex was tempted to continue his investigation.

Then he caught himself.

What were the chances of the Eternal Emperor, when he recovered consciousness from this operation, ordering the death of everyone involved with this project?

Excellent.

What were the chances, even if everyone involved with this wasn't disappeared, of the Eternal Emperor ordering everyone connected with this operation brainscanned to see what they knew about this incredible secret?

Better than excellent.

Poyndex suddenly knew, with an absolute knowledge beyond experience, paranoia, or amorality, that his chances of living, if he investigated where this mysterious signal was beamed at, were far less than zero. Hating this loss of knowledge, but wanting to live even more, he personally destroyed all three devices.

He was not sure of what he had just done. Nor why the Emperor had this bomb in his body, or why he wanted it removed. It made sense for the Emperor to protect himself against kidnappers.

But . . . if he were eternal, as he most provably was, what happened when the bomb went off? How did the Emperor survive the blast?

Psychic projection?

Clot that. Next he would be accepting the wacko beliefs of the Cult of the Eternal Emperor, who thought that their ruler periodically went out to commune with Holy Spheres.

The hell with it. Now was the time to be nothing more than a supremely loyal servant.

"Sir. You are bleeding."

Poyndex came out of his kaleidoscoping thoughts and returned the Mantis soldiers' salute. "Thank you. I must have cut myself. I'll get it treated."

The soldier nodded and continued her patrol, eyes sweeping the wilderness, alert for any signs that an enemy of the Empire lurked out there.

Grateful for the pain, his decision, and the interruption, Poyndex walked toward the infirmary.

He allowed himself one second of pride.

From this moment, the Emperor—aided by his servant—would no longer be controlled by the past.

The Eternal Emperor's eyes opened.

He found himself in a cold, sterile place. Naked.

Was he once more back on that ship? A flash of panic. Had mistakes been made? Was he now that mewling waffler he had grown to hate?

No. He felt some pain. And not the sullen muscles of rebirth.

He remembered . . .

Yes.

He must be on Earth. And Poyndex, as he had promised, had performed his duty.

The Emperor yet lived.

He allowed his mind to wander, still half-anesthetized. But even stuporous, he realized that he no longer felt watched. He no longer felt he had to guard his every thought.

The link was broken.

The eyes of the warden, the assassin, the Voice on the ship, were closed.

Now he was alive.

Now he could rule as his fate, his weird, intended.

Now he was free.

The Eternal Emperor smiled.

BOOK THREE

WALL CLOUD

CHAPTER TWENTY-ONE

THE MASSACRE AT Pooshkan University backblasted across the Altaics. Rumors of the tragedy burst on the streets of Rurik *as the troops were opening fire*. Sten filed this anomaly away as significant while he tried to make sense of the chaos erupting all around him.

Surrounded by Jochi troops whose purported orders were to protect the Imperial embassy, Sten sat in the eye of the storm watching events unfold, filing a blizzard of "Eyes Only" reports.

The massacre itself he had witnessed via two teams of Frick & Fracks, which had swooped over the soldiers as they opened fire on the students. There was no question in his mind that Iskra had ordered the attack. Proof, however, would be difficult. The soldiers wore no identifying insignia on their uniforms. They were clearly human. But they could just as easily have been a rebel Jochi militia. Or even Tork.

Sten also noted that the first rumor claimed the attack was the work of a Suzdal militia unit.

This tidbit of disinformation came *as* he watched Riehl tumble off the barricade. The rumor was followed by its opposite a beat and a half later: It was the Bogazi who had committed the atrocity.

Sten, who had witnessed a great deal of blood spilled in his life, had to force himself to watch the gory drama that unfolded. He heard several young com officers retch at the sight. Even Freston, the chief of the com unit, turned away.

"Th' man's no daft . . ." Alex muttered as he watched the butcher's work on the vid screen. "He's clottin' insane."

Sten ignored him, as he attempted for the tenth time to get Iskra on the embassy line to demand that he call off the dogs. For the tenth time, his call was repulsed by a low-level functionary, who said that Iskra was "meditating" and had left strict instructions not to be disturbed.

"I'll meditate *him*," Sten snarled. Then, to Alex: "Get me some eyes on the palace."

Seconds later he was patched into a pair of Frick & Fracks soaring over the Square of the Khaqans.

The news there was just as bad. A group of protesters, spurred on by the rumors of the Pooshkan massacre, was advancing on the Khaqan's palace.

His stomach churned as, instead of the expected confrontation between the mob and Jochi troops, he saw a contingent of Imperial Guards sweep out of the palace and down the steps.

They charged into the crowd, hitting like shock troops. The confrontation was violent—and brief. In moments the crowd was hammered and put to flight. As the frightened beings fled, he saw many civilian bodies heaped on the ground.

To make matters worse, many of the Imperial Guard soldiers chased after the fleeing protesters, flailing at them with riot sticks.

Cind swore. "They're acting like clottin' cops, instead of soldiers. And bad cops at that."

Sten made no comment. He had his emotions under an iron lid now, but there was a backbrain crawl that wouldn't go away. When this was over many fingers of blame were going to be pointing in many directions. And the Imperial Guard had just made itself a potential target.

"I want the whole station on red alert," Sten told Kilgour. "Notify the kitchen to keep the caff coming. And tell housekeeping to haul in some cots. Until further notice, we all work until we drop."

Alex hustled off to kick the staff into overdrive. Sten turned back to the monitors. His eyes were already red-rimmed and scratchy. He felt Cind's soft hand touch the back of his neck.

She didn't say a word. But the light pressure gave him strength. Sten buckled down to a decidedly ugly task.

As the hours passed, tragedy mounted on tragedy.

A Suzdal militia, hatred stoked white hot by rumor, caught a Bogazi neighborhood napping. They torched it. Then they stood back and slaughtered the frightened Bogazi as they poured out of their hutches.

Revenge came almost immediately. As three Suzdal adults shepherded twenty or more cubs from their homes to a feeding hall, a group of Bogazi burst out of hiding. The Suzdal adults were dead in moments. Then the cubs. One Bogazi lifted a small cub high in the air. She split it with her beak, then swallowed it whole.

"Grandmother was correct," she chortled to her friends. "Suzdal good for nothing. Except eat."

The incident was sure to kick more fuel on the fire. The Suzdal were among the most protective parents in the Empire, genetically predisposed to slaughter anything threatening their young.

More incident reports flooded in.

That evening a small Tork militia unit attacked a Jochi marketplace. But the Jochians were ready. Troops leapt out to confront the Torks, who howled in surprised terror, turned, and fled. The Jochians followed. No sooner had they broken ranks, however, than a much larger Tork force burst onto the scene, striking from the rear. Two hundred plus died at the market. Most of them civilians.

On and on it went. Rurik was one enormous blood feud. Sten could barely keep up with the events. Numbly, he kept filing the reports, putting in calls to Iskra, and getting no answer. He had similar luck with the Eternal Emperor. His boss was indisposed. Sten was mildly surprised. He had never known the Emperor to be sick.

The following day, Sten stared bleary-eyed at the monitor screen as—marvel of all marvels—a *peaceful* group of citizens marched on Pooshkan. It was a mixed crowd, equally composed of the four races of the Altaics. They were carrying wreaths to lay at the site in memory of the slain students.

The group carried large, hand-lettered banners pleading for a return to peace and order in the Altaics. Some of the banners even had nice things to say about Iskra.

Sten was not surprised at what happened next. He chopped the volume and turned away from the screen as soldiers guarding the site opened fire. He looked at Cind. She stood soldier straight, jawline set firm. But her eyes were smudged dark. She gave an involuntary shudder as they both dimly heard screams of terror coming from the university.

Her mouth opened, as if she were about to speak. Then it closed again, with a sharp snap.

She wants me to make it stop, he thought. But she knows there's nothing I can do.

Sten had never felt so low. So unheroic. Not that he believed in such things. And if there were any fantasies of that sort in Cind, they had been thoroughly ground out in the course of the last few hours.

He heard Freston call his name. Sten turned.

"It's Dr. Iskra, sir," the com officer said. "He wonders if it would be convenient to meet?"

Sten went loaded for *Ursus horribilis*. In fact, forget the grizzly. Packed in a blunderbuss, his diplomatic note to Iskra would peel the hide of *Ursus articis*, as well.

Although he didn't directly charge Iskra with ordering the massacre at Pooshkan, he did some heavy denting around the edges. He also lumped in the attack on the wreath-layers, as well as the unauthorized use of Imperial troops on civilian populations.

The wadding he had tamped the charge with was a clear threat that he would recommend that the Emperor rethink his support of Iskra.

Unfortunately, Sten knew he was creeping out on two-mil-thick ice. The importance of the Altaic Cluster was such that the three cardinal rules of diplomacy absolutely applied. A: Check with the boss first. B: Check with the boss first. And, most important of all . . . C: Check with the boss first.

Still, although he was hamstrung by his failure to reach the Emperor, Sten tromped into his meeting determined to carry off his bluff.

Iskra leapt to his feet as soon as Sten entered the room. "Sr. Ambassador," he said, "I protest your failure to support my government!"

Sten buried an unprofessional gape. He buttoned his lip. Raised an eyebrow. Chilly.

"Furthermore, I am going to ask the Emperor that you be withdrawn from service in the Altaics."

"How kind of you to tell me in person," Sten said dryly. "I suppose your request—"

"Demand, sir. Not request."

"Demand, then. Although I suggest you eliminate that word from your vocabulary when you address the Emperor. Back to my question. Does this . . . demand . . . have anything to do with the chaos raging outside your doors? Or is it just you don't like the cut of my formal wear?"

"I blame you for the agony my poor people are experiencing, yes. Can you deny you and your . . . staff . . . have shown a definite lack of enthusiasm in my appointment?"

"I can. Easily. Enthusiasm is for amateurs. My professional duty is to support you. But—and this is a serious *but*, sir—my mission is to restore order to the Altaic Cluster. A mission, I must add, that is sadly in danger—if not doomed as we speak. And you, sir, must take full responsibility for this. As I so intend to inform the Emperor."

"Then I was right," Iskra hissed. "You do oppose me."

"After what happened at Pooshkan, you expect plaudits? A military band to trumpet your accomplishments?"

"You blame that—abominable action on me? Me!" Iskra made his best face of outrage. Sten would have laughed if the dispute had not been over blood.

"I'll have you know I'm sickened over the incident. I've ordered a complete investigation. Headed by a man whose reputation is above reproach: General Douw."

Ho-ho, Sten thought. So that's the way of the land, is it? Douw had been seduced into Iskra's sphere.

"I'll inform the Emperor," Sten said. "He'll be . . . interested. Which is not the word I'd use, doctor, to describe his reaction to the mess you've stepped in."

"Bah! A stronger hand is all they need. These are my people, Sr. Ambassador. You don't understand them. Blood feuds are an integral part of our history. It's a fact of our nature, and always bubbling under the surface. This is why, when your support of me is so lackluster, it only takes a small incident—such as the tragedy at Pooshkan—to threaten chaos.''

"Chaos is what you've got all right," Sten said. "What do you propose to do about it?"

"That is *my* concern," Iskra snapped. "The private business of this cluster. Remember that."

"I'll do my best," Sten said.

He thought about the note in his pocket, the one tearing Iskra a new defecating orifice. If he delivered it as planned, it wouldn't make his future relations with Iskra any easier.

He thought about the young people dying at the barricades of Pooshkan. Clot future relations. Sten determined at that moment to rid himself of this man. He would gather every molecule of evidence. Build a stone bucket. So when he did speak to the Emperor, he would have proof enough to hammer Iskra out of the Altaics.

Besides, the man had already declared himself an enemy. At this point, most diplomatic rule books suggested a body blow—to the gut.

Sten pulled out the note and gave it to Iskra. "A little bedtime reading," he said. "Now, if you'll excuse me . . ." He exited the room, leaving Iskra gobbling after him.

As soon as he was gone, Venloe stalked in.

"That was unnecessary," he snapped. "You've just made yourself a very serious enemy."

"Him? Sten is a mere functionary."

"Another mistake, doctor. Believe me, he's no functionary." With a chill, Venloe remembered his encounter with Sten and Mahoney. He was alive this moment only because they had needed him. "He was also right about the university," Venloe said.

"It was necessary," Iskra said. "As I told that fool of an ambassador, my people need a hard hand to rule them. It's all they understand. The incident at the university gave me a perfect excuse to use that hard hand. My name will be blessed for generations when this is over. Believe me. I know my place in history."

He peered at Venloe with a slight sneer on his lips. "You surprise me. I didn't think you'd be so squeamish over a little blood spilled for good purpose. Strange how you think you know a being.''

Venloe just grunted noncommittally. The thought crossed his mind that if his assignment were of the usual nature, just how easy it would be to kill Iskra. Right now. Without raising a sweat or leaving a sign of foul play.

"I guess you don't," he said.

Iskra stared at him, trying to engage him in a childish battle of stare-down. Venloe's fingers itched to put them both out. Instead, he lowered his gaze.

"Good," Iskra muttered. "Now, I have some things I need. Desperately. I want to go over these requests thoroughly. So the Emperor will understand my requirements."

He began detailing a massive shopping list that Venloe was sure would not be looked at kindly by the Eternal Emperor.

"I'm all ears," Venloe said.

Sten leaned back in the seat of the gravcar. A heavy rainstorm sheeted the windows.

He was damned if he knew how to proceed next. Iskra was one of those beings that all diplomats met at least once in their careers, but were never the wiser afterward.

How did one deal with a ruler bent on his own ruin? The easy solution would be to just walk away. Unfortunately that was almost never a logical alternative.

Difficulty number one: In situations such as this, there is almost never an obvious successor. If the ruler is ruined, so is the kingdom. Which might be just ducky for all parties outside the kingdom, except for:

Difficulty number two: Suicidal rulers are always propped up by outsiders, whose own fate rests on the well-being of the threatened kingdom. In other words, nature is not allowed to take its course. If lightning strikes moral dry brush, many nationalities rush in with a fire brigade.

Sten realized that he was getting a major lesson through Iskra. The Altaics, he realized, had been doomed to their present unpleasantness the moment the first Jochians arrived in the cluster, clutching the Emperor's charter.

The charter—a fancy word for a business relationship between the Jochians and the Emperor—made them special, favored above all others. Their right to rule became as God-given as any ancient monarch. The charter eventually created the Khaqans, who forced themselves on an unwilling populace.

Without the external support of the Emperor, the beings of the Altaics would have been forced to find some other solution. There would have been bloodshed, but eventually the Jochians, the Torks, the Suzdal, and the Bogazi would have hammered out some kind of a consensus.

When he took the assignment, Sten had envisioned working out a situation that would have led to such a consensus government. He had hoped at least to build a scaffold others could stand on to hammer up a building.

Instead . . . Instead, Sten had clottin' Iskra to deal with. What kind of drakh was in his boss's mind?

Sten pulled himself back from irritation. No good to beat up on the boss's decisions. The Emperor might be eternal, but he had never claimed to be perfect. If Sten wanted him to choose a wiser course, Sten would have to help.

The driver signaled. They were approaching the Suzdal embassy, Sten's first stop. It was the first step in his plan to build an outside consensus.

As he looked out the window, one third of that plan went into the crapper.

The Suzdal embassy was empty. Some young Tork ruffians were combing through piles of hastily abandoned personal articles.

Sten slid out of the gravcar. The young beings spotted him and tensed, ready to flee. Sten waved away his security force, which had quickly piled out of its own vehicles. He walked casually up to the kids.

"Good pickings?" he asked the taller one, guessing that size might have something to do with leadership.

"Whotsit to ya?" the smallest of the Torks snarled. So much for guessing. This was not one of Sten's better days.

"Better question," Sten said. "What's it to you?"

He fished out some credits and flashed them before glittering little eyes. The little Tork snatched. Sten yanked his hand back.

He nodded, indicating the embassy. "Where'd they go?"

"Clottin' home is where they went. Whaddya think?" The kid glared at the money, lips compressed. Sten crossed the young Tork's palm with a few credits.

"Tell me more," Sten said. "Start with when they left."

"Three, four hours ago," the kid said. "We was playin' down the street, when all of a sudden there's this big clottin' bust-up. Suzdal yappin' and yippin' way they do. Gravlighters and Suzdal soldiers all over. 'Fore we knew it, they had the whole place packed up and they was gone."

Sten fed the kitty with a few more credits. "Anybody after them?"

"Nope. And nobody showed up later, either. Suzdal left on their ownsome all right. And they weren't talkin' scared, neither."

"What *were* they talking about?" Sten asked, handing over more filthy lucre.

"Killin' Bogazi, whoddya think?" The young Tork was clearly astonished at Sten's woeful ignorance. "We snuck in close, see? Checkin' drakh out for anything valuable they might be leavin' behind.

"We heard the pack leader talkin' to the crooked leg whot runs the militia. Said there was a big fight comin'. With the Bogazi. That's why they was goin' home. To help with the fight."

The kid looked up at Sten. His eyes were old. "I figure the Suzdal ain't got a chance," he said. "They're mean. But the chickens are meaner. Whatcha think? Suzdal or Bogazi?"

Sten handed over the rest of the credits. "Do you care?"

"Clot no! Just tryin' to figure the odds. The money's on the Bogazi in our neighborhood. Ten to one. Thought maybe you'd tell me somethin' so I could shave 'em some. Get down some serious action."

He waved the fistful of bribe money in Sten's face. "Way I figure," the kid said, "guy's just gotta get a bet down any chance he gets. I mean, a person could be runnin' around lucky all day and never know it. If you know what I mean."

"I certainly do," Sten said. He left, thinking even less of his chances than before.

"My vision is a simple one, General," Iskra said. "But I think you'll agree that simplicity of concept is the first definition."

"Without question," General Douw said. "This is one of your attributes I have admired from afar for years. You see a thing, a complex thing, and then with a little rearranging it is no longer complex. It is simple. It is real. It is genius." Douw didn't have the faintest idea what he was saying. It didn't matter. The general was an expert at flattery. He sipped at the water Iskra had given him as refreshment—pretended to savor it as if it were wine.

"It's like the glass of water," he said, grabbing for any kind of analogy at all. "I see water, but you see . . ." His brain slipped a cog. What the clot did Iskra see? Maybe he just saw water. Personally, Douw could see a green-skinned amphibian. One that went croak, croak, croak.

"Yes. Go on," Iskra said. "What do I see, General?"

"A symbol," Douw gasped out. "That's it! Symbolism. Now who but a genius could see symbolism in a simple glass of water?" He quickly checked Iskra's face to see how this bit of verbal dancing had gone down. The doctor was beaming and nodding. Whew. Thank God.

"You strike for the heart of the matter, as always," Iskra said. "This is why I felt I needed you. I knew I would find a kindred spirit."

"Absolutely," Douw said, brushing back his silver locks with a nervous hand. "No question about it."

What an old fool, Iskra thought. "You are perhaps the most respected individual in the military, General," he said.

"Why, thank you."

"It is only the truth. You have a reputation for loyalty. And as a fierce defender of Jochi tradition."

"The old ways were best," Douw said. This was a subject he could warm to quickly. "Sometimes I think the old values have been put aside too hastily."

"That is *exactly* my vision," Iskra said.

"It is?"

"Of course. But it will take harsh measures to return us to the glory days of our Jochi forefathers."

"True. How true. Unfortunate. But true."

"However, I certainly do not wish you to become involved in the *real* unpleasantness. There are things that need to be done that I fear would tarnish the reputation of a true Jochi soldier. I will have . . . Special Duty units trained and outfitted for these tasks, and they will be responsible directly to me, and outside the military's usual chain of command."

Douw beamed. "How perceptive of you, sir."

"However, I wish you to command my conventional forces in the struggle to bring peace to our glorious cluster. It will require cool thinking, and unshakable purpose."

"Then I am your man," Douw said. "And thank you for the honor."

"When our people first came to this cluster," Iskra continued, "they were faced with a hostile territory filled with ignorant species and a barbarian breed of humans."

"Terrible times. Terrible," Douw babbled.

"There were not so many of us, then."

"How true. I've always said that myself. Not many of us in those days. But we made up for numbers with bravery."

"And one other thing," Iskra said.

"Right. That other thing. It was—uh—"

"Wit," Iskra said.

"That's it. Wit. Was on the tip of my tongue."

"To suppress those beasts—I'm sorry, I'm not with the modernists. They are beasts. Nothing more. To suppress those beasts, our ancestors adopted a tactic summed up by a simple, elegant phrase. The phrase and all it stands for, I believe, is a vital part of Jochi heritage."

"I know the answer," Douw said, "but your words are much finer than mine. Please say it for both of us."

"Divide and conquer," Iskra said. "We brought the beasts to their knees by that simple ploy. Our forefathers inflamed the Suzdal and Bogazi. And the Torks, as well. And we put them at each other's throats.

"We even made a tidy profit selling arms to all sides. We let them kill each other. And then we stepped in to rule."

"By God, we should do the same thing now!" Douw smacked fist into palm, his patriotic heart aflutter. "Divide and conquer. A return to hallowed tradition."

"Then . . . you'll accept the post I'm offering?"

"With pride, sir," Douw boomed. "With pride." He wiped a manly tear from the corner of an eye.

Menynder had a shabby little walled estate in the center of a Tork neighborhood.

Sten's professional eye noted that the shabby look was carefully cultured. The walls were chipped and vine-covered. The big entry gate was old and sagging. The garden just inside the gates was overgrown. But the security wire circling the walls was bright and new. The gate was reinforced with steel. And the garden invasion was proofed with thorny hedges or saw-toothed ferns.

Menynder's intelligence profile showed that he had money. Heaps of it, for a Tork. But he was careful not to flaunt it. Just as he had been careful to quickly make himself scarce the moment the drakh hit the fan.

"I'm in mourning," Menynder explained as he cast the fishing line into the green waters of the pool.

Sten sat beside him on the banks of the pond. The rain had turned to baking hot sunshine. But it was cool here under the tree that shaded the old Tork's favorite fishing spot. Menynder reeled in the line, checked the bait and lure, and made another cast.

"A death in the family? I'm very sorry to hear that," Sten said.

Menynder removed his glasses, dabbed at nonexistent tears, and replaced the glasses. "It was a young cousin . . . He died at Pooshkan."

Sten started to say he was sorry again, but caught a cynical glint in Menynder's eye. "How close was this cousin?" he asked instead.

Menynder grinned. "I don't know—seventh, eight removed. We weren't very close. Still, it was a shock."

"I can only imagine," Sten said.

"I'm so shaken," Menynder continued, "that I fear it will be at least a year before I can show my face in public again."

"Do you really think the Altaics will calm down by then?" Sten asked.

"If it doesn't," Menynder said, "I'll have a relapse. Grief is a sneaky disease. It comes and goes. Comes and goes." He reeled in his line, then cast it out.

"Like a fever," Sten said.

"Yeah. Without the trouble of symptoms. A man can grieve and fish at the same time."

"Funny thing about fishing," Sten said, "is that you look wonderfully purposeful. No one ever bothers a person when he's fishing."

"I get the idea I'm not the only one fishing here, Sr. Ambassador," Menynder said. He tried another spot in the pond.

"I guess I'm just trying to think of the right bait," Sten said.

Menynder gave a firm shake of his head. "Forget it. There aren't enough credits and honors to draw me out. I've lived a long life. I'd like to finish it out naturally."

"Hard thing to accomplish these days," Sten said.

"Isn't that the truth." Menynder's line tangled in debris. He gave a flip of the rod and shook it loose. "Frankly, I don't see that it will get better. Not in my lifetime."

"It'll be solved," Sten said firmly. "One way or the other."

"I assume you have plans for me being involved in the solution?"

"Yes, I do."

"You're probably thinking that because I was fool enough to stick my neck out."

"You got some beings talking together whose normal reactions are to fight instead."

"I used to think I was good at that sort of thing," Menynder said. He reeled in the line three clicks.

"You still are. From where I sit."

"Rotten, useless talent. If a talent it even is. Personally, I think I'm just a clottin' good liar."

"Some big things are going to be coming down," Sten said. "A long time ago—under similar circumstances—I advised a being like you to get out of the line of fire. I told him the best thing to do was develop a good hacking cough.''

"Did he take your advice?"

"He did."

"Did he live?"

"He did. He also prospered."

"But—you want *me* to do just the opposite?"

"Yeah."

"You gave the other guy better advice."

"That was then. This is now."

"No offense, Sr. Sten, but I don't have the awesome majesty of an Imperial appointment to protect me. I've got squat for security. Even if I did, this is the first place the good doctor would send the battalions with the jackboots and clubs.''

"You don't think Iskra is going to work out either?"

"Clot, no! What really slays me is that I once mentioned his name myself. Favorably. Tell your boss he fouled this one up good. But don't quote me. I'd rather skip the attention, if it's okay with you.''

"I won't lie and say you're the only hope," Sten said. "But you could be an important one."

"You think I should risk my life—and my family—for some noble tilting at windmills? To save the Altaic Cluster?"

"Isn't it worth it?"

Menynder reeled in his line, thinking. Then he sighed. "I don't know."

"Will you help me?"

"Maybe some other time," Menynder said.

Sten got to his feet. He looked out at the green waters of the pond, wondering why he hadn't seen even the dim shape of a fish.

"Is there anything in there?" he asked.

"Used to be," Menynder said. "I used to stock it every year. Then the weather got real wonky. Case you hadn't noticed. Did something to the water. Changed the balance, or whatever. All the fish died."

"But you're still fishing."

Menynder laughed and cast his line out again. "Sure. You never know when you might catch something."

* * *

Sten found Kaebak, the Bogazi foreign minister, in the embassy compound. She was lowering the flag. Kaebak was alone except for her security force. Everyone else had already departed for the spaceport. Kaebak planned to join them. Hastily.

"There's no need for this," Sten said. "I can guarantee the security of your embassy."

"Bogazi not need security," Kaebak said. "Fear is not in us. Anger is. Suzdal forget Bogazi anger. We make them sorry they forget."

"Why are you blaming the Suzdal for what's happening? Their pups died at Pooshkan, as well."

"Bah. This is lie. Suzdal make propaganda. Blame Bogazi for own bad deed. This is excuse. They want war. Fine. We give them all they want."

As far as Kaebak was concerned, the interview was over. She stepped up into her transport. Sten made one last effort.

"Come to the Imperial embassy with me," he said. "Let me open my intelligence files. You'll see that the Suzdal are dupes as much as the Bogazi."

The transport lurched into life. Sten stepped back. Kaebak poked her beak out the window.

"They fool you, too. Not need to look at Suzdal lies. I go home. Help hutchmates make doggy stew."

Sten's rotten luck persisted throughout the day and into the early hours of the next. He put in call after call for the Eternal Emperor.

But each time he was turned away with the tiresome message that the Emperor was indisposed—and no one would tell him how long this sickly state was going to last.

Sten was flying blind and in desperate need of guidance. The situation was getting worse by the hour.

Iskra, he was certain, had to go.

But there was only one being who could make that decision. The fate of the Altaics hung in the balance.

He took one last stab at it.

"I am so very sorry, Sr. Ambassador," came the soothing

tones of the Imperial secretary. "I am sure the Emperor will return your call as soon as he is able. Yes, I gave him your messages. Yes, I indicated their extreme urgency. So sorry for the inconvenience, Sr. Ambassador. But I'm sure you'll understand."

Sten ground his teeth. Where the clot was the Emperor?

CHAPTER TWENTY-TWO

"I'VE BEEN MEANING to have this little session with you for some time," the Emperor said. "The delay is unforgivable, really. I owe you and your organization a great deal."

The old woman chortled her response. "It is ours (giggle) to serve, Your (giggle) Eminence. After all, isn't that what the (giggle) Cult of The Eternal Emperor is all about?"

"Still. You stood by my . . . memory . . . in difficult times."

"How could any (giggle) time be difficult," Zoran asked, "when you are with us (giggle) *always*?"

The Emperor made no attempt to answer. He let the silence lay there, dark as the room he had had the old woman ushered into. He had wanted to create a certain atmosphere for his task: a gloomy majesty. But Zoran's infernal giggling kept lightening the gloom. It was making him angry.

Which was a rotten way to start. She was such an odd old bird. One hundred and fifty plus years, but with the well-formed body of a young woman under her orange robes. As the high priestess (elected) of a cult, she should have been— or so he had expected—a buzz-brain. That had been confirmed by the constant giggling—until he realized that the giggling was an artifice to throw a questioner off. And her eyes blazed with more intelligence than rapture from being in his exalted presence.

"Is it true," he finally said, "that your, ah, organization believes I am a god?"

"A representation of the (giggle) Holy Spheres, is a better description of our (giggle) beliefs, your majesty," Zoran said.

"Then . . . you *don't* worship me as a god."

"Worship is such a (giggle) nondescriptive word, Your (giggle) Eminence. We don't sacrifice (giggle) fat lambs, or our first (giggle) born. But we do (giggle) honor you."

"As a god?"

"As an eternal (giggle) being."

"Dammit, woman! Am I a god, or am I not?"

The giggling ceased. Zoran sucked in her breath. The Emperor was spooking her. She hadn't expected a halo to be surrounding his exalted presence when she entered the room. Actually, she had expected a sort of ordinary looking human. Which he was—although he was even better looking and taller in person than on the livies.

What was upsetting her—besides the darkness of the room, which she assumed was for her benefit—was the Emperor's eyes. They never looked at her directly, but shifted from side to side. Endlessly. It was almost . . . pathological. Thinking this bothered here even more.

"Excuse my irritation," the Emperor said. "Heavy matters of state and all." He leaned toward her, smiling his most charming smile. Zoran noticed, however, that his eyes still didn't rest. "Will you forgive my rudeness?"

"Oh, Your Majesty," Zoran said, returning his charm with her best gush, "it is I who must beg you for forgiveness. I'm just a silly old woman. And you are being so very patient with me."

The Eternal Emperor grunted. This was better. He noticed the giggling had stopped. Better still.

"Now, perhaps you would be so kind as to explain this god business to me?"

"Oh, certainly, sir. If I sounded obscure, it is only habit. There are so many different types of beings in the order. The word *god* doesn't translate the same to every manner of person."

"This is true," the Emperor said. He prided himself on his knowledge of obscure lore.

"In human terms, however," Zoran continued, "I suppose god is an accurate description of your holy self."

The Emperor laughed. "Imagine. Me—a god."

"Oh, but we imagine it all the time, Your Eminence," Zoran said. "In fact, all members of the Cult of The Eternal Emperor are *required* to imagine this twice a day. In our prayers. To you."

"How very interesting," the Emperor said, eyes narrowing into a smile . . . but shifting, shifting. Back and forth. Back and forth. "In fact this is one of the more interesting conversations I've had in some time."

"So happy to be able to amuse you, Your Highness," Zoran said.

"Tell me, how many beings actually believe in—ha-ha—me?"

"Thousands upon thousands, Your Highness. Possibly even millions."

"Millions, mmh?"

"Accurate figures are difficult at the moment, Your Majesty. But I can say our membership reached record numbers during your, uh, absence. They soared even more upon your return. For a time."

The Emperor's lips tightened. "You mean there's been a falloff?"

"Yes, Your Highness. I'm so sorry to report. But it was only to be expected. Beings are so weak. And they got used to you being back."

"So soon?" the Emperor hissed.

"It is only being nature, your majesty. Also, our treasury isn't what it used to be."

The Emperor knew about her past funding. It had secretly come from Kyes, the only intelligent member of the Council of Five. Zoran had not been aware of Kyes's real purpose. The Emperor intended to keep it that way.

"What would it take to, uh, increase enthusiasm among your congregation?"

"Very little, Your Highness. I tell all potential donors that members of the cult are the most dedicated in the Empire. They are ordinary beings, who live useful, productive lives by day. In their spare time they shed their worldly costumes for robes and spread word of your glory to all who will listen.''

"In other words, no middle-beings skimming the donations," the Emperor said.

"Exactly, Your Highness. Ninety percent of every credit donated goes directly to the cause. Only ten percent goes for administration, transportation, mail, that sort of thing.''

"Remarkable," the Emperor said. He meant it. He had also had his agents confirm this as part of an intensive investigation of the cult.

He pulled a fiche out of his desk and handed it to Zoran. "I've had my people do a little . . . research. You'll find the results here. There's a breakdown—region by region—of my entire empire. As well as a profile of my most, shall we say, *appreciative* subjects.''

Zoran found her hands shaking as she took the fiche. She quickly covered the reaction. "How can we ever thank you, Your Majesty?''

"Oh, it's nothing. Merely a little assistance for your good works. Now . . . to the matter of funding. There can be no connection between us, you understand?''

"Yes, Your Majesty. It would be . . . unseemly.''

"Quite. You'll be contacted shortly. A large donation will be made available. Put it to good use. There will be more, later. When it's needed.''

"Yes, Your Highness.''

"I'm glad we understand one another," the Eternal Emperor said.

Zoran was not so glad. This was proof, she thought, that it is not always wise to pray so hard for a thing. Because there was a great danger your prayers might be answered.

And now she didn't dare reject it.

CHAPTER TWENTY-THREE

"AH HAE OBSERVED," Alex observed, "a wee miracle."

"You're learning to talk right?"

"Hae Ah ripped y' smeller away, recent?"

Sten ostentatiously protruded his tongue, felt his nose's continued presence, and shook his head. Kilgour was a brightener, as always—one of the reasons he had been such a prized member of Mantis.

Besides his seemingly innate capabilities as a murderer . . .

Alex handed Sten a fiche. Sten dropped the fiche into a viewer. It was the Eyes Only weekly report that Jochi police commanders received. He saw nothing beyond the usual crop of homicides, brutalities, and greeds.

"Y' c'n scan i' y' wish, but Ah'm noo a walkin't breathin't abstract."

"GA."

"Thae's arsenals all o'er Jochi bein' ripped, wee Sten. Some copshops, but mostly military. Thae's tearaways beyon't count oot there."

"Somehow, I'm not surprised," Sten said dryly. "Given what we're in the middle of, if I were a resident of this sorry-ass land, I'd be looking to acquire a small equalizer. Such as," he went on, "a *Perry*-class battlewagon. And that'd be for a backup gun."

"Hae a drink, skip. Cind, pour the wee lad a dram. He's wanderin't. He's discons'late an' forlorn, nay, fivelorn, 'cause th' braw Emp dinnae call him back.

"Y' ken, lass, th' problems thae command bring't. Ah reck thae wae a time when Sten wae happy, dancin't i' thae streets,

186

celebratin' nae but a full belly, a empty bowel, a pint backed up ae th' barman an' ae warm blankie t' pass out in.

"Noo, he's bein't cynical an' takin't th' long-range view. He's plain forgot thae'll be no t'morrow unless Ah will it."

"*You*, Alex?" Cind wondered pointedly, as she slid the decanter over. "You mean you're really the Prime Being?"

"A' course," Alex said, pouring rounds of stregg. "An' Ah can prove it. I' this stregg's poison't, an Ah go int' convulsions, writhin' aboot like Ah'm Nessie, an' croak, thae'll be no t'morrow. Right?"

"Not for you, anyway."

"Ah. Th' stregg's nae poison't, so you lightarses c'n drink an' keep up. An thae's th' proof. If thae's no t'morrow f'r me, an' Ah'm th' most important one, thae's no t'morrow f'r anyone, right?"

Sten and Cind looked at each other. Obviously Kilgour was at least two streggs up on them.

"Noo," Kilgour continued, "back t' thae armories bein't thieved. All report'd i' th' class'fied sum'ry ae events th' topper coppers hae, which Ae 'mediately arranged f'r us to get, just after Ah guineapigged thae' local brew an' found it nae fit f'r man, beast, nor Campbell.

"Y' ken an oddity aboot thae thefts, boss. Weapons bein't ripped right, left an' straight clottin' up, but thae's no report ae kill't security."

"Oh."

"What is this 'oh,' " Cind wondered.

"It's real hard," Sten explained, "to break into an armory that's supposedly guarded by the army or the national reservists or whatever, without some patriotic sod objecting to said breaking into, which should have produced some old semiretired sergeant type playing hero and either gunning down or getting gunned down."

"Aye. Th' clottin' army's in on the deal."

"Hell," Cind said. "Maybe I better stick to straight soldiering. This special operations drakh like you two specialize in makes you cynical."

"Ah mentioned thae," Alex said, "aeons ago, back ae Newton, when y' wanted t' be Sten's handholder when he wae slippin' onto Prime."

"You did. I should have listened."

Sten himself wasn't listening to their back-chat. "I would not mind a little independent action," he said. "First, it'd be good for my morale. Second, it'd be nice to advise these local clots the world isn't marching to their particular jodie; and third, I don't like the idea that this local goddamned military thinks they can set up a private terrorist organization—or anyway have one at their beck and call. Let's find out where these guns are going."

Cind looked skeptical. "What do we do? Frick & Frack every arsenal that's still unraided? Takes a lot of sensors."

"Nope. They've got the motive, we'll give them the opportunity. We'll use the gambit that I, hem, hem, call the Ploy of the Singing Gun."

"Zeegrade livie," Cind said.

"Not at all. All we need—"

"Is this," Kilgour finished, sliding a willygun onto Sten's desk. "I' th' clots are lookin' f'r any gun, Ah suspec' thae'll be hemorrhagin' their wee hearts oot frae a bonnie official Imp-issue bang-stick, aye? Ah hae th' thought Ah'm right, since thae's been three villains lurkin't 'crost frae th' side gate's guard post frae a couple nights, noo."

"You never let me be clever, Mr. Kilgour."

"Och, boss. Ah dinnae ken thae's what y' were doing. 'Sides, y' still hae furlongs ae room t' be clever. Such ae, who's goin' t' bell th' cat?"

"We'll just—hellfire and damnation."

"Aye. Ah dinnae trust th' embassy security staff. Colonel Jerety's Guards dinnae hae th' brains t' understand whae's intended. Th' Bhor'd most likely cut their beards off i' y' suggested th' idea to them. An' Ah *know* the Gurkhas'd flat tell you to pack your bum wi' salt an' piddle up a rope."

Sten nodded. Kilgour was right. "I would pay good money for two lousy sneaky, evil Mantis types who'd plant this for me."

"I'm not sure what's intended," Cind said, "but I'll go."

"Nae. Th' oppo's got y' pegged too close, Ah reck."

"Mr. Kilgour. They'd *never* think the ambassador's ace boon would be out on a night like this, would they? Especially wearing soldier-type gear.''

''Ah, boss, Ah tried that one, too. But 'twill nae play. E'en in disguise, thae'll see m' comfortable bulk,'' and Alex patted his solid midsection proudly, ''think Ah'm an ol' soldier, an' nae fall frae such a gimmick. E'en on a night thae's as blust'ry ae this one.

''But now, i' thae peer oot, an' see a young so'jer, a wee lad, who's taken on a dram too much a' th' canteen, an' somehow's walkin't his post i' a military manner or so . . .''

''Kilgour, planting a weapon's something they give you when you're still a Mantis trainee. You want me, Ambassador-type Sten, to—''

''It's braw, lad, t' rediscover an' redefine y'r roots. Teaches humility.''

''Bastard.''

''Y' been talkin't t' m' mum again.''

''Don't wait up. Just leave me some stregg.''

''Maybe,'' Cind said. ''I'm going to need a couple three more while Kilgour tells me I really do know what's going on.''

''On wi' y' lad. 'Tis late, th' relief's goin't oot in a few minutes, an' Ah suspect th' sincer'ty ae the boyos 'crost th' street. Ah'll put a frick ae y'. Sure th' next Mantis reunion th' tape'll be a big hit.''

Sten gestured obscenely, wanted another stregg, but decided not. It was hard to play drunk if you really were brain-burned. Besides, he had to find a security guard's uniform that fit.

Less than an hour later, the Imperial security platoon walked its rounds in a formal manner. The platoon was brought to a halt at each post. An order was bellowed by the watch commander. The relieved guard saluted, came to port arms, and doubled to the rear of the formation. The new guard also saluted and went to his post. Then the platoon moved on.

The new guard walked his post in a military manner for a while, then stopped to relieve himself. Across the wide avenue, the two watchers noted that he set his weapon down and steadied himself against a wall with one hand before he did.

The guard secured his fly and turned. Then he remembered the willygun, hastily turned back, and brought it back to shoulder arms. He walked a few paces, then the weapon evidently became uncomfortable. Against standing orders, he loosened the sling and carried the weapon over his shoulder.

He walked his rounds twice more. One of the watchers thought he saw the glint of a container at the man's lips, and certainly his pace seemed to get a bit more erratic. The guard returned to the gate and hunched into an alcove against the wind, a few meters away from the post's sentry box. The guard was motionless for a few minutes.

The two men exchanged glances. The first started to whisper something, and the sentry box's com buzzed. And buzzed. And buzzed. The guard roused himself, stumbled hurriedly to the box, and answered the com.

The willygun sat, momentarily forgotten, in the alcove—and the sentry had his back to it. By the time the guard finished his loud and laborious explanation and shut the com off, the willygun had vanished.

Kilgour, watching a frick-screen from dry, warm, and semi-drunken comfort in Sten's office, waited a few more minutes before activating Phase Two, which was the sergeant of the guard finding the sentry drunk and the weapon missing and ordering him to durance vile.

He poured Sten a double when he heard the sentry coming down the passageway.

Now for Phase Three, which could take place at any time. Buried in the butt of the willygun was a small transmitter. It was in RECEIVE mode at present. In an hour or two, after it had been moved to wherever the thieves were dumping the stolen arms, Kilgour would activate that transmitter for a directional signal. And, whether the gun had been stolen by profit-oriented thieves or by one or another of the private army members, it would end up in an interesting place.

At that point Sten and Alex could decide what Phase Four might be.

"Clean, lad. Clean like the old days," he congratulated Sten as he entered the office and sank into a chair.

"Clot the old days. Damned wind goes straight to the bone. Where's Cind?"

"Th' lass said she c'd do a better lush'n both of us workin' tandem. An' she muttered some'at aboot some old warrior need-in't his bones warmed."

Sten grinned and slid the untouched stregg over to Kilgour. "Then I'll be saying good night, Laird Kilgour. I'm retiring to meditate on the sudden benefits of old warrior–hood."

"Aye. An' Ah'll be thinkin't, i' m' celibate mis'ry, ae whae nastiness com't next."

The next nastiness, not surprisingly, was provided by the charming beings of the Altaics and was far bigger than a bugged weapon in some death squad's possession.

Admiral Mason, even more grim-faced than usual, informed Sten of the events. There had been little for him or the *Victory* to do of late—praise some benevolent godlet who must have gotten lost and passed through the Altaic Cluster—and so Sten had ordered Mason to assign his ships out to various ELINT duties through the cluster.

Mason had objected, mostly because it was Sten doing the ordering, but had shut up when Sten pointed out that he trusted absolutely no one here in the Altaics including the embassy's own intelligence sources and staff—who, if they had been efficient, certainly should have filed earlier warnings on what had happened.

Mason reported formally, requesting permission to speak to Sten alone. Sten ran a secretary, a code clerk, and his protocol chief out, and sealed the office from all electronic surveillance. This sealing automatically alerted Kilgour to eavesdrop from his office next door.

Mason, without preamble, set up a small viewer and keyed it on. A holograph formed on Sten's desk. It showed the barricades set up at the main entrance to Pooshkan University, the students manning them, and then the students being attacked. The livie, blurry and short, purportedly had been made by a tourist from another world whose cab had gotten lost and ended in the middle of the melee. The livie was a forgery, of course—it did not show the armor that the military had used in smashing the students, and the attackers now wore plain coveralls rather than issue army uniforms.

"You have seen this?" Mason said.

"I have. Once an hour for the last week on every pirate broadcast around."

"Version B," Mason said, and dropped in another fiche.

The same scene, except this time there weren't many humanoids at the university. Now, the barricades were manned by Suzdal pups—and the attackers were Bogazi.

"Wonderful," Sten said. "Where'd you get this version?"

"As per your orders, I punted the *San Jacinto* out to run a bigear between the Suzdal and Bogazi. They picked this up on an open broadbeam that any of the Bogazi worlds could pick up."

"Would you care to bet," Sten said, "that if the *San Jacinto* had waited around for a while it could've snared the same livie, but with the Bogazi as victims?"

"No bet. Sir." The *San Jacinto* was another of Sten's secret advantages—the destroyer was brand new, named after the spy ship that had been the first Imperial warship officially destroyed by the Tahn. The DD consisted of weapons, engines, and sensors, and in fact was only marginally more liveable if vastly larger version of a tacship.

"So everybody's propaganda machine has turbochargers on," Sten said. "How long until the crusade starts will be—oh. You have more."

Mason did—but this was far too touchy for anything other than verbal from the *San Jacinto*'s captain to Mason and thence to Sten.

The jihad was already under way. Two full Suzdal fleets—one the official fleet that the Khaqan had permitted for "local security," the second a ragtag of armed transports, smugglers, and perimeter patrols—were assembling.

Amid the intership and -system raving, the Imperial ship's analysts had determined the target. The Suzdal proposed nothing less than a full destruction raid on the Bogazi's capital world. The cancer must be excised to its roots, no matter the cost on either side. The Bogazi had, for far too long, been allowed to . . .

"Allowed to attack, burn, chop, destroy, eviscerate, et cetera, et cetera, et cetera,'' Sten said. ''And of course the equally level-headed and pragmatic Bogazi are massing to defend their realm.

''The defense, once it is successful, will become a to-the-last-fowl attack on the vile hounds of Suzdal, correct?''

''Yes, sir.''

''This job gets more and more pleasurable by the minute. Kilgour. In with you.''

Alex, without bothering to explain, was through the door.

''You've got the fort. Mason and I are going to wander out and prevent a pogrom.''

''Yessir.'' Kilgour was at attention. If he was angry at being excluded, Alex was too consummate a professional to show it around an outsider.

Mason's expression was incredulous for one beat before it, too, froze into military attention. ''Are you assuming command?''

''I am, Admiral.''

''Very well. I must caution you there is an inadequate amount of time for any Imperial reinforcements to reach us before the Suzdal and Bogazi will be in contact. I already ran the progs.''

''So I figured, as well,'' Sten said. ''Not that we'd be authorized backup anyway—our Empire is spread fairly thin these days if you hadn't noticed.

''So we'll just pick up some indigenous junk, and you, me, and the *Victory* will clean some clocks.

''Shall we saddle up, Admiral?''

''Am I right, Alex, in not getting pissed that Sten left you, me, the Gurkhas, and the Bhor in place because he's officially still here in residence?''

''See, Major Cind? Y're learnin't t' think. Another lifetime a three, an' y'll actually be allowed t' hae an idea.''

''Clot off, Kilgour.''

''Thae's clot off, *Mister* Kilgour t' you. Dinnae y' ken, Ah'm noo th' ambass'dor designate, an' deservin' wee respect.''

''Exactly what you're getting. Very wee respect . . .''

Boredom has killed more soldiers than bayonets.

It was what killed the Tukungbasi brothers.

Not just their own boredom, but their section sergeant had grown a little careless, as had the platoon leader and company commander, up through Colonel Jerety. Providing security for Dr. Iskra and the palace of the Khaqans had become a routine task.

The Tukungbasi brothers, in their first posting to a combat unit, were not happy. They had not joined the Guard to be used as honor guards or riot policemen. They never knew that no one in that Third Guards' battalion liked the assignment, especially the careerists. But, being professionals in a professional outfit, no matter that infantrymen *never* made good peacekeepers, they kept their mouths shut and soldiered.

Soldiered, kept their barracks and equipment spotless, drank the barely palatable local beer in the on-base canteen, and bitched.

Especially about the restrictions, which made no sense to the soldiers. They had been welcomed to Jochi, had they not? So why were they quarantined in their assigned quarters and recreation areas, which were sealed and closely guarded?

Maybe Jochi was a little rough, but they were combat troopies, weren't they? They were in no jeopardy, so long as they watched themselves.

The soldiers didn't realize that there had been too many livie minutes shown of them exerting the minimum-but-necessary force to keep Dr. Iskra safe, and also of them being used to prevent street fights from building into full riots. And they certainly weren't aware of the commentary that frequently accompanied that footage, let alone the stories that were created, built, and spread in the alksoaks and caff shops of Rurik.

Boredom . . .

Fortunately, the Tukungbasi brothers had a friend. One of the old women who worked in the canteen always greeted them with a smile and a bad joke. She said she was sorry they couldn't get out and meet the people of Jochi. Especially her granddaughter.

She showed them a holograph.

Both brothers agreed that the restrictions were more than a pity—they were terrible injustices. That woman in the holograph was very beautiful. The old woman asked if they would like to write her a note. One of them did. The note was returned. The young woman really wanted to meet the brother—and mentioned, in passing, that she had a girl friend who felt the same. Both of them were sorry they were natives of such a stupid world like Jochi, and wished they could have a chance to meet some real men from the outside. From worlds where things happened.

The brothers Tukungbasi, coming from a very rural backwater planetoid, were flattered.

The notes from the young woman and her friend grew more interesting. The Tukungbasi brothers lost all interest in any romance/lust with fellow soldiers. None of the women in the battalion—at any rate none who weren't already attached—could compare in beauty, let alone in suggested areas of romantic expertise.

One off-shift day, a note told them to walk near the perimeter wire. On the other side, tantalizingly close, within one hundred meters, were the two young women. Very beautiful, indeed. The young women waved, and it nearly killed the Tukungbasis not to acknowledge those waves.

They determined to get beyond the wire.

They could be out at dusk and back before dawn, their fantasies fulfilled. They started looking for mouse holes.

And since the Guards unit was infantry, not security specialists, and the perimeter was set to keep outsiders from getting in, not the obverse, they found one.

All that was necessary was to wire across one of the robot sniffers and slip out after the roving patrol passed. Of course that patrol had become routine, as well.

Beyond the wire they slipped out of their night-cammies and stashed them in an entryway. They admired each other, resplendent in full walking-out uniform. Everybody loves a man in uniform . . .

The Tukungbasis, inexpert in seduction, had at least decided to bring a bit of a present. They had bought two bottles of alk in the commissary, a brand neither had been able to afford. But since they had nowhere to spend their pay, both men were flush. Besides, this evening would be special.

The old woman in the canteen had given them a map to her granddaughter's apartment. Neither Tukungbasi thought it a bit odd that the old woman was actively conniving in the seduction of her granddaughter—the barracks rumors had already determined that anybody in the Altaics would do anything to anybody.

Not far from the truth—but not at all what the rumors intended.

The woman lived in an upper story of one of those vertical slum apartments. The Tukungbasis should have found it odd that the building was the only one in the row with a clearly marked address sign and an entryway light that wasn't shattered.

They found the apartment and tapped on the door.

They heard a feminine giggle and a sultry voice. "It's not locked."

The older brother turned the handle. The door swung open. He saw a shabby couch, a table, and two flickering candles. Then two shadows loomed on either side of the doorway, a filthy blanket was over his head, his arms were pinned at his side, and he heard a choked gurgle from his brother.

That was all he saw.

They burned his eyes out as a start.

The three sentries walking their post at the main entrance to Iskra's palace found the Tukungbasi brothers.

Their bodies were suspended from two hastily erected tripods about fifty meters outside the perimeter.

They were identified by their absence at a shouted emergency muster.

Their torturers had left them otherwise unrecognizable.

There was no sane reason, a grim Colonel Jerety growled to his staff, for these young soldiers to be killed.

Which was exactly the reason they had been slaughtered.

They were the first.

"I have a question, Mr. Kilgour."

"GA, Major." For some reason Cind was being formal, and Alex followed her lead.

"When someone is arrested, and held for trial, isn't it customary for them to be allowed some kind of representation? Even if the trial's going to be rigged? Even here on Jochi?"

"Ah'd so think."

"And isn't it normal for a prisoner to be allowed some kind of communication with his people? Even here on Jochi?"

"Thae's a leap in logic Ah'll no make, gie'n thae nature ae these charmin' folk we're dealin' with.

"Stop playin' riddle-me, Major.

"Wha hae y' come up wi?"

Before Cind could continue, Alex started swearing. He had figured it out.

Cind had become curious as to what had happened to those beings purged by Dr. Iskra in time past. Beings Iskra had guaranteed would be brought to trial.

She had heard nothing—and a quick subject scan through the logged media in the embassy records had also produced nothing. Nor did Sten's own highly experienced com officer, Freston, remember hearing anything.

She then checked with Hynds, the already-in-place Mercury Corps station chief. After the ambush in the slums, Hynds had lost complete faith in what little analytical abilities he had and now rated all his sources either Grade III: unreliable; IV: possibly doubled by the opposition; or V: double agent.

He did have three assets in the military, all low-grade and all out of the main circuits. Hynds contacted them. All of them were terrified, none of them would volunteer to find out any data, and none of them had heard anything about what had happened to the soldiers and bureaucrats who had been arrested.

Save one thing: They were, just as Dr. Iskra had told Sten, being held in Gatchin Fortress, far north of Rurik.

Kilgour rolled Cind's data around his mind. "Umm."

"You real busy?"

"Aye. Y' checked th' weather?"

"I did. Pack a parka."

CHAPTER TWENTY-FOUR

"WE HAVE THE full projection—prog sixty-five percent accurate—in the battlechamber, if you wish to see it, sir."

"Negative, Admiral," Sten said. "I sure as hell don't have your skill at deciphering blinking dots of light—and the digest box tells me just how shafted we are."

"I await your orders."

Sten had had about enough of Mason's behavior. "Admiral? If I may speak to you privately?"

Mason nodded for the officer of the deck to take the con and followed Sten into the admiral's day cabin.

"Admiral," Sten began, "I directly requested you for this assignment believing you were enough of a professional to follow orders and leave personalities out of it.

"I was wrong. From the time that we arrived on Jochi, you've behaved like a sulking bratling who's just got his bars and who thinks that makes him God."

"Ambassador—"

"We'll start with that. My civilian rank is meaningless. I have never resigned my military rank, nor asked to be placed on reserve status.

"On Jochi, you asked if I was assuming command. I said I was. Therefore, referring to me by my military rank is perfectly acceptable.

"You will remain silent, Admiral Mason. And I would appreciate your coming to attention. I have neither the time nor the energy to get into a testes-measuring contest with you, nor is it necessary. If you wish, we will step out of this cabin, and I will relieve you of your command in front of your staff and the officers of the *Victory*. You will find that order will be considered quite legal, and will be considered admissible procedure at your court martial.

"Do you wish that?"

Mason remained silent.

"You will, until advised otherwise, refer to me as Admiral. I, in turn, respect your rank, and will continue to channel my orders through you as suggestions. I have no intentions of undermining your authority. Nor do I think it admirable for you to continue to behave in such a childish manner. You lessen yourself and your rank in the eyes of your subordinates."

That got the clot. Mason flushed, stiffened, and took a moment to bring himself back to corpselike control.

"That is all I have to say. Do you have any comments or suggestions?"

"No. No, sir."

"Good. This problem will not repeat itself. Now. Shall we go out there and start keeping the peace?"

Mason's salute sonic-snapped; he about-faced and stalked back out onto the bridge.

Sten allowed himself a grin. Hell, all those absurd cliches that had been snarled at him as he rose through the ranks still worked, given that the person on the receiving end really believed all that drakh.

Oh, well.

He followed Mason—promising himself that when this was all over he *would* decoy the bastard into a dark alley and blackjack him for a week and a half.

Sten's next action was to "request" that Admiral Mason assemble his top four staffers and the *Victory*'s XO in a conference chamber and link, on secure screen, the skippers of the escort ships.

"Gentlebeings," Sten said without preamble, "the situation is pretty obvious."

There were nods from the officers.

The *Victory* was plunging through a rift between two rich open clusters. On a screen corrected for human eyes, human spatial prejudices, and human conditioning, the tiny fleet was flashing into darkest night, with high-banked lightclouds on either side. A more detailed screen would show tiny subsidiary splotches of light to the left and right of the *Victory's* projected orbit. These were, respectively, the Bogazi hastily assembled fleet(s?) ready to defend their capital world and cluster on the left; and, to the right, in the middle of the darkness that was the rift, the attacking Suzdal fleets. The battlechamber, of course, would show each and every world and ship, to the limits of its preset range.

The *Victory* would go hey-diddle-diddle, straight up the middle between the two fleets, in—

"Contact timetick," Sten requested.

"Rough estimate, two ship-days, sir. Exact—"

"Not necessary. Thank you, Commander. Is there any data suggesting they know we're inbound?"

"Negative, sir."

That was unsurprising—one continuing advantage Imperial ships had was vastly superior sensory systems. And one very secret gimmick: before any AM2 was released to non-Imperial sources it was given a "coating" made from a derivative of Imperium X. Any non-Empire ship on stardrive would produce a slight purple flare on Imperial screens, a flare that could be picked up at a far greater range than the unaltered Imperial drive signature. It wasn't much—just enough of an edge to win a war every now and then.

"The object of our little game," Sten began, "is obviously to keep our Suzdal and Bogazi allies from slaughtering each other. And, incidentally, to keep either or both of them from deciding that anybody who breaks up a bar brawl between friends deserves a good one upside the head."

There were suppressed smiles. Admiral Mason did not give briefings like this.

"Right," Sten continued. "Obviously the only way that we can accomplish this is with pure guano. Fortunately, Admiral Mason is, as you all know, one of the most skilled Imperial leaders in deception."

Sten really wanted to phrase it differently and say that Mason was fuller of drakh and therefore more guano-qualified than almost any admiral he knew, but he refrained.

"He and I discussed our problem, and he had some interesting plans. I had a couple of ideas that might be worth considering. There will be five stages to our plan. Stage One is appropriately evil; Stage Two is honorable; and Stage Four might give someone here a medal or two. Stage Five will be pure naked dishonesty, which I shall implement."

"Stage Three, sir?" The question came from the captain of the destroyer *Princeton*.

"That's my own cheap idea," Sten said. "All hands aboard the *Victory* have been spending their off-shifts working on it."

Sten flexed his fingers unconsciously. "All hands" was no exaggeration—his own itched from metal fragments and real wood splinters embedded in fingers and palms.

"We'll get to that in time. Stage One we will begin immediately, while the briefing continues. Order all weapons officers and all Kali crews to action stations."

The Kali missiles, now on their fifth generation, were monster ship-killers. The Kali V class were nearly thirty meters long by now, having grown not only in expense but in size as each generation was given newer and more sophisticated tracking, homing, ECM, and "perception" suites. Power was from AM2—the Kalis were, in fact, miniature starships. All that had not been necessary to improve from generation to generation was the payload. Sixty megatons was still enough to shatter any ship on any military register. Even the *Forez*, the Tahn battleship that remained the mightiest warship ever "launched," had been rendered hors d' combat by Kalis.

The Kali was "flown" into its target under direct control by weapons officers. The control system was helmet-mounted and used direct induction to the brain. Actual control had progressed from the old manual joystick and tiny throttle to involuntary or voluntary neural reaction from the "pilot." The Kali could also be set to use other, automatic homing systems. But those were only used under special circumstances—weapons officers were chosen for their killer instincts, second only to potential tacship pilots, and they preferred playing cheater kamikazi.

Stage One was a launch of all available Kalis.

They burst out from their launch tubes on the *Victory* and its destroyers at full drive for thirty seconds, and then power was shut down. The missiles lanced ahead of the Imperial squadron.

Right behind them came the *Victory*'s tacships, under the same full power/cut power/run silent orders.

This was Stage One—Sten's hole cards.

Stage Two waited for some time, until watch officers reported alarums from the Bogazi fleet. They had "seen" the oncoming unidentified ship that was the *Victory*. Since they were waiting for the Suzdal, their sensors were slightly more efficient, not masked by their own drive emissions. Sten waited a couple of ship-hours, having ordered that no response be made to any challenges from either Suzdal or Bogazi, then assembled his human actors for the next part of the plan.

All Bogazi and Suzdal com channels were blanketed by the *Victory*'s powerful transmitters.

All receiving vid screens showed:

The well-known Imperial Ambassador Sten. Standing on the bridge of a warship, in full and formal garb. He was flanked by two equally grim-faced officers, Mason and his XO, also in full dress uniform.

The broadcast was very short and to the point. Sten informed both sides they were in violation of Imperial and Altaic treaties of long standing, as well as civilization's common agreements of interplanetary rights. They were ordered to return immediately to their home worlds and make no further aggressive moves.

Failure to respond would be met with the severest measures.

The broadcast was not meant to convince, or even to threaten. It was merely a pin in the map to legitimize the real bludgeon Sten had prepared.

The one he hoped nobody figured out was made of metal foil and lathes—quite literally.

The response was as expected.

The Suzdal did not answer the cast, either from their fleets or from their home worlds. The Bogazi, slightly more sophisticated, broadcast a warning that all neutral ships should stand clear of given coordinates. Any intrusion into this area would be met with armed response. Any errors might be regretted but would be considered within the acceptable parameters of self-defense.

There was no response from the *Victory*.

Sten hoped this would worry both sides.

Another timetick. It would be four ship-hours until the *Victory* would be directly "between" the two enemies.

And they, in turn, would be in range of the *Victory* in five hours, and each other in twelve.

The situation was developing in an interesting manner.

"Three hours, sir. And the Bogazi fleet is now under drive."

Sten rose from the weapons couch he had asked to borrow for a nap. This was calculated bravado, intended to prove to all the young troopies that Sten was so confident that he could doze before action.

Of course, he had not slept.

What bothered him was that in the old days he actually had nodded off every three or four times he tried the ploy.

Mason came out of his day cabin. "We're ready, sir."

"Very well."

Mason came quite close to Sten. "You didn't sleep, either, did you?"

Sten's eyes widened. Was Mason actually trying to be friendly? Had that absurd reaming-out caused the admiral to make an attitude check?

Naah. Mason was just setting Sten up so, come another time, he would be the one waiting in that dark alley with the sap.

"Perhaps we might begin Stage Three," he said.

"I shall give the orders."

Stage Three was a truly monstrous bluff.

Back on Jochi, Sten had run a fast list of ways to make people unhappy. He dimly remembered one, told as a joke but also as a mind-jog, back in Mantis training. The story went that aeons earlier, a young guerrilla officer was trying to delay a military convoy. It must've been in the dark ages, because the vehicles were evidently ground-bound, and there was no mention of air cover. The convoy had armor and heavy weapons. The guerrilla officer had twenty men, only half of them armed.

The guerrilla could have thermopylaed nobly and slowed the convoy for five minutes at the cost of his entire band. Instead, he looted a nearby farmhouse. He took all of the dinnerware in the house and carefully positioned each plate, facedown, in the roadway.

Land mines. Sten had objected—the armor's commander must have been a complete clot, since it was unlikely that land mines *never* looked like mess tins, even in those medieval times.

After Sten had finished doing the push-ups that every military school seemed to award its trainees at regular intervals for sins ranging from breathing to buggery, the instructor had pointed out that of course the track commander would not have mistaken them for any land mines *he* was familiar with. They could be something new. They could be booby traps. And if they were real, and he drove over them, and started losing vehicles, it would be his butt in front of the firing squad.

So slowly, laboriously, he had to send forward clearing teams to lift each plate, determine it was a plate, and move on to the next. The guerrilla leader further slowed progress down by regular sniping, in spite of the convoy's counterfire.

"The convoy was delayed by two full E-hours, so the story goes, with no loss to the guerrilla force. Think on that, troops. Mr. Sten, you can stop doing push-ups now."

Land mines . . . space mines. Yes, that was it. Mines—those lethal devices that just sat waiting for a target and then blew it up or, worse, lurked until the target came within range and then went hunting—were never popular weapons. In spite of the fact they were the most efficient, least expensive killers of expensive machinery and beings known. They seemed somehow slimy to "honest" soldiers. Or, anyway, not especially glamorous.

Sten had never imagined that killing one's fellow beings was glamorous. And if he'd had one iota, Mantis Section would have burned it out of him. He had also seen how effective the Tahn use of mines had been. The Tahn operated under the valid if uncivilized principle that killing was killing and needed no particular moral justification.

The Empire's conventional military, being "honorable," knew little and cared naught about mines—therefore, anyone they armed and equipped, such as the Altaic Cluster, would be unlikely to be expert, either.

So, during the flight out from Jochi, the hangar deck of the *Victory* had become a carpentry shop. The lathing Sten had ordered up was wire-tied into rough hedgehog-looking configurations and wrapped with metal foil.

There were several hundred of these blivets stacked on the hangar deck.

On command, these were dumped, a few at a time, into space. They formed a stream, a divider of sorts, between the two fleets. Of course, they were still traveling at the same velocity as the *Victory*, but Sten planned to wreak his next move before his "mines" cleared the field of operations.

They had the immediate and desired effect.

The oncoming fleets went into modified panic mode as the Suzdal and Bogazi sensors picked up the "mines," and their commanders tried to figure out what these strange objects were that were emerging from the Imperial ship like so many bits of candy tossed to the crowds in a parade. On their screens they would have seen the *Victory*, its accompanying destroyer screen, possibly some tacships, and then the mines streaming across their screens.

Very good, very good, Sten thought. They're worried. Now we wait . . .

Shortly both fleets ordered destroyer squadrons forward to investigate.

Now we show them our dinner plates have bangs in them.

"Admiral Mason?"

"Yessir. All ships . . . all weapons stations," Mason ordered. "Targets . . . the destroyers. Mind your discriminators. One target per weapon. Any young officer disobeying that order will be relieved, court-martialed, and cashiered."

Mason, the gentle father figure.

Kalis homed at half speed, or else were told by their discriminators that another missile was swifter on the pickup. Close in, just before the Suzdal and Bogazi destroyers picked them up on their screens, the missiles went to full drive.

Screens on the *Victory*'s bridge flared as the Kalis hit, then cleared to show open space where a destroyer had once been.

Three destroyers from the Suzdal and two from the Bogazi survived to return to their parent fleets.

Any analysis would have shown that these missiles were being launched by those strange-appearing "mines."

Sten nodded to Mason once more—and the tacships smashed in from the high elliptic they had held. Get in, launch, and get back out were their orders.

Two cruisers and five destroyers were killed.

Very good, Sten thought. I am sorry beings are dying, but they are not Imperial beings. And fewer are being killed than if battle were joined between the two fleets. Let alone if the Suzdal fleet was allowed to complete its attack on the Bogazi home world.

Now for the coup de, Sten thought. Again, we start by setting the stage.

Ambassador Sten made another broadcast, once more ordering both fleets to break action and return to their home worlds.

But evidently his 'cast was poorly shielded from other com links. These were being made by the *Victory*, and tight-beamed "back" in the direction the *Victory* had come from.

They were coded, of course. But both computer and staff analysis determined that the *Victory* was linked to other ships, ships out of detector range. And it appeared as if it were an entire Imperial fleet, and the *Victory* was but the scout—a monstrously large and well-armed scout, but still a scout—for the real heavies. Minutes later their prog must have worsened, as the *Victory* changed frequencies and code and began broadcasting to *another*, equally "unseen" war fleet.

The Bogazi and Suzdal may have been less than sane in their approach to civil rights, but in military matters they were quite capable.

Without acknowledging Sten's orders, both fleets broke contact and, at full power, fled home.

Sten whoofed air and plumped down into a chair. "Damn," he said honestly, probably blowing his command-cool facade, "I really didn't think that would work."

"It will only work once," Mason said softly, so that his officers could not hear.

"Once is more than enough. We'll blanket their butts with every straight-fact 'cast we can come up with and hope they come to what passes in the Altaics for senses. And if they try again, we'll come up with something stinkier and whomp them again! Hell, Admiral, a clot like you should *always* be able to think of something.

"Now. Return course. For once we're ahead of their clottin' schemes. Let's see if we can stay that way."

Gatchin Fortress had been built to be both impregnable and terrifying. It had never been intended for use as a real fortress, but as a final prison for anyone opposing the Khaqan. It sat, solitary, on a tiny islet nearly a kilometer out at sea. Great stone walls rose straight up from the tiny island's cliffs. There were no beaches, no flat ground outside those walls. And there was no ground access to the island.

Alex and Cind sprawled near the cliff face on the mainland, watching.

They had prepped for their mission far more thoroughly than just throwing a set of warm undies into a ditty bag. They lay under a carefully positioned phototropic camouflage sheet that now shone a white that matched the snowbanks and dirty rocks around them. Each of them had a tripod-mounted high-power set of amplified-light binocs, plus passive heat sensors and motion detectors focused on Gatchin's ramparts and the causeway.

"Damn, but I'm cold," Cind swore.

"Woman, dinnae be complainin't. Ah been on y' world, an' thae's a summer place compared t'it."

"No kidding," Cind said. "And now you know why so many of us live *off*-world. Besides, didn't you tell me your home world was ice, snow, and such?"

"Aye, but th' ice's gentler, somehow. An' th' snoo comi't driftin' doon like flower petals."

"You see anything?"

"Negative. Which is beginnin't t' make me think you're right."

"We'll know for sure before nightfall. I hope."

''Aye. An' while y're waitin', Ah'll narrate a wee story, thae's got an obvious bearin't ae our present, froze-arsed predic'ment.

''Hae Ah e'er told y' ae th' time Ah entered a limerick contest? Y' ken whae lim'ricks are, aye?''

''We're not totally uncivilized.''

''Thae's bonnie. 'Twas whae Ah was a wee striplin't, assigned t' a honor guard on Earth. Th' tabs announc'd thae contest. Large credits f'r th' prize. Who c'd come up wi' thae dirtiest, filthiest, lim'rick?

''Well, Ah hae braw experience when it com't t' dirty, filthy lim'ricks.''

''I've never questioned that.''

''Ah'm payin't nae heed nor reck t' thae cheap one, Major. So Ah ship't m' filthy poem away, an aye, 'twas so filthy e'en a striplin't like m'self blushed a bit, thinkin't m' name wae attach't.

''But thae credits wae bonny, as Ah've said. An' lord know't a puir wee ranker needs a' th' coin he can secure. So time pass't an' time pass't, an' then one day Ah sees th' tab, an' Ah'm thunderstrick!

''Ah'm noo th' winner! Ah hae nothin'! Th' winner's some clot nam'd McGuire. D. M. McGuire, ae' th' wee isle ae Eire, they name't it, frae th' city ae Dublin. An' th' lim'rick's so dirty thae cannae e'en run thae own prizewinner!

''An a'ter Ah recover frae m' heartbroke, it starts gnawin't ae me. I mean, thae *cannae* be a filthier lim'rick thae whae Ah submitt'd.

''So Ah taki't a wee bit ae leave, an Ah moseys t' Eire, an' thae cap'tal ae Dublin, an' Ah begins lookin't frae D. M. McGuire. Days an' weeks pass, aye, but finally Ah trackit doon th' last McGuire i' Dublin.

''She's a wee gran lady. Sweet, wi' a twinkle i' her eye, an' a smile ae her lips, an' y' jus' *know* she's goin't t' church ever' day, twice't, an' thae's nae been a foul word cross her lips.

''This cannae be th' D. M. McGuire ae the contest, but Ah'm des'prate. So I screws m' courage t' th' stickity point, an' asks.

''Dam't near crap m' kilt, when she says, 'Aye. Ah am.'

''Ah begs her f'r whae it was.

"I's noo her turn t' blush, an' she say't 'Ah'm a respect'ble widow. Ah cannae use language like thae around a man.'

"She talk't funny, she did. 'Twae hard t' understand her, sometime.

"Ah ask't her to write it doon, e'en. But she cannae do thae, e'er. Thae *must* be the scummiest poem e'er wrote. So Ah argue, an' argue, an' plea, an' finally she say't, 'Cannae Ah tell it, but wi' blankety frae th' vile words?'

"A course, Ah says. Ah'll hae nae grief figurin't it oot frae there.

"An' she tak't ae deep breath, an' recites:

> "Blankety-blankety blank
> Blankety-blankety blank
> Blankety-blank
> Blankety-blank
> Blankety river of shit."

After a long silence . . . a giggle. Alex beamed. "Ah knoo frae th' first thae wae someat aboot y' Ah admired. Noo thae's three."

"Three what?"

"Three bein's whae admir't m' stories. One's a walrus, one's a lemur, an' y're the third."

"Exalted company indeed," Cind said. "Now, what's the moral that pertains to our present situation?"

"As wi' any braw preacher," Alex said, "Ah dinnae think m' sermons need further explication."

And silence hung down about them.

In fact, the nothing they had seen so far was grimly productive. Cind and Alex had been in their hidey-hole for two full days. They had seen no aircraft approach Gatchin, nor had they seen any sign of sentries atop its walls. At night, only a few lights gleamed from the ominous citadel.

Two hours later, just before dusk, Alex grunted. "Ah hae some'at. Comint frae th' south. Twa gravsleds. Cargo lighters, Ah reck . . . Whae's th' castle doin't?"

"Nothing," Cind said. "None of those cupolas—I think they're AA launchers—are moving."

"Bad," Alex said. "Worse. Thae's no sign ae guns or guards ae th' lighters, either. An' Ah can make out th' cargo ae th' deck. Clot. Rations. Rations enow frae noo more'n a platoon, Ah'd guess. Y' hae them i' your eyeballs noo?"

"I do," Cind said. She watched as the lighters settled down onto an overhead landing deck. After a moment, she saw a couple of uniformed men come out to meet the lighter. Neither of them was visibly armed, unless they were carrying pistols.

"No security at all," she said.

"No food, no security, no guards, which mean't no prisoners, aye?"

"Right."

"So where'd Doc Isky stash th' usual suspects?"

Cind shook her head. No clues.

"Shall we start lookin't? Knowin't we dinnae want to find?"

And at full dark, they bundled up the surveillance post in silence. Both of them had a pretty good idea where the purged soldiers and officials were. All they had to do was confirm their suspicions.

"Rejected," Iskra stormed. "Rejected. Unable to meet requested quota at this time. Personnel not available. All patrol elements available for client governments are committed for foreseeable future. What the hell is going on?"

"The Empire is still recovering, sir," Venloe said, his voice most neutral. "There's not exactly the cornucopia available that there was before the war."

"I am not concerned with the Empire," Iskra said. "What I am concerned about is the absolute failure of the Imperial system to support its ruler. The Emperor chose me to bring The Altaic Cluster back to stability and order. Yet I am denied the tools I must have to accomplish my task."

Venloe thought of saying something—Iskra's massive shopping list had been either arrogant, ignorant, or insane. Among other items Iskra had requested—demanded—were a full division of Imperial Guards for his security, two first-line battle squadrons from the Imperial Navy, and a flat doubling of the AM2 quota for the Altaics, with no justification given on any item other than "to continue the reestablishment of a legal government and public order."

"Do these bastards want me to fail?"

"I doubt that, doctor."

"The Emperor had best make these bureaucrats aware of one thing. I am certainly the only one who can bring peace to this cluster. My continued success is vital. Not only for my people, but for the Empire, as well. So far, I have been a loyal supporter of Prime World's policies. I doubt if anyone involved with the highest levels of Imperial authority would be happy if I should choose to consider other alternatives."

Venloe, by now, was getting better at covering his reactions to Iskra's pronouncements. This last, however, forced him to suddenly turn his attention to a com screen that was showing nothing particularly important. By the time he turned back to Dr. Iskra, his expression was again bland, pleasing.

He decided, however, that he would not ask Iskra to elaborate. Other alternatives? Such as what? The shattered Tahn? The ghosts of the dead privy council?

Did the good doctor now think the Emperor needed him more than he needed the Emperor?

That information, once relayed, would certainly produce an interesting reaction. Venloe did not, however, look forward to relaying it.

Sten had expected to return to mountains of problems and whirlpools of disaster. Instead:

"Nae problem, boss. Ah did th' important stuff, Cind took th' normal tasks, an' Otho ignored th' dross. Y' c'd a' stayed on y'r wee vacation another year wi'oot bein't missed."

"Shall we kill him, Cind?" the Bhor rumbled.

"Later."

"You'll have to stand in line," Sten said. "I outrank both of you."

"Why are we not drinking?" Otho said. "To celebrate the

return of our warrior-king Sten. Or to celebrate it is the first day of the week, whichever feels more important."

"Because, lad, we're workin't t'night."

Alex, looking smug, indicated that Sten should make the explanation. Sten grinned—the heavyworlder was more than a bit better at keeping Sten's feet buried in firm loam than that slave who was supposed to whisper "This too shall pass" in an imperator's ear during his triumphs. Or whatever the phrase had been.

"That rifle we bugged and let the baddies steal seems to have settled in for the winter," he said. "I think we should exercise visitation rights."

"Hah," Otho said. "Good. I do not truck with these Imperial soldiers. But those two brothers they butchered—they need a blessing sent to hell for them. I hope that rifle is not all alone, concealed in the closet of some pimple-faced alley shooter."

"I don't think so. It's hidden somewhere in the back of a take-out food store."

Otho grunted in pleasure. "Good. Probably not just a single villain. Snack place, hmm. That's a good cover for lots of people going in, coming out. I will remember that.

"So, this is a group, most likely. Does anyone have a clue who they are murdering for?"

"Not yet. That's one of the things we want."

"How hard do we hit them?"

"I want intelligence," Sten said. "Body count is all right if the place is guarded, but it's distinctly secondary. Cind?"

"Ummm . . . do you have an overhead on the area? Thanks. Open access to the rear, we'll need one squad. We'll go in with— let's see, another squad for the front, one platoon backup, four in the door. Keep a company in reserve, I guess."

"We will nae' be beggin't assistance frae Colonel Geraty ae his Guardsmen." It was not even a question.

"Absolute negative," Sten said. "I'm assuming there could be a leak from them and sure as hell a leak if we transmit it through the embassy and into Iskra's com link. And if we start pumping secure signals direct to the Guards, somebody might smell something."

"Are you thinking, my Sten, that scrote Iskra has his own private terrorists?"

"Right now, Otho," Sten said, suddenly feeling tired, "I suspect everyone in this clotting cluster of joining or heading up death squads. Except you two."

"An' whae aboot me, boss?"

"Hah. I say again my last. Hah. I *know* you. Now. Enough frigging about. We'll go in with the Bhor for the terror factor. The Gurkhas stay in reserve."

"They won't like that," Cind said.

"Good. I intend for them to not like it. The way things are going, I think I'm going to need me some *very* angry young men in the very near future.

"Major Cind, write the ops order. We've got complete dark of the moons by 0245. We'll move then."

There was only a single light on in the restaurant, in back of the pay counter. Behind the heavy gratings Sten could see that the interior was deserted, as was the street.

"Who'e'er this place is a cover for," Alex whispered, "hae confidence. Nae e'en a watchman. Or else thae found m' bug an' left it i' th' grease trap f'r a wee joke."

"Confidence—or else they've paid for cover. Look." Sten pointed up as a police gravsled hissed slowly over the rooftops.

"Whae aboot them? Or are we irk't enow t' start killin't cops?"

"Otho has orders to put up some flares and airburst some grenades if there's interference," Cind said. "That should suggest the big boys are playing and they'll stay away. But if they escalate, so do we." The com clipped to a loop on the shoulder of her combat vest clicked. "Rear squad's in position. We're ready."

"Then shall we?"

Blur:

Kilgour was up; at waist level, he swung a solid-steel battering ram with two handgrips, as if it were a pumice fake. Impact—and grating and door and jamb pinwheeled into the building. Alex let go, and momentum sent the battering ram with the debris as he ducked out of the way . . .

Cind thumbed a bester grenade inside . . .

Eyecover and purpleflash . . .

Sten spun through the door, back against solid cover, gun sweeping . . .

Cind rolled in, going flat . . .

Sten ducked forward, toward the kitchen's entrance . . .

Kilgour in the shop, covering; Cind up, leapfrogging Sten into the kitchen; Sten moving, Kilgour providing cover . . .

Back room deserted . . .

Kilgour up with the battering ram . . .

"Laraz," Sten shouted. A password to keep them from getting shot . . .

The door crashing down and dark night outside . . .

Gun barrels . . . hairy Bhor faces peering over sights . . .

"Clear," Sten shouted. "Close up your units, Cind. Keep the reserve platoon across the street.

"Otho. Three troopies!"

"Sir."

"It's o'er here, Skip. Under th' stove."

"Need a hand?"

"Hah."

Kilgour put his weapon down and, seemingly without strain, lifted the huge kitchen range to one side. Stove power lines screeched but did not rupture.

"A wee hidey-hole," he observed, reaching down and pulling up on a small metal ring, inset into the concrete floor. The ring—and floor—lifted smoothly, a counterbalanced trapdoor.

"Y'reka," he observed. "An' Y-not-reka. Boss?"

"Hang on a shake. You three," Sten said to the waiting three gorilla-substitutes. "I want you to tear the place apart. Make it look like somebody's done a rip-away-the-walls search before they found the hiding place. There's no point in giving away all our secrets."

The three Bhor looked at each other. It wasn't as good as killing someone—but at least it was destruction. They went to work happily, smashing and crashing.

"And what do we have?" Sten had to lift his voice over the shatter.

"W' hae a typ'cal terrorist's arsenal," Kilgour observed.

Alex was correct—but it was a very large typical terrorist's stash—a basement room nearly three meters on a side, packed with weaponry. The guns were what Sten expected—just what any private thuggery, or, depending whose side they were on, freedom fighter, would secrete: stolen, bought, or purchased sporting arms in a dizzy array of calibers. Military armament, stolen from or contributed by the Jochi army. Two very elderly crew-served support weapons. Six or seven home-built mortars. A few bombs for same. A half case of grenades. Not enough ammunition for all of the guns. Some knives. Sten thought he even saw a clotting sword. Three or four pistols on a shelf. And two Imperial-issue willyguns.

"Noo, one ae' them's ours," Kilgour said. "But where'd th' other lad come frae?"

"Who knows? Willyguns've been around for a long time," Sten said. "Maybe somebody at the embassy had one before us. Maybe the Third Guard lost one and hasn't realized it yet."

Kilgour tossed one of the sporting rifles up for Sten to examine. Sten then gave it to Cind, who ran a fast, professional eye over it.

"Most of my experience is with real soldiers," she said. "This clot is filthy."

"Nae as bad ae most," Kilgour observed. "Most terrs ae m' acquaintance hae more time f'r rhetoric thae bore-cleanin't. Boss, w' hae th' cheese noo. Are we haein' public ootcry or whae?"

"We'll blow it in place," Sten decided. "You see anything down there that'd link this to anyone?"

"Negative, skip. Thae's professional enow t' no leave callin't cards. Hello. Whae's *this*?"

He passed it up to Sten. *This* was a pistol—but a pistol that fired AM2 rounds. Sten lifted an eyebrow. The Empire, for obvious reasons, tried to keep as tight a hold on the superlethal willyguns as possible. That held doubly true for pistols, even though that weapon, in fact, was suited only for robberies, last stands, plinking, and parades. For such an arm to be in private hands was most unusual.

And this pistol was even more special. It was anodized with what appeared to be both silver and gold. The grips were some kind of translucent white horn. And the entire weapon had been engraved with scrollwork.

Sten examined the engraving closely—no hunting scenes or beings that might give a clue as to what world this surprise had come from.

"Is there a holster?" he asked.

"Aye. An' ae th' finest. Real leather, Ah'd hazard. No initials, no maker's marks, no nothing."

"This," Cind observed, after she had examined the gun closely, "is something an ambassador might give a ruler. Or the other way around. I wonder if we ran the serial numbers, would we find that the late Imperial ambassador happened to be on the sales roster? Or it's recipient—intended, anyway—someone like the Khaqan?"

"Y' hae th' ball," Kilgour cautioned. "Dinnae be runnin't wi' it, no matter how good th' sup'sition might be. All we hae's a muckety's toy f'r sure. Seems a pity t' destroy somethin' like thae."

"It does," Sten said. "It's fitting for a laird. Keep it, Alex—no. Wait."

Alex grinned, most evilly. He was not even slightly disappointed at the evident loss of his souvenir. "Y' hae a dream?"

"You'll get it next time around," Sten said. "When we recover it again. I'd like for that pistol to maybe give us something else. Pull that bug out of the willygun. See if you can plant it in this little beauty."

"Nae problemo, boss."

"Now, when you planted the charges to destroy this assemblage of death," Sten went on, "what happened is that only two of them went off. A third one just burned—but make sure it burned up and the detonator's gone. We don't want to make the scenario so realistic the baddies get some real bangs.

"Since the blast wasn't complete, it destroyed all of the long arms, but blew the pistols up—over there."

"Why," Kilgour complained, "d' all th' schemes start wi' me, th' great powder monk ae th' ages, bein't inept?"

Sten extended his hand, all fingers in a fist except the middle one, which was rigidly extended. "That, Mr. Kilgour, is the only response a drunken, relieved, and stockaded sentry can come up with. Now let's blow this joint before the local yokels hear something or get forced to pay attention."

Kilgour called for a demo pack and started wiring the place. Cind pulled the Bhor outside into a perimeter. Sten left his demo man alone. This wasn't the hardest job Kilgour had ever rigged—among other things, he had once defused a nuclear device under close-range hostile fire and booby-trapped a camel—but it required a bit of concentration.

"How do you know," Cind asked, "that somebody will pick up that pistol and we can track it to another arsenal?"

"I don't—not for sure. But people who make their living around things that go bang seem to get a little wiggy if you show them a trick knife or handgun.

"But I'm hoping for it leading us to something more than just another safe box. I'd be very happy if that lovely, ornate piece ends up in the hands of someone with the authority to appreciate it."

"Like who?"

"Like whoever's running this organization. Which would give us somebody to deal with in the open."

"Sten, you are an evil man."

"You're just saying that to get in my pants."

"This is true. And I'd kiss you, except it'd be bad for discipline."

"Mine or the Bhor?"

"Yours, of course."

But she kissed him anyway.

Venloe tried to read the face on the screen. He could not.

"Is that everything?" the man asked.

"It is, sir."

It was so silent that Venloe could hear the carrier wave hum.

"Do you have any suggestions?"

After a pause, Venloe said, "No."

"Go ahead. We must consider all possibilities." The man on the screen touched, as if unconsciously, the center of his chest.

Venloe chose his words carefully. "When you briefed me for this assignment, I asked . . . about a fallback option."

"And I said I was not prepared to discuss that eventuality. I was not then, and I am not now. My policy is quite firm. Dr. Iskra is to be given the fullest support."

"Yes, sir. I apologize."

Again, silence.

"An apology is not necessary. I do not mean for my servants to be slaves. I want one thing very clear. Dr. Iskra is to be ruler of the Altaic Cluster. That is the primary objective. However . . . however, what you referred to as a fallback option cannot be ignored. Explore its possibilities and ramifications."

The screen went blank.

Venloe nodded in automatic obedience. And, even though there was no one to hear him, he replied, "Yes, Your Majesty."

CHAPTER TWENTY-FIVE

THE ETERNAL EMPEROR listened thoughtfully to Sten's report on Dr. Iskra. He made no comment as Sten took each stone from the bucket and stacked it upon its miserable brother.

Sten told him about the student massacre. The proof that it was Iskra's work. The deliberate disinformation campaign to stir up war among the inhabitants of the Altaic Cluster. The lies Iskra had told to cover his campaign of terror. The mysterious attacks on Imperial personnel. The empty fortress. And much more.

Finally, he was done. Sten waited, hoping to see which way the wind was blowing.

"I assume," the Emperor said, "that your recommendation in this matter does not come down on the side of Dr. Iskra."

"I'm sorry, sir," Sten said, "but it's my job to tell you things you're not especially going to like."

"Quite right," the Emperor said. "Otherwise, you'd be as useless as all these fools I've got around me. One thing I do know, Sten, is that I can always trust you to tell me the truth—no matter how unpleasant."

"Thank you, sir. Now . . . if you'll allow me—"

"Hold on," the Emperor said. "No need to go further."

"I beg your pardon, sir?" Sten was truly bewildered. He was also unsettled by this new habit the Emperor had adopted of never looking him in the face. And those damned eyes. Moving back and forth as if they were active ball bearings.

"I said, no need to say more. I know what your recommendation is going to be. Unfortunately, I have to reject it.

"Iskra stays. You will continue to support him."

"I'm very sorry to hear that, sir. And I hope you won't take this the wrong way—but I'd like to be relieved of my post."

The Emperor's eyes ceased their restless moving. Just for a moment. They bored into him like cold steel. Then the Emperor laughed. "I can see why you'd say that, Sten," he said. "You think I've lost confidence in you."

"Possibly, sir. But that's not for me to judge. It's just that . . . well, you need someone you can trust to carry out your orders."

"I've already said I trust you, Sten."

"Yessir. But I've already made it plain I disagree."

"True. However, agreement has nothing to do with it. These are my orders. You should also know that Dr. Iskra has asked me to have you replaced. I firmly rejected his request."

"Yes, sir." Sten couldn't think of anything else to say.

"And I told him the same thing I'm going to tell you. You're too close to the situation, Sten. Can't see the forest for the trees, as they say."

Sten knew there was probably truth to this. He was not privy to the big picture. Unlike the Emperor.

"I still don't think I'm the best man for the job, sir. Although, I thank you for your faith in me."

"We've been through a lot together, Sten," the Emperor said.

"I know what you can do. And what you can't do. In fact, I believe I'm the better judge of your capabilities.

"Also, the matter with the Altaics has grown even more critical. If I were to pull you out, the bad publicity would be devastating. Now, maybe I was hasty bringing in Iskra. Although I still think he's the best of the poor lot of options I was looking at. Regardless. I've hung myself out with this man. It's vital that I am not embarrassed."

"Yes, sir."

"I'm counting on you, Sten," the Eternal Emperor said. "Perhaps more than I ever have before. Make it work. Do whatever you have to—but, make it work.

"Those are your orders."

"Yes, sir."

"And Sten?"

"Yes, sir?"

"Smile. Be happy. It's all going to come out just fine."

"Yes, sir," Sten said. He made his best salute, as the Emperor's image vanished.

CHAPTER TWENTY-SIX

STEN COULDN'T SLEEP. Every time he drifted off, the Emperor's face floated into view. He was haunted by those eyes. Eyes that were never still. Eyes that swept the edges of his conscience, netting Sten's secret doubts and hauling them in as evidence.

In Sten's nightmare the Emperor would pile up all those doubts into a writhing, eel-like mass. He would turn to Sten, face dark with anger. And those eyes would swivel for him. Sten knew if they ever came to rest, he was through.

Here they came now. Turning. Turning. Cutting a smoking path

along the floor. Then they rose up, searching for his own eyes—
to burn them out.

Sten gasped awake. His body was sheeted in cold sweat. He
stumbled into the lavatory and dry-heaved into the toilet. He knelt
there for a long time, feeling stupid for having such a silly nightmare—but frightened of returning to bed for another bout with
the dream.

A soft rustle and the perfumed warmth of Cind.

"I'm okay," he said.

"Sure, you are. I frequently find perfectly healthy and happy
people crouched on the bathroom floor choking up their guts."

"I'll be fine . . . in a minute."

"I know you will. Now, don't argue, bub. Or you'll be in for
some real trouble."

She hauled him up, stripped him, and shoved him into the
shower. Cold spray needled down, shocking him into full aware-
ness. The film of sweat came off like old grease. Then the cold
water turned to hot, steam billowing in clouds. Cind's naked form
came through the clouds. She was armed with soap and a rough-
surfaced sponge.

"Turn around," she said. "I'm going to start with your back."

"I can do it," Sten said, reaching for the soap.

"I *said*, turn around." She rasped the sponge across his chest.

"Ouch! Okay, okay. You win!" He turned around.

"In case you haven't noticed," Cind said, "I always win."

She wet down the sponge, soaped it up good, and started scrub-
bing away.

It felt good. He forgot the eyes.

Later, propped up on pillows and tucked into fresh bedcloth-
ing, Sten sipped at the hot spicy tea Cind had ordered up from
the embassy kitchen. Outside, he could hear wind howling through
the streets of Rurik. Oddly, he felt peaceful. Cozy.

Cind perched on the bed next to him, a soft, colorful robe
pulled around her. Her normally smooth brow was furrowed as
she considered Sten's dream.

"Did you ever wonder," she asked, "what it would have been
like if the Emperor had never come back?"

Sten shook his head. "Sounds like a worse nightmare to me," he said. "Things were pretty messed up, if you recall."

"I remember all right. And, yeah, it was messy. But the point is, we were *doing* something about it. Everybody had a lot of hopes. Some idea of a future."

"Don't you think we have a future now? Things are tough, I agree. But, once we get over this hump—"

"We'll be back to normal?" Cind broke in. "Tell me what normal is, Sten. I'm young. I don't know about all those wonderful days before the Tahn war."

"Don't be sarcastic."

"You're evading my question."

"Okay. So, it wasn't a paradise."

"What was it, then?"

Sten made a rueful face. "Pretty much like now, I admit. Except . . . there was more of everything."

"Everybody was happier then, huh? The people here on Jochi, for instance, were happier, right? Sure, they had the Khaqan hammering on them, but they had more in their bellies. Which made it all very nice. A veritable heaven for the oppressed."

"You're being cynical again."

"You're evading again."

"It's just the way things work," Sten said. "Somebody has to be in charge. Make things go. Unfortunately, once in a while that somebody is a bastard. A tyrant."

"Like the Khaqan?"

"Yeah. Like the Khaqan."

"Like Dr. Iskra?"

"Especially Dr. Iskra. At least the Khaqan had the excuse of being a senile old fool."

"But we're under orders to shove Iskra down these people's throats," Cind said, "even though we know he's probably worse than the Khaqan. Does that make sense?"

"Not unless you look at the big picture," Sten said. "In the best of times, the Empire is a delicate balance of some pretty hard-case personalities. And these, you will agree, are not the best of times."

"No argument there."

"Good. Anyway, Iskra may be a son of a bitch. But, he's the Emperor's son of a bitch. And he helps the Emperor keep things from going to hell."

"In other words, it's expedient? It's right, even though we're going to make all these people miserable for many generations to come?"

"I wouldn't quite put it that way. But, yeah. It's expedient. Besides, there are billions of other beings in the Empire to think about."

"And how many of them are run by someone like Dr. Iskra?"

Sten opened his mouth to answer. The answer stuck. His jaw snapped shut.

Cind pressed on, not sure herself what she was getting at. "What makes a good tyrant, Sten? A good dictator? A perfect supreme ruler? Or is there such a thing?"

"Probably. For a while, at least. A lot of times people desperately want to be commanded what to do. And they'll squabble and kill each other until a Man on a White Horse comes along to save them. And they'll gladly hand over all their rights to this person.

"If they're lucky, the new ruler will be young, a person with a strong vision. It doesn't really matter what that vision is, just as long as everyone agrees it's worth going after. The actual doing tends to put the rest of the house in order.

"The problem is, I've never heard or read of a case where entropy doesn't apply. Like the Khaqan."

"Explain, please."

"When the dictator is on the job too long, he gets sloppy. Distant from his people. Starts assuming his powers come straight from God on high. He gathers a group of sycophants about him. Jackals who will do his bidding, in return for a share of the carrion.

"Finally, all rulers—absolute rulers, that is—reach a point where they depend on the jackals more than the people. And that is the beginning of the end. Because, they lose sight of who *really* gives them power. Which is, simply, the people they rule."

"Nice lecture, Professor Sten."

"Didn't mean to lecture."

Cind was quiet for a moment. She fussed with the tie of her robe. Then, real low: "Sounds like a pretty good description of the Emperor, to me."

Sten didn't answer. But, he gave a small nod.

"You didn't answer my first question," Cind said. "What do you think would have happened if the Emperor hadn't returned?"

"No point in thinking about it," Sten said. "The crude fact of the matter is, without AM2 we'd all be barbarians. There'd be almost no communication beyond the smallest planetary system. Interstellar travel would either be with the old killer longliners or, if it was under stardrive without AM2 power, would bankrupt a system's resources. No progress. Clot, progress! We'd all regress. To complete ignorance. And the Eternal Emperor—those jokers on the privy council learned to their dismay—is the only one who controls the AM2."

"What happened to it?" Cind asked. "I never really did understand."

"It just stopped," Sten said. "Near as anyone can figure—and the council did a damned great heap of figuring—the AM2 supply stopped the moment the Emperor was killed . . . or whatever it was that happened to him."

"Where *does* the AM2 come from?" Cind asked.

"What?" Sten was truly puzzled. But it was the kind of puzzlement that made a being feel as if IQ had been sadly lacking for a long time. A stunned-ox kind of sensation.

"If it stopped, it has to start from some place," Cind said. "I don't mean a great big secret depot of AM2, or anything. Because even that would eventually be emptied. And have to be filled up again. Which means, somebody—or thing—has to go fetch it. Where is it fetched from? Or is that a stupid question?"

"Not stupid at all," Sten said.

"I didn't think so. It just suddenly occurred to me. Then I figured, someone must have asked that question before."

"Not very loudly," Sten said. "The Emperor does not like people messing about with his AM2."

"Still. AM2 must exist someplace. In great quantities. Mountains and mountains of it. Sitting there for the taking. And whoever finds it—"

"Somebody did," Sten said as a great light dawned. And he wasn't sure the discovery made him happy.

"That's what made him Emperor, right?" Cind said.

"Only partly right," Sten said. "But you're forgetting something. It took more than just the AM2."

"How so?"

"He's also figured out a way to live forever. Or near enough as dammit."

"Oh, that!" Cind said. "Big deal. Who wants to live forever? After a while, everything would be boring. You'd never get a kick out of doing things like—"

"Ouch!" Sten yelped as Cind nipped his nipple with sharp teeth.

"And there'd be no thrill anymore when you—"

"I'll give you . . . a couple of hours to stop that," Sten said.

"Also," Cind said, "you probably wouldn't care a bit if—"

She wriggled her hips and pulled at his head. Sten went where she was pulling, dimly thinking that the woman had a wonderful way of proving her point.

CHAPTER TWENTY-SEVEN

IT WAS STILL on the meadow's floor. But the Place of Smokes was not silent. The wind whipped the tops of the conifers in a steady roar.

Sten, Alex, Cind, and Otho stood near one of the embassy gravsleds. Their Gurkha security element had deployed smoothly from the accompanying gravlighter into a perimeter.

The poacher discovered by Alex's bottomless purse had given them nervous instructions from the rutted road down the track into the clearing. When he had seen Cind unload recording gear, he had wanted his credits on the spot. Alex had paid and asked the man if he would wait: when they were finished, they would return him to his village.

No. The man insisted he would walk home. Thirty kilometers? It did not matter. The poacher walked backward into the trees, turned, and pelted away with devils on his heels.

Sten did not know whether the man had been more afraid of someone recording his face, or of the long, shallow furrows that stretched across the meadow.

"City beings dug those," Otho said. "Rustics would have known earth subsides once it's put back. And they'd have mounded the trench when they covered it over."

No one commented.

"How many?"

Sten shook his head. He had little background as an undertaker.

"There's five thousand that people have had the guts to report missing," Cind said.

"Square thae," Alex said absently, his eyes fixed on the covered trenches. "Which'll mean thae'll be—other places yet t' find." He turned to Sten. "How d' we play th' card, boss?"

Sten thought, then walked to the gravsled and opened an equipment locker. He removed two shovels and gave one to Kilgour.

"I guess," he said, "we'll treat it like an archaeologist's dig. We'll cut a slit one meter wide across one trench. Cind, I want you recording. Make sure the film shows the ground has not been disturbed for some time. There's little plants—"

"Lichen," Alex said.

"Lichen, then, grown up. No footprints except those we'll make approaching the . . ." He let his voice trail off.

"Sir," Otho said. "The soldiers can do the digging."

Sten shook his head and motioned to Cind to start the recorder. Then he walked to the nearest trench and marked the limits of the exploratory slot with his shovel's blade. He started digging carefully. The sandy loam took little effort to dislodge. Alex dug with equal care on the other side of the trench.

Sten was down less than a meter when he suddenly stopped. "Otho. There's a trowel in the locker." He knelt and dug still more gently with the tool. He grunted. Then he coughed hard and threw up to one side of the trench.

Otho brought him a canteen and a breathing mask. He gave a second mask to Alex. "It is a smell you never become used to."

Sten rinsed his mouth out and put the mask on. He was glad it concealed his expression. "Two . . . maybe three months?"

"Thae's aboot th' right time, boss. Cind? I' y' c'd gie us a shot, straight doon int' th' crypt?"

Cind moved closer.

Through the finder, she could see a woman's back. Her hands had been tied behind her with plas cuffs. Next to it, was a man's face. The remains of his eyes were wide, and his mouth was open, the scream silenced with dirt.

Cind told her eyes to stop recording—the machine would do the work. They did not obey.

"Why," Otho wondered, "did Iskra not dump these bodies into the sea? Or burn them with his fire?"

"Being buried alive," Sten said, "is an honorable death here on Jochi."

Otho growled. "And how can murder ever be honorable?"

Sten gave Alex a hand out of the grave.

"Y' dinnae answer m' question, boss, on whae use w' put this atrocity to? Ah cannae say Ah think thae'll be aught good i' we call in th' penny dreadfuls, an' let th' deed be howl't 'crost th' Altaics. Thae'll be more tinder f'r th' firestorm i' we do."

"You're right. We'll cover the hole back up. And all we'll do—at least at first—is ship a copy of Cind's record to Prime."

"Eyes Only frae th' Emp? Sten, this isn't th' first, it's just th' worst ae what we've been tellin't th' boss. Whae makes y' think he'll pay this any more heed—Ah ken he's seen more gashly sights o'er th' aeons."

"I don't know," Sten said. "But he'd damned well better start—because you had it when you said there's a firestorm building. And we're right in the middle."

Then they fell silent.

And there was no sound but the shovels scraping dirt back into the mass grave . . . and the high roar of the wind as it built up force overhead.

CHAPTER TWENTY-EIGHT

THE QUESTION OF whether the revelation at the Place of the Smokes would change the Emperor's course would not be answered.

Her family was not rich, not poor. Or at least not what the citizens of Rurik called poor—on many other worlds she would have been thought a slummer. But she knew both her father and mother, and only two of her brothers had died as babes. She had always eaten at least once a day, and her clothes were clean, if restyled and resewn garments her older sister had owned.

She was a Jochian. But she did not remember, as a child—at sixteen E-years, she of course considered herself adult—having any particular hatred for Suzdal or Bogazi. Even though she seldom saw either of the ET species in her sector. And she never felt anything more than pity for the few Tork families she encountered.

Some years before she had heard stories that her world would change, change for the better. Once that tyrant the Khaqan was gone—she had never thought of him one way or another before—a new day would dawn.

It would be brought by a man named Iskra. Some of her friends gave her pamphlets that talked about how this noble man had always believed in the Altaics, had believed they were to be civilization's center, and that the new fire would be sparked by Jochians.

She did not, of course, actually read any of this doctor's writings. She had been told they were far too complex for someone of her sex and education, and she did not need to waste the time.

She joined a small organization, a secret organization, of course, and was oath-sworn to help bring that new day in whatever way she could.

And then Iskra returned to his home world. She had been part of the roaring throng that welcomed him. She thought she had actually seen him—a dot far away on a balcony of the palace that had belonged to the Khaqan.

Then the stories had started. The new day was not dawning fast enough. The Torks still paraded and showed off their riches, riches that had been ill-gotten from Jochians. And worse, Jochi was still polluted by the presence of Suzdal and Bogazi.

Even when the "aliens" left, there were still evils plaguing Dr. Iskra's attempts to bring a firm hand to the madness. And of course, once her cell leader explained, she saw the real villains clearly: those Imperials who were trying to use Dr. Iskra as their cat's-paw, just as they had used the Khaqan. Now she realized Dr. Iskra was being held as a near-captive in that palace—not ruling freely as she once believed.

She wanted to do something. Something that would bring the change even faster.

Somehow, some way, she could help.

On the livies she saw what others had done. Two young men and a woman—a woman even younger than herself—had doused their bodies with flame, willingly shaming themselves with this dishonorable death, because only by such a stroke would all of Jochi realize *they* were the ones who were shamed.

She told her cell leader of her willingness to die. He said he would ask *his* counselor if such an act would be good.

Two days later, he told her that this was not to be her fate. Instead, she would be allowed to perform an even greater task, a task that would drive the Imperials from their worlds like a great wind from the north.

She was delighted and humbled.

She studied and rehearsed carefully.

Two days after Sten found the bodies buried in the forest, she was told it was time.

* * *

"The clots never listen," the sentry said to the other two Imperial soldiers assigned to the guard post. "Y' can tell them a hundred times this is closed off, you can't get a back way to the market stalls this direction, and they'll nod, smile, and try again next time they come to town. When the Maker asked the Jochians if they wanted brains, they thought he said drains and said 'go ahead and flush.' "

The sentry post was at one of the entry streets that opened on the Square of the Khaqans. It was now secured, because the part of the palace that had been given to the battalion from the Third Imperial Guards for barracks/offices/mess was about a hundred meters away.

He yawned—less than an hour after dawn, which meant less than another hour until the post was relieved and he could eat—picked up his willygun, slung it, and walked out of the sentry shack. He watched as the gravlighter floated toward him. A clottin' antique, he thought. Damned thing actually travels at a cant.

Its cargo compartment was full of what looked like half-ripe, half-rotten tree fruit that no one but a Jochian would have bought, let alone considered eating.

He shook his head. He resolved that when his hitch was up he would *never* bitch about anything on his home world, having seen just how little these Jochians actually had. You would almost feel sorry for them, if they weren't such hate-shoutin' bastards, he thought.

He couldn't see who was behind the controls of the lighter through the cracked, dirty plas shield. The sentry held both hands flat—universal language for "Ground it."

The lighter stopped—but didn't land. It moved back and forth in the gusting wind that came across the wide Square of the Khaqans.

The sentry swore. He moved to one side. Maybe the driver couldn't see him. Then he half smiled in approval. Pretty one, she was. He motioned again—just as the gravlighter went to full power and drove toward and over him.

It may have looked battered, but the lighter's McLean generators were freshly rebuilt and tuned for maximum power. The sentry had one second to think the young woman had misunderstood, then he rolled out of the way as the lighter drove forward at speed.

Imperial—and commonsense—security: the entrance to any secured compound should always be laid out so any entering vehicle, ground or aerial, would be forced to slow to minimum speed. But this particular gateway had but one V-turn in it.

Solid blocks, heavy-duty fencing, or even rolled razor wire had to be stacked to at least three meters above the ground. This gateway had only three rolls of razor wire, the third piled between the second.

The gravlighter snagged wire—but kept on moving.

It was imperative, Imperial security directives continued, that any compound include a secondary vehicle block, in case the outer barrier was breached.

No such block had been constructed.

Under no circumstances, the directives went on, even more sternly, was a troop barracks ever to be vulnerable to a suicide assault. Minimum precautions in hostile areas included monitors, AA posts, ground obstacles, roving patrols with heavy antiarmor weapons, etcetera, etcetera.

The gravlighter was only ten meters from the steps leading into the Imperial Guards' barracks when the young woman pilot—that friendly smile she had forced to the sentry now a rictus—reached down to a small control box that had been hastily welded to the floor.

There were two pull-levers, one sprayed red, the other blue. She had been instructed that the blue lever would start the timer, and she would have thirty seconds to clear the area.

The red . . .

The red was to be used in the event of emergencies.

She never knew that both knobs were the same, because she had determined that there would be no mistakes made. This would be the shot—the blast—heard far beyond Jochi or the Altaics.

It would be heard on Prime World, where that evil puppet master, the Eternal Emperor, would be forced to listen and realize what his machinations had produced.

She pulled the red knob straight up.

She died first as the three tons of conventional explosives that was the gravlighter's real cargo detonated.

The blastwave crashed through the wall of the barracks. Of the 650 beings carried on the Guard battalion's TO&E, more than half of them were still asleep, or being shouted awake by noncoms. Five hundred and eighty total Guardsmen were in the palace building.

Colonel Jerety, caff pot in hand, was about to ask his executive officer and battalion sergeant major if they needed refills when the blast rolled over him.

The explosion smashed down the barracks.

The lucky ones died in the blast.

The slightly less lucky ones never recovered consciousness or were crushed as the building fell about them.

But there were others.

The screams started even before the shock wave died, and while the dust was still boiling.

Halfway across the city the shock wave hit the embassy.

Sten, still abed, was brooding, and Cind was trying to convince him that his day would be vastly improved if he would lie back and let her tongue continue its wanderings, and he felt the rumble and the building shake, and he was on his feet, naked, sure for an instant that the bastards had hit the embassy itself.

He was at a window, ignoring Cind's shout to get down, and staring out as that great pillar of smoke and flame began building.

Deep in his guts he knew this was the turning point.

What would happen next, he had no real idea.

But he had a skincrawl/soulcrawl that it would be something to make all the murder and treachery that had gone before seem like nothing.

CHAPTER TWENTY-NINE

"I KNEW THINGS were going to be pretty bleak when I got back," the Eternal Emperor said, "but, like most of my subjects, I thought all I needed to do was tighten the Imperial belt and slog onward."

The Emperor topped up Mahoney's glass with scotch and refilled his own. "I was stupid enough to think that with a little imagination and a lot of hard work the crisis would pass." He let his gaze rest briefly on Mahoney, then moved onward.

Mahoney had the sudden flash of a lizard searching for a fly. He shoved the disloyal image aside. "I'm sure it will work out eventually, sir. We all have complete faith in you."

The Emperor gave a hollow laugh. "Faith is an overvalued commodity, Ian. And, yes, it *is* a commodity. I should know. I just purchased some for extra insurance."

Mahoney let that go by. He didn't want to know what the Emperor was talking about. "How can I help, sir?"

"That's one of your most admirable traits, old friend," the Eternal Emperor said. "When I call, you're always ready to volunteer."

In other times, Mahoney would have flushed warmly at the compliment of being called the Emperor's friend. Now the words sounded cold, insincere. "Thank you, sir," he said. He sipped his drink to cover confused emotion.

"First, let me tell you what has come to pass," the Emperor said. "I've got a desk full of fiche from my experts"—he thumped the side of his antique desk for emphasis—"which contradict each other on just about every point except one." The Emperor turned a thumb downward. "And that's the direction my Empire is heading.

"The optimists say we're going downhill slowly. They've got

progs of complete collapse within twenty E-years. The boys in the middle say five or six.

"The pessimists tell me it has already happened. They say we're being carried along by economic inertia. That the sheer size of my empire covers up the hard, cold fact that we are dead, dead, dead."

"Surely they're all in error, sir," Mahoney said. "Experts make their fortunes on gloom. Not good news."

"No error. Except, possibly, my own. I've been simply ignoring what's staring me in the face."

"But . . . I don't see how this can be." A bit shaken, Mahoney gasped back his drink, then reached for the decanter to refill their glasses. It was empty. He rose and went to the sideboard to fetch another. Mahoney started to pick up another decanter of scotch, then changed his mind, seeing a flask of stregg. He lifted it up. "Maybe we need something stronger, boss," he said.

The Emperor's face paled with anger. "What's *that* doing there?" he barked. "I don't drink that anymore." Alarmed, Mahoney watched the rage build.

"Dammit," the Emperor snarled. "I told Bleick I don't even want that drakh in my presence." Then he caught himself and gave Mahoney a weak attempt at a smile. "Sorry," he said. "Little things get to me these days."

Mahoney just nodded and walked back to his seat with a decanter of scotch. What the clot was going on here? Why the sudden hate for such an innocuous thing? For the first time, Mahoney felt he was in the presence of a stranger. A dangerous stranger.

The Emperor continued as if nothing unusual had happened, as Mahoney refilled the glasses with scotch.

"When the Tahn war were over," the Emperor said, "the debt we had taken on was astonishing. But I had a firm, workable plan to whittle it away without causing too much discomfort. Unfortunately . . ."

He didn't have to fill in the rest. Mahoney knew quite well that the Emperor had never had the chance to put that plan into motion.

"I could still have pulled it off," the Emperor said, "if it weren't for the actions of the privy council. My God, did they spend. But not for one thing worthwhile. Not a thing that could eventually put credits back in the treasury, or even spur a little mini-boom in the economy.''

The Emperor leaned back in his chair and propped his feet on the desk. ''The Tahn war debt,'' he said, ''now equals only about one tenth of our current deficit. I reckon that same deficit—at current cut-to-the-bone spending—will double again within one E-year.''

Mahoney was not a money man. It did not interest him. Large amounts offended his sense of morality. And he certainly didn't understand it. But, *this* he understood.

''The Empire's problems hit critical mass about four years into the privy council's reign,'' the Emperor continued. ''At that time the impact of the AM2 shortage hit the point of no return. It's put everything into a helluva spin. A big, clotting vortex, sucking us into the hole. And each time a system's economy collapsed and fell in, it tipped another into the funnel. Now the mess has taken on a life and logic of its own. Unless I take drastic action—real quick—even the healthiest parts of my empire are going to get pulled in.''

The Emperor drained his glass, slapped it down on his desk, and turned those scary eyes on Mahoney. A slight flicker . . . and then they swept on.

Mahoney had the sudden feeling that he was being set up. The Emperor's facts were too pat. Too glib: x times y must absolutely equal what I am going to tell you next.

''Not only that,'' the Emperor said, ''but I am personally strapped. Just about broke. As you know, Ian, in the past I have sometimes used my personal resources to help the Empire over some rough spots. But the privy council looted those resources, as well. Now we don't even have my money to fall back on.''

''What do you plan to do, sir?'' Mahoney asked. His tone was neutral.

''I have to rein everybody in, Ian,'' the Emperor said. ''All over the Empire, we've got thousands of different leaders doing things a thousand different ways.'' He casually filled his glass and sipped. ''So, to start with, we need uniformity. Second—and most important—We have to put an instant end to all areas of conflict. Look what's happening over in the Altaic Cluster, for example. Our good and highly competent friend, Ambassador

Sten, is going out of his mind with the trouble those beings are causing. It's those sort of unstable regions and situations that led to the Tahn disaster to begin with.''

The Eternal Emperor shook his head. ''I'll tell you Ian, the only way I can see out of these woods is if everybody follows one being's lead. And from where I sit, I've got to be that guide.

''I want to cut out the middle men, Ian. From here on out, I need to be the only one in charge.'' He shrugged. ''Else, we might as well all give up and go home. Unfortunately, there's no other home to go to.''

''How do I fit into this, sir?'' Mahoney asked.

''I want you to run the whole show,'' the Emperor said. ''I want you to be in charge of putting together my recovery plan.''

''Which is, Your Highness?''

''My pet pols will announce the first stage of my plan in Parliament next week. I'm going to make a one-time offer to all the provinces. I'm going to encourage them to give up independent rule. They'll be offered the chance to become dominions—of my Empire.''

''Excuse me, sir,'' Mahoney broke in, ''but why would they do this? Why would they give up all that power? As you've taught me, that goes against the nature of most beings.''

''Certainly it does. So does the carrot I'm going to offer. As well as the stick. But, to greed first. As provinces they are paying full price for AM2. Plus, they are under strict rationing. As dominions, they will not only pay less for the AM2, but will pay lower overall taxes, as well.''

''What if they refuse, sir? What's the stick?''

The Eternal Emperor smiled. A nasty smile. ''Oh . . . to begin with, I'm also announcing a tenth of a credit tax hike on AM2 for all provinces. That's on top of increased rationing. Which—since economic nature will then take its course—will push the price of AM2 on the spot market into double digits.''

Low laughter. Mahoney shuddered.

''That's just for starters,'' the Emperor said. ''I've got a few other thumbscrews in mind. As a long-time kingmaker, I've gotten pretty skilled at unmaking them, as well.''

''Back to my original question, sir. How do I fit in?'' Mahoney did not forget that his *real* first question had been "How can I help, sir?"

"I want you to be point man with the provinces. I want to heap more glory into your honors chest. As thanks, as well as to boost your prestige in the eyes of the fools you will be visiting.

"And I want you to visit every major province leader. Cajole them. Irish charm them. As well as twist the right arms if you have to. Just be firm, Ian. Make nice promises. But make sure they see the weight in the stick I'm handing you."

"I am deeply honored, sir," Mahoney said quickly. "But I am the worst man for that job. I would be disloyal not to refuse this honor. Such an appointment would not be in your best interests . . . sir."

The Emperor turned a cold face to Mahoney. "Why, Ian?" The question was soft, the eyes looking blankly over Mahoney's shoulder.

"Because I think it's a terrible idea, sir," Mahoney burst out. "You've always asked honesty of me. I've always given it to you. So . . . there it is, sir. I don't want the job, sir. Because I don't believe in it."

"What's there not to believe in? It's a plan. Not a . . . religion."

"First off, sir, in my estimation, the stick will be needed more than the carrot. You'll have to force dominion status on most of them, sir. And they will resent the clot out of it. Which means, your orders will be followed grudgingly at best. Which automatically sets all your actions up for failure. And that, sir, is my humble opinion."

It was also Mahoney's professional opinion that anything micromanaged was doomed. If no one had anything to gain, why chance failure? A "let the big man do it" attitude develops fast. It also offended his democratic, Irish soul.

In Mahoney's view, beings were best left in charge of their own destiny. In the past that had been what he had always loved about the Empire. It had problems, to be sure. But, mostly there was room for all sorts of ways of doing things. Room for genius, as well as for fools.

Now he was even beginning to wonder about his previous view. How much room was there? Really?

"In normal times, I would agree with you, Ian," the Emperor said. "I could list many examples from history."

"The British Crown's takeover of Earth's old East India Company comes to mind, sir," Mahoney said. "One of your favorite examples, sir. As a lesson in failure, I believe."

The Emperor laughed. Mahoney thought the laugh had a little bit of the old spark to it. It made him feel a little better.

"Go ahead, Ian. Throw my own logic back at me. Not too many people would have the nerve. That's the kind of thing that keeps the mental juices going. Keeps me from getting stale."

He leaned over his desk, lowering his voice slightly. "I tell you, Ian, the crew of beings I've got around me are gross incompetents. I miss the old days. When you and I and a few other talented beings—like Sten, for example—kept things going on the fly. I love that old kind of political freebooting."

The Emperor sat back and sipped his drink. Coldness shrouded back over him. "Unfortunately . . . that is no longer possible. And I'm not just speaking of the current crisis.

"Things have become too big. Too complicated. Governing by pure consensus is ideally suited to a tribe. Twenty or thirty beings, maximum. Any number after that weakens the effectiveness of the ideal.

"It's time for a new order, my friend. A universal order. New thinking by right-minded individuals is called for."

Mahoney couldn't help himself. "I'm not sure that rule by an *enlightened monarchy* fits the definition of 'new thinking,' sir," he blurted.

The Emperor shook his head. "You're right, but you're wrong, Ian. You're forgetting I'm . . . immortal."

He settled his gaze on Mahoney. His eyes were like mirrored glass, reflecting Mahoney's image back at him. "I can think of nothing more perfect in the social art of governing, than to have a single-purposed, benevolent ruler, who will keep the course until the end of history."

The Emperor kept those eyes riveted on Mahoney, boring in at him. "Can you see it, now, Ian? Now, that I've explained? Can you see the sheer beauty of it?"

The com buzzed. Mahoney was temporarily saved from answering. Then, as the Emperor spoke to the individual on the other side the reprieve became permanent. He was rescued by the worst kind of news.

The Emperor snarled orders and angrily cut the line. He turned to Mahoney. "There's been a disaster in the Altaic Cluster, Ian," he said. "I mean, Imperial-troops-dead-in-the-most-humiliating-circumstances-type disaster."

He turned his face to the window and looked out at the idyllic grounds of Arundel. He was silent for a long time, thinking.

Finally, he turned back. "Forget the previous job offer, Mahoney," he said. "We'll argue that matter later. I've got something much more important for you to do."

"Yes, sir," Mahoney said. This time, he knew there was no way he could refuse.

CHAPTER THIRTY

DIGGING OUT THE Guard's barracks was three days of grimness. Five hundred and eighty soldiers had been inside when the monster bomb of the gravlighter had detonated.

Four hundred and thirty-seven dead. One hundred and twenty-one injured—most with major traumatic injuries requiring amputation so severe that the embassy's surgical team doubted if more than half would accept limb regeneration. Twenty-three uninjured—physically uninjured.

There had been twenty-six, at first. Three soldiers had been dug out of the rubble seemingly unscathed. One of them had stood up, grinned, said "Thanks, clots, now, who's pourin'?" taken five steps, and dropped dead. The others just died quietly in their hospital beds. And the twenty-three survivors were all psychological casualties, of course. No one ever knew—or reported, at any rate—how many Jochi civilian workers had also died in the blast.

But it was three days before the last screamer, lost in the maze that had been a palace building, rasped into silence and death.

This battalion of the Third Guard had ceased to exist. Otho found the battalion flag buried near Jerety's body and had it cased for shipment to the division's home depot. The battalion might be reconstituted after an appropriate interval. Or it might never exist again.

The wounded, and the injured Guardsmen who had been outside their barracks, were loaded on the *Victory* and evacked.

Sten had put Mason in charge of the rescue operation, and he himself had spent as much time as he could digging with the rest of the Imperials. Then he had ordered Mason to take the *Victory* to Prime and unload the casualties. He had sent Prime a copy of Mason's orders, but had not much cared whether they would be met with Imperial approval or not. He was slightly surprised to receive that approval—and a brief, coded addendum that further support would be provided immediately.

The next communique from Prime had been announcing medals. Some were given to Gurkhas or Bhor that Sten had commended. Others went to Colonel Jerety and the top-ranked officers of the Guard's battalion. If these officers had survived the blast, of course, they would have been relieved and at the very least shot for criminal incompetence.

Sten, Kilgour, and Mason were also gonged. To them the awards were meaningless medals to be tossed in a drawer and forgotten. The disaster should have been studied for its lessons—not memorialized with tin and ribbon. But that is the nature of any military unit.

By then, Sten had other problems.

The blast that destroyed the Guard unit seemed to be the catalyst. Jochi went somewhat berserk.

Suddenly, the Empire was the enemy of the Altaic Cluster. The Empire must be taught a lesson. The Empire must not meddle.

Sten admired—slightly—the campaign. To a degree it *was* spontaneous—peasants never seemed to need much direction for their latest pogrom—but mostly it was carefully choreographed.

At first, Sten had been in a reactive position: filing the correct

protests with Dr. Iskra and what Iskra laughingly called a government; filing the appropriate responses, trying to keep the livie
reporters off his ass . . . and incidentally keeping the embassy
functioning and his staff alive.

He had immediately declared Jochi a high-threat world and
informed all Imperial worlds that any citizen visiting the Altaic
Cluster did so at extreme personal risk. He insisted that Prime
require a visa for anyone coming to the cluster.

He sent out teams of well-armed Gurkhas and Bhor to find all
Imperial citizens and escort them to the safety of the embassy.

Most Imperial visitors—thank some non-Altaic god—had been
professional businessbeings, who were skilled at sensing trouble
and scooting out of its way. But there were always the exceptions:
the elderly couple who were determined to see a part of the universe they had never visited; the honeymooners who, it seemed,
had picked Jochi out of an archaic travel fiche. Sten rescued the
old people. He wasn't in time for the newly married beings.

And then the embassy itself came under siege.

At first it was just small groups of Jochians, and any person or
vehicle attempting to enter or exit the embassy was stoned. Sten
consulted with Kilgour. Yes, Alex agreed. The situation looked
to be worsening.

"Then we'll show them how to throw a real riot."

"Aye, boss."

And Kilgour set to work, readying the response. He could have
done it in his sleep by now. This was hardly the first time he and
Sten had been besieged by "civilian mobs" on a "peaceful world."
They had a very effective standard defusing order prepared.

The crowds grew bigger. Instead of rocks, they were throwing
firebombs and nail-wrapped improvised grenades built out of low-
grade explosives.

According to Dr. Iskra's flunky, J'Dean, these people represented the righteous wrath of Jochi. Wrath about what, Sten did
not bother to ask. J'Dean told him that Dr. Iskra, who was quite
busy at the moment, would happily send out troops to clear the
area, if Sten so requested it. Right, Sten thought. Another massacre, which will be clearly and positively laid at my hands, since
I know this conversation is being recorded.

"No," Sten said politely. "The Empire will not harm innocent Jochians freely expressing their political opinions as is their right." He broke the connection. He didn't think even Iskra's tape doctors could butcher that into a statement of slaughter.

Then the sniping started. Projectile weapons, being fired by marksmen who had seen at least some training. One secretary was shot in the leg, and one clerk was temporarily blinded when a near miss shrapnelled rock from a wall into her face.

That was enough. Sten ordered everyone nonmilitary inside, and only essential movement to be made during daylight hours even by troops.

Naturally, the next stage would be a direct attack.

Sten put all nonessential personnel into the many levels of subbasements under the embassy building. He stationed anyone with any military training or weapons familiarity near the entrances and exits to the compound buildings.

The Bhor had been quite busy following Kilgour's blueprints. The somewhat monstrous beings may have been thought of as barbaric killers—which they were, of course—but they were also sophisticated traders and pilots. Which meant that each of them had, by now almost at a genetically transmitted level, talents as shade-tree mechanics. Any of them could, for instance, weld anything, up to and including radioactive materials, by hand, safely, and with minimum shielding. Or rebuild a broken engine never seen before—given no more than hobbyist's machine tools and an hour to puzzle it out.

The embassy already had two elderly riot-control armored vehicles. The guns were stripped off, and Alex rearmed the clunkers with his own choice of devices. Four embassy vehicles, including the stretched luxury ceremonial gravlighter that Sten had inherited from his predecessor, were stripped, given improvised armor, and equipped with the same weaponry as the riot vehicles.

Four of the Gurkha trooplighters were also modified, with heavy iron vee-blades welded to their prows. These four were stationed near one of the embassy compound's sally ports.

Sten and Alex were building and camouflaging bombs, then planting them at ground level on the compound's outer walls.

That night, Lalbahadur Thapa, who Sten had commissioned

Jemedar, took two unmodified lighters and a platoon of Gurkhas out a side gate on a smash and grab on a central hardware depot. He returned having taken zero casualties and having accomplished his mission, although, he told Sten, he had never seen a mongery so large but with so little stock in trade. "How can these Jochians find so much time to be killing their neighbor and have so little time to be taking care of their own food and shelter?"

Sten didn't know, either.

Kilgour told off twelve members of the embassy's own security staff for special duties. They would be armed with the stolen "weaponry" and were dubbed, with Alex's archaic sense of humor, Tomcat Teams.

By dawn, the embassy was ready. Sten thought the assault would come sometime between noon and dusk—it takes time to organize, fuel, oil, and motivate any mob.

The Gurkhas and the Bhor were put on standby for reaction forces, in the event the mob made it through the gates or over the wall, or if a charge became necessary.

That left two tasks.

Alex took care of the first—he ran a last-minute, complete check on the embassy's security, concentrating on any structures outside the embassy grounds that had line of sight on the compound and could be used as command centers. These included two buildings— one a new office structure, the other one of the near-abandoned vertical slums. Each had a new com antenna on the roof.

They were marked.

Cind had her best riflemen in the embassy courtyard, and targets set up. The range was subminiature, of course, and was intended only to let the snipers make sure the sights of their weaponry hadn't been jarred or shifted since fired last.

Cind was grateful that the rounds to be fired were AM2 and not projectile-type, so she did not have to calculate at what centimetric range a target would give the same zero as the desired thousand-meter flat zero or any other stone-age nonsense. The AM2 went, without deflection and with a straight-line trajectory, straight for its target.

Their weapons were Imperial sniper rifles. These ultralethal devices were modified-issue willyguns, using the standard AM2 round.

But the "propellant" was not a laser, as on the standard infantry rifles, but modified linear accelerators hung around the barrels. A conventional-looking sight automatically found the range to the target. If the target had moved out of sight—behind a wall, perhaps—the scope was twisted until its cross hairs were where the sniper imagined the target to be, invisible on the other side of the wall. A touch of the trigger, and the weapon shot around corners.

Cind had her own personally modified sniper rifle, fitted with every comfort known, from thumbhole stock to set trigger to heavy barrel. One of the Gurkhas, Naik Ganjabahadur Rai, spotted for her.

Sten hoped the crash of gunfire from behind the embassy walls might deter some of the prospective rioters' enthusiasm, but he doubted it.

They waited.

The day built, with shouts, rocks, bottles, and chants coming over the embassy walls. It was midafternoon before Sten felt the mob was all frenzied up and ready to be dealt with. It probably took so long since the day was raw and windy—not exactly perfect weather to destroy an embassy.

He moved Cind's snipers to the roof of the embassy. One floor below, lurking in an office with the windows removed, Alex waited with two Bhor antimissile teams.

All of Sten's assault troops were on a single command freek, which normally would produce instant com babble. But since he was using the superexperienced Gurkha and Bhor soldiery, Sten thought he could keep the gabble within reasonable limits. Their coms were also set for an instant-override section band.

"All sections, all troops," he opened. "On standby, this band. Section leaders, make your com check, both freeks, and report. Sten, out."

He was broadcasting *en clair*, since there was no time for codes, and no particular need, either. If whoever was masterminding this "spontaneous demonstration" wanted to listen in and try to react, that was fine with Sten.

All elements checked in five-by and zed probs, except that one section leader had to replace two com units. One of these centuries, Sten thought, they will actually come up with an infantry radio that is reliable five meters beyond the manufacturer's bench. But not this one.

Sten moved a tripod-mounted high-power set of binocs into position and decided it was time to check the street scene outside.

Shouts. Banners. Horn blasts. Screaming rabble-rousers. Barricades blocking the side streets. The dull crack of a couple of small-caliber weapons, aimed at he knew not. The embassy was completely surrounded by a sea of madness. The mob swayed, roaring.

Roaring like that wind in the Place of Smokes, he thought, and then turned that part of his mind off.

Quite a crowd, he estimated. Nearly . . . let's see. He guessed over a hundred thousand beings.

"How do you know there's that many?" Cind wondered, from her sprawl two meters away from him.

"Easy," he said. "I just count their legs and divide by two. Hang on. Cind. Targets. Alpha. Thirteen thirty. Five hundred meters. Bravo. Fifteen hundred. Four—correction, three hundred seventy-five. Charlie. Sixteen hundred, four hundred. One more—Delta. Zero nine hundred, six hundred meters. Looks like he might be the big Limburger. Monitor, please. Sten, clear."

He was using a clock locator, with twelve hundred being the central boulevard that ran from the embassy to the palace, and ranges in meters.

The spotters reported promptly. All targets that he had suggested were beyond the crowd swirl. He had looked for beings who were standing on top of things, speechifying, organizing, rabble-rousing.

Crowd roar was getting louder. Now, Sten thought, if these speech makers are just angry citizenry, concerned about injustice, in a few moments they'll shout their way to the front of the mob.

But they were not moving.

Professional-type rabble-rousers, then. Ones that whoever's throwing this masked ball would rather not sacrifice if bullets start zipping about. Or else they're just cowards, in which case I'm almost sorry for what's about to happen.

"Alex."

"Aye, lad."

"When you take your two, we'll take the windbags."

"Aye, skip. Hae y' a mo' f'r some incidental intelligence?"

"No . . . yes."

"Ah hae m' wee ticky ticky wi' me. Th' one thae's th' twig f'r thae flashy popper w' hae oot there?"

Sten thought . . . oh. Alex was talking about the detector that was linked to the bug in that elaborate pistol they had bugged in that back-alley arsenal.

"GA."

"As y' said. Th' whoppin' Camembert hae i'."

Son of a bitch, Sten thought. So. As he had thought, this "mob" was being created, built, and driven. And whoever was running this operation was also involved with a little private terrorism. And, he was morally willing to believe, even if it wasn't justified enough for an intelligence summary, willing to send a suicide bomber in to kill over four hundred Imperial Guardsmen.

"You're detached, Alex. Don't lose that ticker."

"Ah thought y'd say thae, boss. An' Ah' wish't y' t' be impress't, an' owe me one, frae bein't so self-sacrificing. Ah'm off th' net, an'll be mon'trin' frae com central. Alex, clear."

"Cind?" Sten had his hand over the com mouthpiece.

"I heard." She spoke into her open mike to her sniper section. "This is Sniper Six Actual. Delta is a negative target. I say again, Delta is a negative. Over."

That target—that being—that Sten had spotted far beyond the mob's reach and surmised to be the horde-officer-in-charge was carrying the bugged pistol. As much as he wanted to hit Delta now, the target must be taken later.

"Here they come!"

"Unknown unit! ID yourself!"

"Sorry. Main Central."

Sten swung his binocs. Indeed, here came a thrust of people toward the main gate.

A stumble, really. Sten gave an order.

Irritant gas hissed from projectors atop the embassy walls. A very thin spray, and the gas was cut ten-to-one. It was dyed yellow and would stain anyone it touched. This was in case Sten or anyone else needed to ID any rioters at a later date, since the dye would take at least seven baths to scrub off.

The gas was intended to be no more than an annoyance, but was also intended to be a suggestion that worse things could happen.

The first wave fell back, blinking. Then the now-tawny troublemakers surged forward. This time they were brandishing knives, improvised spears, and firebombs.

Sten touched buttons on the det panel in front of him, and his and Alex's bombs went off. They were not bombs so much as high-pressure spray cans. They had been disguised as trash bins, streetlight bases, and anything else that would have been part of a believable street scene. Each bomb contained at least twenty liters of lubricant.

It became quite hard to walk on the slick streets just around the Imperial embassy.

Then the Tomcat Teams hit, darting out from the embassy's quickly opened and shut sally ports.

They were two-man units, one man with a willygun and orders not to use it unless the team was trapped, the other with a great pack full of what had been looted from that warehouse. Ball bearings. Many, many ball bearings, grabbed by the handful and scattered underhand.

Ball bearing mousetrap.

Tomcat.

It got *much* harder to be a raving rebel and not be in a seated or prone position.

The mob hesitated. The front rank was suddenly unsure of what was going on, and the rear ranks wanted to find out what was going on and get in on the looting that could be no more than seconds away.

The embassy sally ports opened again, and the two riot-control vehicles, along with the four others Sten had modified, lifted out and opened fire.

Water.

Under medium pressure. Not even at a firehose blast.

The first several ranks of the crowd decided they wanted to go home. It was cold out.

Sten would oblige them, as his second wave of gravlighters boomed out of the embassy. Screams, and people dove out of the way as the dozer blades closed on them before they realized that the gravlighters were deliberately attacking at three meters above the ground.

The lighters weren't intended as weapons—they drove on at speed, toward the barricades down the side streets. They shattered against them once, spun back, and hit again, piled debris and civilian gravsleds spinning out of the way. Now the streets were clear.

The lighters turned and sped back into the embassy grounds. No casualties. Sten sighed in relief—this had been the most dangerous part of his plan, the most likely to produce Imperial casualties.

The mob was swaying, indeterminate.

That gravlighter attack was Sten's bit of humanitarianism, planned to give "his" mob a back door when the next part of the plan was implemented. He, too, wanted them to go home.

"Now!"

And now people died.

Bhor fingers touched firing switches, and missiles spat out of launch tubes. They were fire-and-forget, but even a guided or unaimed missile could not have missed. Both impacted at point of aim: one on the top floor of that slum, the other in the penthouse of the office building.

Beings who had had no intention of involving themselves in real physical violence, let alone in real jeopardy, had bare seconds to blink, as two fiery lines homed, and the missiles blew.

Blastwaves curled out . . . and other fingers touched triggers.

Alpha . . . Bravo . . . Charlie . . .

The street speakers were dead, too, even before they had time to look up to see the plume of death smoke from their superiors' lairs.

The mob was frozen.

And the gates of the embassy swung open.

The yammers, shouts, and screams stopped.

There was utter silence.

And then there came the even crunch of boots on rubble.

Sten, flanked by twenty Gurkhas, strode out the embassy gate.

All of them held kukris, the half-meter-long curved-blade knives, held at a forty-five degree angle to their chests, at the ready.

They came forward ten paces. And stopped, without orders.

Ten Bhor, willyguns leveled, came out, veed back for flank security. They, too, crashed to a halt.

There was a murmur from the crowd. These were the killers. The little brown men who took no prisoners, men who, the wild stories had said, killed and ate their own children if they were not murderous enough. All of the slanders the most skilled propagandists on Jochi had spread on the Nepalese warriors, slanders that the Gurkhas had paid no mind, now back-blasted. These men were even more terrible than the tales said. These were not men, even, but killers, who went in with the long knife, and came out leaving nothing but blood and silence behind them.

Again with no orders, Sten and the Gurkhas took one measured pace forward, then stopped.

Another pace.

Another.

In five more paces, they would close on the rabble.

The crowd broke. That mob, intent moments before on obliterating the embassy and tearing apart every being within it, became a scatter of frightened souls, interested only in getting tender behinds out of harm's way.

Howling, screaming, they pelted away, away from the knives, away from the terror.

There was not a flicker from Sten or the Gurkhas.

Sten barely nodded, and the Gurkhas, in unison, about-faced. With equally measured pace, they walked back inside the embassy grounds. The Bhor waited until the Gurkhas were inside, then port-armed and doubled after them.

The gates clanged shut.

Sten moved to a wall, made sure that he could not be seen outside, and sagged against it. A little close, he thought.

Jemedar Lalbahadur Thapa marched to him, came to attention, and saluted.

Sten returned the salute. "Very good."

"Not very good," the Gurkha said. "Anyone can frighten

sheep. Or children. The dead of the Imperial Guard are unavenged.''

Sten, too, turned grim. "Tonight," he promised. "Tonight, or the next night. And then we will not be playing child's games, nor with children.''

It took, in fact, three nights before that moving dot that was the telltale pistol came to rest.

Sten's operation order was verbal, with no record being made, and very short.

Twenty Gurkhas. Volunteers. Standby for special duties at 2300 hours. Sidearms only. Barracks dress.

Alex had lifted an eyebrow at that last: Why not the phototropic cammies?

"I'll want no one to wonder about this later," Sten said shortly. "This is authorized slaughter, not private revenge.''

The entire Gurkha detachment volunteered, of course.

Eight Bhor. All master-pilot rated. Four gravlighters. Basic weapons.

Again, Cind told him her entire team wanted to go in. Starting with her, she added.

Sten had said nothing about the nature of the special duties. Evidently he did not have to.

The soldiers assembled at 2200 hours. Outside, the sky was partially overcast, black clouds racing across the face of the four currently visible moons.

There was none of the Gurkha's usual prebattle barracking. They knew. As did, somehow, everyone in the embassy. The canteens and hallways were deserted.

Sten and Alex blackened their faces, put on cammies, and checked their weapons. Sten had his kukri, the knife, and a pistol. Alex had a handgun and a meter-long solid-steel bar he had wrapped with ordnance nonslip tape.

Alex went to the com room for a final look at the target—they had not only the pistol's beeper broadcasting, but four Frick & Fracks orbiting the area, and eight more grounded for area intelligence.

The Gurkhas and their eight Bhor pilots were drawn up in an embassy garage. Cind was in front of the formation.

Sten returned her salute and ordered the troops to open ranks for inspection. The Gurkhas had their kukris drawn. The chin straps of their slouch hats were tight under their lower lips—and their eyes were fixed on infinity.

Sten passed down the ranks. Merely as a formality, he checked one or two of their blades. They were, of course, hand-honed into razors.

He turned the formation back to Cind, and she ordered the weapons sheathed and ranks closed. Alex hurried out of a stairwell, a most grim smile on his face.

"'W' hae a feast a' friends," he said. "Alive-o, alive-o she cried. Th' sensors hae fifteen vultures gatherin't. Thae'll be havin't a conference or p'raps a party, but i' looks like th' whole clottin' cell's i' place."

Sten's acknowledging smile was equally humorless.

He gave the mission orders:

Four-man teams. After grounding, move to the target zone. Wait for the assault command. No guns to be used unless in complete emergency.

And:

No wounded. No prisoners.

They doubled out into the courtyard, where the gravlighters waited. The Bhor slid behind the controls, the Gurkhas boarded the first two—the others would be used for cleanup—and the lighters lifted, flying nap of the city toward the attack zone.

The target was less than twenty minutes flight time away. No one spoke. Sten, hanging over the pilot's right seat, saw the large-projection map on-screen and the blinking dot that represented that pistol and their objective.

It had come to rest two days earlier in a large mansion, surrounded by extended grounds, on a riverbank just outside and upstream from Rurik. A headquarters? A safe house?

Sten did not much care. He and Alex would shake the place— afterward.

The lighters grounded a few hundred meters from the sprawling house.

There was a half-alert sentry at the front and another at the rear. They were silenced.

Alex checked the main entrance for sensors or alarms. There were none.

Sten drew his kukri, and in a ripple, twenty-one other knives flashed in moonlight.

Then the corpse-glow vanished, obscured by clouds.

They went in.

The task took five minutes. There had been no outcry. When it was over, the bodies of fifteen butchered terrorists, and the two sentries, were lined up on the overgrown lawn. Cind searched the bodies for identification and anything intelligence-worthy. There was very little.

Sten and Alex took porta lights from one gravlighter and searched the mansion, in the high-speed, fine-tooth manner they had learned in basic intelligence. Neither of them spoke.

Alex broke the silence. "Ah hae indicators. Th' mob wae big fans ae Iskra. Look't all th' prop'ganda. All th' same. Jochi for Jochians an' thae. But Ah noo hae aught thae'll link th' quack solid."

"Nor do I."

"Clot. Whyn't the bassid happen t' slip oot ae th' evenin', t' hae a brew wi' his thugs, an' we'd find him here."

"That only happens in the livies."

"Ah know thae too. But a lad can dream, canna he? C'mon, Sten. Thae's nae f'r us here. Do Ah fire th' place?"

"Yes."

The bodies had already been loaded onto the two spare gravlighters. Sten waited until he could see flames build inside the mansion, then he ordered withdrawal.

The seventeen bodies would be weighted and dumped far out at sea.

Terrorism, properly implemented, was a double-edged sword. Dr. Iskra's people might have a bit of trouble recruiting more action cells after this one vanished into the night and fog.

Then the killers departed, having gone in with the long knife, and come out leaving nothing but blood and silence behind them.

CHAPTER THIRTY-ONE

FEW SOCIO-HISTORIANS WOULD argue that at the height of his reign the Eternal Emperor held more raw power than any being who had come before him.

His admirers—and they had always been legion—wrote that for most of that reign he chose not to exercise that power. The cynics say that was the key reason he held it for so long: The Emperor was the ideal third-party solution to many heated and bloody disputes.

In short, power was conferred because it was the safest place to put it.

So, when the Emperor set out to win more power still and to wield it against his enemies, he faced a formidable task. As soon as his intentions became clear he knew he would be opposed by despot and democrat alike.

He also knew that the first target his opponents would choose was his competency to rule. The Emperor was too much of a political fox not to understand that all his pluses had a flip-side negative.

The Emperor's triumphant return from death had thrilled his billions of subjects. Grand parades and public spectacles were staged for nearly two years. He was a hero beyond heroism.

But parades all have an end—usually in a back alley where the colorful bunting is revealed to be dull tatters. The thrill of victory soon turns to boredom with mundane daily life. Finally, the victory itself raises problem-solving to an impossible standard. Average beings become frustrated that their own personal problems persist.

They usually lay this to a gut belief that their leaders simply don't care. Socio-historians like to dodge this point. It's one of those basic truths that kick the pins from under their science. Which is why there's nothing a historian distrusts more than the truth.

To counter this political prime negative, the Emperor had to show success. In normal times, he could have pumped up the volume of any number of his efforts. Now, there was nothing but ruins and suffering all about him. To be sure, he had the Tahn war to blame for the ruins; suffering was laid to the excesses of the privy council.

Unfortunately both of those causes had become—in the words of that mythical pol, Lanslidejons'n—pretty old dogs to whup.

The Emperor didn't need excuses. He needed positive action.

When the Khaqan died he saw his opportunity. Here was an entire cluster in shambles. But it was a fixable shambles. Once it was repaired, the cluster would be portrayed as a mini portrait of his empire: Humans and ETs living and working happily together in the warm glow of Imperial benefice.

This is why he chose Dr. Iskra. The being had performed dully but well as a territorial governor. His books were politically correct, his passions tempered. And he surveyed well in the Altaic Cluster. When his name was added to a list of potential rulers, it was viewed favorably by all.

In the survey of Jochians, he came in first. With the Torks, he placed second—after Menynder. Just as he placed second after the favorite sons—an archaic political phrase, no longer implying gender or species—of the Bogazi and Suzdal.

Iskra seemed the safest of bets. The Emperor got into trouble by coppering that bet, then publicizing it Empire-wide.

Sten wasn't sent to the Altaics just because of his undisputed skills of turning ascorbic acid into a tasty, hot-weather drink. His accomplishments were so high-profile that his name guaranteed the attention of the media, hacks as well as pros.

Next, the Emperor launched a sophisticated, although purposely blunt, public relations campaign on Iskra's behalf.

There were thoughtful front-page think pieces planted in scholarly publications, discussing the plight of the citizens of the Altaic, pointing up the gulf between species in the past, and laying that division at the feet of the senile Khaqan. Praise was lavished on Professor Iskra in these pieces. There were frequent mentions of Iskra's abilities as a "healer of wounds."

The yellow press was fed the common touch. Iskra was portrayed as an intellect with a heart, a being sworn to live a Spartan existence as an example to his people. His dietary oddities were turned into sidebar recipes and columns on sure-fire ways to health and long life.

The PR clamor over Iskra was so loud that only a fool—and that fool a hermit—wouldn't know the Emperor's prestige was hung out to dry in the Altaics.

So when the bomb blew at the Imperial barracks on Rurik, more than the lives of the Emperor's troops were destroyed. His own plans were in danger of going up in the same smoke.

Sure, he had that big dog Mahoney waiting in the wings. But he couldn't unleash him yet. There was much political groundwork to prepare.

The Emperor needed a momentary, stopgap solution.

He acted swiftly. The solution was a news blackout.

Ranett was an old-fashioned see-for-herself newsbeing. She was also a legendary combat reporter who had covered the Tahn war from the front lines. She had kept her head low during the murderous years of the privy council. But she had kept on scribbling notes during those years. When the Emperor returned she had turned those notes into a stunning series of livie documentaries detailing the atrocities and stupidities of the privy council.

The last installment ran just as Iskra was assuming power in the Altaics. The broadcast was viewed by billions. It would be cynical to say that this was the reason the Eternal Emperor had insisted on personally thanking her in a tag to that final broadcast.

Ranett took this praise from on high in typical stride. When the vid camera shut off she turned to the Emperor and asked, "Your Majesty, what's with this clown, Iskra?"

The Emperor's smiling face went blank. He pretended he hadn't heard. His attention suddenly shifted to important matters of state. Before Ranett could repeat the question, the Emperor's front men had hustled him out the door.

So Ranett decided to learn the answer to the question herself. Her editor was not pleased.

"I got Altaic Cluster stories and Iskra beeswax comin' out my clottin' ears, Ranett. Who needs more? Besides, good news does not sell vid casts."

"I don't think it's all that good," Ranett answered. "Otherwise I wouldn't ask."

"That's a lotta drakh, Ranett. Anything happens in that cluster is good news. They been down so long, everything looks up to them. No, what we need is for you to go find some nice little war to cover. With lots of blood."

"If I go to the Altaics," Ranett said, "I think I'll find all the blood you want."

"Whatcha got besides reporter's instinct?"

Ranett just stared at her editor in eloquent silence. Then she shrugged, meaning: *instinct was all she had, but it was by-god bankable instinct*. The editor stared back at her. Hard. His silence was equally eloquent in this routine battle of the wills. Then he lifted an eyebrow, meaning: *are you really, really sure?* Ranett shrugged again.

The editor sighed. "You clottin' win. Go, already."

Ranett went low profile. She got a spare berth on a freighter bound for the Altaics. The only beings aware of her journey were her editor, the company clerk who made out the expense chits, and the freighter captain, a reliable drunk.

Ranett was one of those individuals who habitually find themselves in the right place at the right time. "I'm just lucky that way," she would tell her colleagues at the press club bar. They never believed it. They attributed her good work and fortune to "lies, bribes, and looks." Ranett didn't lie, would rather skip a story than grease a palm, and her looks were merely adequate.

Her luck struck again two E-days out of the Altaic Cluster, when she caught word of the disaster on Rurik. As she listened to the confused broadcasts on the ship's communicator, Ranett chortled. She would be the *only* major-league newsbeing in place to report on the incident and its certain nasty aftermath.

Ranett hustled off to her cabin to double up on her homework.

She had hauled along a big case of fiche on the cluster's dirty little history.

Eighteen E-hours out of Jochi, the captain came sober and shamefaced to her door. "Got some bad news, lady," he said. "We gotta go back."

Ranett pierced him with that look famous for buckling knees far sturdier than his. "Explain, please."

The captain shook his head. "I can't. Company veep wouldn't say why. Just said, do not deliver cargo to Jochi. And to get my butt back to Soward."

"So, forget the cargo," Ranett said. "You can still deliver me."

"No way, lady. Sorry."

"I'll pay extra. Double fare. Hell, I'll charter your whole damned ship!"

The captain sighed. This was wounding his mercenary soul. "I was ordered not to set down on Jochi. In any circumstances."

Ranett came to her feet. "You people have a contract with my company," she snapped. "And I expect it to be carried out—in full!"

She racked the captain up against the wall. "Now, get that buttwipe veep on the line. You hear?"

The captain heard.

She started with the veep and worked her way up to the president of the shipping line, scorching space from the Altaics to Prime in the process.

It was hopeless.

As the freighter turned maddeningly around and set off on its return journey, Ranett learned two things: The shipping line was as upset as she was at the action—there was an expensive and perishable cargo aboard the freighter. And the order had been initiated outside the company.

Meaning it was political.

Meaning the action could only be aimed at her.

Someone real important wanted to stop Ranett from getting the story on Jochi.

And there was nothing she could do.

Her editor was equally irked. "Nobody will admit it, but this has Imperial interference written all over it," he fumed on the deep-space hookup. "I jerked chains all the way up to Arundel, but it's no good. Everybody's scared."

"How'd they find out I was on the way?" Ranett asked.

"Snoops. Bugs. What else? I'm having our offices swept by security right now."

"What's our competition doing?" Ranett wanted to know.

"That's the only good news," the editor said. "It's not just us. Nobody but nobody with press credentials gets to the Altaics."

Enough details did leak out, however, to put the Emperor into a high rage.

BARRACKS BOMB TOLL SOARS, read one vid screamer. SHAME ON THE ALTAICS, read another. And there were many more: GUARDSMEN'S FAMILIES IN SHOCK . . . TRAGIC IMPERIAL FOUL-UP ON RURIK . . . The more thoughtful vid casts weighed in with: ALTAIC TURMOIL TIED TO ISKRA . . . QUESTIONS RAISED ON EMPEROR'S CHOICE OF OBSCURE PROFESSOR . . . ISKRA: THE SCHOLAR TYRANT.

"Next time I write a constitution," the Emperor railed, "I want an Official Secrets Act with *real* damned teeth in it. I want prison terms. I want firing squads—I want clottin' torture chambers, dammit!"

The woman with the lush young figure and old pol eyes applauded. "No problem with that drakh," Avri said. "Last polls I ran on the media showed the rubes are with ya, boss. Ten percent think a free press is important. Sixty-five percent say kick those rabble-rousers off the sleigh. And the other twenty-five percent were so dumb they thought the Evening News was a livie sitcom."

The Emperor's rage turned to booming laughter. "That's what I liked about you from the start, Avri," he said. "You always cut to the chase."

"I got my masters in scalp hunting on Dusable," she said. "But I got my Ph.D. watching you in action . . . sir." Avri looked the Emperor up and down in frank admiration. "I never met or heard of a politician living or dead who coulda pulled what you pulled."

The Emperor made humble noises. "I didn't invent anything.

I just stole from the masters." He gave Avri a wolfish grin. "Of course, I put a few new twists on the rules."

"I'll say you clottin' did, uh, sir."

"Knock off the sir," the Emperor said. "When we're in private, of course. There's no room for respect in a business that votes graveyards."

The Emperor had met Avri on his long road back from death to the Imperial crown. He had needed to fix an election on Dusable, and she was handling the perfect candidate for the job: an empty-headed pretty boy who would sit and heel and fetch in those votes like a good little political doggy.

At the time, he had mainly appreciated Avri's crooked brain. But as he looked at her now, poured into a black body suit, other areas of interest came to mind. Avri caught the look. She gave him a "don't mind at all" smile and stretched back in her seat to give him a better view. The Emperor felt a stir. He put it aside for a while. Let it age in the cooler.

"How are things lining up in Parliament?" he asked.

"Real nice," Avri said, a bit disappointed. But she brightened quickly as she took up her favorite game: counting yeas and nays. "Tyrenne Walsh has been practicing that speech we worked up for him. The dumb clot doesn't understand a word he's saying—but he *sounds* positively yummy." Walsh was the pretty boy Avri and the Emperor had put into the top job on Dusable—toppling one of the canniest and dirtiest old political bosses in the Empire, while they were at it.

Now the Emperor had called in Avri to launch his plan to turn the independent Imperial provinces into under-his-thumb dominions.

"Here's how I have it mapped," Avri said. "Walsh gives the lead-off speech, just like you said. He makes with the high-minded buzzwords to start: duty, loyalty, patriotism . . . all those words that hit the symbolism buzzer hard."

The Emperor nodded. "Fine. Fine. Then he makes the big statement, right?"

"That's what you wanted," Avri said, "but I think you're moving for the bottom line too fast. I mean, we don't want him to sound like your stooge."

The Emperor chuckled. "Heaven forbid."

"Well, that's how it'll sound," Avri said. "What we want him to do is announce that he's going to be the first big boss to turn over his system to you."

"You mean, to become one of my dominions," the Emperor said.

"Sameo, sameo," Avri said. "Of course, in Walsh's case it don't matter. He's already being run. By yours truly. But some of the other types are used to calling their own shots. They're not gonna go that easy."

The Emperor saw her point. "What did you have in mind?"

"A hero sandwich," Avri said. "If we put enough garbage in this bun, nobody'll notice how thin the slices of ham and cheese are. And they'll have voted and be halfway home before the heart-burn cuts in."

"Go on," the Emperor said.

"Okay, so we wave the flag like you said." Avri made a crude pumping gesture with a closed fist. "Then we lay on some personal suffering biz. You know: the letter from the little old lady who's sending in her last credit to help bail out the Empire. And I did a vid layout on some starving infants. Good creepy drakh. Orange hair. Swollen bellies. Real neato heart tuggers."

"Blood, sweat, and baby urine," the Emperor said. "It always works."

"Sure. With your left hand. Okay, now get this. While they're still gaggin' on the screwed up kids, I wanna smack 'em good with an old soldier's routine I worked up."

"This is getting pretty interesting," the Emperor said. "I might vote for this thing four or five times myself."

"You better," Avri said. "You need *margin* on this sucker . . . Now. I dug up some old general of yours. Been retired thirty some years. More dirt in his head than brains. I got him all worked up about the quote 'plight of the Empire' end quote. Got him good and weepy. At the end, he struggles to his feet—I put him on crutches—and calls on all the beings in your Empire to pull together.

"He does a terrific unity whine. Says this is the greatest emergency in his lifetime. And that no sacrifice is too great to ratchetaratcheta—it'll work like a charm. I guarantee it. Laid it on a test group last night. Not a dry eye in the house. Best of all, the audience emptied its pockets for the Imperial relief fund. Best bucks per capita those frauds have ever seen."

"Then Walsh makes the announcement?" the Emperor asked.

"Then Walsh makes the announcement."

"Great job," the Emperor said. "But I have one wrinkle to add to your problem."

"What's that?"

"That boost I'm planning in the AM2 tax?"

Avri nodded. "Yeah. Good idea. Scare clot out of the holdouts. What about it?"

"I want to make it retroactive. To all the AM2 since the end of the Tahn war."

Avri whistled. "Might scare 'em too much."

"Sorry. You're going to have to work around it, somehow."

Avri's eyes suddenly brightened. "Maybe if the general died at the end. On-camera collapse type of thing. So we're leading with quote 'dying last words' end quote. He's pretty feeble. I imagine the techs can give him a stroke for the retake."

"Bad idea," the Emperor said.

"Yeah. Somebody might find out. Leak it."

"I'm not worried about that," the Emperor said. "It's just his dying words will upstage Walsh. And he's the boy carrying this thing."

Avri caught his logic. "That's why you're the boss," she said. "I'll figure something. It'll be easy."

The interview over, Avri was giving the Emperor "the look" again—eyes misting over, squirming in her seat. "Anyway," she husked, "that's the plan."

"No quarrels from me," the Emperor said. "Put it into action."

He returned the look. Let his gaze run across her body. Starting from the toes . . . working slowly up.

"Will there be anything . . . else?" Avri asked.

The Emperor let it wait. Then: "Maybe . . . later."

"Did I mention my secretary?" Avri asked. She licked her lips. "She's been a lot of . . . help on this thing."

"I'll have to thank her some time," the Emperor said.

"I could call her . . . now."

"Make it personal?" the Emperor said, voice low.

"Real personal. Just the . . . three of us."

"Call her," the Eternal Emperor said.

CHAPTER THIRTY-TWO

POYNDEX SCREENED THE report yet again. It had not changed since he had last read it, three minutes ago. If it had not come from a long-trusted—as much as any spymaster ever trusts a source—field agent, he would have thought either someone was trying to shuck him, or else the report was on a loop from years before in the days of the privy council.

Poyndex had promised himself, back on Earth, that he would be "good," that he would quit running agents and trying to figure out what was "really" happening. Of course, he could not. No one who had ever walked in the shadow world ever believed that the truth was what was in the spotlight.

According to the report, someone was putting large credits behind the Cult of the Emperor. Just as Kyes of the council had years earlier. And this someone was not an easily findable "anonymous benefactor." The credits were coming in through multiple sources, all of which could be traced just so far, and then hit a stone wall.

Poyndex idly ran the cult through an open-search function to see if anything else of interest was going on.

In a few minutes he had an answer.

A great deal was occurring. High-ranking cult members that a file had automatically been opened on, back in Poyndex's Mercury Corps days, were realizing their dreams. They were being promoted—frequently over the heads of their former superiors—quite rapidly.

Hair lifted suddenly on the back of Poyndex's neck. His fingers slashed keys, and he bailed out of the search. His forehead beaded sweat.

Poyndex considered, then grimaced.

He was probably being paranoiac. But the same sense of danger shrilled that had howled through his system after that bomb in the Imperial guts had been removed.

He was grateful he had programmed his computer to work with cutouts. The search, for instance, could be traced by a sufficiently skilled expert. But the trace would lead to an open library terminal on a faraway frontier world.

The Cult of the Emperor was active . . .

He slid open a hidden cover on the side of the keyboard and forced two tabs together, activating an OVERRIDE command and breaking a fingernail in the process.

There was but one being Poyndex could think of who could play that many cultists like puppets on a string, and who would also have that many sterile channels to pour money down . . .

His computer instantly wiped itself sterile and was overwritten, just as standard military procedure dictated. Then it was automatically wiped yet again . . . and again overwritten.

The Eternal Emperor himself . . .

Poyndex's computer clicked, and the third, final program was added, files and a program that excluded any action that Poyndex had taken within the last E-week.

But what benefit could the Emperor gain from the Cult of the Eternal Emperor?

Poyndex felt a little safer.

Did he want to have himself made a god, for pity's sake?

And now there was a chill beyond zero Kelvin, and Poyndex felt that never again would he be safe, never again could he not look over his shoulder knowing what he now believed true.

Sr. Ecu, the universe's diplomat emeritus, banked, nearly spun out, and wished that his race understood the unquestionably leavening benefits of profanity and obscenity.

Below him was arctic desolation.

Gray seas crashed high against a solitary rock pinnacle to his right. To his left a monstrous iceberg floated. It was bright blue on the slate seas—the only primary color as far as the eye could see. An achingly lonely color.

Ecu did not wish to judge this world, but he found it had all the charm of the Christian religion's hell, with the fires out.

On an ice floe far below, a dot moved. He focused on the dot, and the dot became a huge, obese aquatic creature, a creature whose blubbery hide, tusks, and skin suited it for this frozen hell, who probably thought the weather a pleasant spring freshet.

It made little sense that the unknown being on that ice cube below appeared to be a primitive fish-eater—but in fact could well be one of this world's premiere philosophers. Or poets.

A shearing gust caught him, and Ecu almost lost control once more. His three-meter-long tail thrashed air, trying to stabilize, as his great white wings curled, reconfiguring lift areas to the blast—their red-tipped winglets trying to damp Ecu's overcontrolling.

He was too old and too dignified for this nonsense, solo-flying through a polar storm as if he were a spratling who had just discovered flight.

He also thought that everything to do with this self-appointed project of his smacked of the low-grade melodramas that children and bumpkins appreciated, with clearly marked heroes and villains—One Being against the Forces of Evil, and so forth.

Let alone that Sr. Ecu actually believed, and winced from the belief, that he was the only being who seemed to be aware of this great evil, an evil that could bring everything shattering down. This, his thoughts continued, was absurdity, and he prided himself on being someone who had learned that there was seldom truth and almost never light. Everything was shades of gray, to be analyzed and interpreted most carefully.

Perhaps Rykor would have attendants waiting, who would skillfully sedate the Manabi and escort him to a padded room where he could spend the rest of his days babbling about the Eternal Emperor.

Perhaps that was why he had sent the material ahead of him,

material that he had laboriously transferred into an exotic code they'd used back during the days of the tribunal—when the members of the privy council were to be brought to trial for their crimes.

Sr. Ecu tried to bring his thoughts under control, just as he wished, with equal lack of success, that he could cause this williwaw to subside into a calm. He thought, ruefully, that one reason his mind was so undisciplined was that he was frankly terrified. Fear was a feeling that always prevented logical analysis.

Not that he was irrational to feel it.

Sr. Ecu might have served the Eternal Emperor on many occasions, and even convinced his race to ignore their long-held neutrality and clandestinely back the Empire during the Tahn war, but he was under no illusions as to what the Emperor would most likely do if he was aware of Sr. Ecu's thoughts, beliefs, and mission.

Which was one reason he had vanished from his own world, telling no one his mission or destination. His passage to Rykor's home world had been made on one of the Romany free-trading ships. Another relationship, he realized, that had come from the tribunal days, and had originally been created by that man who had wanted anyone to be able to fly: Sten.

Sten had drawn Ecu into his involvement with the tribunal with a simple gift: a kit-built holographic display of an ancient Earth "air circus," where ground-bound humans jeopardized their lives by riding in twin-wing combustion-powered aircraft any self-respecting *archaeopteryx* would have sneered at.

Seeing the model, Sr. Ecu had marveled:

"Did they really do that . . . I've never really appreciated before what it was like to be permanently grounded by an accident of genes. My God, how desperately they wanted to fly."

"Beings will risk a great deal," Sten had said, *"for a little freedom."*

He wondered how the human was doing in his assignment in the Altaic Cluster. He hoped well—but he suspected, especially considering the recent news blackout on the area, that the situation, already bad, was growing worse.

He considered if Rykor somehow thought his mad theory to be

correct, whether Sten would be brought in. How? In what capacity? he jeered at himself. And to do what?

Are you starting to do what these humans do, and think that any time a seemingly irresolvable problem appears, the solution is to collectively throw up your hands and turn everything over to a ruler in shining armor, who, of course, turns out to be a tyrant?

That was what had created the present situation.

That, Ecu corrected himself, and AM2.

AM2. That was the stumbling block. Without AM2 everything in the Empire, its triumphs as well as its crimes, would be lost.

And AM2 was what would prevent, Ecu finished morosely, finding any real solution to this problem.

The horizon cleared, and he saw an island ahead. It was as grim and uninviting as the rest of this world, jagged rocky spires jutting up from bouldered shallows. Desolate—but his white sensing whiskers told him there was life down there.

Then his eyes confirmed his other sense, as he saw movement on one of the island's rocky "beaches." More beings, like the one who had waved to him, were sprawled on the icy wave-washed slabs as if they were humans basking in a tropic sun.

He heard a bellow over the wind-howl as one of those beings stretched to its full height on rear flippers, and *hoonked* a greeting. Rykor . . . it must be.

The being humped a few awkward meters on land, dove, and became eely grace into a breaking wave, then vanished.

Now, Sr. Ecu thought in irritation, how am I supposed to emulate her behavior? Am I supposed to follow her underwater like I'm triphibious?

Then black rock moved aside and there was the entrance to a wide tunnel yawning in the middle of one of the island's cliffs. Around it and above, on the cliff top, antennae bristled.

Ecu tucked and plummeted, reflexively curling his winglets even though the tunnel was more than wide enough to allow a medium-size starfreighter entry.

This was Rykor's home—and her office.

Ian Mahoney frequently compared Rykor to a walrus in jest. But in fact, the similarities were only physical—to a degree—and

Rykor's species was also aquatic by evolution and preference. The physical resemblance wasn't that great—Rykor was a third again as big as the biggest Earth *Odobenus*, with a body length of over five meters and weight of more than two thousand kilos.

Her species, however, was known for its intellect, particularly in areas requiring intuitive analysis and the ability to draw extrapolative conclusions from fixed data. Therefore, they were poets. Philosophers. City- and world-planners. And, as in the case of Rykor, psychologists.

When she retired, she was the highest-ranked psychologist in Imperial Service. She also had been used, sub rosa, by Ian Mahoney—then head of Mercury Corps and Mantis—as his specialist in the headworkings of spies, saboteurs, assassins, and traitors, Imperial and unfriendly.

She had been convinced to come out of safety and seclusion by Sten, when he had set up the tribunal. She had then, like everyone else involved in what had seemed triumph at the time, been offered anything and everything. But after the Emperor's return, she had realized why she had retired in the first place: there were volumes to be written on human and other species' behavior patterns that she and no one else had experienced and could possibly explain.

Plus Rykor had a surfeit of what was, truthfully, bending her skills into the service of someone else to convince the analyzed person/culture to behave in a certain manner.

Now she was being asked to use her talents once more. But for a far greater purpose—this time by Ecu.

"This is most unusual," Rykor apologized. "I had this chamber constructed to deal with my land-bound friends and clients. And also as a personal joke, since I spent so many years serving the Empire from either a saltwater tank or a gravchair."

Sr. Ecu waggled his sensing whiskers, politely indicating amusement—his species needed no ego reinforcement for being clever.

This chamber *was* fitting revenge. It was a high-ceilinged, wide-mouthed tidal cave, whose above-water entrance had been closed with a transparent wall. Ecu thought the wall was probably mobile and would rise and fall with the tide. Looking out to sea, there appeared to be nothing between the crashing surf and the viewer except those spray-drenched boulders that formed a partially sheltering lagoon outside. Wind and sea sounds were miked and their level controlled by a mixboard. Entrance to this cave was by diving under the wall for Rykor and her fellows, or by solid passageways for land beings.

Ecu hovered just above the artificial shelf Rykor had built for land-bound visitors. It, too, was tide-responsive and would rise and fall so that it always was a few centimeters above the gentle waves inside this cave.

The shelf was fitted with all sorts of comforts and devices, from viewers to coms to computers. Above this conference room were apartments and dining areas.

Rykor's own quarters and work areas were reached by underwater tunnels that led from chamber to chamber. The equipment Rykor used in her normal course of work was either environmentally insensitive or sealed.

"I am," Rykor said, "somewhat unfamiliar with the . . . etiquette, let alone the practicalities, of entertaining an aerial being. Do you, well . . ."

"Roost?" Ecu's whiskers twitched once more, and, after a moment of slight embarrassment, Rykor's own face bristles ruffled and her sonic-blast laughter echoed around the chamber until the active acoustic system damped it.

"No," he said. "My race lands but seldom. And then for specific purposes." He did not explain; Rykor did not ask.

"May I offer you refreshment? Since the Manabi are not the most commonly entertained race in this Empire, it was most hard to learn what you preferred to ingest. But I gather the following, in spray form, is considered pleasurable. Even though these microorganisms aren't exactly duplicated on this world, we have synthesized the mixture."

Her flippers stretched and touched keys on a floating panel beside her. An overhead screen flashed a chemical formula. Ecu scanned it. Again, he "laughed."

"Your source was correct, Rykor. We do enjoy that organic compote. But it also renders us hors d' flight, and we become 'pissed as newts,' as our mutual friend Kilgour puts it. Perhaps later. Perhaps when we have begun our discussions I will feel less like a fool, less worried, and more able to relax.

"Or you may wish to sedate me with that formula, since I fear my basic neural reactions are becoming unpredictable."

"Manabi," Rykor said flatly, "don't go insane."

"I may be the first."

The cave was still, except for the sound of the sea and the wind, dimly in the background. Rykor floated motionlessly for a while.

"No," she said, firmly. "You are not insane. I have gone through your material. Analyzed it both intellectually and electronically. Further, I allowed my most trusted aide—do not start: he is, in fact, one of my sister's pups and is to be trusted, since the corruptions of the Empire don't interest us, and thus far nobody has attempted to subvert us with fishing rights on an Imperial river on Earth."

She laughed again and Ecu felt himself relax.

"First, though," she said, "let me express my thanks for that parcel you sent. It's the first real 'book' from ancient Earth I've owned. A question: Was the volume originally waterproofed?"

"I had that done."

"Ah. I surmised. I found it most interesting, and charming, in a sad sort of way. I imagined this primitive human, writing in the darkest of dark ages, sitting there and staring out at what must have been terrible times.

"In those days, there would have been nobody but witchfreuds, I think they were called, who cast spells and made vile potions in cooking pots, their couches spread around the great tribal fire that kept out the real and imagined monsters of the dark." She whuffled sympathy. "And so this poor man imagined that one day there would be rules for psychology. That it would become a science. Except that—what did he call it? Psychohistory? It was a fascinating conceit.

"I, myself, find that dream fascinating. Although I realize that if we can't solve the n-body problem in astronomy, the tera-cubed-tera-plus bodies that constitute intelligent life will never be fitted into a computation.

"I must say, however, I found the scribe's hero, that Selden human, rather repellant. Far too reminiscent of some of my creche tutors, full of false truth, wretched prejudice, and themselves.

"But I digress.

"I see why you sent me that present, however, and how this fictional, fumbling attempt to find order in an entropic universe and equally entropic Empire pertains to the data you provided.

"A question. Were you selective in the material—choosing only data that supported your theory?"

"I was not," Ecu said. "I attempted to provide as complete an assemblage as I knew how."

"Your experience in diplomacy suggests that you do know how to be fair," Rykor said. "I took the liberty of reducing your raw data into symbolic logic."

Again, she touched keys, and several screens lit. Ecu, even though he did not use symbology a great deal in his art, knew the discipline.

It took almost an hour for the data, even crunched into computer language, to screen.

As gibberish to most people, it may have been a little less depressing. But not to the two experienced beings in the sea cave. Finally the last screen blanked.

"Is my reduction approximately correct?" Rykor asked.

"Not approximately. Exactly." Ecu's wings sagged. The situation was as bad as he had thought it was.

"Summarizing your theses verbally," Rykor went on, coldly, clinically, "it's evident that the Empire is in the direst straits. Not cause for total panic, though, since this isn't the first or the fiftieth time that Imperial catastrophe has loomed. However, you have further theorized that this economic, social, and political decline is being accelerated by the Empire itself. Specifically, by the actions the Eternal Emperor has taken since his . . . return."

Sr. Ecu said, "That was where I feared I was becoming less than competent in my thinking."

"Not at all. Since I've reassured you as to your sanity, would you now care for that refreshment? Because it's now my turn to reason, and to add some interesting data that I have gotten on my own, since your package arrived."

"Thank you. I shall indulge."

"It is in a pressure container, just to your right. Activated—yes, with that rather large lever."

Moisture hissed into the air. Sr. Ecu felt himself lifted and momentarily was reminded of the time, once on Earth, when he had seen simple avians frolicking in a spray of water.

Rykor treated herself to what appeared to be a slab of flame-dried peat. "Piscean leather," she explained. "Hung just beyond the highest reaches of the ocean spray, and wind-dried. It's as close to a narcotic as my sometimes simplistic race has managed. Although research goes on.

"Continuing. I noticed that you included in your data the disaster our young crusader, Sten, is trying to solve. The Altaic Cluster. He's sustaining a madman, as you're aware. A Dr. Iskra. Did you know that this Iskra is a being who's been supported in exile for years by the Emperor? To control on the former ruler.

"I further found that Sten is under direct orders from the Emperor that Iskra must be kept in office, regardless of cost."

Ecu's body rocked in a nonexistent blast of wind. "What is your source on this?" he asked.

"I cannot say. My colleague remains in the system, and therefore in danger."

Rykor stopped and her tail flippers crashed down against the water's surface. "How odd," she mused. "To hear myself say a friend's life is in danger because that friend is close to our respected ruler, and because this friend speaks a bit of the truth."

"I, myself, have felt potentially in physical jeopardy," Ecu confessed.

Rykor did not answer that, but went on. "A second fact. I don't recall when I stumbled upon it. But I assure you it was in the course of some legitimate field of inquiry. As I said, I disremember the circumstances, but I found myself wondering just what the Emperor gained—directly, monetarily—from his rule. Or was the mere exercise of power adequate recompense? So I investigated.

"Obviously I was most careful in my curiosity. But I found that, indeed, the Emperor had rather incredible funds, invested in various arenas where his governing policies would also prove financially rewarding. The investments were made with multiple cutouts that could never be traced back to the Emperor. I found such an action neither moral nor immoral. These investments, I further learned, had been used during times of disaster to support the economy . . . as well as his policies. Which would suggest these profits would be considered 'moral' by most. I think they're called a slushy fund by humans.''

''Slush.''

''Is the spray affecting—oh. Yes. Slush would be correct. A few days ago, I very carefully rechecked a couple of those funds.

''The Emperor's personal wealth is increasing at a monstrous rate, second by second. In these times, which most would call depressed, our own ruler is vastly profiting from his own Empire's poverty.''

''That's insane,'' Ecu said, his normal smoothness broken.

''For the first time, I agree with your application of the word, even though it is clinically without meaning. By the way—some support for what you just said. Have you been watching the Eternal Emperor when he appears on livie casts lately? More and more rarely, of course, and when he does the angles are favorable and remote. But look closely at the way his eyes shift, like a whipped Earth canine waiting for another beating—or else someone who is slipping further and further into what used to be called a manic-depressive psychosis.''

Again, Sr. Ecu wished that profanity provided a meaningful form of expression to his race. Rykor was suggesting that the Empire was now ruled by a madman, and the thought was monstrously inconceivable. Yet, his backbrain reminded him how many times had he dealt with insane rulers and felt vague, impersonal sympathy for the poor beings they tyrannized.

''Another piece of the puzzle,'' Rykor continued. ''The Emperor has ordered large increases in military development. The Cairenes, for instance, were desolated when the Tahn war ended. Military shipbuilding was no longer necessary, and their patron, Sullamora, was killed.

''Then, and I do not understand this, the Cairenes somehow became AM2-fat during the course of the Imperial return. You'll recall that the Emperor's physical return was on a ship from the

Cairenes's central system of Dusable. Very well, somehow the Emperor was helped, and the beings of Dusable were rewarded.

"That is the way politics has worked. So ignore the original Golden Calf and his Eggs, or whatever creature it was.

"But their prosperity has continued. Within the last E-year, I've learned, nearly a hundred contracts have been placed with the shipyards of the Cairenes. None of them were put out for open bids. In these times, when there is peace, why build warships? There are more than enough left from the wars. In fact, the scrap yards are full of never-commissioned hulks."

"Could it be," Ecu theorized, deliberately playing devil's advocate, "what I have heard the Emperor call pork-barreling?"

"It could. But I dislike using anything nonsentient to reason from. It's my discipline's prejudice, of course.

"But here is another part of that same puzzle piece. A colleague of mine—actually she was one of the humans I attempted to train into logical paths—had an interesting assignment. She's an expert at the psychology of military recruiting. She prepared a campaign, under very exact orders, for the Tahn worlds."

"What?"

"Yes. Our former enemy, now even further depressed than the Empire. Nothing is being done to improve their economic lot, by the way. But recruiting officers are blanketing these worlds and signing up recruits."

"It's evil," Ecu said, "but it happens that the military, historically, offers its shilling most loudly where poverty is the worst."

"Correct. But if you remember, the Emperor was determined, at war's end, that the old military ravings that the Tahn called their homicidal/suicidal 'culture' would be destroyed. But today these Imperial recruiters are using a campaign that rings every change on the idea that it's time for the warrior Tahn to rise up and redeem themselves. Prove they still have the thews of their elders, even though those elders fought in an evil cause. Now it is time for you to help defend the Empire. And so on and so forth."

Ecu drifted high up, near the cave's apex, while he thought on this. "It might make sense, to an economic babe, to spend your way out of a depression by purchasing unneeded weaponry," he said. "But you do not hire soldiers or sailors. They are simply too expensive and too troublesome in time of peace. Simple welfare and breadlines are more cost efficient, if you are one who can think that cold-bloodedly. Why look for soldiers,'' he finished, ''if there is no enemy?''

''Possibly the Emperor *does* see an enemy,'' Rykor said softly.

''Consider the nature of kings,'' she said in a near-whisper. ''Consider what they become.''

''But the Emperor is Eternal,'' Ecu said, his normal equanimity shattered. ''This has never happened before.''

''No. It has not. Something has changed. But that is not my concern.'' She tapped keys again. ''It's deceptive, and very easy, for each generation, as it ages, to whine about Armageddon. But computers do not become irascible and curmudgeonly.

''I ran progs. Predictions.

''We'll go through this later, after we have both rested, to make sure that there is no error. But the conclusions I've ended with are these: The Empire is finally proving that it is no genetic sport. Like all Empires before it, it is following the path of hardening, corruption, decay, and is now doomed to destruction. Not from any historical process, or from any external enemy. But because of one being: The Eternal Emperor.''

That had been Sr. Ecu's final judgment exactly.

''I assume,'' Rykor said, after some time and thought had passed, ''that you came here for more than confirmation of your sanity. You are far too rational a being to travel this far, at this risk to your race and person, just to want reinforcement.''

''Yes,'' Ecu said. And suddenly the thought flashed through him: Here he was, master diplomat. Consultant. Expert adviser. Gray eminence for half a thousand rulers, and a being who had even proffered advice to the Eternal Emperor himself, and whose advice had been accepted. Here he was, needing Rykor's advice, as if he were an emotionally troubled spratling.

He understood just why Rykor was held in the respect she was.

''You want to know,'' Rykor said, ''what we must do to prevent this.''

''Yes,'' Ecu said once more.

''I do not know. I have considered, and will consider again. But I have no answer.

"However, I will offer you one thought, since everything I've said is slightly bleaker than midnight. Consider this. What would have happened if the Emperor had not returned? I mean, returned at all, not returned at a later date."

"We would have had chaos," Ecu said. "A collapse into barbarism."

"I agree. But it would've stemmed from one reason only—the loss of AM2, correct? The presence or absence of the Emperor is not a significant enough factor to bring everything crashing down."

"Yes," Sr. Ecu said cautiously. "I agree with that."

"Thank you. Now, isn't it true that every race, every culture, has had dark ages? Sometimes many of them?"

Sr. Ecu's body ducked—an assenting nod.

"And they are always recovered from?"

"I cannot say always," Ecu said. "Races might well have slipped into total barbarism, and we have not encountered them. Or degenerated into complete anarchy and race-suicide."

"Eliminate the always, then," Rykor went on. "But it is true, generally. Isn't it also true that once the blight of savagery is thrown off, the next stage is a renaissance?"

"Yes. And you cheer me, even if I don't believe that would apply to the Empire. Its presence is too large, too ancient, and too omnipotent."

"Not if AM2 is taken out of the equation."

"But the Emperor is the only being who knows where AM2 exists in its raw state, or how it is synthesized."

"Sr. Ecu," Rykor reprimanded gently, "you're far too educated and sophisticated to allow yourself to think there is but one inventor who can produce a particular invention. One painter who can produce that picture. Or one philosopher who is capable of producing a social system."

Sr. Ecu said, "Again, you have cheered me. But I'm afraid I don't believe that putting together some sort of manhattan project to look for AM2 would be successful. The privy council seemed to have tried hard enough."

"The privy council was, and again I've got to use semantically loaded words, evil. A less charged word would be self-oriented.

But I'll use evil. Evil, being the opposite of good—both words are in quotes—is, by definition, shortsighted, self-serving, lazy, and dishonest. Therefore their search could only be limited and doomed to failure."

"Rykor, how can you remain such an optimist, after all your experience?" Ecu wondered, amused. "I have seen evil triumph at least as frequently as good."

"As Kilgour would say in that primitive dialect he believes to be an understandable language, a clean mind, a clean body. Take your pick.

"Now," she said, heaving her bulk out of the water, onto the shelf, and into a gravchair, "shall we move to an upper chamber, where food and more of your spray awaits? We needn't panic tonight. Even entropy moves at a measured, slow pace."

Ecu floated above her gravchair as they moved up, deeper into the crag's depths, still considering their ultimate problem. He realized that somehow both of them had rather casually accepted the fact that the Emperor must be removed, or at least rendered harmless. Putting aside the matter of AM2, the next question would be, Who could conceivably, in the human phrase, bell this colossal cat?

A name passed through his brain once more:

That man who wanted anyone to fly.

Sten.

CHAPTER THIRTY-THREE

THE ECHOES OF the barracks bombing were still reverberating when Iskra moved to consolidate and extend his power. The Eternal Emperor's news blackout played right into his hands.

Iskra hit the airways with a blistering attack on those (unnamed) traitors who had humiliated the Altaic Cluster by their cowardly attack on the Emperor's peacekeeping forces. He declared martial law. Set a one-hour-after-dawn and one-hour-before-dusk curfew. Banned all demonstration, public protests, and strikes. He also hinted darkly at "other measures" that would be "revealed at the appropriate time." He ended with an impassioned plea that all citizens search their "souls and their neighbors' souls" for any sign of disloyalty.

After generations of violent repression, people knew what was going to happen next. Some dug into mattresses and gardens for bribe money. Some made lists of enemies they could nark on. Most cowered in their homes and waited for the crash of bootheels and rifle butts thundering on doors.

But experienced as they were in the politics of fear, the beings of the Altaic Cluster were not braced for what followed.

Milhouz was lean and proud in his new black uniform with its rakish beret and silver "Students for Iskra" badge. He had a captain's tab on one shoulder and a Purity Corps patch on the other.

He hoisted his pistol and snarled orders to his eager, youthful forces. "I want this timed perfectly. Get into position—quietly, dammit! And when I give the signal, we all rush at once. Got it?"

There was a hushed chorus of "yessirs."

Milhouz made imperious go-for-it motions with his hands. The Purity Corps sprang into action.

His battering ram squad took point. Milhouz and the main force followed behind. They all trotted down the dark, tree-lined lane that led to the central Rurik library. Jochi's moons dimly lit the scene.

The lights were burning late at the library that night. The head librarian—an elderly Tork named Poray—had lobbied hard for a permit to ignore the curfew and work late that night. His official reason: to comb through the stacks for seditious material banned under Iskra's emergency decrees.

The librarian's real intent was to rescue as much of this material as possible. Poray and his staff put out a call to all like-minded intellectuals. It was a drill they had performed many times during the rule of the Khaqans. In the past, this tradition had saved the most valued texts in the library system.

As the dark shapes of Milhouz's Purity Corps fanned out around the building, Poray was once more mourning his choices. He couldn't save everything. Enough seditious material had to be turned over to make a large display of the intellectual community's loyal intentions.

He eyed the trolleys of fiche and books being rushed to the secret vaults in the library's basement. To one side was a mound of material he was planning to give to Iskra's book burners.

It was a very small mound.

Poray sighed. He was not doing well. He had to cut harder. He hefted two elderly volumes. They were real books—the library's sole copies of the works.

One was a much-thumbed *Fahrenheit 451*, by Ray Bradbury. The other was a pristine copy of *Common Sense*, by the ancient thinker Thomas Paine.

Poray hated playing intellectual god. It tormented him that his tastes were the sole judge of what should stay and what should be destroyed.

He looked at *Common Sense* again. Then at *Fahrenheit 451*. He shrugged.

Bradbury went on a trolley of books to be saved.

Common Sense was for the burning. Forgive me, Sr. Paine, Poray thought.

There was a smash of glass and wrench of metal as Milhouz struck.

Poray gaped as black-uniformed youths thundered into the library. There were screams of terror from his staff and volunteers.

"Down with the intelligentsia!" someone bellowed.

Milhouz thundered toward Poray, pistol coming up. Poray instinctively raised Thomas Paine as a shield.

Milhouz fired.

Poray fell to the ground.

As dead as *Common Sense*.

* * *

The line from the grocer's stretched half a kilometer. Hundreds upon hundreds of hungry beings were lined up, ration cards ready for the moment the doors opened.

They had been waiting since the morning curfew lifted, which meant seven hours for the first being in line. All under a sun that had dawned a scorcher.

"It gets later and later every day," grumbled one elderly woman.

"And less and less food to buy," muttered another.

"All garbage," said a third. "Dr. Iskra should come down here and look at this slop. He'd have the storekeep's head for being such a thief."

Before anyone could answer, the line surged forward. "They're opening!" someone shouted. Then the line came to a jolting halt. There were shocked gasps. People in the back craned their necks to see what was happening at the front.

The grocer's was not opening.

Instead, a line of troops was trotting out from the alley, weapons ready.

An officer's voice bullhorned over the crowd: "No one will move. This is an inspection of papers. You will have ration cards displayed in the left hand. Citizenship papers in the other."

The crowd grumbled, yet moved quickly to do the officer's bidding.

But the old woman who had complained about the long wait for food had other ideas. She stepped out of the crowd and hobbled up to the officer.

"You should be ashamed of yourself, young man," she said. "We are all hungry. And we have waited hours and hours to buy food for our families."

The officer shot her where she stood. He kicked her still-twitching corpse. "There you go, grandmother. Now, you don't have to wait."

The Bogazi neighborhood watch commander picked her way along the barricade, checking for gaps in the protective jumble and inspecting the guards at their posts. The barricade proved as sound as her last inspection, her guards alert as when they first came on duty.

She looked over the sleeping neighborhood. Not a light in a window, a stir in a hutch. This is good, she thought. This is very good. Then she heard a low sound from behind her. She whirled around. The sound was gone. Imagination only, she thought. I am silly being.

The gunship popped up above the barricade, chain guns yammering.

The watch commander was cut in half before she had time to gurgle a warning.

Two more gunships jumped into view, opening fire on the neighborhood. Within minutes the hutches were burning and Bogazi were streaming out. Some were wounded. Some were carrying wounded. All were paralyzed with fear.

Jochi troops smashed through the barricade. They were followed by a long line of gravlighters.

One hour later the trucks were loaded with the Bogazi survivors and heading out into the night.

The next day, dozers scooped up the dead along with smoking rubble. By nightfall the neighborhood was bare ground.

The following evening the Jochi vid casts announced the availability of new home sites for "qualified citizens." They were snapped up by morning.

A letter from Sapper-Major Shase Marl, to Direktor-Leader S!Kt, Seventh Military Front commander:

. . . and while I realize sending this letter violates the military chain of command, I felt I had no one else who would have the authority and distinction to solve this problem, as you will see.

I write you not only as my supreme commander, but also because I remember, years past, before that evil one who used to rule (cursed be his memory) forced you into retirement. You spoke before my firster class at Kuishev Academy, and I never forgot your words. How an officer has a duty beyond his written orders, a duty to his honor and his race. This letter is my last chance to fulfill that duty.

The problem arose when my unit was ordered to lead a clearing operation on Ochio IX, one of the Disputed Worlds, Sector

Seven of your front. Only partially pacified, there were still Suzdal combat elements on the world who were insisting by force of arms their right to possess this planet which, of course, is rightfully Jochi. I was briefed, assigned an area to quiet, given certain supporting units, the names and duties of which do not matter, except for one. This unit was Third Strike Company, Second Saber, Special Duties Corps, led by a Captain L'merding.

I inspected the unit prior to deployment, and formed the impression this soldiery appeared to be adequate in their parade-ground bearing, and particularly well equipped in their weaponry for antipartisan operations. This was in spite of the fact I did not feel they were sufficiently trained, nor were their noncommissioned and commissioned leaders particularly impressive. I made no criticism, of course, to Captain L'merding, but merely welcomed his unit and said I would attempt to give them special opportunity to excel and prove their new corps worthy of belonging to the Jochian Army and serving Dr. Iskra.

Captain L'merding's only response was they had their orders and would fulfill them.

At this point I should have approached my superior, Colonel Ellman, and requested a clarification of command. I did not. The troops were landed, and we moved out into the rural areas, which were inhabited by a mixed population of Torks, Jochians, and Suzdal, where the Suzdal bandits had their strongholds. As usual, the Suzdal resisted bitterly (see OpRept 12-341-651-06, three month, weeks one, two, and three), and inflicted casualties on my force. Very few prisoners were taken, since, as you know, the Suzdal prefer death to surrender.

The first problem I encountered with Third Company was that Captain L'merding refused to deploy his unit into the countryside, answering my orders with a flat statement that the real enemy was not bogtrotters—those were his exact words—but rather the evil conspirators behind them in the towns and cities. I chose not to examine this odd statement, being a soldier, not a political person.

My attention was primarily focused on combat, of course, and it was not until the third week of the clearing operation that I was given information I found impossible to believe at first, but knew I must investigate to protect the honor of Jochi.

This report accused 3/2, Special Duties Corps, of the most appalling atrocities. I personally went to the area Captain L'merding's company was responsible for and found that these accusations were true. The Special Duties unit *was* killing Suzdal civilians in violation of accepted standards of war. Their targets were, in particular, any educated Suzdal, particularly those who were teachers or lawgivers. They also seemed to pay particular attention to any Suzdal with wealth. These beings were removed from their homes and vanished. Captain L'merding refused to specifically say what had happened to them, but their fate was obvious.

There were confirmed reports of children being slaughtered, rapes of Jochi civilians, and buildings being looted. In addition, murders of unarmed Suzdal civilians had been committed in broad daylight and their bodies left in the street. Clearly, this so-called strike company was composed of nothing but gangsters and hooligans. Captain L'merding had posted directives throughout the area, under his own signature, saying use of the Suzdal language, written or spoken, was banned and all Suzdal were forbidden to gather together in groups of more than two. Immediate execution was the penalty for violating any of his commands.

He had posted other orders that were equally as illegal, but the worst by far was his announcement that any criminal act committed by any Suzdal would be responded to with the most extreme measures, which would include razing of that Suzdal's home warren, extirpation of that Suzdal's breeding line, and the execution of one hundred Suzdal, to be chosen at random, as retribution. I told Captain L'merding he was relieved. He laughed. I attempted to place him under close arrest. My aides and myself were disarmed, beaten, and told to leave the area or face the ultimate consequences.

I returned to my own unit and notified my battalion commander of Captain L'merding's actions, and requested a combat unit be sent to seize this shameful being and his murderous thugs. I was first told by Colonel Ellman to mind my own affairs. I argued, and was given a direct order to leave L'merding's monsters alone.

In fact, Colonel Ellman informed me, this company and the other elements of the Special Duties Corps were obeying orders given from the very highest—orders that might be disagreeable to hear, but orders that must be obeyed to accomplish their vital mission. I refused to accept this and went over Colonel Ellman's head and appealed first to my brigade commander and then, when nothing happened, to the division leader.

I was told I was guilty of insubordination and behavior shameful to Jochi. When I persisted, I was quite illegally reduced one hundred numbers on the promotion list, without hearing or trial. I am now desperate, direktor-leader, and am appealing to you.

Is there no honor left in the Altaics? Is there no dignity left in our noble race? Has our own army, the army that I dedicated my life to serve, become nothing more than back-alley assassins?

The letter was never answered.

Six weeks later, Sapper-Major Shase Marl was shot to death in a rear area. His unit's day-report said that there had been an accidental discharge of weaponry, and that the culprit could not be identified.

Sapper-Major Marl was promoted one rank, posthumously, awarded a campaign ribbon and one star, and honorably interred on the Disputed World of Ochio IX.

The main road leading into Rurik's spaceport was a solid sea of miserable life. Thousands upon thousands of beings slogged through a heavy downpour, pushed, prodded, and flogged onward by Jochi troops.

There was no species division in this forced march. Suzdal was jammed into Bogazi into human.

The crowd of refugees was so thick that if a being fell the body would be carried along by the mass. People cried out mournfully for family members, or for simple pity.

Waiting for the refugees at the spaceport were scores of ancient freighters Iskra had pressed into service. More troops manned the gangways of these freighters, shoving beings into the holds until they were packed beyond reason.

At the signal, the hold doors were slammed shut, and the

freighters blasted off their pads. They had barely reached orbit before the next ships took their places.

Professor Iskra watched the scene with intense interest. He palmed controls for a variety of vidscreen views: wide shots of the jammed avenue; close shots of hopeless faces; another long shot showing the spectacle at the spaceport. As one freighter lifted off, he leaned back in his chair and allowed himself a long, pleasurable swallow of his herb tea.

Iskra looked over at Venloe, a rare thin smear on his lips that Venloe supposed was a smile.

"I hope you realize that we are watching history unfold before us," Iskra said. "Who could imagine such an exodus? Such a vast cleansing of our world?"

Venloe just grunted.

"Come now," Iskra pressed. "Surely I deserve at least a small compliment for my handling of this crisis?"

"Not my job description, professor," Venloe said. "Besides, you've got a big enough cheering section."

Iskra was enjoying himself too much to be angry. "That's all right. I don't expect compliments from the ignorant."

Venloe thumbed at the vidscreen. "You think that's genius?"

"What do you call it, my uneducated friend?"

"Crazy," Venloe snapped. "Or just plain stupid."

"My, my. Humanity bleeds in that cold heart."

"Don't mistake professional opinion for a warm and cuddly nature, professor," Venloe said. "It should be obvious to anyone other than a pedantic fool that you're just making things worse. This is all not only unnecessary, but dangerous. Every time you do something like that"—he jabbed a finger at a picture of a soldier hammering a lagging refugee—"you make yourself five or six more enemies."

"This isn't a popularity contest," Iskra said with a laugh. "Besides, I would think you'd be pleased. After what happened at the barracks, I'd think you'd be delighted that I'm revenging your poor, dead Guardsmen."

"Don't put it on us," Venloe warned. "You were never requested to take this kind of action. Don't drag the Emperor into this thing."

"But he already is," Iskra purred. "And quite vocally. Why, the entire Empire knows how important I am to him." He gestured at the vidscreen. "Just as everyone in the Altaics will soon know that it is in his name all these sacrifices are being made."

Venloe's eyes narrowed. "What are you talking about?"

"This is just the beginning." Iskra laughed. "Oh, it will take much more work to purify the Altaics."

"Meaning?"

"Watch my next vid cast," Iskra said. "I think even you will be impressed at my new emergency decrees."

Venloe looked away from Iskra's sneer. On the vidscreen he saw a refugee break out of the crowd. The being quickly unfurled a handmade banner.

He had just time to make out the words on the banner before the man was hammered down by soldiers: WHERE IS THE EMPEROR?

CHAPTER THIRTY-FOUR

"THERE'S NO WAY, Your Highness, anyone could have foreseen what Iskra has become," Venloe said, adding one milliliter of concerned sympathy to his tone, "let alone yourself. The last time I checked, you had to worry about an entire Empire."

To Venloe's concealed astonishment, a flickered expression crossed the Eternal Emperor's face. Surprise that anyone should care? Venloe could not—would not—interpret what he had seen on the screen. The Emperor's countenance swiftly reverted to calm authority.

"Yes," the Emperor said. "You're right, Venloe. You understand a bit of the reality of ruling. I can see why Mahoney thought highly of you, even though you were on opposite sides."

It was now Venloe's turn to poker-face. Ian Mahoney had, in fact, not only refused to touch palms with him as a gentleman should have when the game was over, but had said he would like to kill Venloe. Slowly. Venloe had believed him. Absolutely.

The Emperor didn't appear to have noticed Venloe's studied lack of reaction.

"These latest actions of Dr. Iskra and his regime that you, Sten, and . . . other agents have reported are completely psychopathic," the Emperor continued. "So we must deal with the problem directly and immediately."

"Yes, Your Majesty. Thank you for clarifying the situation. I'm afraid I was confused about which option should be used," Venloe lied, deliberately laying it on a trifle thick, trying to see at what point the Emperor's famous antisycophant snarl would cut in.

The Emperor, however, was looking off at another screen Venloe could not make out. "I've called up," the Emperor said, "the fiche you prepared on what we called the fallback option. A thorough job, Venloe. My compliments."

"Thank you, sir."

"I will tell you which option I want implemented shortly. One thing, though. There'll be a change to the one I'll order. I wish you to be directly involved. It isn't enough to control the exercise at long range. There must not be—cannot be—the slightest error."

Venloe bristled a bit. "Your Highness, my operations have been uniformly successful, and I've always kept one thing foremost in my planning."

"Which is, that if the drakh comes down, you're safely on a stage headed out of town."

"I've never before been accused of being a coward, sir. The reason I prefer to work by remote control is to keep my client's hands clean. If the operative is caught and then plays true confessions, it doesn't matter, because no one beyond a field agent or two, who's been deliberately given misinformation, will be caught in the net." Venloe thought, but certainly didn't say, that his clotting plans worked well enough to have speared the biggest fish of all: the clotting Eternal Emperor himself. But he was hardly suicidal.

"That's not a concern here," the Emperor said. "And that was an order. I want you on-scene and capable of personally rectifying any error, if an error is made."

"Yes. Sir."

"Very well. I've told you that Mahoney has been assigned to the Altaics, and in what capacity. He knows nothing of this plan, by the way. And I want you to extract yourself from the Altaics as soon as possible—after the operation has been completed. Now, adding Mahoney to the equation, your option must accomplish several things.

"First. Dr. Iskra is to be killed. Instantly. He must not be allowed to suspect anything before the moment of removal."

"Obviously, sir."

"Second. In view of Mahoney's orders, his task will be made much easier if some of these lightweights who've been flocking around Iskra, those ineffectual power-seekers Sten has mentioned in his reports—it would be well if some of them ceased to exist. The confusion of their replacement is desirable, in the eyes of the Empire."

"That would suggest that Your Highness will order either Option C or R."

"Correct. And you will know which of the two when I give you the final condition.

"The Empire cannot be implicated in this matter. Not even in whispers or the vaguest of paranoiac rumors. And the best way I can see for us to remain beyond suspicion is if one of our most highly respected and honored servants is unfortunately killed in the debacle."

"The—ambassador? Sir?"

"Yes," the Eternal Emperor said. "We all exist but to serve. And this will be his greatest service to me.

"Sten must die."

BOOK FOUR

VORTEX

CHAPTER THIRTY-FIVE

VENLOE FORESAW NO major problems carrying out the Eternal
Emperor's orders—at least as far as the murder of Iskra and any
other Jochi politico who could be decoyed into the trap.

He wasn't especially in love with killing Sten to cover up the
conspiracy. Not because he had any feeling for him—Sten and
Mahoney had, after all, tracked Venloe to his hiding place and
forced him to undergo the racking brutality of a brainscan—but
he thought the Emperor was planning a flight when no one would
pursue.

Venloe did not think that anyone in the Empire outside the
Altaic Cluster would care if a slimeball dictator was assassinated.
Many would even cheer a little, even if they suspected the Eternal
Emperor had masterminded the killing.

But he had his orders.

So Sten would die.

It might, the more he considered it, be beneficial to Venloe
himself. Sten was too slippery, too good at the double- and triple-
think of intelligence ops. If he were in his meat locker, that might
make Venloe's extraction less risky.

Venloe was still angry at the Emperor's orders that he, himself,
had to be part of the murder plot. Stupid. And it showed a measure of distrust. But he eventually shrugged and forgot it. The
Eternal Emperor wasn't the first to require the absurd—and he
certainly was the biggest client Venloe had ever worked for and
must be kept satisfied.

So the Emperor wanted Venloe to go back to the days of his
youth and show his talents as an iceman once more. So be it.
Venloe added an extra E-hour to his day's normal physical con-

ditioning while he pondered where he would actually station himself on the day.

He was too wise to ignore the Emperor's orders. Most likely the Emperor's mention of ''other agents'' in the Altaic Cluster was bluff—but why take the chance?

One—or a dozen—more corpses didn't matter to Venloe. After some thought he had figured out his back door. It was a simple and clean Break Contact and Exit, which meant it would work. Occam's razor also cut in wet work.

Once away from the butcher's floor, all Venloe had to do was get off Jochi and out of the cluster. Fine. He had had a private yacht secreted on an auxiliary field outside Rurik within two weeks of his arrival on-planet with Iskra.

Venloe, someone had once said, didn't even use a latrine without making sure there was a way out—even if it meant jumping directly into the drakh below. Venloe had chosen to take the statement as a compliment.

Having figured his egress, he also knew what weapon he would carry. He would have preferred an Imperial-made weapon for its quality, but since he planned to abandon the tool at the site, he thought it better to procure one of local manufacture. Since Venloe prided himself on his taste, he preferred even his murder weapon to not be an off-the-shelf item. He ended up with the perfect device: an obsolete sporting arm that had been custom-built a century before, to slaughter a wild animal that was now extinct. He had found a bullet mold and cast new bullets and then hand-loaded propellant into shell casings for the weapon.

Now, for his assassin.

Assassins, since the Emperor wanted the biggest bang for his buck.

That, too, was simple.

He started with Dr. Iskra's Special Duty units. Every dictator, public or corporate, that Venloe had ever worked for or heard of had his own private thuggery, with its own label—from the Fida'is to the Einsatzgruppen to CREEP to Mantis to the Emperor's newly formed Internal Security to this unit of Iskra.

Venloe didn't think much of them. He referred to them publicly as ''beards,'' or ''bearded ones,'' and refused to explain why.

Actually, Venloe was making a private reference to one of the least-competent murder organizations of all time, far back on ancient Earth.

The first and—so Iskra had thought it—preeminent cell of these Special Duty units, this one a deep-cover team, had been vanished from its supposedly secure safe house in a mansion outside Rurik. There had never been any rumors, nor had any of Jochi's other private hit teams claimed credit for the deed. Venloe had wondered idly, since that cell had been assigned to harassing the Imperial Guard battalion and had almost certainly been responsible for the barracks bombing, if Sten hadn't given himself a little private pleasure and obliterated them.

Regardless, the effect was immediate—and chilling. Several entire "units" of Special Duty people requested reassignment to active duty status on other worlds, perhaps to fulfill duties against the Bogazi, Suzdal, or Torks. Still other cell members went inactive. That ended when beings still loyal to Iskra hunted them down and dealt with the traitors.

In any event, the Special Duty units were, to Venloe, a joke. But that didn't mean he could not use them. He had enquired of their "Supreme Intelligence Leader" what beings, now serving in the Jochi armed forces, were considered potentially traitorous and capable of armed resistance that the Special Duty teams hadn't gotten around to dealing with yet.

That got him one list.

He got a second list from the army's own Counter Subversion Department. A list that was a little less hysterical.

Any name that was on both lists Venloe put on his own roster of possibly dangerous service types. He could not believe how big this short list was—hell, Iskra wasn't even all that good at purges.

Which gave him the direction for his final cut—anyone who had been friendly with or assigned to the same unit as any of the beings Iskra had purged when he arrived on Jochi, beings Iskra still swore were imprisoned in Gatchin Fortress. Venloe knew better, but had not bothered to find out where Iskra had disappeared the bodies to, so long as no trace could ever be found.

This final list he was quite pleased with. He was still more pleased when he found that some of these beings, all of whom had excellent reason to hate Iskra, had been carefully applying for assignment to certain units.

Venloe positively beamed, and permitted himself a single glass of Vegan vintage wine that night. The only thing more perfect than creating a false conspiracy was finding one already extant that could be used for his own purposes. Then he sent two of his most trusted free-lance aides into the field, to find out who was running this conspiracy a-birthing.

The answer was four young officers. None of them appeared to have any idea on what specific mission their conspiracy would take—but it would be used, and used soon, to destroy Iskra. They weren't particularly clever or Machiavellian. If Venloe hadn't found themselves, they would undoubtedly have been picked up by Counter Subversion or the Special Duty teams and body-bagged.

There were thirty of them he could use, he finally decided. Very good. The murder technique that would be used on the day, Venloe kept mentally filed as Crimson Ratpack. He collected, using Iskra's never-to-be-questioned authority, their dossiers from the counter-intelligence unit, and burned their files. They now owed him greatly. He had saved their lives. The least they could do now was sacrifice themselves, but this time to fulfill their dreams instead of ending as futile cinders at the Killing Wall.

His two aides approached the four officers, without saying that Iskra's behind-the-scenes adviser was planning to cut his boss's throat. Venloe had been right—they were more than happy to volunteer for the sacrifice.

Venloe had half of his players. Now all he needed was the other half—the victims.

And a theater.

That, too, was simple.

"I do not see," Dr. Iskra said, having scowled his way through Venloe's memorandum, "what purpose this farce would have. What will I—which means the government of the Altaic Cluster—gain?"

"Solidarity," Venloe said.

"In what way?"

"First, peasants love a dumb show, as you said in your essay, 'The Revolution's Need to Understand the Soul of the People.' "

"Correct."

"Secondly, there have been some stories about certain offworld events involving both the military and the Special Duty Corps."

"Idle talk should be punished."

"It is," Venloe said. "Your Special Duty units are especially effective in that area. But we now have the opportunity to provide a positive image. How could anyone seeing the noble soldiery of Jochi parade past imagine them culpable in what these rumors hint."

"Ah."

"Plus such a parade is a magnificent opportunity for you to show that your government is solidly supported by everyone, including the Torks, when livie viewers see the Torks' leader near you on the reviewing stand."

"Menynder will not attend."

"Yes, he will," Venloe disagreed. "Because the alternatives that will be presented to him won't be to his liking."

Iskra considered. "Yes. Yes, Venloe, I see your thinking. And it has been too long since I showed myself to my people. As I pointed out, as part of my analysis of the Kha—that forgotten monster's tyranny, how he was planting the seeds to his downfall in many ways, not the least of which was hiding, invisible, in this palace. It was in the second volume."

"I am sorry," Venloe said. "I have been too busy for any off-duty reading. One other thing," he went on. "The Imperial ambassador should be invited."

"Sten? I have requested his relief," Iskra said. "Yet another necessity that's not been responded to by that *man* on Prime. Why should he be invited? And why would he attend, anyway?"

Venloe did not quite roll his eyes, but he wanted to. Iskra, for all of his millions of words and speeches about politics and ruling, knew less than nothing about it.

"He should be invited because that will show the populace you are supported by the highest. And that their worries about this new AM2 shortage must be pointless.

"And Sten will attend for one reason: He is a professional."

* * *

Sten looked out the window at the weather, listening to Kilgour filter through the incoming messages behind him. The weather continued to fulfill Sten's expectations, alternating from humid, overcast, and oppressive, to humid, overcast, and raining, cloudbursts passing so rapidly that no one knew how to dress when going out.

"Clottin' kilt maker. Ah dinnae know th' clot'd hae th' brains t' track me doon. He'll whistle 'Bonnie Bells' throo hi' fundament ere he gies credits frae Laird Kilgour.

"Gie'in me ae kilt thae's th' ancien' Campbell sheep-futterin' pattern, an' claimin't he c'd nae tell th' difference tween thae ae' th' tartan ae th' Kilgours.

"Hah.

"Noo, whae hae we here. Mmmph. Mmmph." A chortle. "Hah. Boss. Noo thae's int'restin'."

Sten turned back around. "Whatcher got, myte?"

"Y' rec'lect wee Petey Lake? Th' navy weatherman w' hae assigned, way back, i' Mantis?"

"Not really."

"I' wae th' time we were t' be blowin't thae dams ae thae planet wi' the bein's thae lookit ae weasels an' smell th' same? We were suppos't t' bring thae boom jus' when th' rainy season broke, so's t' nae cause max damage, but jus' enow t' topple th' gov'mint an' send i' th' Imperial peacekeepers?"

"Oh yeah. Wait a minute. The weatherman? Human type? The guy we called Mr. Lizard?"

"Aye. Thae's th' lad."

"How the *hell* did he stay out of jail? Let alone beat the court-martial?"

"Ah hae noo idea. P'raps we w're wrong, an' th' lasses an' their ridin' hacks were enjoyin't whae he wae doin't, an' were just hollerin' frae their clothes. Ah dinnae ken. Anyway, Ah've hae letters frae him e'er noo an' then.

"He's doin't quite well. Runnin't a stables wi' real Earth horses f'r rich little girls noo. At any rate, Ah wrote an' asked why this clottin' weather's so clottin' clotted ae Rurik. He's tellin't me thae any big planet wi' fast rotation, braw seas, small landmass, tall bens, an' multiple moons'll most likely always be bloody.''

"Sure," Sten said, not having thought about the weather much beyond just watching it—it was just another part of the general sewer that was Rurik.

"He hae a wee warnin't. Aboot thae cyclones Ah, at any rate, hae been takin't wi' a grain ae haggis. Here. P'ruse f'r y'self.''

Alex passed the long, handwritten letter across Sten's desk. Sten scanned it, until he hit the section Alex had referred to, then read hastily—he *did* remember Mr. Lizard, and he wanted to get his hands off the document and into a sterile bath as quickly as possible.

. . . so it's going to be miserable on Jochi—miserable cold in the winter, miserable hot in the summer, and, oh yeah, capable of being either one out of season.

Serves you right, you clot, for sticking with the uniform drakh.

One thing you want to be careful of—and you can push that clot Sten in front of one for me—is tornadoes. Tornadoes are trick little circular winds that'll blast you straight out of your shorts if you aren't either underground or out of the way.

Take these suckers real serious—the whirlwinds'll get up to 4-800 kph rotational wind speed in the vortex, and will honk right along anywhere up to 112 klicks an hour. About here is where the measuring instruments break, so don't assume any of those numbers are maximum. You *can't* run, so you'd better hide.

I got a whole bunch of statistics in my files that I can ship along if you're morbidly curious as to what a tornado can do—kill a thousand people in forty minutes, punch a blade of straw through an anvil, throw five tacships weighing a few hundred kilotons each a quarter klick, without bothering the crews inside by the way, and so on.

The best example I've got is on Altair III, and the clots there who were dumb enough to build their capital city right in a tornado belt (sounds just like this Rurik place you're in)—and yeah, tornadoes have patterns. Anyway, summer afternoon, and the city, est. pop. of around five million, gets hit with seventy-two twisters in one afternoon. Killed one-fifth of the city's population—guess they didn't believe in storm cellars.

Just to show you what a good guy I am, I'll even give you a couple clues as to what to look out for, before the funnel lifts you into low orbit.

First, you get convection currents that overcome the usual inversion layers. The air will lift to up to 10,000 meters or so altitude, and will be affected by any jet stream you've got running overhead. This is gonna lift air from all over the region, and it'll destabilize the inversion layers.

The air from the jet stream is like a giant tube, rotating at altitude, and when the tops of cumulus clouds encounter that tube, it bends in the middle from the rising air, due to the rotational wind increasing with the height.

As the tube becomes more vertical, the winds increase with altitude, but more importantly veer from the southwest . . . right now you have a giant, rotating tube, embedded in one big mother thunderstorm . . .

. . . if you've got anything as primitive as a radar set, about now you can see this tube, which will look like an extended cat's-paw. Sometimes it's called a figure six or a hook echo.

This is the wall cloud . . . think of it as a horizontal tornado, usually black, but sometimes even green . . . wall cloud tilts . . .

Down on the ground you're gonna be sweating bullets, getting cranky if you believe in positive ions and getting wet, because there's almost certainly going to be a helluva thunderstorm going on.

You ought to be getting a little scared, too.

Sten scanned on.

. . . hail and storm . . . downdraft ahead of the updraft . . . an overhanging cloud . . . all of a sudden funnel clouds drop out of the wall cloud and rotate around the mesocyclone—the southern-most tube—don't remember right off the top how many tubes you get.

But only a crazy clot would stick around to count them, because right now, your basic vortex is about to ruin your entire week . . .

* * *

The letter went on and became a gibberish of equations—evidently Mr. Lizard had gotten tired of ghosting it and looked the subject up.

Sten flipped the letter back. "Thank you, Mr. Kilgour, for giving me yet something else on this clottin' world that will try to kill us."

"Nae prob, wee Sten."

A screen dinged, and Alex scanned the scrolling letters. "Noo, here's e'en better'n Lizard's wee whirlwind. Doc Isky's throwin't a review. Ae th' troops. An' he'd appreciate th' pleasure ae one Ambassador Sten, on th' stand. Th' intent i' plain. T'bore y' to death wi' his bootskies, bootskies, movin' up an' doonsky . . ."

Alex spun the screen around for Sten to look at. Nobody except a circus throws a parade just for drill. Why this one? He considered. To build the morale of the civilians, first. Second, to give Iskra a chance to pose nobly—all dictators liked that.

Not enough.

There was a tap at the door. A secretary entered and gave Kilgour an envelope. Alex opened it.

"Ah hae here th' confirmation ae th' review. Handwrote, i' Isky's braw scrawl, i' is. An' on real paper, Ah reck.

"Ah do wonder," Alex mused, "jus' whae villainy th' good quack's plannin' t' hatch?

"D' y' pass, lad?"

"No. I go."

"Ah dinnae think thae's wise. Cannae y' d'velop a case ae clap, or aught?"

Sten just shook his head—both of them knew better. This was part of being an ambassador—even one that was not held in the highest regard by the current government he represented Imperial interests to. Sten would have to appear and lend authenticity to whatever Iskra's scheme was.

"I' y' go," Alex announced with finality, "y' dinnae do i' wearin't nae but y'r new spring frock, flowers i' y'r hair, an' ae doofus smile. An' noo Ah'm speakin't ae y'r security adviser. I' y' hae t' play that clot's games, y' dinnae hae t' play by his rules."

Sten grinned. What Alex was evidently proposing was a fairly severe violation of protocol—for an honored diplomat to consider going armed, with backup, to a celebration of the host government.

But considering how events in the Altaic Cluster had been, and the honorable, upright beings Sten had encountered, he thought it very reasonable to consider double-armoring his own privy.

Kilgour's large, horned fist slammed down on the metal bench. Being intended for use as an engine stand for gravlighters' McLean generators, the bench's legs bulged but did not give way.

"If Ah c'n hae y' attention," he bellowed, and the murmur of conversation died away. Kilgour stood in front of an assemblage of Gurkhas and Bhor, in one of the embassy's garages.

"Ah wan' y'r eyeballs hooked t' thae chart ae the wall, there.

"Ah'll keep this brief," he went on. "Y' c'n find y'r own duty assignments up ae they're listed. Thae garage's swept, no more'n an hour ago, by myself an' Cap'n Cind, and it's unbugged. So we dinnae hae t' use circumlocutions.

"Th' skinny is like so—th' boss is goin't twa thae review t'morrow. I' th' square ae th' late Khookoos. An' we dinnae think the deal's square-up.

"So we'll be i' position, aye?

"Ah wan' you Gurk's i' squad format. Two squads per gravlighter. Otho, y're pr'moted sarg'nt, an' i' charge ae th' Bhor. Four per gravlighter, plus two heavy-weapons teams. Aye?"

"As you say," Otho rumbled. "But what of our captain?"

"Cap'n Cind hae th' countersniping detail. She's tucked e'er sniper-rated an' expert-qualified rifle shot under her wing. We'll be saltin' them, twa by twa, ae th' rooftops afore dawn.

"Now. Here's th' orders. I' there's aught attempt made ae Sten—Ah wan' thae hitter dead. Dead 'fore he can think ae violence, an' we'll nae consider gie'in th' lad th' chance t' touch th' trigger.

"We'll hae all coms open, so i' there's an attempt, Ah wan' all a' y' t' swarm th' reviewin't stand. Dinnae be worryin't aboot prisoners or such."

"Question?"

"Aye, lad?"

"By my mother's beard," the young Bhor growled, "but you send in the lances just on the suspicion there will be danger."

"Aye?"

"I am not arguing, sir. But what would you do if there was a confirmed threat to the ambassador?"

Alex's face went still, and his eyes glittered. After a pause, he said, "In thae case, Ah'd hae Sten lock't i' th' cellar, an' th' reviewin' stand'd be a nuke ground zero afore th' ceremony'd begin.

"Noo. Thae's all. Y' ken y'r duties, y'r weapons, y'r gear. See to it. Stand-to is one hour before dawn."

"Kilgour, this isn't my tailcoat."

"Aye. Shut y'r lip an' be puttin' i' on. Th' piss i' review'll be nae more'n twa hours away."

"Fits lousy," Sten growled, frowning at his reflection. "Who tailored this? Omar th' Tent Maker?"

"Th' coat's 'flatable, an' thae's inserts t' be put i' place."

"For what? If somebody shoots at me with a cannon?"

"Ah." Kilgour smiled. "Ah always ken y'r noo ae stupid't ae Cind keep't sayin't. Cannon i' th' watchword.

"Noo. Bolt y'self up.

"I' y' rec'lect, all a' thae silliness Ah been doin't since yesterday's i' y'r cause. C'mon, lad. Ah hae t' put on m' own wee drag. I' y're braw, Ah'll buy y' a pint a'terward."

If, Kilgour thought, there is an afterward . . .

Sten evaluated the thick crowds on either side of the wide boulevard as his gravlighter approached the palace.

If this is supposed to be a holiday, Dr. Iskra has miscalled it, he thought. The faces were angry, sullen as the darkling skies overhead. At first Sten thought the hostility was pointed at the two Imperial flags fluttering from the gravlighter's stanchions, then corrected himself. The rage was free-form and unprejudiced—Sten saw a man look up as one of the constantly patrolling military gravsleds slid overhead, then spit into the gutter.

Otho grounded the embassy's ceremonial stretch gravlighter just behind the huge reviewing stand that had been special-built to one side of the Square of the Khaqans. The gravlighter looked even worse now—the weapons mounts and most of the jury-rigged armor had been cut away, but there had been no time to refinish the body or repaint. The craft looked as if it had failed to qualify in a demolition derby.

Two Gurkhas in full ceremonial dress, which included kukris and willyguns, snapped out of the lighter and presented arms, first to the Jochi flag to one side of the stand, then to the main riser, where Dr. Iskra's chosen symbol was mounted. Iskra had not yet materialized, but he was the only dignitary not in appearance.

Sten stepped out, Alex slightly to his rear. Kilgour had chosen to wear the full ceremonial rig of his home world: flat shoes, tartan stockings with a dagger tucked in the top, kilt with sporran—containing a pistol—another dagger at his hip, silver-buttoned black velvet and vest, lace jabot at his throat, and lace at his wrists. On his head was his clan's bonnet, and slung over one shoulder was a tartan cloak.

The outfit was not, however, exactly what he would wear on Edinburgh turned out as Laird Kilgour of Kilgour. The flat shoes were strapped on, so as not to come off if Kilgour had some running to do. The tartan pattern was very dark, which Alex blandly explained was the correct ancient hunting tartan of his clan. Sten had never been sure whether there really was a Clan Kilgour, or whether Alex, and the several thousand people on his estates, were making it up as they went along. The Scots were fully capable of doing something entirely that elaborate just to pull the chain of the sassenachs.

He was not carrying the usual ceremonial broadsword, again for efficiency. Swords got in the way. And the cloak thumped if banged against—Sten thought that the heavyworlder was likely carrying a full weapons shop in the drape.

Behind Sten came two more Gurkhas. Sten bowed to the Jochi flag and, mentally gritting his teeth, to Iskra's emblem. Otho lifted the gravlighter away—he would keep it ready in a park just behind the palace with the other backup units.

Two of Iskra's Special Duty goons were at the foot of the stairs, with detectors. Alex looked at them once. Even hooligans occasionally were guilty of sense, and the two stepped out of the way, awkwardly saluting.

The Gurkhas remained at the rear of the stand. Sten felt a bit more secure about his back. In front of the stand's base, standing shoulder to shoulder, were more of the Special Duty troops.

"A wee bit of info," Alex whispered. "All th' troopies thae'll pass i' review hae been told i' their weapons point anywhere close t' th' stand, Iskra's murthrers hae orders t' ice 'em wi' no questions. Whidney y' like a wee career i' th' Jochi gruntery?"

Sten was twice surprised at the top of the stand. First he saw Menynder. Interesting. Someone or something had winkled him out of his period of mourning.

The second surprise—and it took him a moment before he recognized the being—was seeing Milhouz the rebel, now in the black uniform of this new "student" movement that Iskra had created and Sten had vaguely noted.

There were two older beings beside Milhouz—his parents, Sten thought. Milhouz met Sten's gaze, started to flinch, then stared boldly.

Sten frowned, as if trying to remember the face, couldn't, but to be polite nodded slightly: Perhaps we were introduced at a social function some time?

Sten almost felt sorry for the clot. Turncoats were never trusted—and everyone knew that, especially those who doubled them. True in espionage, true in politics. Milhouz had only one future—to be used by Iskra as long as needed and then dispensed with.

Iskra being Iskra, Sten thought, that dispensing would almost certainly involve a shallow grave rather than an obscure retirement.

No more than Milhouz deserved.

Sten, Kilgour beside him, worked his way to his assigned seat. A polite greeting to Douw, who was wearing a full dress uniform hung with decorations old and new. Nods to other dignitaries and pols.

He stopped beside Menynder.

"I am glad," he said, "to see you have recovered from your family's tragedy."

"Yes," Menynder said, his head moving a bare millimeter sideways, toward Iskra's emblem. "Nobody'll ever know how grateful I am to have some new friends who just cheered the drakh out of me, telling me how much the rest of my family means, and how my ancient estates should be worried about, and, in general, convinced me to dump the widow's weeds."

As Sten had thought. Menynder had been blackjacked into attendance.

A military band blared what might be considered music, and Dr. Iskra, aides at his heels, came down the steps from the palace's terrace and walked slowly across the vast open square to the reviewing stand.

"Any idea," Sten whispered to Kilgour, "why the doctor isn't reviewing his troops from the usual place?"

"Ah ask't," Kilgour hissed. "Ah wae told because th' terrace i' distant. An' the doctor wishes t' be closer t' his wee heroes."

"That's a real cheap lie."

"Aye. An' wha' worries me, is th' stand wae no built right."

Kilgour was correct—it was no more than a meter and a half off the ground. A basic part of preriot crowd control was to build the bandstand high enough to make it difficult for the madding throng to rush the stage successfully.

The dignitaries came to the salute as Dr. Iskra mounted the stand.

Cymbals crashed, and the military band crescendoed and broke off.

In the sudden silence, Sten heard, from a great distance, the twitter of a panpipe being played by some street minstrel working the crowd.

And then, as if cued, the clouds broke, a high wind rolling them up like they were dirty linen, and an impossibly blue sky shone above.

The band cacophonied into life again, and the review began.

The Square of the Khaqans was a crash of cleated bootheels, an eerily grating rumble of tracks, and the bash of marching music. Every now and then Sten could hear the cued cheers from the crowds watching.

He applauded with his forearm against his side, Altaic style, as yet another range of rankers bashed past the stand.

"Fifth Battalion, Sixth Regiment, The Iron Guards of Perm," the unseen commentator told them over the square's PA system.

"Didn't we just see them?"

"Nae, skip. Thae wae th' *Sixth* Battalion, *Fifth* Regiment. Y' hae t' pay tighter heed."

"How much longer can he keep running troops past us?"

"Damfino," Alex whispered. "Till our eyes bleed an' we start burblin' ae th' wonders ae ol' Isky. It's mass hypnosis, lad."

"Time," Cind said. Obediently, her spotter rolled away from the scope, behind his own rifle. Cind slid into position and began her own shift, sweeping endlessly across the palace rooftops and windows that she had taken for her sector.

Her other sniper teams were doing much the same—one being watches, the other waits behind the gun. A spotter could only work effectively for a few minutes before starting to see motion that was a curtain blowing in the wind, menace that was the shadow from a chimney, or just simply things not there.

The architectural style of the Palace of the Khaqans didn't make their job any easier, having been built and then redecorated in a style that could be referred to as Early Unromantic Gargoyle.

Cind and her spotter had taken position on one of the palace's roofs, finding a fairly level area to keep their backup arms and ammunition in, then slithering very slowly to the roof's peak to observe. A dull scarlet hood, just the color of the metal roof they were lying on, hung over the scope, and both snipers had their faces camouflaged with a flat medium-brown wash.

Cind's eyes were watering from the strain in a few minutes. She swept the roofline, then swept it again, routinely. She stopped and moved the scope back.

"Earle," she said, unconsciously and needlessly whispering. "Three o'clock. That dormer window."

"Got it," the man behind the rifle said. "The window's open. Can't see inside. Too dark."

"Come left half a finger," Cind ordered.

"Oh-ho."

"I'll take the gun."

Earle started to protest, then took the spotting position. Cind moved up, hands automatically readying her own rifle.

Across the square, to the side of that dormer window, a hatch onto the roof had been lifted clear—a hatch that had been closed earlier. And very close to that hatch was a low parapet that would make excellent cover for someone to use to move the thirty meters or so to where a wall zigged out, that provided a hidden crevice that would make an ideal escape route.

The window was about six hundred meters away from the reviewing stand below, and about . . .

"Range?"

"Twelve . . . twelve twenty-five."

"I have the same . . ."

. . . twice that to Cind's post.

Cind slid her shooting jacket's fasteners shut, pulled the rifle sling tight around her upper arm until there was no circulation anymore, and was in the rigor mortis that was her firing position.

All that existed was that open window twelve hundred meters away.

She barely heard Earle reporting that they had a possible target and ordering another team to take over the routine scan.

Venloe was ready. He had his monstrous sporting rifle braced firmly on a tabletop, the table solidly sandbagged.

He was about three meters back of the open dormer window, in clever concealment. Neither the human eye nor a scope would be able to see him in the gloom, and if some extraordinarily paranoid security type was using an amplified-light scope the glare from the rooftops outside would blank that device.

He looked again through the rifle scope, then rubbed his eyes. He had forgotten how exhausting sniping was, and how short a time before the edge was lost.

Six hundred meters away was the reviewing stand.

Venloe had his targets chosen, and six cigar-sized solid projectiles resting in the rifle's box magazine.

If there was an error . . . first Iskra.

Then Sten.

Then . . .

The tiny com beside him, tuned to the review's public broadcast, spoke:

"Eighth Company, Guards Combat Support Wing. The Saviors of Gumrak.

"Afoot, Scout Company, Eighty-third Light Infantry Division."

This was it.

Now for the Crimson Ratpack.

The combat support wing's gravlighters swept forward, three abreast, at low speed. Just ahead of them trotted the lightly armed scouts.

Each gravlighter carried a full complement of troops, sitting at rigid attention. The gravlighter's pilot concentrated on his formation, and the lighter's commander saluted.

Six ranks back, in the center row, was the first of Venloe's assassins. The gravlighter's pilot was one of the young officer/conspirators, as were all of the other soldiers.

"Sixteen . . . seventeen . . . eighteen . . ."

At a count of twenty, the gravlighter was, as calculated, about fifty meters out and twenty meters short of the reviewing stand.

The pilot punched full power to the McLean generators and pushed the control stick hard over to the right.

The gravlighter pirouetted, crashing into its fellow, which went out of control and dominoed into the parade formation.

The young officer fought his craft level, then slammed it to the ground, the lighter skidding forward toward the reviewing stand, skewing crazily.

It spilled out soldiers, soldiers who hit the ground running—and firing, semiautomatic grenade launchers blasting the Special Duty soldiers.

These guards took a bare moment to recover—but a third of them were dead by then. Then they opened up, rounds sheeting into the middle of the review.

The support wing's formation broke, gravlighters climbing for the sky and getting shot down as other Special Duty units obeyed orders to kill anyone or anything irregular.

A platoon of the scout unit broke from *its* formation and went flat. Orders were bellowed, and rifles crashed.

Their target was the reviewing stand.

One burst and—''Grenades!'' came the shout, and the platoon charged the stand.

A quarter second earlier, Sten's four Gurkhas had been at attention, at the rear of the stand. Now, most suddenly, they were on the stand, knocking fear-maddened pols aside, willyguns braced on their hips, AM2 slugs slashing out and cutting down the scouts.

Sten dug under his monkey suit for his pistol and was down as Kilgour bodychecked him flat. Alex recovered, his cloak pitched away and the willygun hidden under it up and chattering rounds.

Douw was suddenly in an underwater trance, as he saw the grenade thud down on the planking just in front of him—how annoying—and he kicked it, grenade dropping off the stand and then exploding, blasting him back into Menynder. Both men sprawled, Douw half stunned.

Menynder started to shove the general's crushing weight off his body, then reconsidered. What better shield could there be, he realized, and then turned his thoughts toward camouflage, concentrating on being the very model of a modern major corpse.

Dr. Iskra's eyes were wide open, his brows just beginning to furrow like a professor about to chide a favorite pupil for being unable to answer an easy question, when the blood-covered woman levered herself up onto the stand in front of him.

Iskra's hands went out, trying to push this horror away.

The woman shot Iskra four times in the face before her body was shattered by a burst from a guard's weapon.

Sten rolled sideways, pistol coming out of a rear holster, and was coming to his knees, mind recording screams from the crowd, gun blasts, crashes from the pandemonium that had been an army in review seconds earlier, and the whine of gravlighters at full drive.

Out of a corner of his eye he saw the Bhor lighters rip out of their park toward the stand, then there were two men just below

him, aiming, and he fired . . . tap, tap . . . tap, tap . . . they
were down and dead . . . looking for another target . . .

The pleased smile was frozen on Venloe's face as he touched
the sight stud, and it zoomed tight on the target, his field of vision
narrowing.

Iskra was dead. Absolutely.

Menynder and Douw were hit—probably. It did not matter—
they weren't major targets.

Now. Now for Sten.

There he is. The bastard's not killable. He's coming to his feet
now . . .

Just coming up . . . hold the breath . . . exhale smoothly . . .
touch the stud . . . brace for the recoil . . . firing pressure . . .
now!

Shock-recoil-slam, gun butt against shoulder. Action crashing
back, sending the smoking shell case spinning out, *clatter*, another round chambered, bolt locked in battery, dammit, the sights
are off target . . .

"Sten is down," an unemotional voice on the com said.

Shut up, Cind said. Don't look. Don't turn. Just hold on that
dormer window and see the curtain flung out by the muzzle blast
inside, bastard's trained, had enough sense to pick a stance back
in the shadows, and she pumped three AM2 explosions through
the window . . .

Sten's formal dress may have been bulletproofed by Kilgour.
However, there is no way the human animal can withstand the
impact of a solid bullet weighing just over one hundred grams
being delivered at a velocity of around eight hundred meters per
second, unless he or she is inside a tank, any more than a bulletproof vest is worth drakh to a pedestrian hit by a bus.

But it had been too long for Venloe's old training, as his mind
flinched away from that shoulder-cracking kick-to-come.

Six hundred meters is not significant with a modern weapon.
But it is a factor. It is especially a factor if a projectile weapon
uses conventional propellant to punt an enormously heavy round

to its target. So the trajectory taken by the bullet from Venloe's dinosaur-killing rifle was a high, looping howitzer-arc, subject to crosswind and heat/cold waves.

The bullet should have hit Sten in the stomach. Instead, it first struck the heavy chair beside him, and shattered. Most of the bullet ricocheted away to who-knew-where. But its solid jacket impacted directly on Sten's monkey jacket, just on the base of one of those solid plates Kilgour had sheathed his boss with. Sten was knocked spinning off the stand. The self-inflating shock cushion realized that its finest hour had arrived, and suddenly the Imperial ambassador greatly resembled a floating bath toy; then, as he touched down on corpses, the shock cushion deflated, and there was somebody just in front of him with a bayoneted rifle.

Somehow the pistol was still in Sten's hands, and he shot the man dead, and was looking for a target, then realized he was still alive, and able to hear that wonderful wonderful *Ayo . . . Gurkhali* as his backup arrived.

Cind's AM2 rounds blew the attic room apart, sending Venloe stumbling back, dazed for a moment; then he recovered, staggering toward the open hatch, but no, there'll be someone out there, remember you planned for this, too, reach down, reach down.

Venloe's hands found the pull cord on the two smoke grenades he had taped on either side of the patch, and yanked.

Wait . . . wait . . . wait for the smoke . . . now. Through the hatch and away with you.

"Clottin' missed him," Cind muttered, then her sights swung as the open hatchway gouted smoke.

"The ambassador is all right! I say again, the ambassador is all right," the com bleated.

Did the explosion start a fire . . .

Hell. It's a smoke screen, she thought, seeing a flicker of movement that disappeared behind the parapet.

Oh, you cute thing, she thought.

"Earle. Three rounds rapid. Into the middle of that wall. Forward one meter from that rainspout. Now!"

Crash . . . crash . . . crash.

The ancient stone of the parapet shattered. Cind could see a tiny, jagged hole through her scope.

Now, you behind that wall, what are you thinking? Do you think you're quick enough—or that I'm not a good enough shot—to wriggle past that little crack?

Cind sighted and fired. Her single round slammed through the crack and exploded somewhere on the parapet's far side.

Yes, you. I *am* that good a shot that I can slip a bullet through the hole if I see any movement.

Now, it would seem to me, were I stupid enough to be that man over there, thinking that twelve hundred meters and only one way out makes you bulletproof, I would now be considering modifying my avenues of egress.

"Earle, watch the smoke."

"NG for him. It's thinning."

Very good. So what do we have? We have you out there, lying prone behind that parapet. Your exit route is blocked by that hole Earle drilled and by the knowledge you have that I can see through it and shoot through it.

About twelve meters back of Earle's spy hole, the parapet ends against the dormer window. So you are lying somewhere within that twelve meters.

First we access the area . . .

She sent another round into the dormer window's sill, shattering away. Yes. Now, if I were lying there, would I be closer to the dormer, or to that little crack? I'd be closer to the crack, and waiting for some kind of miracle to cross that two-centimeter "gap."

Range to the dormer sill . . . *that*. She locked the range finder.

Cind moved her scope sideways, sweeping the cross hairs along the blank face of the parapet but keeping the barrel aimed exactly at the shattered window sill. About . . . there. The linear accelerator hummed. Ready.

Cind fired.

The AM2 round spat across the twelve hundred meters. Then, at the appropriate range, it turned a sharp right.

Venloe was lying flat, trying to figure what his next option might be, just where Cind had estimated.

The bullet hit him at the base of his pelvis and exploded.

Half of Venloe's body pinwheeled up into the air and over the parapet, and splattered down on the rooftop. Then it slid, greasily, hands splayed as if trying to hang on, over the edge of the roof and fell two hundred meters into the square.

The time elapsed since Venloe had set off his smoke screen was just under two minutes.

Milhouz stood alone on the reviewing stand. At length, he realized he was still alive.

He was the only one.

There . . . there were the bodies of his parents.

He would mourn them.

But the dynasty would continue.

Iskra was dead.

But Milhouz lived.

The beginnings of that look of saintly self-satisfaction crept across his face.

It was still there as the kukri slashed from behind, and his head rode a crimson fountain to bounce off the stand and paint a red semicircle on the square's paving.

Jemedar Lalbahadur Thapa stepped back as the headless corpse dropped. He sheathed his kukri and nodded once, in satisfaction.

The Gurkha had been at Pooshkan University.

The Square of the Khaqans was almost quiet, except for the moans and screams of the wounded and the roar of runaway engines from crashed gravlighters.

Sten heard wails and screams from the crowd as the equally stunned security forces began clearing the square. A few meters away was a sprawled body he identified as that of Dr. Iskra.

Overhead, the bright cheerful day was gone, and storm clouds were rolling in. So much, Sten thought, for weather prophesying hurly-burly, witches, or anything else.

He walked over to the body and used a toe to turn it over.

"Th' lad's aboot ae dead as Ah've e'er seen."

"He is."

"Well," Alex said as he walked up beside Sten. "Th' king's

croaked, an' long live th' king an a' thae. What the clot are we goin' t' do next?''

Sten thought about it.

"I will be double-damned if I have even the slightest," he said honestly.

CHAPTER THIRTY-SIX

THIRTY-SEVEN E-HOURS LATER, thunder rolled across Rurik.

Sten was carefully composing his dispatch on Iskra's assassination that would give the full details—following up the initial flash sent to the Eternal Emperor and Prime within minutes of Sten's race back to the embassy.

Someone at the spaceport buzzed the embassy—an Imperial unit or units had just broadcast that they were inbound for landing.

Neither Sten nor Alex had time for more than a fast wonderment: Was this support? Some Imperials that had nothing to do with anything? An invasion?

The sky rumbled louder than one of Jochi's super thunderstorms, and ships swept overhead.

"Sufferin' Jesus," Alex swore. "Ah dinnae glim s' many putt-putts since th' war ended. Thae must be . . . twa, no, three squadrons. Wi' battlewagons. Somebody's through muckin' aboot—or else they've finally found us oot, lad.''

Sten didn't answer—he was also watching the sky. The second wave was coming in, behind the warships.

Troop transports, auxiliaries, and their screens.

Sten estimated that a full division of Imperial soldiers was arriving.

Now, just what in the hell . . .

". . . are you doing here, Ian?"

"You want the answer as of the day before yesterday," Ian Mahoney asked, "or what it is after we intercepted your charming message to Prime?"

"Whichever one I can handle," Sten said. They were on the flag bridge of the Imperial battleship *Repulse*, flying Mahoney's command flag. Outside, Rurik's once-deserted spaceport was studded with ships and looked like a central military field on Prime World.

Sten and Alex's estimates had been quite correct—Mahoney's force consisted of three battleship squadrons and Mahoney's "home" unit, the First Guards Division.

Mahoney had greeted them, introduced them to the admiral in charge of the naval forces, a rather officious sort named Langsdorff, chased him off the bridge, and opened a bottle of the special liquor made for the Emperor called Scotch.

"I'll give you both sets of my orders, then. The Emperor ordered me to put together a peacekeeping force just after the barracks bombing. He told me he wanted me to arrive, with muscle, at the proper time. My job description was to be Imperial governor. I was supposed to back you up, and make sure Iskra stayed on his throne."

Sten pursed his lips. "So nothing changed his mind, then? About Iskra."

"Was something supposed to?"

"Yeah. About twelve metric tons of the best stones I could polish and a solid silver bucket to keep them in. Never mind. I'll show you my rock collection later. The Iskra situation has taken care of itself."

"So I got my orders changed," Mahoney said. "The Altaics are now to be put under direct rule from Prime."

"Home rule," Alex wondered. "Thae's clottin' *ne'er* an answer. Sorry, sir."

"Kilgour, the day you can't put in an oar is the day I'm ready to go back to wearing a uniform. I don't like it either. But that's the direct orders from the Man."

"For how long?"

"I wasn't told."

Sten rolled his yet untouched drink between his palms, looking for the right way to ask his question. "Ian—what did your orders say about me?"

"Nothing. Should they have?"

"I don't know."

Sten explained that he had asked to be relieved previously, and that the Emperor had refused. Now, with Iskra dead, and the Altaics even closer to the cliff edge of chaos, he assumed he would either be headed for home in disgrace or at the least offered another assignment.

"I guess," Mahoney said, "that you're to continue as ambassador. At least until the shock waves settle down. Then I guess one of us will be moved on. I can't picture the Emperor keeping both of his high-dollar troubleshooters in the same forty-holer for very long. There's too many barns burnin' out there."

"Yeah."

"I don't think we need to worry about any kind of pecking order, do we, Sten?"

"That wasn't why I was asking."

"Okay. Everything's settled. Let's see if we can't jerk these clots into something resembling armed truce, starting tomorrow.

"Now, would you slug that back? You're getting touchy, being out here with all these murderous clots, touchy and paranoiac."

"I guess I am," Sten said, and followed Mahoney's orders, trying to relax.

Now, at least, he has something and somebody to lean on with some real clout. But the back of his mind told him that somehow, in some way, the Altaic Cluster would find a way to drag Mahoney, the navy, and the Imperial Guard down, into the bloody anarchy they seemed to love all too well.

CHAPTER THIRTY-SEVEN

THEY SAT ON the banks of Menynder's desolate pond. The old Tork was silent as Sten painted the bleak future facing the Altaics.

"You're at one of those moments in history," Sten said, "when disaster and opportunity are equal options. What happens next is your choice."

"Not mine," Menynder said. "Choices are made by people with hope. Right now, I have about as much hope for my people as I have of ever catching a clottin' fish in this pond." He gestured at the dead waters.

"Someone *will* replace Iskra," Sten said. "Chances are, all you'll do is trade one despot for another. Why leave it to chance?"

"Because no single person can successfully lead the Altaics," Menynder said. "In case you haven't noticed, none of us are very clottin' easy to get along with."

"I've noticed," Sten said dryly.

"In fact, we're rotten at it. We'd as soon as kill each other as breathe. So the top man is top killer. By definition . . . It's the way our stupid system works. The biggest and baddest tribe kicks drakh out of everybody else as often as possible. Which is how it stays big and bad."

"I was going to suggest something else," Sten said. "I was going to suggest putting together some kind of coalition government."

Menynder snorted. "Coalition? On the Altaics? Not clottin' likely."

"You almost put one together before," Sten said flatly.

Menynder's eyes narrowed. "What do you mean?"

Sten didn't bother with being casual. "The infamous dinner with the old Khaqan," he said. "I've never believed that story."

"What *do* you believe?" Menynder's voice was cold.

"I think the Khaqan was never invited at all," Sten said. "He wouldn't sit down with a bunch of Suzdal, Bogazi, and Torks. Much less *eat* with them.

"I think you . . . General Douw . . . Youtang and Diatry . . . had no idea he was even going to show up. In fact, I think you were all sitting together in that room trying to figure out how to get rid of him. And *you* are the only being in this cluster capable of hammering together a plot involving all representative species."

Sten gave a chilly smile. "If that's true," he said, "it only follows that you are also the only being capable of putting together the kind of coalition government I have in mind."

Menynder was silent. Sten's praise also included accusation.

"What I can't figure out," Sten said, "was how you killed the old bastard."

"I didn't," Menynder said. A beat. Then, "*We* didn't."

Sten shrugged. "It doesn't matter to me one way or the other."

"You'd have a murderer as a ruler?"

Sten looked at him. "Name one who isn't."

Menynder thought awhile. Finally, he said, "What if I don't go along with your idea? Will you just let it rest?"

Sten gave him a hard look. "Not this time."

"So I really don't have a choice," Menynder said.

"Maybe not. But it'll work a whole lot better if you *believe* you have a choice."

"Then I'd better say yes, real clottin' fast," Menynder said.

"That's the way I see it," Sten said.

"Menynder again," the Eternal Emperor snapped. "Why do you keep bringing up his name?"

"Because, sir, he's the best being for the job," Sten said.

The Eternal Emperor fish-eyed him. "Is that an 'I told you so,' Sten? Are you saying I screwed up by picking Professor Iskra?"

"It's not my place to judge your decisions, sir."

"Why do I keep hearing reprimands in your voice?" the Emperor said.

"Professor Iskra was the best choice from a poor lot, sir," Mahoney broke in. "Anyone can see that. Which is why, sir, I think Sten's idea now has merit."

"Committees make rotten law," the Emperor said. "They always have. They always will. Before you know it, every committee member has his own agenda, based on pure ego. Consensus becomes a joke. Paid for by power or money or lust or all of the above."

The Emperor drained his drink. His holographic image gestured across millions of light-years for Mahoney and Sten to do the same. "Clot a bunch of rule by committee," he said. But his mood had changed.

Glasses were emptied and refilled. Sten started to speak, but Mahoney tipped him the wink, so he buttoned his lip and let Mahoney grab the ball and run.

"I couldn't agree with you more, sir," Ian said. "Government by committee tends to be bloody useless. But, in this case, sir, might it not be a temporary solution? In fact, might it not eventually lead to a permanent one?"

"Explain," the Emperor ordered.

"The act of putting together a coalition," Mahoney said, "might also have the side benefit of calming things down. Putting a lid on the violence."

"I can track that logic," the Emperor said. "Go ahead."

"So, what if we give the coalition a time frame, sir? Such and such must be accomplished in such and such time. After that, the coalition ceases to exist. Automatically."

"Some kind of sundown law," the Emperor said.

"Exactly," Mahoney said. "The committee *must* be replaced by a more stable system by the date you mandate."

The Emperor thought. Then he said, "All right. You win. Put it into motion."

"Thank you, sir," Sten said, hiding the relief in his voice. "One other thing . . ."

The Emperor waved this down. "Yeah. I know. You need some

kind of dramatic gesture that says I am going along with this coalition idea.''

''Yessir,'' Sten said.

''How about a royal audience? Get Menynder and the others to Prime. I'll make a fuss over them in court. Bless their holy mission of peace, and all that rot. Send them back heroes. Will that do?''

''It'll do just fine, sir,'' Sten said.

The Emperor reached for the button that chopped the connection. He paused. ''This had *better* work,'' he snapped. Then his image was gone.

Sten turned to Mahoney. ''Ian . . . I owe you real clottin' big.''

Mahoney laughed. ''Put it on the tab, lad. Put it on the tab.''

''This is Connee George reporting live from Soward Spaceport. The delegation from the Altaic Cluster is due to land at any moment, gentlebeings. And look at that welcoming party waiting for them on the landing pad, Tohm!''

''A big Prime World welcome it is, Connee. My goodness. What an historic moment! I'm sure our viewers are glued to their livies, waiting to get an exclusive KRCAX Prime look at this distinguished delegation. I wonder what's going through our viewers' minds, now, Connee.''

''Probably the same as me, Tohm. Which is—wow! What a story!''

''Indeed it is, Connee. Indeed it is . . . uh . . . Give us some of your thoughts on this . . . uh . . . historic . . . uh . . . moment, Connee.''

''Well, the official release from the Emperor's press office tells us that on board are four beings bound for destiny. A destiny of peace. But, the release doesn't tell us the whole story, Tohm.''

''No, it doesn't . . . uh . . . does it?''

''Excuse me, Tohm, while I see if Captain P'wers can put us in a little closer. Can you get in over to the left of the landing pad, Gary?''

''I'll try, Connee. But the traffic is pretty fierce and the tower is giving us a hard way to go.''

''Just doing their jobs, I'm sure, Gary. And what a job that is!''

"Right, Connee . . . Okay . . . Hold on . . . Geesh, where'd that lighter come from?"

"Probably our competition, Gary. Ha-ha. Forgive my gloat, Tohm, but I'm sure the viewers at home will understand."

"Absolutely, Connee. They know that's why we're the number one news team on Prime. KRCAX Prime, Connee."

"It sure is, Tohm. Now, look at that view!"

"Sure is impressive. Good work, Captain P'wers!"

"Thanks, Tohm. Clot! Get outta my sky you bas—"

"Watch it, Gary. Kiddies at home. Ha-ha . . . Now that we've got an exclusive view for our exclusive live coverage, Connee, why don't you finish that rundown."

"Right, Tohm. Well, in the wake of the tragic death of Professor Iskra, the Eternal Emperor has come up with what most authorities agree is a sheer masterstroke of a plan to solve the troubles of the vital Altaic Cluster.

"On board that ship are the beings who will lead their region into a new era of peace. Heading the distinguished delegation is one Sr. Menynder. And his fellow Torks are one thousand percent behind this effort, Tohm."

"As they should be, Connee. Now, tell us about the . . . uh . . . others. A pretty distinguished group, themselves, right, Connee?"

"Right, Tohm . . . The Suzdal are lead by Youtang, one of the most able diplomats in the Altaic Cluster. On the Bogazi side is a being of equal importance, Diatry. Last, but certainly not least, is Sr. Gray—the leader of the all-important Jochi population."

"Great rundown, Connee. Now, tell our viewers what festivities lie ahead for these . . . uh . . . distinguished . . . uh . . . delegates."

"Well, you can be sure, Tohm, that Prime Worlders are not going to stint on our famous hospitality. First, there's the big welcoming at Soward."

"Excuse me, Connee, but I want to remind the viewers that we'll be covering that live. As soon as the delegates land."

"Go ahead, Tohm."

"Uh . . . I just did, Connee. Ha-ha."

"Ha-ha. Okay. After that, the Eternal Emperor has scheduled

a big public celebration at the palace. Which we shall also be covering.''

"Exclusively, Connee. Live and exclusive.''

"Right, Tohm. Following the celebration, there's a big royal ball set for tonight. Then—''

"Sorry to interrupt, Connee, but the tower reports the ship is coming in.''

"Don't be sorry, Gary, you're just doing your job. Ha-ha. Now, let's see how close we can get. We'll give our viewers a real KRCAX Prime look at things.''

"Tower's gonna be mad.''

"Don't worry, Captain P'wers. They're all pretty good sports in the tower. Besides, they're just—''

"I know, Connee . . . doing their jobs.''

Menynder peered at the ship's vidscreen as the spaceport rushed up at them. He grudgingly admitted to himself that he was excited.

As excited as a kid, you dumb old Tork. But what harm is there? Let's be honest. You've never been anywhere in your life. And now you're actually going to get to see Prime World. Which has to be every being's dream since . . . since clottin' forever.

Menynder chuckled to himself and glanced over at the other members of his party. Damned if they weren't as excited as he was. He noted that Youtang's sharp grin had a silly pup tilt to it. And Diatry's beak was wide open, looking at all the marvels of Prime. He couldn't see the Jochi, Gray. But he heard him sniggering.

Knock it off, Menynder. There is serious business ahead. Yeah. Sure. But just for now, can't I be a kid again? I mean, I gonna meet the clottin' Eternal Emperor. At a big clottin' for-real castle. Maybe even shake the Emperor's hand. Damn. Damn. Damn. If Momma could see me now.

Menynder saw a gravlighter darting across the screen. The sign on the side read: KRCAX Prime. Some kind of livie news crew, he assumed. He idly wondered if the lighter captain might be cutting it a little too close. Nah. These were the best of the best, weren't they? A by-God news crew from by-God Prime World. Absolute pros. He was sure.

But—oh, my clot. It was still coming! Hey . . . What's going on?

"Look out!" Gray screamed. "We're gonna—"

Menynder had an instant to feel the jolt and see the screen go from white to black to collapse. And then he felt the great heavy hand smashing into his back. Heard the crack of his seat giving away.

And then Menynder was ramming forward. The far cabin wall rushing at him.

He heard screamsscreamsscreams. And he thought . . . Aw, drakh!

"This is KBSNQ, reporting live from Soward Spaceport. For those viewers joining us late—there's been a terrible tragedy here at Prime World's main spaceport.

"A delegation of high-level beings from the Altaic Cluster—arriving here for crucial peace talks with the Eternal Emperor—has collided in midair with a lighter carrying a local news team.

"All beings aboard both craft are believed dead. Imperial investigators are at the site now. The Eternal Emperor has ordered all flags lowered to half-mast for a one-week period of mourning.

"We now return to our regular programming. Be assured we will interrupt if further developments warrant. This is Pyt'r Jynnings reporting live for KBNSQ. You give us twenty-two minutes . . . and we'll give you the Empire."

CHAPTER THIRTY-EIGHT

STEN SAT BROODING at the dark skyline of Rurik. The only light showing was the faint, far-off glow of the eternal flame burning in the Square of the Khaqans. All was silent . . . waiting.

He felt Cind's hand touch his arm. "Menynder was our last hope," he said.

"I know."

"I talked him into going. All he wanted to do was sit by that damned dead pond. In peace."

"I know that, too."

"He was a crooked old dog. But—clot. I liked him."

Her answer was a tighter grip.

"I haven't the faintest idea what to do next," Sten said.

"Maybe . . . the Emperor will think of something."

"Right."

"Mahoney, then."

"He's as lost as I am. Right now, he's battening down the hatches. Getting ready."

"You think it's going to be that bad?"

"Yeah. Real bad."

"But it wasn't anybody's fault. Except maybe that damned news crew. It was an accident, for clot's sake."

"That's not what *they* think." He pointed out at the silent city. "They think it was a plot. That the Emperor lured Menynder and the others to their deaths."

"That's ridiculous. Why would he?"

"They don't need a reason," Sten said. "They just need someone to blame. We screwed up last. So we're it."

Cind shivered. Sten put an arm around her. "Thanks," he said.

323

"What for?"

"For being here . . . with me . . . That's all."

She snuggled into the arm. "You just try to chase me off," she said. "You just try."

Even in his gloom, Sten was comforted. He leaned back and pulled Cind closer to him.

They sat there until dawn. The sun came up huge and red and angry.

A few minutes later, they heard the first gunfire.

"W' hae snipers 'n rioters 'n looters, oh my," Kilgour said. "Which is noo ver' good. But it's noo ver' bad, either."

"What could be worse?" Sten asked.

"Ah'm feared w' hae thae comin' up, lad."

"Which is?"

"A braw clottin' absence a' army."

"Come to think of it, I haven't seen any Jochi troops about, either. But I thought that was good news. Go ahead. Tell me different. I'm getting used to this depression. I'll probably miss it when it's gone."

"I's th' puir bein's here thae's turned matters topsy-turvy i' y'r wee nog," Alex said. "Bleak's happy. An' joy i' bleak. Afflicted by their clottin' weather, puir things. Eat hate 'n ill will wi' breakfast haggis."

"Thanks for reminding me about stuffed sheep's stomach, Kilgour. Yum yum. I feel much better, now."

"Ah'm rejoicin't t' be lookin't oot frae y', lad."

"Tell me about the army."

"Absence of army, son."

"Yeah, that."

"Well, i' ain't clottin' there, aye? Nary a trooper or trooper's whore t' be glimt i' Rurik. Had m' frick 'n fracks up f'r hours, snoopit an' poopit aboot. Zed th' barracks. Zed th' ossifers' and noncompoops' mess."

"Where the clot did they get off to?"

"Braw question. So Ah query't an em'nent silvery-haired fox."

"General Douw?"

"Aye. He's away, too."

Sten sat up straight in his chair. "Where'd he go?"

"Off wi' his troopies. Maneuvers, his ferret of a press officer said. Annual maneuvers in yon alps." Alex pointed off in the general direction of the mountain range that half-ringed the wide Rurik valley.

"Maneuvers? Oh, bulldrakh. You don't believe it, do you?"

"Noooooo. 'Less th' Jochi troopies—brave lads an' lassies a'—go on maneuvers wi' ammunition all alive, alive-o."

"Drakh," Sten said.

"Hip high, old son. 'N risin' fast."

Douw may have been a silvery-haired fool with a pennyweight brain. But perched on a camp stool in his mountain command center, he looked every inch a general. And acted like a very angry one.

"We don't need proof," he snarled across the war table. "Insisting on proof is the last refuge of cowards."

"No Suzdal has ever been called a coward," came a growl. It was Tress, warlord of the Suzdal worlds.

"Don't be so quick to take offense," Snyder said. He was Menynder's cousin and, now, the de facto war chief of the Torks. "That's our problem in the Altaics. Every time we consider unified action, someone gets his nose out of joint and the whole thing collapses."

"Respect we must have," Hoatzin said. His voice was harsh, weary. His wife, Diatry, had died with Menynder and the others. It was now Hoatzin's task to lead the Bogazi hutches into battle. If there was to be one.

"Divide and conquer. Divide and conquer. That's always been the Emperor's way," Douw said. He was not being hypocritical. He had truly forgotten that Iskra had used those very words, though in a different—and Jochian—context.

"So, we fight," Tress said. "What chance do we have? Against the Eternal Emperor? His forces—"

"Who cares about the size of his forces?" Douw broke in. "The terrain is ours. The people are ours. If we all stand together . . . we must prevail."

"Emperor not so strong as he thinks," Hoatzin said. "Fight

Tahn many years. He had victory, yes. But not so good a victory. Very long war. Soldiers, I think, are tired. Also, as general say, this not their land. What they fight for?''

"Still," Tress said, "the Emperor has never been defeated before."

"It happen once," the Bogazi said. "Must have. Why else the Emperor disappear? I think he flee privy council."

No one had ever put the Emperor's disappearance in that light before. It was wrong thinking. But it was the kind of wrong thinking that leads to treacherous conclusions.

"We must all join together," Douw said. "For the first time in our history, we must stand united in one cause. The cause is just. Our soldiers are brave. We only need the will."

There was a long silence around the table. A nesting bird fussed overhead.

Tress rose to his haunches. "I will speak to my pack mates," he said.

"What will you tell them?" Douw asked.

"That we fight. Together."

The sniper still made no sense to Cind.

"Dinnae fash, lass," Alex advised. "Th' shooter's peepers hae big crosses on 'em noo."

"By my father's frozen buttocks, you're thick sometimes."

"Now y're cussin' a' me in y'r heathen Bhor tongue. No respect f'r y'r puir gray mentor. Shame, shame on y' lass."

"Come on, Alex. How did he get into the palace? Why was he able to pick the best window to shoot from? How come he had all the time in the world to set up shop, find out where Sten would be sitting, plus create a diversion for his escape?"

"We hae a team pokin' 'n a probin' on th' dread plotters, wee Cind."

"No hope, there," Cind said. "Too many suspects. Too many possible combinations. They've got better chance at winning the Imperial lottery."

" 'N y're believin't y' c'n do better?"

Cind thought a moment, then nodded. "Sure. Because they're looking in the wrong direction. The guy was a pro. From his choice of positions, to that old rifle he chose as a weapon, down to the hand-molded bullets.''

''Ho-kay. Yon dead shooter wae a pro. This is noo unusual i' a sniper. Wha' else is buggin't y'?'' Despite himself, Kilgour was getting interested. Cind was maybe onto something.

''Two things. The first is personal. He was trying to kill Sten. Clot, he almost did!''

Kilgour knew this, tsked, and waved for the key point.

''What really gets me,'' Cind said, ''was that he was the *only* sniper. Dammit, that makes no sense. Under the circumstances, there should have been a whole host of rooftop shooters. Or none. Not unless somebody wanted to be extra sure of exactly who died.

''Fine. We know he didn't have to go for Iskra. The coroner's report tells us the attack on the stands got him. But the same attack missed Sten. So . . . Wham! He tries to take him out. Thanks to you and your chain-mail tailor, it didn't work. But . . . still . . .''

Alex was thoughtful. ''Aye . . . Thae hae t'be more.''

''More of what?'' came Mahoney's voice. ''What trouble are you two cooking up?''

They whirled to see that Ian had entered the room. Cind was used to big beings moving silently. Look at Alex. Look at her Bhor comrades. But Mahoney still astonished her. It wasn't that he was just, well, getting on in years . . . But his large Irish body and round friendly face didn't look as if they belonged to someone who could cat around corners and into rooms.

She started to snap to attention and acknowledge her superior officer. Mahoney waved her down. ''Just tell me what you two are plotting.''

Cind filled him in on the mysterious sniper. Mahoney listened closely, then shook his head. ''It's an interesting mystery, I agree,'' he said. ''And the man was certainly a pro. Which means he was hired. Which also likely means whoever hired him would have had a cutout. Therefore, if you find out who the sniper is, *that's* all you'll learn. He even might be an interesting fellow, in an evil sort of way. But, I'm afraid in this case, x plus y can only equal: who cares?''

''I don't think so, sir,'' Cind said. ''Not this time. And it's not a feeling, but an instinct. Professional instinct. See, when I was hunting him, I did my clotting best to try thinking like him.''

"Naturally," Mahoney said. "Go on." The former Mantis chief found himself getting drawn in.

"Pretty soon I *was* thinking like him. Even named him 'Cutie' in my mind.''

"So, what makes 'Cutie' different?'' Mahoney wanted to know.

Cind sighed. "It boils down to his knowledge of the terrain *and* his target. Which means, I think Cutie had been around the palace for a while. I think he checked out every square inch of it.

"I also think he would have done his damnedest to get to know his target. Otherwise he wouldn't have been comfortable. No. Cutie would've wanted to know Sten. Real well. Have an idea about his private habits. Know which way he would duck when the attack started.''

"Aye . . . Quite logical, lass," Alex said. " 'N maybe . . . Jus' mayhap . . .''

Mahoney smacked the table. "Of course! He would have tried to visit the embassy. Or, at least attend some official functions that Sten would have been at.''

"Exactly," Cind said. "Which means either Sten, or Alex, might recognize him.''

She looked up at Mahoney. "I want Sten to go to the morgue, sir," she said. "To see if he can ID the remains.''

"Tell him, not me," Ian said, quite sensibly.

Cind lifted an eyebrow. "He'll think it's a waste of time, sir,'' she said. "Maybe if you . . .'' She let it dangle.

"I'll drag him along by the ear," Mahoney said. "Come on Alex. Let's go chat with the ambassador.''

The basement morgue was white and cold, with antiseptically filtered air that didn't cover the occasional whiff of odor that put a rusty taste on the tongue.

"Hang on a sec," the human attendant said. "I ain't finished me lunch.'' He waved a thick sandwich in their faces. Tomato sauce seeped through the bread.

Cind was about ready to rip his face off. Even with Mahoney

and Kilgour prodding, Sten had stubbornly refused to go. He was too busy, he said. Up-to-his-ears-in-drakh busy.

Remarkably, however, she now watched him step in. Instead of barking orders, he slipped a sheaf of credits out of his pocket and waved it under the attendant's nose.

"You could always bring your lunch along," he said.

The attendant snatched the bills, motioned with the sandwich-filled hand, and trotted off. They followed.

"It's the only way to get a bureaucrat's attention," Sten muttered to her. "Yelling just makes them stubborner—and stupider."

The attendant was moving along the drawered crypts. "Let's see . . . Where'd I put that Jon Doe?" He aimed a remote box, pressed the button, and a corpse drawer rolled out with a crash. Cold air blasted from the crypt.

The attendant peered into the drawer. A drip of red sauce fell onto the body. He wiped it up with a thumb, then licked his thumb clean.

"Nope. Wrong guy." He jabbed the button and the drawer slammed shut. The attendant laughed. "Sorry to stiff you with the stiff."

Nobody laughed at his joke. He shrugged. "We been pretty busy since the Khaqan died," he said. "Got more clients than we got time."

He laughed again. "My wife's happier'n pig in drakh. I been on golden overtime for months. One more big shootin' match and we can go buy that retirement cottage we been dreamin' about."

"How fortunate for you," Cind said.

The attendant caught her tone. "Wasn't me that put 'em here, lady," he said. "That's *your* job. You frag 'em, I bag 'em. That's my motto."

He aimed the remote at another crypt and pressed the button. The drawer slid out. He peered into it. "Yep. That's the Doe you laid down your dough for. Still dead, too. Ha-ha. Belly up to the bones, boys. And see your future." He snickered at Cind. "You too, lady."

But it was Mahoney who looked first. His reaction was quick. And it was massive.

"Mother of Mercy," he intoned. "It's Venloe!"

Sten was rocked back. "It can't be." He took his own look. "Damn! It's Venloe all right."

"Thae's noo possible," Alex said as he was confirming their view. "But i' bloody is!"

Cind didn't know what they were talking about at first. Then she remembered. Venloe was the man responsible for killing the Emperor!

"I thought he was—"

"In a maximum clottin' security prison," Sten finished for her. "Last I heard, he was so far under the ground they had to pipe in the sunlight."

"He must have escaped," Cind said.

"Another impossibility," Sten said. He looked again. "But . . . there he is."

"Top part a' him, anyways," Alex said.

Mahoney frowned at the waxen features staring up at him. He remembered the day he had brought Venloe to ground. And their subsequent conversation. Venloe was a being who could squirm out of just about any situation—even the Emperor's most secure prison.

"But—what was he doing here?" Cind asked. "Who could have—"

The rest of her question was cut off by Mahoney's emergency beeper. He whipped it from his belt and keyed in. "Mahoney, here."

The officer's voice rasped through the speaker. "You better get back here fast, sir. We just picked up a fleet heading for Jochi. They're confirmed unfriendlies, sir."

Mahoney was already running as he keyed out. The others sprinted after him.

Venloe lay cold in his drawer behind them, his mystery forgotten in the impending attack.

The morgue attendant—who had overheard the news—hustled off to make his wife an even happier woman.

CHAPTER THIRTY-NINE

ADMIRAL HAN LANGSDORFF had obviously either slept through or cut his class in Basic Military Mistakes some fifty years earlier.

He took the three Imperial battleship flotillas out to stop the Suzdal/Bogazi invasion fleets full of confidence and contempt. This would be a simple, if bloody, mission. First he expected these primitive beings—Langsdorff concealed it rather well, but he was a xenophobe—to freeze when confronted with the mailed fist of the Empire. After they recovered from their awe and terror, they might, at worst, form a battle line and attempt a frontal engagement.

Langsdorff dangled one cruiser squadron as bait and arranged his main battle force in a lopsided wing behind and to one side of the decoys.

The enemy would attempt to attack the Imperial force, and it would be simple for Langsdorff to turn their flank and have all of them enfilade.

It was not a complex plan. But simplicity was a virtue in battle. Besides, how could any consortium of oversize avians and canines stand against the Empire?

He certainly wasn't the first battle leader to hold his foe in utter contempt. History has made a very full list of occasions when the same thing happened:

The Hsiung-Nu long-term disaster in Turkestan. The Little Horn. Isandhlwana. Magersfontein. Suomussalmi. Dien Bien Phu. Saragossa. And on, and on, and on.

Even the name of his flagship might have helped. Langsdorff vaguely know that the *Repulse*, many incarnations before, had been a water-borne warship. He even vaguely remembered it was something called a battle cruiser. That was the sum of his knowledge.

He did not know that the *Repulse*'s namesake—and an accompanying battleship—had sailed calmly into harm's way, confident that the mere presence of battleships would create paralytic terror in the enemy; that no one would hazard land-based aircraft over the open sea; and that certainly no one from the never-sufficiently-despised Mongoloid subspecies of the human race would *dare* confront these magnificent examples of Empire.

It took the Japanese land-based atmospheric bombers just under one hour to sink both warships.

Langsdorff scanned the screen. The longer-ranging Imperial sensors had picked up the Suzdal/Bogazi fleets. He snorted. These beings could do nothing right. If he were invading a cluster's home world, he would certainly have come up with more warships than he was looking at—even if he had to bolt missile tubes to every lunar ferry he could requisition.

Two hostile cruiser squadrons smashed at the Imperial cruisers in a frontal assault. Bare minutes later, two more Suzdal/Bogazi formations—these formed around tacship carriers and heavy cruisers—came down on the Imperials from above and below, like the closing jaws of a nutcracker.

The Imperial cruisers fought back—but were outgunned.

The battle was joined. Admiral Langsdorff ordered his battlewagons in, to envelop the Suzdal/Bogazi left flank, just as the human Turks had attempted in the sea battle called Lepanto. But unlike the Ottomans, he kept none of his forces in reserve.

The Suzdal/Bogazi fleet commanders believed, just as Langsdorff did, that in battle simplest is best. Their tactics were taken from the clichéd drawing of a minnow being swallowed by a slightly larger fish being swallowed by a shark being swallowed by a whale.

Because farther above and below the jaws that had closed on the Imperial cruisers were the real Suzdal/Bogazi heavies. Their admirals waited until Langsdorff's battleship formations were irretrievably committed.

And then they closed the bigger jaws on the far richer prize: the entire Imperial strike force.

Langsdorff was dead before he could bleat for help—help that just didn't exist.

The battle was a catastrophe—for the Empire.

The Suzdal/Bogazi lost five cruisers, fourteen destroyers, and a scattering of lighter craft.

The Imperial *survivors* were one battleship, three cruisers, one tacship carrier, and twenty troops.

The Suzdal/Bogazi fleets reformed triumphantly and drove on toward Jochi. Their victory would not, however, be studied at many military academies, even those of the victors.

Massacres, for some reason, aren't vastly interesting to soldiers.

Langsdorff's disaster left Jochi wide open for invasion—and the First Imperial Guards Division stranded on a hostile world.

CHAPTER FORTY

THE EMBASSY SHUDDERED under the heavy storm blasting down from the mountains. Even here—in the conference chamber buried far under the building—Sten could hear lightning crack and thunder roll.

He shivered. Not from the cold rain outside, but from the words being spoken by the strange being hovering a meter above the chamber floor.

". . . I regret to say, my reasoning did not prove faulty. Perhaps that's why I went to such risk and trouble to visit Dr. Rykor. False hope that I was in terrible error. And that our wise friend would gently guide me back to reality."

Sr. Ecu gave a flick of his tail and drifted to Sten's side. A sensitive tendril whiskered out and touched Sten's hand.

"But there was no error. The Eternal Emperor is quite mad—and only certain disaster can result."

Sten said nothing. He felt orphaned for the second time in his life. He had worked and fought for the Emperor since adolescence—after his real family had been killed.

"I can barely bring myself to believe this," Mahoney said. Although he had suspected as much for some time, he found the hard truth difficult to choke down.

"I am very sorry, my old friend," Sr. Ecu said. "But you of all people know just how correct I am. However . . . there are two other things I should tell you both."

He shifted position, dropping a little lower to the floor. A tendril whiskered through the open case. Mahoney found himself holding a fiche.

"That is an intelligence file my operatives have put together. You see, when I became convinced the Emperor was insane, I wondered who was advising him now. Who had his ear? Who was doing his bidding?"

Mahoney stared at the fiche. "And you learned?"

"Poyndex," Ecu said flatly.

Sten sucked in air as another blow fell.

"But the man's a turncoat," Mahoney protested. "He betrayed the Emperor to join the privy council. Then he betrayed them to save his own life."

"This is true. And now he commands the Emperor's efforts to bring the Empire's provinces into dominion status. A job, my sources tell me, you rejected. On moral grounds."

Mahoney slumped in his chair, a portrait of despair. "How could things come to such a pass?" he said. "After all these years?"

The Manabi's tendril drew forth more bad news. It was Sten's turn. He was presented with two paper-jacketed files. One was blue, the other red. He duly saw his name on both.

"Your personnel records," Sr. Ecu said. "Forgive my intrusion into your privacy."

Sten shrugged. What did it matter now?

"The first file—the blue one—is your official file. A record for public consumption of your many achievements in Imperial Service.

"A close analysis shows there are gaps in that record. Gaps that are artfully covered over." Sten and Mahoney both knew that those so-called gaps were the secret missions Sten had undertaken in the service of the Emperor.

"Don't bother trying to explain those missing years to me," Sr. Ecu said. "I'm sure I can easily guess the nature of missions you undertook in the Emperor's name."

"Thanks," Sten said wearily. "I guess."

"Please open the second file, Sten," Sr. Ecu said.

Sten thumbed back the red jacket, revealing a cover sheet, with the letter head of Internal Security. Sten looked up at Sr. Ecu, bewildered.

"I'm being . . . investigated?"

"The investigation has already been accomplished," Sr. Ecu said. "When you have time to look it over, you will see that the gentlebeing at the Internal Security office had a different view of those gaps.

"A view that leads to the unalterable conclusion that you are a traitor, Sten. You, the most loyal of all the Emperor's subjects, have been the tool of his enemies."

Sten quickly thumbed through and saw evidence piled upon evidence. He closed the red file. "Ammunition, I assume?" he asked.

"Exactly. If you fail in any undertaking—or somehow anger the Emperor—that is the file which will come into play. And your achievements will go the way of the shredder."

Sten felt the room swaying around him. It wasn't the storm. He steadied himself. "I thank you for this warning, Sr. Ecu. But—I assume you have more than just my reputation in mind."

Sr. Ecu was taking a terrible risk with this visit. Yes . . . he had used an absolutely secure transport provided by Ida of the Rom—Sten's old Mantis team friend. If anyone learned the nature of his mission, Sr. Ecu was not endangering only himself, but his entire species.

The Manabi dropped all pretense of diplomatic fine wording. "I was hoping you could help," he said.

This shook Sten. "Help? But—how? I don't control armies and fleets. I'm just—"

"Don't get alarmed, young Sten," Sr. Ecu said. "I'm not sure what I'm asking you to do. Except . . . think . . . think hard. When this ugly business in the Altaics is over . . . come to me on my home world. You, too, Ian. We accomplished a miracle once before, did we not?"

"But that was just the privy council," Sten said. "Not the Eternal Emperor."

"I think we should listen to him, Sten," Mahoney said, his voice a rough whisper. "I swore my allegiance to a symbol. Not a man."

Sten was silent. How could he explain? There were no words for the loss he had just suffered. The king is dead, indeed. Long live the king. Suddenly, he thought: What's to hold me now? Whom do I owe? Besides Cind? Besides my friends? He thought about his retreat on Smallbridge. He ached for its forests and hills and his cabin by the frozen lakes.

"Find someone else," he told Sr. Ecu. "I don't mean to sound like an ingrate—but I'm going to do my best to take your warning and make very selfish use of it."

"I'll still be waiting, young Sten," the Manabi said. "I have faith in you."

"You'd better go," Sten said brusquely. "My people will get you back to your ship. Have a safe journey. And thanks for your trouble."

Sten headed for the door. Mahoney came slowly after him.

"Rykor said you would refuse me at first," Sr. Ecu called after him. "But in the end, she said you'd come around."

Sten was unreasonably angry. He snarled back at the gentle being who had come so far. "Clot Rykor!"

"Just think about it, Sten," he heard the Manabi say as he went out the door. "It will save us all a great deal of time."

Sten stormed through the reception hall, his guts a knot of white-hot anger. He wanted to get away. Anyplace. Anywhere. Get drunk. Chew on a pistol barrel.

He barely noticed the pale, frightened face of the reception officer as he swept past the main desk and headed for the embassy doors.

Mahoney's big paw came down on his shoulder and swung him around. It was all Sten could do to keep himself from striking out at his friend.

"Sten! Listen to me, dammit! Remember what I said back on Prime? Before all this started? Now—I think I know where our answer might be."

Sten shrugged off the hand. "I've had enough with these games, Ian," he said. "Let somebody else look for answers for a change. Clot! I don't even care what the question is anymore."

Four large individuals in the gray uniforms of Internal Security stepped into view. Sten's heart lurched as the meaning of their presence sunk in.

The IS beings strode up to them. The commander flashed his warrant card. Another whipped out plas manacles. Sten braced himself.

The IS commander pushed past him. Sten's head reeled as the man addressed Ian. "Governor Mahoney, you will come with us, please."

Sten gaped. What the clot was happening? Why weren't they after *him*?"

"By what authority?" he heard Mahoney's voice boom.

"By the authority of the Eternal Emperor," the commander snapped. "You have been charged with incompetence in the face of the enemy. You are hereby relieved of command. You will be escorted to Prime World where you will be indicted . . . and if an indictment is returned . . . you will be tried."

Sten tried desperately to make sense of this. They must be talking about what happened in the Disputed Worlds. Admiral Langsdorff's foolish and humiliating defeat. He stepped in between the IS officers and Mahoney.

"But—he had nothing to do with that," Sten protested.

"Out of the way, Ambassador," the commander said.

Sten turned to call for help, wondering, even as he did, what fool would rush to his aid.

"That's all right, Sten," Mahoney said. "Let's not make things worse."

He pushed Sten aside. "I'm ready," he told the commander.

Sten watched helplessly as they shoved Ian against the wall, kicked his feet apart, and put him through a thorough, spirit-grinding search. Mahoney's hands were bent behind his back. The manacles were snapped on—so tight that Sten could see Ian's hands engorge with blood.

A moment later, Mahoney was being marched out of the embassy.

"I'll call the Emperor," Sten shouted after him. "It's a mistake. I know it. A terrible mistake."

"Just go home, lad," Mahoney yelled as he was shoved through the door. "Remember what I said—and go home!"

A hiss of doors . . . and he was gone.

Sten raced to the com room and pushed the night officer aside. He hammered out the code himself and punched the send button.

"I want to speak to the Emperor," he shouted at the official who finally took his call. "Right now, dammit!"

"I'm sorry, Ambassador Sten," the official said. "But I have been given explicit instructions. The Emperor does not wish to speak with you. Under any circumstances."

"Hold on, you clot!" Sten snarled. "This is Ambassador Sten, calling. Not some jerk-off clerk."

The official pretended to scan a list before him. "Sorry. No mistake. The Emperor specifically asked that your name be removed from the personal access list. My apologies if this inconveniences you . . . but I'm sure you can get what you need through official channels."

The screen blanked.

Sten sagged back. The only thing he could do for Mahoney now was pray.

And this was impossible for a man who, quite suddenly, had no gods at all.

CHAPTER FORTY-ONE

MAHONEY'S RELIEF AND arrest sent what little morale there was among the Imperial Forces into free-fall. To Sten, Mahoney was not just his mentor and friend, but the man who had saved his life back on Vulcan.

To Kilgour, a man who had little faith in officers, Mahoney was, among other things, a respected leader—he had been Alex's CO back in Mantis Section, years before he had met Sten.

To Cind, Otho, and the Bhor, Mahoney was an honored war leader and elder. If he had somehow offended the Emperor, they agreed, he should have been given a chance to cut off his own beard in council and await the verdict—rather than being escorted off by armed beings as if he were some kind of criminal.

To the First Guards Division, Mahoney was not just one of them, having begun his military service in their ranks, but their most venerated commander. During the Tahn war, he had been their commanding general.

Their current commanding general, Paidrac Sarsfield, had even been a company commander under Mahoney, back on a hellworld called Cavite.

None of them understood what mistake, let alone what nameless crime, Mahoney had committed.

Not that they talked about it.

The event, and the situation, were too objectionable for that. The soldiers didn't even bitch about what had happened.

Sten would have had to take some sort of action to build the esprit back up to a functional level—he was unsure what it could be—if there weren't a worse nightmare approaching:

339

The Suzdal/Bogazi invasion fleet, oncoming at full speed. There was no way Sten could see to stop the invasion.

Two elements kept their own council on the relief of Mahoney:
The Gurkhas.
And Fleet Admiral Mason.

Alex slammed into Sten's office, crashing the door behind him. The jamb splintered, but held.

"Ah hae," he said, sans preamble, "jus' decoded our marchin' orders. Except thae'll be none ae us marchin't. Eyes Only. Nae frae our clottin' respected Emperor, lang may he wave, but frae some clot i' th' Imperial office."

He spun the printout across to Sten.

It was brief:

CONTINUE MISSION AS OUTLINED. IMPERIAL DIRECT RULE WILL CONTINUE. MAINTAIN PUBLIC ORDER.

"Wi' no suggestion ae how," Alex said. "There's some clot oot there gone sarky—an' Ah know who. Thae braw flyin't ray was right."

Sten wasn't paying any attention to Alex's ravings.

"So whae d' we do?"

Sten made up his mind. "Can you mickey the code log?"

"Wi' m' left foot. Y' wan' a bogere message sayin't 'tis time t' haul, or what?"

"Negative. Too hard to back up. We just never received this."

"Aye, sir."

Kilgour turned to go. "Y' know, lad. When we gie our arses off an' away, Ah'll no be servin't th' Emp. F'r better 'r worse, he dinnae deserve m' oath no more."

"Let's worry about asses and away first. That's unlikely enough to happen anyway," Sten advised in as neutral a tone as he could manage.

"Admiral Mason, I'm detaching you from command of the *Victory*."

"Yes, sir."

"I want you to take over what remains of that clot Langsdorff's fleet—and the escort ships that were left with the Guard's transports."

"Yes, sir."

"The *Victory* will be detached and placed under my direct command, as with the tacship carrier that made it back."

"The *Bennington*, sir."

"Thank you."

"What are my instructions?" Mason asked, still in that chilling neutral voice.

"We're preparing to evacuate all Imperial elements from Jochi and the Altaic Cluster. How that'll be done, with the minimum casualties, I'm not sure."

"What about the First Guards?"

"I'll be responsible for them, as well."

"Yessir. May I comment?"

"You may," Sten said.

"Do you really think you're qualified as a general?"

"Admiral, I don't think *anybody* is qualified to lead a retreat under fire, which is what we're going to undertake. But I'll remind you I've stumbled through one. During the war. On a planet called Cavite. Now, if you have any other insults?"

"No. But I have another question."

Sten nodded.

"What changed things? I thought the Emperor wanted the Altaics held. I thought this armpit had some great diplomatic significance that I'm not aware of."

"I filed an operations order this morning to Prime," Sten lied. "Saying the Altaics cannot be held. I've had no response. So I propose to proceed with the withdrawal. If the situation changes, you'll be among the first to be told.

"That's all."

Picket ships announced that the Suzdal/Bogazi fleet was three E-days from Jochi's solar system.

* * *

"General Sarsfield, if you're alone?"

"I am, sir."

"I want you to saddle up your division. Get all noncombat items wrapped and ready. Anything that's not absolutely vital to an on-planet combat mission can be stashed on the transports. What's the minimum time your division requires for a move?"

"The regs say ten E-hours when we're at full alert. We can do it in five."

"Good."

"Might I ask where we're going?"

"Home. I hope. But there might be a few detours on the way."

"That's enough," Sten ordered, rubbing eyes that were feeling, from the inside and out, like hard-poached eggs. He blanked all of the screens in the conference room, and as the yammer of impending doom stopped, the room fell silent.

He went to a table, where a previously unnoticed covered tray sat. He lifted one of the salver covers and picked up a sandwich. It was only a little stale. He tossed it to Alex and took one for himself.

Beside it was a decanter. He took the stopper out and sniffed. Stregg.

Was that advised?

Why not? Disaster would be the same sober as boiled.

He poured drinks, handed one to Alex, and they toasted.

Bless Cind. She must have had someone slip the refreshments in sometime after she had taken over as commander of the embassy guard.

"Y' hae any gran' strat'gy developed?" Alex wondered as he inhaled the sandwich and scooped for another.

"Not much more'n it better be better than Cavite," Sten said. Mahoney had begun the withdrawal of the outmanned, outgunned Imperial Forces from that world, and Sten had finished the task. He had gotten the civilians out, and less than two thousand of the Imperial soldiers. Sten himself had ended up a prisoner of war.

He had been given the highest medals for this accomplishment, and he had been celebrated as a brilliant war leader. Sten had never considered that true—he thought Cavite a complete disaster and his efforts no more than damage control at best.

At least this time there weren't very many Imperial civilians, beyond the embassy staff.

"Aye," Alex agreed, although he had never judged Cavite as harshly as Sten did.

"I have a couple of ideas," Sten continued, "but right now my brain seems to have spun out."

"'Tis nae wonder," Kilgour said. "It's lackin' but an hour 'til dawn. P'raps we'd best have a bit of a lie-down."

Sten yawned, suddenly very sleepy. "Good thought. Put a wakeup in for two hours."

There was a tap on the door.

"I'll chase th'—"

"Enter," Sten said.

The door opened. Three Gurkhas stood there. Sten felt quite grimy suddenly. In spite of the hour, all three of them were dressed as if for barracks inspection.

He held back a groan. The Gurkhas were Jemedar Lalbahadur Thapa, and newly promoted Havildars Chittahang Limbu and Mahkhajiri Gurung.

The last time the trio had confronted him was on Prime, when they had offered themselves and twenty-four other Gurkhas for Sten's service, breaking the long tradition that the Nepalese mercenaries served only the Eternal Emperor, an offer that had visibly put the Emperor's teeth on edge.

The Gurkhas saluted. Sten returned the salute and told them to stand at ease.

"We are sorry to both you at this hour," Lalbahadur said formally. "But this was the only time we could find. We would like to speak in private, if it is possible."

Sten nodded—and Alex swallowed the sandwich, washed it down with stregg, and vanished. He offered them seats. They preferred to stand.

"We have a question or two about the future that we are unable to answer," Lalbahadur went on. "This is utter foolishness of course, since without question those evil feathered capons who are flocking toward us will peck us into tiny bits and hurl those bits into the garbage pits, to be torn at by their jackal friends. Am I not correct?"

"You are without a doubt correct," Sten agreed. All four of them smiled—or at least bared their teeth.

"But once we have withdrawn from this dung heap of a cluster, what will be our next duties?"

"I—I guess you will return to the service of the Eternal Emperor. At least until your enlistments are up." Sten puzzled at this total irrelevancy, wondering why the Gurkhas were wasting his time now, but his backbrain told him that these soldiers often went obliquely to a vital interest that concerned the moment.

"I do not think so," Lalbahadur said firmly. "We must consult with our king, back on Earth, and with our superior officers in the bodyguard to be certain. But I do not think so.

"We Nepalese withdrew from Imperial Service when the Emperor was killed, refused all offers from those yeti afterbirths who called themselves the privy council and other gangsters, and returned only with the Emperor."

"Ancient history, Jemedar. And I am very sleepy."

"I will make my point rapidly. It is our opinion that we were in error to come back. This Emperor we agreed to serve is not as the last one my people served. I think it is not he who was reborn, but a Rakasha, a demon who wears his face."

"My grandfather's grandfather," Mahkhajiri Gurung added, further confusing the issue, "would have said his aspect is now that of Bhairava, the Frightful One, and can only be worshiped in drunkenness."

"As much as I'd like to get sloshed with you gentlemen," Sten said, feeling waves of exhaustion crash down on him, "could we get to the point?"

"Very well," Lalabhadur said. "If we are not in violation of our contract, and even then I will consider breaking it, we would wish to enter your service on a permanent basis, sir. And once more I speak not just for the three of us, but for the other twenty-four as well."

Wonderful, Sten thought. That would further endear him to the Eternal Emperor.

"Thank you. I am honored. And I shall keep your offer in mind. But—and I am not saying what I shall be doing when we get out of this dung pool—I doubt I shall need bodyguards."

"You are wrong, sir. But you will see that, later. And thank you for honoring *us*."

The Gurkhas saluted and withdrew, leaving Sten to wonder what the blazes *that* had been about.

The hell with it. He was too tired. And he still had to figure out a way to get out of the Altaics.

"Base . . . this is Little Ear Three Four Bravo," the com drawled, in a voice that had been carefully built to *never* show strain, stress, or fear.

"I have many, many hostiles on-screen, headed yours. Estimated time of arrival, two AU off yours, twenty E-hours.

"Units' main course, main orbit—"

The signal from the picket boat stopped.

The officers in the com room of Mason's new flagship, the *Caligula*, knew Four Bravo would not make another one.

"Admiral Mason," Sten said. "Stand by for orders."

"Yes, sir."

"I want you to lift clear of Jochi with all fleet elements. I want you to take an *offensive* position—of your own choosing—about five AU off-planet."

"Yes. Sir. I am not arguing, but I assume you are aware my ships are outnumbered at least eight to one."

"More exactly about twelve to one by my calculations. But that does not matter. You are not, repeat not, to engage the enemy. You are only to engage any Suzdal or Bogazi ships attempting to attack you in your holding pattern. You are to maintain, as much as possible, the integrity of what we're going to keep a straight face and call our fleet. Is that clear?"

"It is. So you want to try a bluff?"

"Exactly. Feel free to make any kind of threatening feints or ugly faces, so long as they don't violate my orders."

"What makes you think I'll be able to draw them off, or at least get their attention? I'm not sure they'll believe I've either got some kind of secret weapon, or else I'm about to make a suicide run."

"If you were Suzdal or Bogazi, and you'd just seen the number that imbecile Langsdorff pulled, wouldn't you think that the Empire's capable of almost anything? Just as long as it's stupid?''

Mason considered. "Worth a try."

Without saying more, he palmed his screen switch and broke contact.

Sten really hoped Mason survived this. Clot the dark alley and the blackjack—Sten was going to turkey-gobble-stomp Mason into the pavement in broad daylight—in the middle of the parade ground at Arundel Castle.

"Okay, troops. Gather around." Sten's shout echoed through the *Victory*'s vast tacship hanger. All of his tacship pilots, and the pilots from the other two squadrons from the *Bennington*, had been ordered to this briefing.

"We'll make this quick. You can brief your crews independently.

"Here's what's going on. The invasion fleet is coming in, hot and heavy. We can't stop them. What we're trying to do is make life difficult enough for the bastards so us cowardly civilians and the crunchies can haul ass.

"You guys are gonna do it for me, and justify those clottin' white scarves and the flight pay that comes out of my taxes."

The pilots laughed and relaxed. All of them knew Sten's killer record as a tacship pilot/combat commander.

"Admiral Mason has what heavies we've got left offworld. He's going to do a tap dance and convince our friends he's about to attack. They'll *have* to at least form some kind of defensive line between the troopships and our BUCs. Then it'll be your turn."

Sten was suddenly serious. "Flight commanders . . . squadron leaders . . . attack in any formation you wish. Your targets are the transports. *Only* the transports. Kill them. If you hit them offworld, don't hang around for the finish. If they're in-atmosphere, make sure none of them will be able to make a forced landing. If they deploy troop capsules before you kill the mother ships, take out the capsules.

"If you're in-atmosphere, and close to the ground, and you see any enemy troops—hit them. This includes Suzdal, Bogazi, Jochians, or Torks. Draw double units of fire for the chain guns. If your ships are fitted for antipersonnel bombs, carry them and use them.

"That is a direct order.

"I want a big butcher's bill on this one. And any pilot who decides to play ace or dogfight star, I will personally ground and break.

"And remember—every soldier you let land on Jochi is a soldier who'll do his damnedest to kill an Imperial Guardsman.

"That's all. Dismissed."

Sten was getting very tired of saying "That is a direct order." But he wanted to make sure none of his pilots or captains labored under any illusions this battle was anything other than a last-ditch fight for survival.

He had seen, years, centuries, geological epochs ago, what happened when one side attempted to fight a war in civilized fashion—and he not only had seen his first command wiped out, but had personally buried too many bodies of friends to feel anything other than murderous purpose toward the bloodthirsty beings of the Altaics.

The Suzdal and Bogazi admirals analyzed the situation as their fleets closed on Jochi. There appeared to be no Imperial units in-atmosphere or immediately offworld.

In fact, the only warships in the system were those of the small Imperial fleet far off Jochi, orbiting in a ready position between two of Jochi's moons. First question: Could this fleet be ignored? Negative. If the Imperial ships attacked they could wreak havoc among the troopships. Second question: Should the landings be postponed until the Imperials were destroyed? Also negative— the threat was not that significant.

Besides, as one politically perceptive Bogazi pointed out, "Our confederation glue not sticky. Torks. Jochians. Suzdal. Sooner, later, they behave as normal and stab backs. Best sequence: Secure Jochi. Destroy Imperial soldiers. Destroy Imperial ships. With Jochi as base, any changes with allies easy for response."

The Suzdal and Bogazi main battleships moved out from Jochi

toward Mason's fleet and formed in a defensive perimeter. Waiting.

The thin-skinned transports gunned toward the ground, protected by only a thin screen of destroyers.

The first wave of Imperial tacships hit them in Jochi's exosphere.

Hannelore La Ciotat was a drakh-hot pilot—her phrase. Everyone agreed, including the other pilots in her squadron. Not as drakh-hot as she thought she was, and certainly not as drakh-hot as *they* were—but drakh-hot.

She had slaved a secondary weapons-launch helmet from her weapons officer's station to her own post at the controls. She claimed it helped to be able to see on-screen not only what her tacship was doing, but what the enemy was about to get bashed with.

The transport bulked large in the screen. Readouts blurring on either side, indicators moving across it, read, deciphered, understood yet ignored by La Ciotat.

"Closing . . . closing . . . range . . . range . . ." her weapons officer droned.

"Stand by . . ."

The transport grew larger.

"Downgrade launch from Kali," La Ciotat snapped, and the weapons officer changed the weapons choice from the huge, long-range ship killer to the medium-range Goblins.

"Range . . . range . . . range . . ."

"Stand by . . ."

La Ciotat felt herself drakh-hot as a pilot—but more importantly, she had a secret: she was *not* a drakh-hot shot. So she never launched outside point-blank range, and preferred to get closer.

"Stand by . . . clot!"

The transport's sensors must have seen the incoming tacship and emergency-launched its troop capsules, spattering long tubes full of troops into Jochi's atmosphere.

"Transport . . ."

"Still acquired."

"Launch One! Cancel backup!"

She flipped the weapons helmet to the back of her head, ignored the ghost image of the missile slamming into the transport as it futilely lifted for space, fingers and boots dancing on the controls, and brought the tacship back—a lethal hawk swooping as the waterfowl scattered.

"Range . . . range . . ."

"Goblins . . . Multiple launch, single target distinction . . . set!"

"Set! Range . . . range . . ."

"On automatic . . . fire!"

The tacship held eight Goblin missile launchers, each loaded with three missiles. The launchers chugged . . . the tacship shuddered as the 10 nuke-headed missiles blazed out.

Nineteen troop capsules shattered, spewing screaming, dying soldiers into the high atmosphere, soldiers clawing at emptiness as gravity spun them down and down toward the ground far below.

Suddenly for La Ciotat these targets stopped being inanimate simulations on a battlescreen and became beings—whose deaths had come swiftly in the blast, horribly as their lungs froze in the frigid atmosphere, or mercifully as they spun into unconsciousness.

And "Bull's-eye" La Ciotat saw the deaths from very close range. Her stomach recoiled. She was violently sick, vomit splashing over the screen and controls.

She turned back for another pass, to kill the twentieth and last capsule.

Sten watched the slaughter from a battlescreen in the embassy's control room, refusing to let his mind translate those points of light appearing and vanishing into what they represented. He could have gone out of the subbasement to an upstairs window and seen the great battle raging over the mountains ringing the valley that contained Rurik. But that would have been still worse.

Around him the last embassy staffers hurriedly packed what files and equipment they would take offworld.

Outside, in a courtyard, high fires raged, as the rest of the embassy's records were destroyed.

Sten had been somewhat surprised that there had been no panic or trouble. Kilgour had explained: he had borrowed a company of Guardsmen for embassy security, told the Bhor and Gurkhas to rack their weapons and help with the evacuation. With one experienced combat veteran to every four civilians, it was hard to start a proper panic.

"A'ready, boss, w' hae i' better'n Cavite." On Cavite, Alex had been in charge of evacking the civilians—and had sworn his own oath of never again. "Whae'll we do wi' th' embassy? Blow it? Or jus' leave some wee booby traps?"

"Negative on both. There might be another ambassador show up one of these years. Why make life hard for him?"

Kilgour's stare was glacierlike.

Who cared what happened with the next regime, or the next clot dumb enough to take the Imperial shilling?

But he did not say anything.

"Do you have a prog on the landings, General?" Sten asked.

"Tentative," Sarsfield said. "They appear to have come in with, oh, call it twenty divisions. Say five for the first wave, five for the second, the same for the third, and five for reserve. That's my guesstimate, and that's what I'd do. But none of the Intel progs disagree, so that's what I'm going with."

"GA."

"Right now, I'll say—and these are pretty firm—that they've managed to put no more than eight on the ground. The rest either were lost in the landings or are still in orbit after the invasion was aborted."

Sten repressed a wince, even though the body count was enemy. The First Guards Division, at full strength, numbered about eighteen thousand beings.

Assume—and a screen nearby showing Imperial Intelligence's order of battle said the assumption would be fairly correct—the same book strength for the Suzdal/Bogazi landing force.

Three hundred and sixty thousand beings, and only eight made it—the invasion force had taken over fifty percent casualties before real battle had even been joined.

"Of course," Sarsfield went on briskly, "casualties were not total. Elements of all invading units are almost certainly on the ground. But as stragglers, casualties, and so forth—not to be taken seriously.''

Sarsfield was a true Guardsman, Sten thought. He didn't appear worried that at least 150,000 enemy were now on Jochi, reinforcing whatever Tork militia were deployed—probably around a hundred thousand beings, and then the half a million more serving in the Jochi army. Three-quarters of a million, versus eighteen thousand.

''I'm grateful they don't appear, at least so far,'' Sarsfield added, ''to have landed any heavy armor or artillery.''

They wouldn't need it, Sten knew. Douw and the Jochians had more than enough to go around.

Now, he wondered, how long would it take for them to reform and attack the city?

He knew that answer, too. No more than three E-days.

Imperial losses were slight—only five tacships had been shot down. But those five were irreplaceable.

Sten, Sarsfield, and Mason were on a three-way sealed beam, trying to plan what next.

What should have happened was that the Imperial personnel should have been onboard their ships and scooting for deep space and home.

But there were two small problems: the Suzdal/Bogazi fleet off Jochi, and the oncoming allied army.

Almost a dozen Frick & Fracks had been infiltrated and blown out of the sky before Kilgour had a firm report that the Altaic Confederation was on the march.

Sten had two advantages: First, Mason's ships off Jochi—which were enough of a threat to worry the Suzdal and Bogazi fleet admirals. Second, he had in-atmosphere aerial superiority, or at least enough units to make the air overhead contested territory.

The Suzdal and Bogazi heavies would be unlikely to hang in space and lob heavy missiles down on the Imperial Forces inside Rurik. None of the allied forces, including the two ET races, would define noble victory as having destroyed the longtime capital of the Cluster. That was a shade too Pyrrhic even for these beings.

Nor would the fleet, except as a last resort, sacrifice maneuverability and come down to smash these sprats that were tacships—sprats that very likely could kill more than one-for-one as they died, and no one would trade a battleship or cruiser for a fifteen-being spitkit.

On the other hand, Douw's advancing army would slowly provide an AA umbrella that would deny the air to the Imperial ships, so this was only a temporary standoff.

He suddenly found two more shafts of sunlight in his mental sky. First was he had a trained, disciplined force—the First Guards—who were fresh and not brought to battle. Second was the realization that, if he *was* able to get his Imperial bodies off Rurik, there would be only limited pursuit.

Just bashing the Empire out of the Altaics would be defined as enough of a victory.

At least that's what the Altaics would think.

He listened in silence as Sarsfield and Mason ran various options through and shot them down, trying to figure a way to get out of this Altaic sandwich the Imperial Forces were trapped in.

Something glimmered. He rolled it back and forth. It seemed worth exploring. It probably wouldn't work. Even if it didn't, the situation couldn't worsen. Could it?

"Mr. Kilgour," he asked formally to Alex, who sat somewhat off-screen. It slightly jolted Mason and Sarsfield—they had been unaware of Kilgour's presence. "Do we have a code that's sort of compromised? Not a complete joke, but something they'll be able to break, at least partially, without too much strain?"

Alex shrugged and called up the embassy code chief. Mason started to say something, but Sarsfield waved him to silence. Five minutes later, Kilgour presented a choice of three codes that the code chief was morally certain were splintered, if not completely busted.

"Very good. Why don't we . . ." and Sten outlined the first stage of his plan.

Sarsfield, since the first stage did not involve him or his command, didn't say anything. Sten could see Mason trying to be fair—but wanting to say that anything that clotting Sten could come up with was worthless.

"My biggest objection," Mason said after a while, "is that we already tried it."

"Not quite, Admiral," Sten said. "We tried the simple version of the con. Did you ever play which hand's got the marble?"

"Of course. I *was* a child once."

Sten doubted that, but continued. "First time you tried it, you just lied. Then you told the truth. Then you lied again. Escalating dishonesty.

"That's what we're going to attempt, unless someone's got something better—or can point out where I'm completely full of it."

And so the Bluff, Stage Two, was begun.

First a destroyer was detached from Mason's fleet and sent in the general direction of Imperial worlds and Prime itself.

Once beyond the range of any of the Suzdal/Bogazi units, it broadcast a coded message, both to Mason's fleet and to the besieged Imperial post on Rurik.

Sten waited for six hours, watching Alex's Frick & Fracks, as the Altaic army ground closer toward Rurik. Thank somebody, what the clot, give it to Otho's gods Sarla and Laraz, they were moving slowly. Sten attributed it both to caution, none of them ever having fought Imperial Forces before, and the inevitable incoherence of trying to coordinate an alliance, particularly one where everyone hated everyone else.

He had ordered his tacships up as aerial artillery, lobbing air-to-ground missiles at predetermined targets—crossroads, major roadways, and the like.

Then both his com officer, Freston, and Mason's equivalent officer reported: there had been a sudden flurry of intership transmissions in the Suzdal/Bogazi fleets, transmissions that had been sent in a rarely used—which suggested high-level—code. Blurt transmissions were also beamed out in directions suggesting they were intended for the capital worlds of the Suzdal and Bogazi.

"Mr. Mason?"

"Yes, sir. We're on the way."

The fish were nibbling, it would appear.

Sten had, indeed, just come up with a second version of that bluff he and Mason had run, pretending to send messages back to an oncoming Imperial fleet.

The destroyer he had ordered sent out had transmitted a message, in that breakable code, that appeared to come from the vanguard of a heavy Imperial strike force. This mythical strike force ordered Mason to abandon his position off Jochi—the besieged forces on the planet would have to fend for themselves for a while—and serve as a forward screen for this strike force.

The transmission continued, saying that Mason would be fully briefed at a later date, but that this strike force had been specially detached to punish the dissident Suzdal and Bogazi—cleverly making no mention of any human dissidents—by attacking the ET capital worlds, returning tit for tat.

Sten was too elaborate in his deception—he forgot to allow for the fact that this was exactly what any of the races or cultures in the Altaics would have done if they were in the same situation as the Empire.

Three E-hours later, the Suzdal and Bogazi heavies broke orbit and struck, at full speed, for their own systems.

Sten, trying to keep the elaborate geometry of astrogation in his mind, thought they would probably set a course in x direction for their home worlds. A course that would be more direct than the one Mason was supposedly on, and certainly one that was predicted never to coincide with the y direction or directions the huge Imperial strike force would most logically track.

Uh-huh. All this exotica from someone who had needed coaching in basic one-ship astrogation back in Flight School. It would not work—at least not for very long. Sten hoped it worked long enough for the next step, and for Mason to duck around the Suzdal/Bogazi fleet and get back to where he would be needed.

Regardless, at least one layer of the sandwich had been stripped away.

Four hours later, scout elements of the Altaic Confederation's army entered the outskirts of Rurik.

* * *

Sten had told Sarsfield his hopes, not his orders. He did not want the First Guards to feel they were being commanded to pull some kind of impossible Bastogne or Thermopylae.

Stop them. Try to get them to dig in. Make them think we're counterattacking.

Sarsfield, like Sten, had counted noses. Neither of them thought this third ruse would work. It's very hard, after all, to bluff someone who's got three aces and the joker showing and both elbows keeping his hole card from being turned over, when you've got four different suits and one slice of bologna.

The enemy scouts proceeded unmolested.

However, their nerves were tested. Here they found an abandoned barricade. There vehicles were overturned. Up there, some kind of antenna spun. Cryptic codes had been sprayed on the pavement.

The scouts proceeded, more and more cautiously.

They saw no signs of Imperial soldiers.

It was unlikely they would—the Guards' forward recon elements were specialists in not being seen.

The Confederation's progress was reported.

Frick & Fracks were behind the lines, waiting for the first heavy armor and gravsleds to creep into the city. No one likes to risk his expensive track or even more expensive gravlighter in the rat trap of city fighting. But the Altaic soldiers had no choice.

They were in the trap.

Sarsfield ordered the artillery to open up. His own cannon and surface-to-surface launchers opened up on predetermined targets, targets that were now obscured by enemy vehicles.

The tacships were launched from the mother ships, which were grounded near the huge park back of the embassy, where Sten had ordered the transports grounded.

Drakh-hot pilot Hannelore La Ciotat popped her tacship up, saw the track platoon's cannon begin to swivel, blasted a volley of rockets from the rack jury-rigged on her ship's belly, ran two cases through her forward chain gun, and disappeared.

La Ciotat was swearing almost continuously. Clot. She might as well have joined the clotting *infantry*. She gunned her tacship down a street, well below the building roofs, looking for another target.

The platoon was destroyed—and the momentum of the attack temporarily broken.

But they kept coming.

The Jochi armor-infantry Combat Command moved swiftly and efficiently toward the city center. It was a highly trained force on familiar ground. The tracks would hit anything the infantry couldn't, and the grunts kept antitank gunners from killing their big friends.

"Battery A . . . fire!" and the four Imperial gravsleds appeared to explode. Each explosion was, in fact, forty-eight rockets salvoed from the racks mounted on the gravsleds' rear. The unarmored sleds lifted at full speed and headed for another location.

The rockets were just that—propellant, guidance vanes, and warhead. Their accuracy was plus-minus fifty meters at four hundred meters. Appallingly bad. But when 192 rockets, each with fifty kilos of explosive in its warhead, simultaneously impact on an area one hundred meters on a side, and that area is occupied by a crack armor-infantry unit, the results can be impressive.

The Jochi infantry died to a man.

A few of the tracks had been hit and crippled. But most of them were still combat-capable.

Then the two-man antitrack teams rose out of their hiding places in the rubble, fire-and-forget missiles streaking fire.

But the Confederation kept coming.

The skies were black, and there were high, building storm clouds in the distance.

Kilgour wiped sweat from his forehead. "Th' weather'll break, noo, an' we'll lose th' wee tacships."

Cind grimaced. The ships had all-weather capability. But no one had ever meant that to mean a spacecraft could fly in the heart of a city, fight an enemy on the ground, which meant with mostly visual target acquisitions, and not spend a lot of time revamping the local architecture.

Or, if the architecture was as solid as on Rurik, crashing.

Seconds later the storm broke, huge raindrops shattering down. Kilgour swore, ducking for shelter that wasn't there, and then his language went doubly purple as hailstones spattered him.

Clottin' wonderful, he thought. Tis nae enow we hae th' hands ae all men agin us here, nae t' mention a few ETs, but th' weathergods hae us on the list ae well.

Warrant Officer La Ciotat stood beside her tacship, oblivious to the rain spattering in through the *Victory*'s open hangar doors. The ship was grounded just behind the embassy, and the other tacship carrier, the *Bennington*, nearby.

"Sir. I'm willing to try it," she argued. "We'll just use the Kali sensors out the front of the launch tube, and I'll go on instruments and get targets from the missile."

"Negative," her flight commander ordered. "We're grounded. We'll be pulling drive offworld next.

"Or if not, we're *really* going to be making kamikaze runs, instead of just getting close like you want. That's an order."

"I have reports," Sarsfield said, tonelessly, "that my artillerymen are firing sabot charges over open sights. They're getting close, Sten."

"Tell them to blow their guns and move to the transports."

"Yessir."

"What's the loading status?"

Sarsfield consulted with an aide.

"I have all battalions loaded, except the one boarding now, and the First Battalion in its defensive position back of the square. Plus the arty batteries that are hauling for the ships right now.

"I guess," Sarsfield said, "the First will have to fight the rear guard action. Clot. At least," he said sadly, "they volunteered for it." As had every other battalion of the First Guards, Sten knew.

"All embassy personnel are loaded," Sten said. "As ordered, you are to lift all Imperial ships when First Battalion has the attacking units engaged and counterattacks. The *Victory* will hold on the ground until the last possible moment for pickup for any

Guards elements that can disengage after you lift. I'm shutting down this station now."

"Roger you're last. You're transferring now to the *Victory*?"

"Negative," Sten said. "I'll be with First Battalion. Sten. Out."

Sarsfield had not even time to register his protest. Sten stood, stiff muscles stretching, and reached for his combat harness.

Alex, similarly outfitted for battle, held it ready. They went for the stairs. Kilgour turned and pulled a wire, then they went on up toward the ground floor.

Ten seconds later explosives shattered the coms and conference room.

"Y' hae a plan," Kilgour wondered.

"Sure," Sten said. "Many, many plans. To pray for peace. To not get killed. To make it to the *Victory* before she hauls. To break contact at nightfall, and exfiltrate into the country and go to ground."

"An' how long d'ye think," Kilgour wondered, "thae clottin' Emperor'll take t' send a rescue party f'r a man who disobeyed orders?"

"Have faith, Alex," Sten said. "Sooner or later, we'll just learn to levitate home."

In the courtyard Sten saw Cind, the Gurkhas, and the Bhor drawn up. Waiting.

He wasn't surprised.

But he almost started crying.

Cind saluted him, rain dripping from her nose.

He returned the salute, and his pissant little formation doubled off—up the wide boulevard toward the Square of the Khaqans to join the last stand.

Fleet Admiral Mason glowered at the screen, which showed the Jochi system rushing toward him. This whole assignment has been clotted, he thought.

First I am chauffeur to that popinjay Sten on that clotting yacht he was given. Then I spend time dancing around playing peep-bo and now you see it, now you don't with a bunch of geeks and ETs.

Hither, yon, hither yon, and it is all shadows, just like I told Sten, back on Prime, a world where everything is gray and there is no truth.

He deserved better from the Eternal Emperor, he thought furiously. And wondered how, once this disaster wound to a close, he could remind his Emperor of that.

At least there will be no relief and court-martial, as happened to Mahoney for some reason, he thought. I have followed my orders exactly.

And a soldier cannot go wrong when he does that.

"Jochi planetfall . . . two E-hours," his watch officer said.

The Altaic soldiers moved confidently into the Square of the Khaqans. Opposition had lightened, and then disappeared. Now they would take the palace, and move on to destroy unutterably the hated Imperials.

A cheer rose. This was the center, was the throne. From this place, all power came. Now—and each soldier's thoughts differed, depending on his race—the rulers of the Altaic Cluster would be different.

The counterattack struck.

The multiple rocket racks had been dismounted from the gravlighters and concealed behind balustrades, terraces, and even statues. Firing studs were touched, and the rockets crashed out, ripping horizontally across the square.

Explosions shattered and echoed, and then the First Battalion counterattacked, rolling up the Altaic soldiers and sending them reeling back.

Bare seconds later, more thunder crashed. But this was not from the storm or from the Guards' rocketry.

Fire blazoned into the darkness that was technically day as the Imperial transports lifted clear of the park and drove at full power for space.

Sten watched them disappear into the storm clouds. Very good. Very good, he thought. Better than Cavite.

Now let's see if there's any way to save my own young ass.

* * *

The rain was slamming in now, wind-driven, and thunder was crashing as the wind roared across the great square in front of Cind.

She was stretched prone, using a projectile-chipped staircase for cover, and paid no mind to the puddle she was lying in, the puddle that was scarlet from the blood draining from the Guardsman next to her.

Her own rifle lay beside her, disregarded.

A precision sniper weapon was no use here. Far across the square, which was littered with crashed gravlighters and destroyed tracks, fire flickering from their hatches in spite of the storm, the Confederation Forces were getting ready for another assault.

Time had passed. How much time, she didn't know.

The enemy had reformed and attacked.

They tried first with armor—but Guardsmen with AT weapons were stationed in the upper floors of the palace, firing down into the always-vulnerable top deck of the tracks.

Then fast gravlighters swept forward, trying to punch through the increasingly thin lines of the Guardsmen. They were stopped.

Next the Confederation began human wave attacks. Shoulder to shoulder infantry attacks, men and women shouting cheers and marching bravely, suicidally, into the near-solid gunfire.

They died—but so did Imperial Guardsmen.

She had seen Alex cursing and putting a field dressing on a bloody, if superficial, shrapnel wound on his upper leg before he had gone back to the slaughter. Otho, too, had been hit. But after his wounds had been dressed, he had returned to the line, spotting for a Guards' mortar crew.

Cind wondered if they could stand two, three, or just one more assault before that wave washed over them.

There had been no opportunity to break contact and try for the *Victory*, assuming the ship was still on the ground.

Sten splashed down beside her.

The two of them were grimy. Bloody—but at least the blood was not their own. Their eyes were glaring.

"Well?"

"Two tubes left, boss."

"Here." He passed her another magazine of AM2 rounds.

"Be melodramatic," she suggested. "Kiss me."

Sten grimaced, started to obey, and then jerked back as he heard the grind of oncoming tracks once more. "Well, I shall be clotted. Look."

This time the attack was combined armor and infantry. And, standing in that lead track was . . .

Cind grabbed her exotic rifle and sighted. She saw the handsome face and silver hair. "It's him! You want the privilege?"

"Go ahead. I've had all the fun lately."

The man in the track was General Douw. Cind supposed he thought this would be the final attack that would overrun the Imperial Forces, and had chosen to lead it himself.

Brave.

Brave, but dumb, Cind thought as she touched the trigger and the AM2 round blew Douw's chest apart.

"Thank you," Sten said.

Cind scrabbled for the willygun. The death of their leader hadn't even been noticed by the oncoming soldiers.

Wave after wave of them poured into the square. Cind swept their ranks—then decided to wait until they were closer.

She lifted her head to see—and her eyes widened.

"Jamchyyd and Kholeric," she whispered, her tone wholly reverent, actually calling on the Bhor gods as if she believed they might exist. "Sarla and Laraz."

Coming over the city's rooftops, swaying like a great dark snake, came the cyclone, cutting a solid swath as it came. And behind the first funnel cloud . . . another. One . . . two . . . Cind counted six of them, swinging back and forth like a dancer's hips as they came.

Sten remembered: ". . . kill a thousand people in forty minutes . . . punch a blade of straw through an anvil . . . throw five tacships . . . a quarter klick . . ."

The tornadoes picked up debris as they came. A roof. A shed. A gravsled. A personnel carrier. A crashed tacship. A man. Spun them, ruined them, broke them beyond recognition, and then used them as weapons.

Cind's ears cracked, and she swallowed.

The roar was louder now than the gunfire, and the Altaic troops stopped. They turned—and saw the cyclones.

Then the first vortex entered the Square of the Khaqans.

It swept through the soldiers and their weapons like a vacuum cleaner picking up dust balls. It picked them up and cast them aside.

Sten was on his feet.

Shouting. Screaming. Unheard.

He was waving—back. Back—away. For the *Victory*!

The second tornado entered the square. Both funnel clouds twisted and spun, hesitating, as if unsure if they should continue.

Imperial soldiers pelted away from this new demon that no one could be expected to stand against.

But they were not in panic. They ran—but slowly, helping the limping walking wounded. Bringing their weapons with them, or abandoning them to pick up the ends of stretchers.

Sten and Alex held, just where the broad boulevard opened, the boulevard Sten had sent the *Victory* roaring down toward the embassy, lifetimes earlier.

The square was a black swirl, as yet another tornado came onstage. Palace walls ripped away, spinning out into the near-vacuum low-pressure area, and were caught by the cyclone and lifted thousands of meters up, into the overhanging cloud.

Then the vortex stalked forward once more, wind roaring and speed building, toward and through the palace that had once been the pride of the Khaqans, then had briefly housed Dr. Iskra.

The palace vanished in a swirl.

The tornado's fellows, spawn of that great brooding wall cloud, came on, inexorably planing the soldiers of the Altaics, the shaky Confederation they had fought for, and that meaningless vanity of a palace that meant power from the face of Rurik.

They left nothing—nothing but chaos.

The *Victory* was still on the ground, waiting.

One AU off Rurik, Sten sent the message *en clair*, punched through with max power, direct to the Emperor's private channel, second transmission to the Imperial office:

ALL IMPERIAL UNITS SUCCESSFULLY EVACUATED FROM RURIK IN
GOOD ORDER. IMPERIAL UNITS NOW ON DIRECT COURSE FOR PRIME
WORLD. ALTAIC CLUSTER NOW IN OPEN REVOLT AGAINST THE EM-
PIRE.

                                                          STEN

Now, court-martial me, he thought.
You insane bastard.

CHAPTER FORTY-TWO

MAHONEY WAITED IN a prisoner-for-transport cell beneath the
large new building that was Internal Security's headquarters. It
was a small room, with white plas walls, a fold-up sleeping bench,
and a hole in the floor for body wastes.

In a few minutes they would take him to his hearing before the
Imperial grand jury. He was dressed in the pure white coveralls
required by law for indicted criminals. The color was symbolic.
White indicated presumed innocence. It also indicated that the
prisoner's statements had not been produced by torture.

Mahoney had to admit that in his case the latter was true. So
far. He had been treated with rough but professional courtesy.
Sure, he had been beaten. The first time when they loaded him
on the transport to Prime. But that had only been to alert him to
his new station in life—bruises and blood to show him who was
boss. There had been no emotion in the beating. Nothing personal. The same all along the processing line, as he was transferred from one IS group to another.

When the beatings stopped, Ian knew his hearing date had been
set. It was a routine precaution. To make sure everything had
healed in time for his appearance.

Mahoney had weathered the experience well. Not that he was philosophical about his fate. He refused to think about it at all. To dwell on the betrayal would only serve to soften him up—for the probably inevitable brainscan.

Instead, he thought about old adventures. Friends. Lovers. He never thought about food. Mahoney was glad that prison fare was efficiently bland. Otherwise, those meals the Emperor had fixed for him with his own hands would have come back to haunt.

Ian's hackles rose, his old Mantis senses prickling. Someone was watching. He made himself relax. Then he heard rustling at the cell door.

Ah, they've finally come, Ian. Be still, heart. And you there, lungs. You're not needing so much air. Steady on, boyos. Be of good Irish cheer.

Poyndex looked through the two-way as the IS screws hustled Mahoney out of the PFT cell. He was surprised at how well the man looked and wondered if he could do the same in Mahoney's position. He pushed that thought away. It was a talent he would just as soon leave undiscovered.

He stepped out into the hallway to intercept Mahoney and the guards. Ian saw him. From the flicker in his eyes, Poyndex knew he was recognized. The flicker vanished and was replaced with a grin.

"Oh, ho. So the boss sent the first team in," Mahoney said. "I'd say I'm honored, but I'd be lying."

Poyndex laughed. "I don't want to be responsible for a lie," he said. "We wouldn't want to start the grand jury proceedings on the wrong foot."

He told a guard to remove Mahoney's restraints, then waved the guards away. "I'll be your escort," he told Ian. "I'm sure you won't try anything . . . foolish."

Mahoney rubbed life back into his wrists. "Why would I? I'm an innocent man. Joyfully waiting for justice to be done." He laughed.

Poyndex grinned back and indicated the far corridor door. They both started walking, Poyndex just a half step behind Mahoney.

"Actually, I've come along to make sure that's exactly what

you get," Poyndex said. "The Emperor wants complete fairness."

"Oh, certain he does," Mahoney chortled. "And tell him his old friend, Ian, is humbly thankful for this courtesy."

Poyndex forced a small chuckle of appreciation. He had decidedly mixed feeling about his mission. On the one hand, Ian Mahoney was his sole competition for the power he now wielded. Disgrace had ended that competition.

"Tell him not to worry," Mahoney said. "When questioned I'll stick to the facts. I have no intention of bringing his name into these proceedings."

"An unnecessary promise," Poyndex said smoothly. "But, I'm sure he will be pleased you're still thinking of his best interests—that you remember your past relationship."

On the other hand, Mahoney *had* once stood in Poyndex's shoes. He had been the Eternal Emperor's faithful servant for decades. As he watched Mahoney walking tall toward his fate, Poyndex feared for his own. This is what will happen, he thought, if you should fall from grace.

A whisper in the back of his mind hissed: Not if . . . but *when*.

"Tell the boss I remember," Mahoney said. "I remember *very* well."

"I'll do that," Poyndex said. "And that's a promise."

His hand dipped into his pocket, then came out. As they reached the door, Poyndex pressed the silenced barrel against the soft spot at the back of Mahoney's neck.

There was a quick flinch of skin from sudden cold.

Poyndex fired.

Mahoney tumbled forward. Slammed into the door. Sagged down.

Poyndex stood over the body, amazed. Mahoney's face still carried that damned Irish grin.

He bent down, pressed the barrel against Mahoney's head, and fired again.

With a man like Ian Mahoney, you had to make double damned sure.

CHAPTER FORTY-THREE

"FARE THEE WELL, you banks ae Sicily, fare thee well, thee brooks an' dells, frae thae's noo Scots soldier thae's mourn th' last of ye," Alex hummed from memory, thinking fondly of a very tall brew as soon as the fleet was absolutely clear of anything, including vacuum, that resembled the Altaic Cluster.

He was idly punching through various public channels being cast from the Imperial worlds ahead. Nearby, Sten was collapsed in the *Victory*'s CO station—but no one asked him to move. Both of them still wore their torn, filthy combat uniforms.

The bridge was near-silent—probably because no one thought they would actually have gotten away with this one.

"Sports," Kilgour muttered, finding another cast. "Ah dinnae ken whae thae's bein's thae think thae's virtue in puntin' a wee sack ae leather frae one chalk't line t' another.

"Reminds me," he said to Freston, who sat near the console, "ae th' time thae tried t' make m' play a clottin' sport ae gentle-bein'ts call't crickit. First Ah thinks thae's mad, goin't chirp—"

And his mouth snapped closed.

No one exactly remembered what the liviecaster on-screen was saying. But it was very clear:

Disgrace . . . once hero of the Tahn war . . . Governor General . . . supreme penalty . . . Ian Mahoney . . . name to be stricken from all records and monuments . . . traitorous . . .

Sten was standing beside him. His face was white.

"That's torn it," he whispered.

Kilgour started to say something, then shook his head. He swallowed.

366

He heard the snarl from the watch officer behind him: "Watch your screens, mister. What's that com that just ran?"

"Uh . . . sorry . . . it's coded."

"I can tell it's coded," the watch officer said. "Who's it to? Who's it from?"

"Sir . . . I think . . . Prime. And . . . and it's intended for the *Caligula* . . . I think."

"Don't think, mister. Know!"

"Sir . . . we don't have the code. It's not indexed."

Sten forced shock and anger about Mahoney's murder away. "What is the signal?"

"We don't know, sir. From Prime to *Caligula*, sir."

"I heard *that*. Patch me to Mason."

"Yessir."

Caligula, *this is* Victory, *over*.

. . .

. . . *This is* Caligula, *over*.

This is Victory. *What was the transmission you received?*

Wait one . . . *signal being decoded* . . .

"How th' clot," Kilgour wondered, hair on the back of his neck starting to lift, "d' thae hae' th' code an' we dinnae?"

"Sir! The *Caligula*'s broken contact."

"Reestablish."

Caligula, *this is* Victory, *over*. Caligula, *this is* Victory. *Do you receive this transmission?*

"Sir, the *Caligula*'s broadcasting."

"GA."

"Not to us, sir. To its DD screen. Burst transmission. I didn't get it."

Sten was trying to figure out what the hell was going on. Then he noticed the main maneuver screen.

The *Caligula* had broken fleet formation, together with the four destroyers that normally screened the battleship. It set a new course . . .

"What's the *Caligula*'s new orbit?"

"Wait one, sir . . . it appears to be a near-reciprocal track from the fleet's. Straight—I'm estimating—back toward Jochi!"

There was a rumble of surprise.

"Quiet on the bridge."

Sten forced his mind to function. What the clot was going on? He found he had spoken aloud.

"Sir?" It was Freston. "I think I might know."

"One ray of light. Talk to me!"

"Uh . . . sir, before I was assigned to you, I was com officer on the *Churchill*. And the captain had been given a private code when he took command. There was another copy in the ship's safe, to be given to the XO or whoever took over if the CO was a casualty."

"GA. But why the clot would the *Caligula*—or Mason—have a code that we don't? We're the flagship."

"Yessir. But—but we're not carrying a planet buster."

Of course. The Empire did not like even to admit that it had weaponry heavy enough to shatter a planet. But it did. Planet busters were *never* used—even during the height of the Tahn war they had not been launched.

For the Emperor, it had little to do with morality. Genocide made lousy politics, he used to say. That *had* been the Emperor's view. Apparently, went Sten's grim thoughts, the Eternal Emperor had changed his mind. Perhaps it had never been a moral issue for the Emperor. But it certainly had been for Sten.

"Is the *Caligula* answering?" Sten asked.

"Negative, sir."

"Commander, do you have a tacship flight on standby?"

"Of course."

"I want one ship. The best pilot on the *Victory*. Kali-armed. Launch time as soon as I get to the hangar deck."

Kilgour was on his feet, starting for the companionway.

"Alex! I want you here on the bridge. I'll be broadcasting from the tacship, but I want the com linked to the *Victory*."

"Y' dinnae need me frae that, skip."

"And I want a synth that'll match analysis."

"Right. Ah hae it noo. Away wi' y' lad."

And Sten was running for the *Victory*'s hangar.

The tacship flashed out from the *Victory*'s port and, barely clear of the mother ship, went to full AM2 drive.

"What's the IP?"

La Ciotat didn't need to look at a screen.

"Fifty-three . . . fifty-one minutes, sir."

"Fine." Sten sat at the weapons officer's station, adjusting the control helmet to his own head.

"Here's the drill. The *Caligula* is headed back for Jochi. It's going to launch a planet buster."

La Ciotat, priding herself on her poker face, wasn't able to control her expression. "But what—is Admiral Mason mutinying, or—"

"You do not need to know, Ms. I want you to hold a closing course on the *Caligula* and have your com person keep an open link to the *Victory*. I want you to notify me when we're within . . . five minutes of the *Caligula*. Do you have any trouble with those orders?"

"No, sir."

"Keep us from getting tagged by the destroyers. I'm pretty sure they'll have orders to stop us."

"*That's* not even a concern. Sir."

Sten almost smiled—it sounded like La Ciotat *was* drakh-hot.

"*Caligula*, this is *Victory*. Admiral Mason, this is Sten, over."

"Still no response."

"*Caligula*, this is Sten, over. Patch me to your Six Actual. That is an order, over."

"Seven minutes to intercept, sir."

"God dammit . . ."

The screen on the tacship suddenly cleared, and Sten saw Mason's face.

Mason—or so Sten hoped, at least—would be seeing Sten, or a computer synthesis of Sten, back on the bridge of the *Victory* and never think that his response had been almost immediate and that he was, in fact, aboard a tacship bare minutes behind the *Caligula*.

"Admiral Mason, I think I understand your mission," Sten began.

"I am under orders, sir, to not discuss my assignment with anyone."

"I am not interested in discussing, Mason. This is not a debating society. And I know that you've been told to bust Jochi. You can't do it."

"I have my orders, sir."

"Did you verify them? Mason, do you want to be the first man in—who the hell knows how long?—to wipe out a planet? Not everybody down there's loony, Mason."

The on-screen figure made no response.

"I see no point in continuing this transmission," Mason said finally, mechanically.

"Mason . . . stand by for one moment . . ."

Sten closed his mike and pulled the weapons helmet down over his head. "Ms. La Ciotat, I am launching the Kali."

"Yessir. At full drive . . . IP will be one point three minutes . . . ship IP is now two minutes."

Sten touched the red key on the weapons panel—the only physical act that he needed to do.

The monstrous missile was launched from a tube that was the tacship's spine. It was twenty meters long, and its warhead was a sixty-megaton deathstrike.

The missile spat out from the tacship, and Sten aimed it through the helmet at the rapidly closing tiny constellation that was the *Caligula* and her escorts, holding at three-quarter drive.

He opened his eyes, and Mason ghosted at him on-screen.

"This is my last attempt, Admiral Mason. You know you're working for a madman. We just heard—the Emperor had Mahoney shot."

Mason's eyes flickered, then he became the automaton once again.

Sten tried once more—knowing it was futile. "Look, man. Do you want your name to go down like this? Mason the planet-killer?"

Mason suddenly almost-smiled. "Sten, that is the difference between us. You think that you have some sort of god-given privilege to judge what orders you should or should not obey. That's seditious behavior, and you know it. Maybe that's why Mahoney was executed. Did you ever consider that? I'm following direct

Imperial orders, mister. No, Sten, I'll not be the traitor. Mason, clear.''

The screen was blank.

Sten closed his eyes and became only the Kali. He hit full emergency.

"Closing . . . closing . . ." he dimly heard La Ciotat's chant.

"You are spotted . . . you broke a DD's screen . . . I have a Fox-launch . . . closing . . . prog cannot intercept . . Closing . . . Target impact . . . Mark!''

Sten's world fireballed.

He pulled the control helmet off and saw, on screen, the *Caligula* cease to exist. There had been a hint of an explosion, and then simply nothing. The screen might as well have been trying to look into a black hole. He wondered if the Kali had sympathetically detonated the planet buster.

He guessed the *Caligula*'s destroyers would still be trying to launch countermissiles, if any of them had survived—the screen stayed dark, overloaded.

He didn't care. Evading them was La Ciotat's job.

"That's it, Ms.,'' he said, tiredly. "Back to the *Victory*.''

Mason died as he lived—following orders.

Sten did not give much of a damn about that.

But more than three thousand beings had died with him—and Sten doubted there would ever be a monument to them, out here, in the darkness and silence of interstellar space.

CHAPTER FORTY-FOUR

STEN WAS STILL on automatic. Back aboard the *Victory* he had gone to the bridge and numbly given the order to secure from general quarters.

"We're frae th' hangman now, son," Kilgour said. His voice was low. But it dashed Sten back to reality.

He looked at his friend. The Scot's round face was as calm as if he were discussing dinner arrangements.

Sten glanced around the bridge of the *Victory*. It was suddenly crowded.

There was Otho with a knot of Bhor. The wiry forms of the Gurkhas, headed by Lalbahadur Thapa. And many others.

Faces he remembered—but names he shamefully didn't.

And there was Cind.

The expression on her face was the same as the others. Expectant. Waiting for his decision.

Sten wiped moisture from his eyes.

They were with him—all of them.

Sten badly wanted to haul Cind into his arms. He wanted to be comforted, soothed.

He wanted soft lies that everything would be well.

Then the full force of what he had just done hit him.

Sten was an outlaw, now.

And through his actions he had damned all these trusting souls.

Soon, the Eternal Emperor would learn of Sten's betrayal and loose his coursing hounds.

Sten had to run. They *all* had to run.

He started to speak. He knew dozens of places to hide. Sten only had to choose and issue the coordinates.

He stopped.

No place was safe. Eventually, the Emperor's forces would run them to ground.

Sten looked around at the loyal faces again. There might be others.

He thought of Sr. Ecu. And his proposal.

What was the use?

He wished Mahoney were there. Ian would have known what to do. He would have said, Quit your whining, lad. You've got your health. You've your lady. You've got that ugly Scot, Alex Kilgour. And many other loyal friends. And you've got a bloody great battlewagon. The Emperor's own ship!

At that moment, Jemedar Lalbahadur whispered to his group. They all snapped to.

In the formal, Kukris raised Gurkha salute. "We are at your command. Sah!"

And Sten decided.

If he ran, the Emperor would get him.

So he had to get the Eternal Emperor first.

Sten issued the orders.

About the Authors

CHRIS BUNCH is a Ranger- and Airborne-qualified Vietnam vet, who's written about phenomena as varied as the Hell's Angels, the Rolling Stones, and Ronald Reagan.

ALLAN COLE grew up in the CIA in odd spots like Okinawa, Cyprus, and Taiwan. He's been a professional chef, investigative reporter, and national news editor of a major West Coast daily newspaper. He's won half a dozen writing awards in the process.

BUNCH and COLE, friends since high school, have collaborated on everything from the world's worst porno novel to more film and TV scripts than they care to admit. They stopped counting at one hundred when they suffered the total loss of all bodily hair.

Lured from a safehouse above an Azerbaijan bar by promises of fame, fortune, and an early publication date, Bunch and Cole were immediately leapt upon by a team of Black Ops editors.

Hauled before a tribunal of Sten readers, they were sentenced to return to Los Angeles as writer-slaves. A high-placed source in a mail order firm specializing in locksmith courses claims they are currently chained to their desks and working on the final Sten adventure.

Allan Cole and Chris Bunch

present imaginative,

suspenseful adventures

for die hard science-fiction fans